To Wayne
joy THE Book!

Davie x

The Lost Boy,
the Doodlebug
and the mysterious
`number 80`

Stevie Henden

Matador
9 Priory Business Park,
Wistow Road, Kibworth Beauchamp,
Leicestershire. LE8 0RX
Tel: (+44) 116 279 2299
Fax: (+44) 116 279 2277
Email: books@troubador.co.uk
Web: www.troubador.co.uk/matador

ISBN 978 1780885 186

British Library Cataloguing in Publication Data.
A catalogue record for this book is available from the British Library.

Typeset by Troubador Publishing Ltd, Leicester, UK

Matador is an imprint of Troubador Publishing Ltd

Printed and bound in the UK by TJ International, Padstow, Cornwall

*Dedicated to Vince Lively you wonderful, mad man.
I'm sure we will both get to have tea with
Eva Peron one day.*

With all my love.

With huge and heartfelt thanks to Ingrid and Eleanor whose hard work proof reading and editing helped make this book possible. Also thanks to everyone who encouraged me to write it, particularly Penny and Pier and to Neil who is always there for me. Last but not least to my wonderful Aunty Iris, who is also in her 80's with hardly a grey hair and who was the inspiration for the character Iris. Her story is not the fictional Iris's story but she once committed a great act of kindness for me and for that I am eternally grateful.

Cover artwork by Marnie Pitts
www.marnietpitts.com

Prologue One: A Vision in the Blitz

South London Suburbs, November 1940

The girl looked around her rather untidy bedroom trying to find the pack of Tarot cards that she had been given as a birthday present earlier that year. It was a mysterious birthday present indeed, as the cards had arrived carefully wrapped in brown paper but with no indication who they were from. There was just a small card with a picture of a black cat on it and on the other side the words in blue ink, 'Use these cards, you have a talent.' That was all. Brief and mysterious.

The strange thing was that the girl suspected herself that she had a talent. Nothing much; small things came to her. Sometimes she knew things were going to happen before they did. Her mother Lily, a great sceptic on these matters, always laughed it off, but the girl would often say, 'I'm worried Mummy that something bad is going to happen,' and then Grandma would be ill or the cat would get lost again. Everyday things but enough to make the girl realise that she had some kind of sense that not everyone shared.

The door of the bedroom opened slightly and Tiger, the family's huge tabby cat, came in and nuzzled round the girl's legs. They had a close affection for each other and Tiger spent many nights asleep on her bed, much to the disgust of her mother, who thought it was dirty.

The Germans had been bombing London heavily for the last 3 months and the girl was often very scared of what might happen to her and her family. They had been lucky so far, although on one occasion a parachute mine had fallen at the bottom of the garden and brought all the ceilings down, blown the windows out and cracked the washbasins. The house had been patched up somewhat since then but it was still looking in a sad and sorry state. It was so difficult to get anyone to do repairs and money was very tight. The girl's mother had refused to allow her and her two sisters to be evacuated to the country along with their school friends and she had therefore spent numerous nights huddled in the Anderson shelter in the garden until it flooded so much it became unusable. They now braved the worst of the German raids under the stairs or sometimes in a neighbour's shelter.

A loud voice shouted up the stairs. 'What are you doing up there darling?'

'I'm just looking for something Mummy. I'll be down in a minute.' Her mother didn't know of her mysterious gift and would have been most disapproving. She was a very conventional woman and always keen to keep up middle class appearances and the girl was sure that the Tarot cards would not fit in with these aspirations. Being middle class was a new-found status for the family. They had previously lived in the East End near the docks and hated the dirt and grime of the area. In 1932, having saved hard, they were able to buy a house in a new South London suburb.

It had previously been a small village on the outskirts of the city but at that time roads and roads of modest mock Tudor semi-detached houses were being built and it was to one of them that the girl moved with her mother, father, two sisters, grandmother and uncle. Quite what the neighbours made of this large, motley crew that descended from the East End, the girl was never quite sure, but her mother was convinced that their new life had levitated them to middle class status and she was going to hang on to it whatever happened.

The girl finally gave up looking for the pack of Tarot cards and went down to the kitchen to help her mother prepare the evening meal. She would resume her task later.

At bedtime she went back up to her room and almost immediately found the cards. They had been beneath a book on her dressing table. She took them out of the cardboard pack and spread them on the floor. She had been practising using them for a few months now and loved all the different pictures of the major and minor Arcana. Sitting cross legged and spreading the cards out into a fan shape, she started to focus on them. Nothing came to her. She pushed her long, dark, almost black hair from her face and breathing deeply refocused on the cards. She felt something inside her shift slightly; she couldn't describe the feeling, she just felt slightly different. She closed her eyes, the images of the cards now fading, and gradually the sounds of her house were switching off around her. She could no longer hear her mother washing up in the kitchen, the gurgling of the hot water tank disappeared and the distant thud of Ack-Ack guns firing their shells into the night sky at another German raid drifted away. Tiger nuzzled up against her leg and she absent-mindedly petted him. She was totally oblivious of anything apart from the gentle purring of the cat. She started to see images moving before her; she was aware she was awake but at the same time it was like a dream. Her vision began. The Tarot was just a memory now, unused on the floor before her.

A beautiful long sandy beach, dunes behind, a lovely English summer's day, not too hot but warm enough to make you feel all sparkly and happy. She becomes aware that the beach does not look like all the beaches she has seen recently on the news reel: no barbed wire. The sea is turquoise, unusual for England, and quite still. Seagulls call raucously overhead. In the distance three figures fade into view, slowly walking along the surf line, sometimes jumping in and out of the small waves, getting wet and laughing. To her surprise she can see herself and she is walking alongside two men, who are hand in hand. She feels herself blush. She doesn't really know of such things and is a little shocked. Her mother would be horrified. They giggle and whisper things to each other and the girl quickly comes to understand that the two men are deeply in love. She doesn't really know how that could be, how could men love each other in the way that a man and a woman could? But she knows love when she sees it and accepts it with an open heart.

They are both handsome, one broad, dark and swarthy, the other fair with wonderful blue-green eyes. She feels their love and their warmth for each other and although her conventional upbringing makes her struggle with it she feels herself rejoicing in their love. She knows it to be very special, something written in the stars, something deep and ancient.

What the girl also notices is that although the men are clearly intimate with each other they include her in their giggling and sometimes reach out and put an arm around her as well. The scene dissolves and she is a little sad. She wants to know more of the lovers and how somehow she is their special friend.

She breathed deeply and opened and closed her eyes. The cat was still warm against her, but the sounds of her house, the Nazis and South London, were still blocked out.

Images begin to appear before her again; nothing that she can distinguish at first, then gradually settling down into things she can recognise, like a blurry film coming into focus. A light and beautiful room full of sunshine and flowers. The most beautiful room the girl had ever seen. The same two men. The dark swarthy one sits in an armchair, the fair one sitting between his legs as his lover tousles his hair.

'I love you so much,' the dark one says, 'I know it was always meant to be, and I know that we will be together for all time. To have had the honour of meeting you, to have you as my lover and my dearest friend, is a great privilege for me. Let's go out and do something good today. I feel like celebrating, let's go to our favourite spot on the river and if the weather is kind to us let's swim naked in the cool waters.'

'That would be so special,' the fairer man replies passionately. 'I feel that every day that we have together is something that is to be celebrated and to be thankful for, we must have every moment of enjoyment that we can, no time must ever be wasted.'

The girl was now so lost in her vision that she had forgotten she was having one. Everything was too focused to be a dream, too ordinary for that. No, this was more like going to the cinema and watching a movie.

The scene changes and she's now watching the two men in a little wooden rowing boat on a river. The river is broad and winding and lined on either side with willow trees that dip down into the water. It looks like it is late afternoon because there is a beautiful golden sunlight that brushes the water and makes everything look terribly alive. The sky is stunningly blue with just one or two little puffy clouds lolling about as if to further emphasise the colour of the background. Every now and then as they meander slowly up the river another vessel passes, a little motor cruiser or a rowing boat, and the occupants always wave happily at the two men who return the greeting cheerfully.

After what seems like an age the darker man says, 'That looks like a nice spot over there, shall we go and moor up?'

And at that they change the direction of the boat towards the bank. It is a secluded spot, just a little inlet a few feet across, flanked by tall trees. On the opposite side of the river are fields, and just a little upstream, the rushing of water over a weir. Yes, a perfect spot. The dark man jumps out of the boat into the shallow water. He has shorts on, and secures the mooring rope to a fallen tree. The fairer man quickly follows him carrying a small wicker hamper and a rug. They decide that they are going to have a late afternoon picnic and the basket contains their meal which is quickly retrieved and laid out in front of them. It is simple fare but perfect for the summer's day they're enjoying. They have chicken legs and some green salad and then a bowl each of the reddest, glossiest, tastiest strawberries. Accompanying the meal is a bottle of the crispest, coldest white wine, kept cool in a bag of ice cubes.

During their picnic they say little, they don't need to. They know each other so well, so intimately that each knows how the other is and what the other feels without having to say anything. There is pleasure in the silence, never awkwardness. Finishing the food they pack the remains away. The dark man gets a packet of cigarettes out of the hamper and lights two, handing one to his lover who now lies with his head in his lap. The fair man holds the moment, feeling the gentle warmth of the sun on him, listening to the lap of the water at the shore and smelling the strong cigarettes and the male scent of his lover, feeling his presence and the love that flows between them.

'What are you thinking about?' he eventually asks.

'Ah now that would make you big headed, you get far too many compliments from me.'

The fair man sits up and then, as if in reprisal for his lover refusing to say anything, starts to tickle the dark man roughly.

'Stop, stop, please I can't breathe,' the latter giggles

uncontrollably. They are soon both rolling around on the ground, tickling each other, play fighting and getting covered in dry earth.

'Come on, let's swim,' the fair man says. At that they both remove their clothes and are soon naked. The dark man is muscular with a broad hairy chest and thick strong arms and legs. The sun catches the definition of his muscles, accentuating them. The fair man is much leaner, not muscular but wiry and very fit. His abdominal muscles are perfectly defined. They run out into the water and are soon swimming, playing, sometimes jumping on each other's backs and pushing each other under. Eventually they rest, and standing on the muddy bottom, the water comes just up to their stomachs.

The fair man reaches out and puts his arms around his lover and looks him directly in his eyes. 'This moment, this special moment, this wonderful summer moment on the river with you on this amazing day, this is how I want it to be forever, for all time my love. I believe we will go on many journeys together and if each of the journeys is as wonderful as this then I am happy. A man can wish for no more.'

Before anything else could be said or could happen the scene suddenly dissolved yet again. There was no warning and the girl was startled at the interruption. It was replaced by the two same men standing hand in hand in the dark. She could see nothing else, just the two men, surrounded by empty blackness.

It is a cold, empty, heavy and threatening darkness; the change from the happy sunlight and joy filled day to this dark empty place is shocking. She feels a cold chill through her body. Suddenly everything around the men is lit up with a fierce orange light and a terrible burning wind blows. Even the girl can feel this fierce, hot current and there is an ear splitting roar. The men desperately try to hold onto each other's hands but gradually their fingers are wrenched apart and they are blown off into different directions. The girl can hear the roaring terrible wind, she can feel it tearing at her face, but what distresses her most and tears at her very heart is that she can hear an awful howling, a crying, a screaming as the two men are ripped apart and propelled to she knows not where. It is like the terrible noise made by a mortally wounded animal as it is attacked again and again by hungry predators and has the life ripped from it. Then nothing, a dark, dank, heavy silence falls.

The scene dissolved and disappeared for a final time and the girl realised she was returning to normality.

The girl didn't understand what she had seen and was highly disturbed at the nature of her vision. The happiness that she had felt at seeing herself and the men, their enormous, passionate love for each other and their awful violent separation. She now had tears running down her face. She also started to understand something else; with her limited sight she knew that the vision had a deep meaning not just for the men, but also for her. She sensed unwillingly that in some manner she was going to be involved in the events that she foresaw. In some way she was going to have to help these men, these men who she didn't yet know. That she was sure of.

The heavy two-toned wail of the air raid siren finally snapped her out of her visionary state and she could hear her mother's voice calling her to the cupboard under the stairs. She went, carrying Tiger with her, still deeply disturbed and puzzled.

★ ★ ★

Prologue Two: Gestation

Peckham, South London, November 1940

Not far away, around the same time that the girl had her vision, the boy finished pleasuring himself with a grunt. He was alone in the house and had taken the opportunity whilst thinking the dark thoughts that he always did at such times. He lay on the bed in his bedroom; the small dark room in the Victorian terrace was made even more dingy than normal by the blackout.

He was pleased that his parents were out at some event at the Rye Lane Social Club. It had allowed him time to give himself some much needed relief without the worry that his hated mother, Doris, would burst into the room. She never knocked and he would be horrified, and blushed at the thought.

He reflected briefly on his parents and how much they troubled him. His mother was a coarse, greasy-haired woman who smoked heavily and constantly berated the neighbours in her harsh voice, about some slight or another. But what the boy really hated about his mother was her weakness. She did nothing to stop his father from what he did. His father, Sid, was a rough, brutal man who worked at the iron foundry in Bermondsey. He would often come in late from work having been drinking heavily and the boy would avoid him as much as he could as he knew he was likely to receive a beating if he crossed his father's path. His mother would stand there saying nothing whilst his father meted out the punishment; the boy hated his mother more than his father for this.

He was revolted by his parents' ways, attitudes and lack of education; he knew that he was better than that and had decided to educate himself.

He borrowed copiously from the library and would spend most of his time when he wasn't at school poring over books, mainly history. He rarely played outside with his school friends and the amount of time he spent in his room meant that he was very pasty faced.

A waft of something unpleasant came up the stairs and into the boy's room. His mother had always been a dreadful cook and now with rationing it was even worse. Some ghastly stew was bubbling on the stove waiting for Doris and Sid's return from the social club. He hoped that his mother wouldn't go off with her friend Elsie who lived two doors down for a cup of tea afterwards. His father might be drunk, he may beat him or he may do that *thing* again.

A few weeks before, with his mother away seeing an aunt in Ramsgate, his father had stumbled home after several too many pints. The boy had heard the front door slamming and assumed he would be safe from the normal beating as he was up in his room and his father would probably forget his presence. But a few minutes later his father came staggering into his room and sat on the bed. The boy saw with revulsion that he had his flies undone and was groping himself. And what happened next the boy couldn't really bring himself to think about. His father did that *thing* to him. That *thing* that didn't have a name in the boy's head but that he knew was deeply and terribly wrong. The boy's misery was now complete.

Since the *thing* had happened he had hidden away in his room more and more, only going out when he had to go to school and having dark and tortured fantasies. He flipped between profound black depression and elation after he had had one of his frequent dreams.

He dreamed of dark acts to come. Things he would do. He knew that *people* would be involved with his plans; he knew that in particular one boy repeatedly appeared in his dreams. The boy in his dream had wonderful blue-green eyes; sometimes in his dreams he did the *thing* to the boy. And then sometimes in his dreams he killed him. He knew it was his destiny.

★ ★ ★

Prologue Three: Tea in the Park

Dulwich, South London, February 1953

The man sat on a bench, silently staring into the little lake that was a focal point in the park. If a passing stranger had observed him they would have thought that he was staring at *something* in the lake, but actually he was just staring, completely oblivious of where he was or what his surroundings were. It was a cold winter's day, grey and overcast, and he wasn't really dressed for it, wearing only his normal sports jacket, having forgotten his overcoat. He didn't notice the cold. He was far too lost in his own misery.

He had walked for a couple of hours mulling over his thoughts, trying to reach a final decision as to what his actions would be. Starting at his house in the road that ran alongside the park, he firstly walked down to the shops to buy some cigarettes. He was saddened at the amount of gaps there were in the line of houses from various wartime bombs. Some of the houses had already been rebuilt whereas in other places a weed-covered emptiness still prevailed. In the village he dropped by the newsagents and bought himself a packet of Embassy. He walked up the main road, and aimed for Dulwich Woods, which he had loved as a boy. He thought that maybe he would bring things to a conclusion there. His loneliness was total and complete, his parents were dead, he was friendless and even the neighbours avoided him now as they thought him slightly odd.

'He's never recovered from losing his parents in that awful bombing in Kennington you know.' He was a handsome man; dark and a little swarthy with flashing dark eyes that would make many hearts miss a beat with excitement. But he had still not found love. He didn't know how to find love. He thought that maybe he had had love once, he was not sure. Maybe it was a dream. He didn't know. But now in his abject misery he knew that there was only one thing he could do to bring peace to himself, to purge him from the terrible blackness, and that was to release himself from this life. In his pocket he carried a bottle of sleeping pills.

He walked slowly through the woods alongside the railway line that ran up to Crystal Palace. He had heard they wanted to close it down; few people used it now. He thought he would find a quiet place, sit down and finish it, release himself from the dark terrible grip of his life, but just for the moment he kept walking. He didn't really know why. Once a woman with a black Labrador startled him.

'Good morning, little chilly,' she cheerfully gestured … He just grimaced back.

A little further on he found somewhere that was almost right then had second thoughts as someone might find him too quickly. He was so confused. He really didn't know what to do. He wanted it over, wanted the pain to go but somehow couldn't find the moment, the energy or the will to complete the act.

Walking back down the main road past yet more bomb sites, he found his way back to the entrance of the park and made his way to the lake, a favourite spot since childhood. This is where he sat, pondering his fate.

And that is where the woman found him several hours later. She walked over and sat on the other end of the bench to him. 'Do you mind if I join you? I saw you as I walked up the path by the side of the lake and I'm not sure but I think I've met you before'. The man tried to smile but it came out as a horrible grimace.

'I'm so sorry,' the woman said quickly, 'I can see I'm intruding, I will say goodbye and go and have a cup of tea in the café.' The man realised he was being rude and for the first time spoke.

'Please forgive me for my manners; I was lost in my thoughts. I must seem so terribly rude.'

The woman giggled a little, almost shyly, 'Well you didn't exactly give me a warm welcome.'

There was something about her that the man liked. He was not interested in meeting women for dates, with their constant demands, but there was something about this particular woman that he trusted. He noticed her dark, almost black eyes and her dark, shiny hair piled up into a fashionable sausage on the back of her head. He felt now for some reason that he wanted to continue their conversation.

'I'm not sure that we have met. I have a good memory for faces, but perhaps you would like to have a cup of tea with me now in the café.'

'That would be most charming,' the woman replied.

They walked slowly and wordlessly up the path from the lake towards the café, entered the main door and found an empty table. For a reason, which neither of them could articulate, they felt very comfortable with the silence. If the woman was really truthful with herself she had found the dark handsome stranger very intriguing and rather sexy. She had split up with her boyfriend a few weeks before and would be more than happy to go out on a date with this handsome man.

The tea was quickly brought to them. It was too strong but they both drank it gratefully, still in silence, and the brew took a little of the February chill away. 'You looked so lost when I saw you sitting by the lake,' the woman gently ventured and at that moment she saw a tear escape from the corner of the man's eye and slide down his cheek. He coughed and, embarrassed, quickly wiped it with a handkerchief he withdrew from his pocket.

As he did, something fell to the floor and the woman politely dipped down beneath the table and retrieved the object, which she identified as a small brown bottle. She saw in a moment that it contained sleeping pills. With a sick feeling an inner knowledge welled up in her and she knew, without asking, what the man had intended. She said nothing, passing him the bottle back and giving his hand a gentle squeeze as she did.

'I'm feeling a little lonely,' she said after a few moments. 'You look like you are too, how would you like to go to the cinema in Peckham with me next week?' The man was rather shocked by her boldness, girls always waited to be asked out on dates, and he blushed a deep red hue.

'I'm sorry, I've offended you,' she quickly added, 'I really shouldn't have been so forward.'

He pondered his reply for a few moments. 'No, that's fine, it would be nice to spend some time with you.'

She was pleased at this response. She had a sense that this was a man that she wanted to share something with. She didn't really understand why. She was deeply troubled by the bottle of sleeping pills and was not sure how she could help him.

They had a second cup of tea and a toasted muffin dripping with hot butter. The man and woman spoke a little and made polite enquiries about each other's lives, where they lived, what their jobs were, and most importantly they finally told each other their names. By the end of the second cup of tea they chatted away easily and their conversation was punctuated with laughter. The man, finally taken out of his black misery, forgot for a moment his tortured and lonely thoughts and the woman realised that he was opening up to her and that she may be able to extend a hand of friendship to him. She was a woman with a great amount of kindness and love to give.

They noticed that it was starting to darken and that soon the park gates would be closed, so almost reluctantly, not wanting the encounter to finish they paid the bill, tipped the waitress and walked out together.

'So what are we going to see at the cinema next week?' he enquired.

'I'm not sure what's on at the moment but I will get the local paper and we can plan something,' she replied, rather excited at the prospect of a date.

'I am so, so very lonely,' the man whispered. 'I don't know why I am saying this because I barely know you, but I would be so pleased if you would become my friend.'

She replied, 'I think we can be good friends with each other, and by the way, you will be okay now won't you?'

He fully understood the nuance of what she said and smiled, 'I promise.'

He wrote his telephone number on a piece of paper he had in his pocket and gave it to her, folded. 'Please call me so we can plan to go to the cinema.'

'Yes of course I will.' They parted and the man strolled off up the road towards his house.

As the conversation had been developing the man had realised with stunned amazement who the woman was. At some point when he had got to know her he would tell her what he knew. She would be involved in what had been and what was to come. But he would have to gain her trust first. This meeting changed everything for him, and for the first time in a long time he felt hope. He remembered again what he had intended to do that day.

He pulled the bottle out of his pocket, unscrewed the lid and poured the contents down a drain grating.

The girl walked the other way up Hurst Court Road. She had to get a tram from the end of the road and then change to get a bus to her final destination. The handsome stranger intrigued her and she wanted to befriend him. She kept turning over and over in her mind the thought that she had recognised him when they first met. It troubled her greatly, she kept searching and searching thorough the memory of all the people she knew but nothing came to her. Finally she gave up thinking and pushed her way onto the crowded tram. For a while she forgot about the stranger and reflected on why she had come to the park that day at all.

She was still wounded and miserable from splitting up with her boyfriend and she had felt that some fresh air in the park a few miles from her home would do her good. She had felt drawn to that particular park; she didn't really know why, it was several miles from where she lived and she had only visited it once before.

It was only many years later that she fully understood it was meant to be and that the meeting in the park was part of her fate and part of a much larger story. Getting off the tram after a 20 minute ride, she joined the queue at the bus stop. It was dark now and penetratingly cold. Suddenly, with a blinding flash that made her gasp (and making the old woman behind her enquire kindly, 'Are you alright ducks?') she knew. She knew where she had seen that face before. A face she had only known briefly all those years ago. She knew now why she was so comfortable with the man. An icy chill probed her stomach; she felt slightly sick not knowing if it was with fear or excitement. She was at the same time consumed with a sense of wonder and bemusement. But she knew.

★ ★ ★

Part One: The Making of Charlie

Chapter One: Rites of Passage

South London Suburbs, 15th June 1956

Rose Rogers busied herself around her tiny but immaculate kitchen preparing the food for her son's christening guests who she would be entertaining later that day. She was in a very good mood. The sun was shining so strongly through the little window that she had to pull the curtains. These were printed with one of the bright new designs featuring a tomato motif.

On the teak draining board of the sink that she used as a work surface she was slicing cucumbers carefully to make the sandwiches. Rose was very specific about how cucumber sandwiches should be made, no crusts and a little bit of salt and pepper. The sun only enhanced her mood and she smiled to herself as she reflected on how good her life was. She had a wonderful husband, David, who she had been married to for seven years. He was handsome and kind and had a good job with the bank. Rose's mother had always instilled into her, 'Marry well', and Rose had. David would go off to the station each morning with his bowler hat and rolled umbrella, getting the steam express up to the City to do his desk job and returning home promptly at 6.30 each night having walked up the long hill from the station. Rose spent the day washing, ironing, buying and preparing food; that's how things were and she was content.

They didn't have a lot of spare money; things had been tough since the end of the war and food rationing hadn't long finished but they had enough to have a modest home in a new suburb, and just about managed to buy an ageing black Ford car which enabled the young family to take day trips out to the seaside or the country. Rose knew that in the future her husband would do well in his job, he worked so hard, and she was sure one day they would be able to afford holidays, perhaps even abroad.

And of course there were her two wonderful children. Susan Mary, born in 1952, and Charles Stephen, born in 1955. They were a bit of a handful if she was honest, but she loved them dearly and gave them all the love that she had been used to in her family home when she was brought up with her rather chaotic, but close and loving family.

Charles Stephen: today it was to be his christening, 11 months old and ready to be welcomed into the Church. Not that Rose or David were particularly religious but they just felt it was the right thing to do. Charles Stephen was a particularly beautiful and happy baby. He had the most winning smile, little dimples in his cheeks and the most wonderful pair of blue-green eyes.

Rose finished making the sandwiches and ran through a quick mental checklist to make sure she had everything ready for her guests. She did like everything to be just so. She then ran upstairs to finish getting ready herself. She looked at her reflection in the long mirror in her bedroom and was quite pleased with what she saw. She was very pretty, dark and still quite slim in spite of having given birth to two children. She had dressed simply and smartly for Charles's christening day in a grey pleated skirt and crisp white blouse. Round her neck was a string of imitation pearls.

She went to the dressing table, sat down and adjusted her make-up until she was entirely pleased with her appearance, finishing off by dabbing a little of her favourite perfume, Tweed, behind each ear. She felt very content.

Finishing her preparations she walked down the stairs and met her husband in the little hall. She kissed him on the cheek and then hugged him. 'I love you,' she whispered.

'You too,' he returned and kissed her back. The door knocker clunked and they separated. Rose quickly adjusted her hair again in the hall mirror; she was after all a very conventional woman and appearances were so important.

She opened the door and there stood her sister Iris, the first of her guests for the afternoon. She was pleased that her sister had come first as they were very close and Rose, although excited about the afternoon, was actually quite shy and was going to find welcoming the large number of guests a little difficult.

'Hello darling, come in, you're the first here,' and her sister came into the hall. Like Rose, Iris was also very dark haired and extremely attractive with a beautiful hour-glass figure, which meant she had a constant trail of boyfriends, none of whom seemed to last very long.

'How was your journey?' asked Rose.

'It was fine,' replied Iris. 'I got the train from the junction and then walked up the hill from the station. Mummy and Daddy are coming in the car later, but they couldn't fit me in as well as Gran and Uncle Tom.'

'Are you ready, have you got all the food done?' Iris enquired rather hoping that the answer would be yes. Whilst Rose was a homemaker and loved to cook and look after her family, Iris's main mission in life seemed to be to go to as many parties as possible and to have a long list of handsome boyfriends.

'All done, you'll be pleased to hear,' replied Rose with a little smile; she well knew of her sister's lack of interest in the kitchen. 'Do you think we should serve tea and sandwiches in the garden or shall I leave it in the dining room for people to help themselves?'

Iris glanced out at the weather then replied, 'I think leave them inside, we could have a shower later so that will be better I'm sure. Oh and by the way, Stephen called just before I left for the junction and said he was running a little late.'

Rose was a very punctual woman and the thought of one of the godparents being late or missing the service was troublesome to her. Her anxiety level went up about five notches.

'Bloody Stephen,' Rose snapped, 'he'll be late for his own funeral.'

'Don't worry,' Iris reassured her, 'he'll be here, he knows how important it is.'

Over the next half hour most of the guests arrived. Rose kept checking her watch anxiously and made a mental check list of who was and wasn't there. Finally at 2.30 she was sure that everyone was there *except* bloody Stephen and she started to herd her guests together for the short walk up to the parish church where the service was to take place.

They set off and as she went up the path of her little suburban detached house Stephen came running up the road, red in the face and out of breath.

'Late as ever,' laughed Iris.

'It was the train,' Stephen gasped.

'It always is,' said Rose, no longer cross with him and just pleased that all three of the godparents were there and that the service would be able to go as planned.

Rose and David had considered the choice of godparents for Charles very carefully. Firstly as godmother there would be Iris. Rose and David felt that Iris, with her loving and kind nature, would be a good influence on their son. A good aunt is someone a child always needs, they agreed. Then there were the two godfathers. Stephen Foster had been introduced to the family by Iris and had become very good friends with the couple. Rose and David liked him and he was also quite wealthy and when considering him they felt that should anything happen to both of them, then Stephen would look after Charles financially. Lastly Frederick, who was the husband of Rose's other sister Violet. Frederick was very conventional and solid, working as an accountant in the city and an occasional churchgoer. The couple felt that at least a little religious influence in their son's life wouldn't go amiss.

They arrived at the church, met all the other guests, and the christening service took place. Rose and David felt a great sense of satisfaction at this rite of passage having been completed.

The christening reception, with its cups of tea served in Rose's best bone china and accompanied by her carefully cut cucumber sandwiches was, everyone agreed, a great success and Rose felt slightly smug that it was all due to her very careful planning. She was that type of woman. Everything should be just so.

The only thing that slightly spoilt the day for Rose was Great Uncle Harry on David's side. David had insisted that he was invited, as he was one of his father's brothers and convention dictated that all of the family was there but there was something about him that gave Rose the creeps. He was 56 years old and unmarried which she found a little strange.

There was something rather grubby about his appearance and

his nails were bitten down to the quick. And there was something in his eyes, something that Rose couldn't quite put her finger on. Once, out of the corner of her eye, she had caught him looking at her baby Charles in a most odd manner, staring, staring far too long for her liking. But she put all these thoughts out of her head on this day, on this wonderful sun filled family day (Iris's prediction of rain never happened).

So, Charles Stephen Rogers, born 21st July 1955, was christened 15th June 1956. Loved by his parents, secretly adored by his big sister Susan and doted on by his three godparents. A very lucky boy.

September 1959

Charlie (as he was now known to everyone) adored his Aunty Iris. He often went and stayed with her. Iris had finally settled down and married one of her many boyfriends, Roger Wilson, and now lived just down the road in the same South London suburb. Iris and Roger didn't yet have any children of their own so Charlie and Susan knew when they went over to see their favourite aunty that lots of fuss would be made of them. There would always be sweets and cakes and there just didn't seem to be the same amount of rules as there were in their own household.

Charlie did love his Mummy and Daddy but at times he would, at four years old, be tearful at yet again being forced to tidy his little bedroom that he loved keeping in a mess. But that's what his parents were like. Tidy. Aunty Iris was a different kettle of fish entirely. She always encouraged Charlie to have fun, she would play the piano for him and sing songs from the latest Rogers and Hammerstein musicals and she never seemed to be tidying up after him. Her home was, well, chaotic. He loved it. It was a big, rambling Edwardian house and to Charlie the corridors seemed to stretch for miles and he could never work out exactly how many rooms there were. Sometimes Charlie, Susan and Iris would play hide and seek all afternoon and there were so many places to hide that it could take ages for the seeker to find the hider. Charlie's favourite place was up in the little eaves cupboards in the attic, which was accessed by a proper staircase (not like the loft ladder at home).

He would sneak in there and hide amongst the old trunks and suitcases and would probably never be found if it wasn't for the fact that he couldn't suppress his giggles when either Iris or Susan came into the room.

On this particular day Charlie got on his little bicycle that he could already proudly ride without stabilisers and rode off by himself the few hundred yards to where Iris lived. He was sobbing and red faced and when Iris answered the door she was immediately concerned and threw her arms around him in a big hug.

'Now darling, what's wrong? What can Aunty do to make it better?' After a few minutes of gentle coaxing Charlie finally became coherent and Iris managed to get out of him that: 'Daddy made me throw Teddy on the fire because he was broken and he doesn't understand and I love Teddy.' Charlie became almost hysterical at this point. Iris consoled Charlie with a glass of milk and some ginger nuts and assured him that the bear was now in Teddy Heaven. She mentally cursed David though. Why did everything have to be so bloody organised? If the boy wanted a torn, worn out old bear then he should be allowed to have it. She would have a word with Charlie's father next time she saw him. He must learn not to be so strict.

Charlie soon forgot his tears and enjoyed the rest of the afternoon with Iris playing in the sunshine in her huge, overgrown garden. Iris had phoned Rose to let her know where her son had gone so that she wouldn't worry, but stopped herself telling her sister that David shouldn't be so strict with the boy. She knew that Rose would just get defensive and she would reserve her criticisms for when she could speak to David face to face.

At 4 o'clock Iris decided it was time for Charlie to go home and went and called him in from the garden. 'Have you had a nice afternoon Charlie?' she enquired as he ran in.

'Yes Aunty, I've been making a dam in the stream.' She looked at the state of his hands and knees covered with mud and thought that she should clean him up a little before she took him home. Rose would be so horrified at a muddy urchin arriving at her front door. She took him up to the bathroom and applied warm water and soap with a flannel and soon Charlie was ready. 'I love you Aunty Iris, I wish you were my mummy.'

'Now Charlie,' Iris gently replied. ' I love you very much too but you know your mummy loves you as well don't you, just in a different way?'

'I suppose so,' he replied mournfully, his blue-green eyes filling with sadness.

Iris hesitated for a moment unsure that she should say much, but then continued. 'Charlie, as I say, I love you very much, I will always be here for you, and one day you will understand how important I am going to be to you. I'm sure you don't understand what I mean now, but I am going to be a very, very special person to you. You will always have your Mummy and Daddy but I will be here to love you in a special way and to fight off any big nasty dragons for you. In the future, when you are grown up, I am going to be one of the most important people in your life. Will you promise me you will always remember that darling? Is that a deal?'

Charlie smiled and nodded his head. Iris had said too much she knew but she felt that she had a duty to make the boy feel the strength of her love and support. It wasn't that Rose and David didn't care for her nephew; it was just that she thought they were a little hard on him sometimes. She would 'protect him against that prude of a sister of mine,' she laughed to herself.

Charlie was safely delivered home at 7 o'clock as usual. He said goodnight and kissed his parents and went up to his little bedroom. He quickly went to sleep and before long was dreaming the odd dream that he often did. It wasn't really a nightmare.

He wasn't frightened but even with his limited, childlike understanding he thought it a little strange. All he could remember about the dream was the number 80 written on every possible surface. 'Very odd,' thought Charlie when he woke up.

2nd December 1959

Not too far away, a few months later, the boy, now a man, sat reflecting on what he had done the previous week with smug satisfaction. It had been a smoggy night, London was at a crawl and he was barely able to see where he was going as he walked down the street from Peckham Rye station towards his house. He had made plans. He knew what he had to do. There was no choice. The cellar was ready. And tonight he knew that he was ready to complete the act that he been born to do. His bloody parents were dead, so he wouldn't be interrupted. He had already decided on who the boy would be. He had seen him a few times in the street and knew that 14-year-old Tommy Dawson was a neighbour's son. He didn't know why it was to be this boy but he knew that he had to do the *thing* to him. The thought of that sent a flush of sexual arousal through his groin.

Reflecting with some satisfaction, he remembered how he had followed the boy home from the station and at the corner of the street stopped him and asked him if he could come round and help him move some rubbish from the attic and he would pay him two shillings if he did. The boy happily agreed; he got little pocket money and anyway recognised the man so felt comfortable with him.

The man had been very satisfied with the arrangements when he had strangled Tommy Dawson with the electrical flex. Yes, very satisfactory. He knew that he had taken *control*. It was his duty and his destiny. Things needed to be controlled and the horror that was played out in his cellar was, he sighed contentedly, *'under control'*. That's what he liked. For it to be *'controlled'*.

But of course the man also knew that before long he would have to take *control* again. 'More planning,' he sighed, like a housewife considering all the daily chores she was going to have to do. He would feel that need starting to burn in him. But he also knew it to be a pathway and that there would be several steps along the long path but at the end the final prize, the final *control*. And if he planned well he would ensure that he took that prize. The boy with the wonderful blue-green eyes that he dreamed of.

Dreamland

The dark woman tosses and turns in her sleep. There has been a disturbance, a tremor; she knows instinctively that something terrible has happened. She gets up and goes to the lavatory then goes back to bed hoping that sleep will only bring oblivion. She is wrong; sleep returns her into a nightmare state. But she also knows, with her small fragment of sight, that this is more than a dream. It is a foretelling. She finds herself in a dark, dank space. Very low ceiling and lit by a single, mingy light bulb.

She is no longer herself and knows that she is seeing with the eyes of her nephew, now a young man. She sees through his eyes. She has his body. She has his memories and his consciousness. She feels his terror. His hands are restrained behind his back and a man blocks his way to the exit. He cannot see who the man is but can see the bulk of him in the semi darkness. His hands are outstretched and between them is a piece of electric flex. He knows what is going to happen. He screams. He keeps screaming. The scream will never stop.

The woman awakes, sweating and frightened knowing in her guts that this is more than a dream. Knowing with every fibre of herself that this is a vision of what is to come. And she knows something else. That she will stop this. She has to stop this. She is the sworn guardian of the boy and she also has a great duty placed on her to make sure that another story is written.

'Dear God, why me? How do you expect me to deal with this? How can I be capable of preventing this horror?' And she lies down again and weeps.

★ ★ ★

Chapter Two: A Cessna and a Brontosaurus

21st July 1960

Charlie, now a very grown up 5 year old, couldn't really contain his excitement.

The previous weekend his Mum and Dad had told him that his godfather Stephen was, for his birthday present, going to take him up in a little airplane at Biggin Hill, which was not far from where he lived. Charlie had never been in a plane before and apart from being excited he was also a bit nervous. He wasn't going to admit that to anyone though. He was a very determined boy. In truth when Stephen had first suggested the treat to Rose and David they really weren't sure it was a good idea and thought that it was perhaps too risky, but after a long discussion they agreed that Stephen was very experienced as he had gained his private pilot's licence 5 years before. They also checked out the credentials of the flying club. Finally they agreed in spite of their caution, seeing what an amazing opportunity it was for their boy.

On his birthday Charlie was so excited he had woken up at five in the morning. It was already light as it was high summer and peering though the gap in his curtains it was promising to be a sunny day. For a couple of hours Charlie amused himself reading and when he heard his Mum and Dad get up about 7 o'clock he dashed down to the kitchen in his pyjamas. 'Mummy, Mummy, can I have my presents pleeeeeease?'

Rose was very particular about meal times and she made Charlie sit and impatiently eat his fried egg before presents could be considered. His sister Susan, two years older, had followed him downstairs and they ate together at the little red Formica table in the kitchen. Soon it was ready for present time and Susan dashed off, coming back with an odd shaped package, rather badly wrapped in some colourful paper. 'I got this for you myself Charlie, and wrapped it,' she said excitedly.

Charlie pulled at the parcel roughly and it quickly came away. Inside was a large, golden furred teddy bear. Charlie's eyes widened with glee and he smiled his beaming smile. He was very pleased to have another bear to add to his growing collection. 'Thank you Susan,' and he hugged his sister.

Charlie's father had now joined the family in the little kitchen. He was already dressed for work in his normal pin-striped suit.

'Charlie, I've got your present for you. It's something very special.' He was carrying a big oblong box, carefully wrapped up with a card on the side. Charlie took the box from his father, which his little outstretched arms could barely grasp.

He started to try and unwrap the present, but his mother, seeing that he was having trouble, bent over with a pair of scissors and helped him cut through the paper.

'There dear, you should be able to do the rest yourself now.'

Finally, having removed all the paper from the box he could see what it was, proudly labelled 'Triang Brighton Belle train set. OO Gauge'.

Charlie was now beside himself. 'Wow Dad that's what I really wanted. WOW'. Rose and David smiled at each other. They were so happy that Charlie liked his present. He wasn't always an easy boy to please and there had been plenty of tantrums recently, but clearly they had got this right.

Charles Stephen Rogers. Five years old, 21st July, 1960. A very loved boy.

Charlie spent the morning starting to put the tracks of his train set together. He was frustrated that he would have to wait until his dad got home before he could actually get it running as it had to be 'wired in' whatever that meant.

At 1 o'clock prompt the doorbell rang and he ran and opened it to find his godfather Stephen standing there. Charlie jumped up and hugged him. 'Hang on there Charlie, you're going to knock me over,' Stephen laughed, walking into the kitchen and kissing Rose.

'Hello Rose, do you think Charlie's ready for his big day?'

'Well,' she replied, 'I think he is, but I'm not sure that I am, I'm so worried that something awful is going to happen.'

Stephen carefully reassured Rose how safe flying was and how much experience he had and she felt a little better. In truth, despite her nerves she was rather envious. She had never flown and thought the prospect exciting.

She was also excited by the presence of Stephen who she had secretly fancied ever since she had met him seven years before. She would never do anything about it of course. She would never betray her husband, believing firmly in the sanctity of marriage. That didn't stop her having naughty thoughts about him, blushing and getting rather giggly when she was around him. He was just so dashing and handsome. She suspected that he knew, as he would sometimes flirt a little in return. Rose had a suspicion that there may be more than a friendship going on between Iris and Stephen, and was highly disapproving at the thought as her sister was already married.

'You ready then Charlie boy?' Stephen shouted out into the hall and Charlie came dashing into the kitchen, shrieking, 'Yes Uncle Stephen.' Stephen said his farewells to Rose and Charlie kissed his mother. They walked out into the drive and there was parked Stephen's gleaming green Bristol which Charlie thought was so wonderful.

It had something called 'overdrive' and Charlie had no idea what it meant apart from the fact that it sounded very modern and rather exotic. Stephen skilfully reversed the car out of the drive and it purred off down the road with its dashing driver and excited passenger.

Biggin Hill was only 20 minutes away and normally Charlie would have been disappointed that a drive with his favourite uncle (he called everyone uncle or aunty even though they were not related) was over so soon but on this occasion he willed the car towards the airfield knowing what treat lay ahead. Before long the Bristol was smoothly turning into the entrance to the flying club and Charlie could see the little blue and white single engine Cessna lined up on the tarmac. He could now barely contain himself. He tugged at Stephen's hand to try and hurry him on and Stephen compliantly followed. He was so pleased to see his godson's excitement. They went into the flying club building and Stephen went through the pre-flight formalities including checking the weather, which, as he suspected, was going to be perfect.

A lovely English summer day, barely a wisp of cloud in the sky. Having completed the formalities Charlie and Stephen walked out together across the little tarmac apron.

'Uncle Stephen,' Charlie enquired, 'will I be able to fly the plane?'

'Yes you will be able to take the controls as you are so grown up now. But of course with a little help from me,' Stephen added mentally.

They reached the plane and Stephen went round the other side and opened the cockpit door then lifted Charlie up and put him into the leather passenger seat. Stephen slammed the door and double-checked it was secure then reached over and made sure that Charlie was belted in. He went though the pre-flight checks – flaps, rudder, elevators all waggled satisfactorily – and all the time explained to Charlie what he was doing. 'You see when I push the stick to the side, that will make us turn,' he finished. Everything done, Stephen started up the engine, which spluttered into life and emitted a large puff of grey exhaust.

Charlie was beginning to feel quite nervous but determined not to let his uncle see this. Stephen opened the throttle a little and the tiny plane started to move, initially hesitantly, across the grass. Charlie's big adventure was about to begin.

Childhood memories are often of those things that are different, things that are not part of everyday routine. Throughout Charlie's life he would remember this special day. He wouldn't be able to recall all the details but he would think of the funny feeling in his tummy as the plane lifted off. He would remember how grown up he felt when Uncle Stephen let him put his hand on the joy stick (with Stephen's bigger hand covering his to guide him of course). He recalled Stephen pointing to an airplane taking off way below them to the west from London Airport and also the long silvery thread of the Thames running out to the east.

Strangely though, another thing always came back to him when he thought of the day, and he often thought of it when he was feeling unhappy or troubled. He would feel somehow safe, somehow special and somehow very important. He could never quite explain that to himself, never understood why and it would be many years later that he would find out the answer.

Two days after his birthday Charlie got a letter addressed to him. He recognised Uncle Stephen's handwriting and opened it excitedly.

23rd July, 1960

Dear Charlie,

Thank you for coming flying with me the other day. I think you flew the plane very well and I was very proud of you. Charlie, I have to tell you that I am going away to somewhere called New Zealand, which is a long way away on the bottom of the world. I have some very important business to do there. I will come back to England sometimes and perhaps when you are older you will be able to visit by airplane. I'm sorry to go away so suddenly without saying goodbye.

Be a good boy for your Mum and Dad.

Stephen

Charlie was inconsolable for several days and Rose was angry at Stephen's apparent cruelty and the brevity of his letter. Charlie was eventually calmed down when Rose showed him New Zealand on his toy globe and explained how one could fly there on a 'big plane'. Charlie immediately started making plans in his head for his visit which he thought might be in the next school holidays.

Charlie never made the trip to New Zealand; his parents couldn't afford the air fare and he missed his uncle most terribly for many years.

October 1960

It was the half term holiday and Charlie had been getting really bored so was quite pleased when he heard that Uncle Frederick was going to take him up to London to a museum. Charlie was still very sad that he didn't see Uncle Stephen any longer but he had had a postcard from him and was looking forward, before long, to going to see him on a big airplane.

Uncle Frederick was a different kettle of fish altogether. Charlie didn't find him nearly as exciting, if truth be known. Frederick was a rather dull man but he had taken Charlie on some outings (mainly to cricket matches) and on this occasion Charlie understood that they were going to somewhere called the 'Natural History Museum'. That sounded okay to Charlie.

Frederick picked up Charlie at 11 o'clock in his little grey Morris Traveller. 'Not like Uncle Stephen's car,' Charlie thought sadly as they set off down the hill to the station.

'Are you looking forward to your day out in London Charlie?' Frederick enquired. 'We are going to a very exciting museum.'

'It sounds great Uncle,' Charlie replied sounding more enthusiastic than he felt for his uncle's sake.

'I've brought lunch with us so we will be able to have something to eat on the train before we get there.'

Frederick had brought a very carefully prepared, if meagre, packed lunch of liver-sausage sandwiches and Kit Kats. When Rose heard of this she had grimaced to herself thinking, 'Too bloody tight to take the boy out to lunch at the museum.'

They arrived at the station car park and Frederick gave Charlie some money to give to the man behind the ticket office window. 'Ask for two day returns to Charing Cross,' he instructed. Charlie duly complied and came away armed with two little green card tickets, which they presented to the ticket collector at the gate.

'Which platform for the fast train to Charing Cross?' Frederick enquired. Now that got Charlie a little more excited than he had been. He wasn't sure what the 'fast' train meant but reckoned it sounded exciting. He had never been up to London before on the train and this was a new adventure for him. They were duly directed to Platform 2 and Charlie held Frederick's hand, taking in the sights and sounds of the station around him.

He had been on a train a few times before but only a couple of stops up the line. After what seemed like an interminable wait,

Charlie saw the front of the train approaching around the bend in the track. It drew into the platform with a squeal of brakes. It was a dark green electric train and was crowded with passengers who had got on at some distant coastal resort. Frederick reached up and opened the door and helped Charlie step up over the big gap from the platform. The tinny sound of the tannoy sprung into life: 'The train on Platform 2 is for Waterloo and Charing Cross only.' They climbed into the little single compartment and squeezed into two spare seats between a rather fat woman who smelled of cigarettes and a business man who was heavily engrossed in the Daily Telegraph.

Charlie was a little disappointed that he wasn't given the seat by the window so he climbed up onto Uncle Frederick's knee to get a better view. The train hissed as the air was released from the brakes and soon it was accelerating up the track towards the city. As it got faster the wheels made a clickety-clack sound over the rails. Charlie thought it was a very exciting noise and began to think that Uncle Frederick might not be such a boring uncle after all.

During the 20 minute journey to London through the southern suburbs, the noise, smell and sights of the railway enthralled Charlie. He noticed that as they got closer to the centre of the city, there were fewer trees and the houses looked much dirtier and closer together. There were also a lot of empty green spaces that had been bomb sites not that many years before and which were now covered with long grass and buddleia trees.

After going through London Bridge station without stopping, the train got slower and slower and it seemed to Charlie that they were travelling over the roof tops of people's houses. Sometimes the windows were so close that he could see people in their kitchens. He also noticed that the train was making a very loud screeching noise as it negotiated the many bends into the city. There was a brief stop at Waterloo where quite a lot of people including the fat woman got off. After a few moments the train crossed the bridge over the Thames (Charlie worried briefly that the bridge might fall down) and eased its way into Charing Cross.

As it did so Frederick exclaimed, 'Oh no, we forgot to have our lunch Charlie!'

Charlie had in fact remembered but had been avoiding the meal as he thought liver-sausage sandwiches sounded scary and hoped they would be forgotten.

'We can have them later at the museum.'

Charlie's heart sank.

At Charing Cross they got off the train and Charlie was immediately taken with just how many people there were rushing around. He had never seen so many people before in his life. They pushed through the crowds and went down some stairs. 'We are now going on the Underground train,' said Frederick. Now Charlie had started out the day without a great deal of enthusiasm and the whole concept of liver-sausage sandwiches had weighed heavily on his mind, as they would later on his stomach. However things seemed to be getting more and more exciting by the moment; not only had they been on a 'fast' train, they were now going on an 'Underground train'.

As they descended the stairs to the District Line, Charlie noticed how musty and gloomy it was. They waited on the platform with what seemed like hundreds of people and in a few moments a red train came snaking into the station. Charlie was amazed when instead of having to open the doors like they had on the previous train, they slid open as if by magic, with a hiss. They got in; it was very crowded and they had to stand up. The train pulled out of the station and accelerated and Charlie immediately put his hands to his ears as the train made awful squealing and rattling sounds. He was actually quite frightened for a few moments and looked to Frederick for some reassurance. His uncle, seeing the concern on the boy's face, smiled and took his hand and squeezed it. 'Don't worry we'll be there shortly.'

The train arrived at South Kensington and they disembarked and walked up the long tiled subway to the museum. As they arrived at the entrance Frederick recalled the forgotten lunch again and to Charlie's dismay they found a bench and he had to make the best of the sandwiches, which as he feared were disgusting, and the Kit Kat, which he enjoyed. Having finished the food they went to the entrance and Frederick brought two tickets.

They went through the huge hall and Charlie was amazed at

the size of the place and before long his mouth dropped open in awe as they encountered the first of the wonders of the day: a huge skeleton of something called a 'Brontosaurus'.

Now Charlie was really starting to see that Uncle Frederick was a little more interesting than he thought. He had tried to like him before, it was just that his birthday and Christmas presents from him had always been so boring.

Last year it had been a jumper. 'It will keep the boy warm this winter, Rose,' he had said. 'And Marks and Spencer had such a good autumn sale.' Frederick had tried to enthuse the boy with the outings that he had taken him on but Charlie really couldn't get excited about cricket, he hated sport anyway, it just seemed so slow. But this was different.

They spent a couple of hours walking through the halls of the museum and Charlie would often stop and go 'Wow,' or 'What's that uncle?' He had a thoroughly enjoyable afternoon looking at dead creatures in tanks of formaldehyde and butterflies pinned to boards. At the end of the day they got the train home again but Charlie didn't remember anything about the journey as he was totally exhausted and slept all the way home.

The next day Rose made Charlie write a thank you letter to Frederick. She was very proper in those things. It read:

Dear Uncle Frederick,

Thank you very much for the day out yesterday. The train was very exciting and I loved the dinosaur. (Rose had to spell that for him.)

Love
Charlie XXX

Dreamland

Things could not be better for little Charlie. That was of course apart from his dreams. They had become darker over the years. On the night that he went to the museum with Frederick he had the dream again. It was always the same; he would be in a room, an empty room, a dark room.

*Nothing there, just an awful sense of being scared. Then he would see the number **80** written on every surface. Huge numbers that looked like they had been written in chalk.*

He had no idea what it meant. He had no idea why it was frightening. It was just a number but it made him very scared and he woke up screaming for his mother. She came and comforted him back to sleep. Then he had the good dream that he often had. In the good dream he was a bird flying high up in the sky and he felt happy and secure and comforted and the number 80 was a forgotten mystery.

★ ★ ★

Chapter Three: A Cricket Bat

July 1961

The man sat in deep thought in the grim little parlour of his dead parents' house. He was pleased they were gone. His mother was a stupid, common, dirty woman. And as for his father. The man could barely bring himself to think about his father. The years of beatings he had endured were bad enough but then his father had started doing that *thing* to him. When it first happened he was frightened and he had no word for it, he just knew it hurt and was deeply wrong. Since he had become a man he had fully understood his father's perverted actions and despised him deeply but at the same time hated himself for not having been able to stop the man from doing this.

The bitch mother had died 10 years before of a heart attack and his vile father had lingered on another 5 years before stomach cancer took him.

The man smiled to himself, he was happy and contented. Life was good. He had this house; that pleased him. His parents had never amounted to much, they were both too stupid, he thought, but they had been able to pay off the small mortgage on the property. When his father died he was surprised but delighted to find that everything had been left to him in the Will; no one else in the family was mentioned. Perhaps, this was some measure of atonement in his father's mind for what he had done. Probably not, probably more it was an act of spite toward them.

He was also pleased about how his plans had been going. He knew that he had a destiny, and the destiny was to control and the ultimate control was to kill. He knew that when he had murdered Tommy Dawson two years before, he had loved him dearly. During the act of doing that *thing* to the boy, he had found a physical expression of that love and at the moment of climax had tightened the electric flex around the boy's neck until the life faded out of him. The sense of bond and unity with the boy were complete.

Dreamland

*As well as the dark thoughts he has during the day, at night the man dreams and he dreams of the boy with the wonderful blue-green eyes. He now knows who he is and he senses the intricate jigsaw puzzle of events starting to draw together. He knows what is fixed, what is to come. He knows his own destiny and the boy's destiny. They will bond and be together. He had begun to understand this a few years before when his dreams of the boy had begun to be more detailed. He now sees in his dreams the despicable **thing** that other men will do to the boy and he knows deep in his loving heart that the only way of saving him will be to bond with him in a final act of loving.*

Christmas 1961

Charlie opened his eyes; although he hadn't really been asleep he was so excited. It was Christmas morning and Charlie knew full well what that meant: presents. He was pretty sure he would be getting what he wanted this year. He had asked for an extra train for his train set. He had seen a little blue freight locomotive he liked and had written a letter to Santa with the exact description. He was sure it would work. If Charlie was really honest with himself he wasn't quite sure that he believed in Santa Claus anymore. He had been struggling with the concept since he had found his presents at the top of his mother's wardrobe the previous Christmas. He wasn't really bothered. Presents were presents wherever they came from, but he kept up the pretence for his parents' sake.

Charlie could hear his mother busying herself in the kitchen that was immediately below his bedroom. He knew that Christmas lunch this year was going to be at his house with all the family. He sighed slightly at the thought, yes the turkey would be great, he liked that and of course there would be crackers ... but he also knew that he would have to endure being kissed by loads of grandmothers and aunts, which he hated. Apart from Aunty Iris of course. He loved Iris very much and although he didn't have a name for it, Charlie probably had a little bit of a crush on her.

Rose was approaching the lunch preparation with gusto. As normal she had made numerous checklists to ensure everything was just right. Ingredients, timings, seating plans, everything organised to the last detail. She was already a little weary from all the preparations, but determined to give her family the best possible Christmas.

There would be 14 people for the festivities that day; it would be a squeeze getting them into the dining room but they would just about fit. Rose had got David to extend the dining room table with some folding card tables and borrowed chairs from the neighbours.

Her next job was to write out the little place name cards that she had bought, each one decorated with a snowman. She liked things just so and thought that who sat next to who was very important. She wanted to get everything just right. She wrote out the cards in biro. The last one she did was Uncle Harry's. She grimaced as she did this. She didn't really want him there but David had insisted that his uncle should come. Rose didn't like him, he always had a slight odour about him, she couldn't say of what, and he said so little. The biggest reason why Rose hated Harry though was the way that he had looked at Charlie at his christening. She wasn't sure that she wanted to define the look but it just didn't seem right. She quickly brushed all these thoughts away and decided that irrespective of Harry the day was going to be perfect. There were so many people coming that she would barely notice him anyway.

Rose had had the turkey roasting in the oven for an hour and checking that things were on schedule against her timetable, she decided it was time to give the children their breakfast. As there would be so much to eat at lunchtime she wasn't going to do a cooked breakfast, a quick bowl of Rice Krispies would do.

'Charlie … Susan,' she called up the stairs, 'breakfast is ready.'

The children came bounding down from their bedrooms knowing that as soon as they had eaten up their cereal it would be time for presents. In a few moments the Rice Krispies were scoffed down and they ran into the sitting room where the big spruce Christmas tree was, covered in colourful decorations and with a pile of presents underneath it.

Rose and David both came into the room and David went over to the tree and started giving out the presents to their children. Charlie as always had the biggest pile. He excitedly started the process of unwrapping. He had a plan in his mind and that was to leave his parents' present to last, because that would be the best. There was a scarf for his favourite teddy bear, hand knitted by his sister Susan, which he was very pleased with. He groaned as he found yet another jumper from Granny Rogers. She wasn't a very good knitter and the family was always in fits of laughter as one of her victims would try on another shapeless item she had lovingly made.

He eventually reached the bottom of the pile by which time he was surrounded by crumpled bits of Christmas paper and ripped off labels. He picked up the present his Mum had said was from them and as he did his heart sank. He could immediately tell from the shape that something was wrong. Instead of a big oblong cardboard box which he knew would contain the train he wanted, this contained a long but narrow and very hard object. Although Charlie was sensitive he was also a very polite boy so he tried not to show his feelings. Perhaps it was something else for his train set he thought. He pulled away at the paper and gradually revealed the wooden object beneath.

At first he had no idea what it was but then with a sinking feeling in his tummy he understood with horror that it was a cricket bat.

'There Charlie,' David said, 'I thought it was about time that you started to learn a sport. I always enjoyed cricket as a boy.'

Now as much as Charlie wanted to keep his feelings from his parents, this revelation was simply too much. He had desperately wanted the freight train for his train set, he had been forced to play cricket a few times at school and hated it, and was now overwhelmed with the idea that his father wanted to encourage it further. So Charlie's response to this grim news was to promptly burst into tears and wail, 'But I wanted a train, it's not fair.'

Perhaps if his father had picked him up and hugged him and re-assured him, then what happened next wouldn't have and Charlie might have been gently persuaded that cricket wasn't a great evil.

However David's response, in his normal brusque manner was: 'Don't be so damned ungrateful Charlie, that was a very expensive bat. Get up to your bedroom and learn some manners and whilst you're up there tidy up your mess.'

Charlie wailed even louder, ran upstairs and slammed his bedroom door as hard as he could. He was crying so much that he was breathing in huge gulping breaths. He hated his father, he hated cricket and he wanted his train.

After a few minutes he started to calm down a little and began to think more rationally. If his father couldn't give him the train that he wanted then he would find someone who would, and he knew who that was. He was going to find Uncle Stephen who was in somewhere called New Zealand. He didn't know how to get there but suspected it would be quite a long journey.

Charlie found his little red bag that he took his sandwiches to school in and started packing for his trip. He was still crying but now very determined. The first thing he packed was his teddy bear. Then he went to the bathroom and put in his toothbrush and lastly from his bedroom the book that he was reading and loved, 'The Lion, the Witch and the Wardrobe'. He shook his moneybox and a small pile of coins came out. He quickly counted up: seven shillings, surely that would be enough for a plane ticket to New Zealand?

He pulled his duffle coat off the back of his bedroom door and slipping his school bag over his shoulder he quietly crept downstairs. Some of the family had arrived and he could hear his Granny Rogers barking out commands to Rose in the kitchen. Charlie thought she was a very scary grandmother. He checked that there was nobody in the hall, quickly made for the front door and shut it quietly behind him. His tricycle was parked just outside and he got on it and rode off defiantly down the lane. He would head for Biggin Hill and find a plane there. It would take a long time but he was pretty sure that he would be in New Zealand by the afternoon, maybe evening at the latest.

Over the next hour the rest of the family all arrived at the house in various cars. The other set of grandparents, Rose's mother and father, Violet and Iris and their husbands and Violet's daughter Wendy. The only person that wasn't there was Uncle Harry and Rose was rather hoping that he wouldn't turn up. That would make her day she thought as she put the sprouts on to boil.

Rose ticked the sprouts off the checklist with a little pencil she kept hanging on a string on the wall, always very useful. As she did so Iris came into the kitchen. She of course looked as glamorous as ever. She had on a big green swirly taffeta skirt and cream blouse, which set off her dark good looks very well. She used a lot of make-up by Rose's standards and her lips were a particularly bright red today. Although she was now 36 years old she still had a wonderful figure. 'Hasn't had any children to spoil it,' thought Rose a little uncharitably.

'Where's Charlie? I want to give him his present.'

'Damn boy is sulking in his bedroom again; he's had another tantrum, and been up there for an hour at least. '

'Don't worry dear, I'll go and find him and see if I can dry his tears.'

Rose felt a small pang of jealousy go through her at the thought that her sister had a better way with her son than she did, but she quickly dismissed it.

Iris went upstairs and knocked on the door of Charlie's room. 'Charlie, it's Aunty Iris, I've got a present for you.' There was no answer, and worried that Charlie may be particularly upset Iris pushed the door open a little and immediately saw he was not there. Unconcerned she went back downstairs.

'Rose, he's not up there, where else could he be?'

'Probably skulking in his den in the garden. He's such an awkward boy sometimes. Susan can you go and find Charlie please?' Susan ran off only to come back a few minutes later.

'Mummy he's not there.' At that moment Rose felt a cold shiver of fear but immediately tried to be rational.

'He must be somewhere, let's have a good look round the house and garden together.'

But as they searched Rose had a rising tide of panic that she didn't know where her 6-year-old son was. Within 10 minutes the tide of panic had overflowed into hysteria as she realised he was nowhere to be found, and her fears were confirmed when Susan spotted that Charlie's tricycle had gone.

'David,' she shouted tearfully, 'I think Charlie has gone off on his bike. Where could he be? Please someone do something. Anything could have happened.'

She fell tearfully into her mother's arms who tried to comfort her daughter whilst David and the other men decided what to do. They agreed that they would go out separately in different directions. He couldn't have gone far. It was too soon to call the police though. So David, Frederick, Roger and the boy's grandfathers walked off into the cold Christmas morning on a mission to find the lost boy. 'Damn him,' sniffled Rose. 'The lunch is going to be ruined.'

The next hour Rose spent in an agony that can only be understood by a parent who has had a child go missing. One by one David, the uncles and grandfathers came back, grey faced and now deeply worried. They had searched all the nearby streets where they thought Charlie could have gone and he was nowhere to be seen. 'Rose,' said David gravely, 'I think we should call the police, don't you?'

'Oh my god what are you suggesting? Do you think he could have been abducted?'

'Now please try and keep calm Rose, I'm not suggesting that at all but the police are much more experienced at finding lost children than we are. I'm sure they will find him really quickly.' David wished he actually believed what he was saying but he felt he had to try and reassure his wife. He went over to the little black Bakelite phone and dialled 999. 'Hello, is that the police? Yes? I want to report a missing child.'

At that moment he heard a gasp behind him and turned around. Rose had her hand to her mouth. In the porch stood Uncle Harry, dishevelled as ever, and smelling of that Uncle Harry smell that Rose could never define. In his arms was Charlie. Charlie was clearly conscious as his eyes were open, but they seemed to have a distant vacant look in them. His shorts were ripped down one side and he was covered in blood. Harry initially didn't say anything. He rarely did, but finally he spurted, 'Found Charlie, love him, wanted to help him.'

At this point all sorts of terrible ideas went through Rose's head. She had a great distaste for Harry and awful thoughts of what might have happened to or been done to Charlie went spinning through her mind. 'Give me my child you freak, get your fucking hands off him.' Harry looked confused but meekly passed the traumatised boy to his mother.

The rest of the family were probably more horrified by Rose's use of the F-word than Charlie's appearance, but quickly rallied round Rose to check the boy was alright.

'Call the doctor NOW David.'

Rose took Charlie in her arms up to his bedroom and laid him tenderly on his bed. He still hadn't spoken a word and his eyes had a glazed and terrified look in them. Out of the bedroom window she saw Harry skulking off up the street.

Over the next hour the doctor came and confirmed that Charlie was suffering from a gash to his head, but no concussion. Rose was persuaded that the police shouldn't be called as it was starting to look like Charlie had perhaps just had an accident on his bike, which was still missing.

Rose still had a nagging feeling that something else was wrong. She gave him a couple of aspirins as the doctor had suggested and held him in her arms until he drifted off to sleep. She was going to get to the bottom of this she thought. What the hell had Harry done? She wouldn't be persuaded that he hadn't done something to the boy, she thought determinedly.

The family managed to have their Christmas lunch but the atmosphere was grim. Rose was trying to put a brave face on things and even managed to joke about the fact that the sprouts were overcooked, but David could see she was still deeply troubled.

When the meal was over, Rose and Iris stood together in the kitchen making a start on the washing up. 'This really is the last straw Iris. He is such a difficult boy. He has spoilt Christmas Day running off like that and then I want to find out what the hell happened.'

'I think you're being a little over dramatic,' replied Iris. 'It looks to me that Charlie came off his bike somewhere and that Harry happened to come across him as he walked over here for lunch. Can you not give poor Harry any credit?'

'Poor Harry. You must be joking Iris. I reckon he's some type of pervert.'

'Rose that is ridiculous, just because he's a little odd doesn't make him evil. Now shall I go up and see if Charlie is awake? Maybe I can get something out of him.' It was the second time that day that Iris had presumed she could mother Charlie better than Rose but this time Rose was pleased. She knew it to be true. Blast Iris, she had a way with the boy that Rose didn't fully understand.

Iris talked gently to the boy for a few minutes, told him how much she loved him again and how she would protect him, but even to her he wouldn't open up.

No one would find out the truth of what had happened that day for many, many years. Charlie would never talk about the subject and Harry was never invited to family celebrations again. But this was also the start of something else, a pattern of Charlie running away when things got difficult.

Dreamland

Many intertwined dreams are dreamed. In South London a little boy dreams repeatedly of the number 80 and still doesn't know why it is so frightening. Gradually, each time he has the dream it changes and gets more and more scary. He will find himself in a dark damp and terrible place and he is with a man but he doesn't know who; he knows that the man is going to do something very bad to him but he doesn't know what. On waking he makes himself feel better by thinking of being a bird in the sunshine, soaring in the summer air and being loved.

*Not far away a bitter and twisted man with black evil in his heart dreams of what he will one day do to the boy with wonderful blue-green eyes. He has happy and contented dreams knowing that what he will do is **right**.*

A woman dreams a dream she had many years ago and knows that one day soon she will have to ensure that the dream comes true.

Far away a broken and lonely man dreams of something that he had and lost and wakes crying and desolate, his wife on the other side of the bed unable to comfort him.

The dreamers' lives are tangled up like strands of wool. Some of them know much of how events will be played out, some have no inkling at all. But all, including the boy, have a sense that none of this can be changed. It is already written and they are just actors in a play reading someone else's lines.

★ ★ ★

Chapter Four: The Tattooed Rent Boy
and a Polish Countess

August 1970

What man can ever really recall the moment that they know they are gay? Charlie would often reflect on this through his life and when he talked about it with his friends he would describe it as a gradual awakening rather than a sudden realisation.

From when he was a little boy he knew somehow he was different. He hated the rough and tumble of having to play sport at school and he was often lonely and isolated as he found it difficult to make friends. He didn't know in his young mind why he was different but there was an inner sense that he was.

Family life for Charlie could be trying; he loved his Mum very much but found her sense of everything being 'proper' rather difficult.

His father had given up years ago trying to involve Charlie in any 'boys' activities like sport and would refer to him in an irritated voice as 'That odd boy'. Everything always had to be tidy at home, excruciatingly tidy and as Charlie grew up there were constant clashes. Charlie knew that his close family were good people, they didn't treat him really badly but there was a distance as they tried to deal with the feeling that he was different.

Charlie first noticed other boys in the showers after gym at school when he was 10 or 11. Their bodies intrigued him. He didn't know it was a sexual attraction. Actually this being the 1960's he didn't even know what sex really was, but there was a fascination in looking at boys' naked bodies that he didn't have a word for and didn't understand.

Now, aged 15, he was lying on his bed in tears. There had been another row with his father, this time about his school work (or lack of it as Charlie did as little as possible) and he had stormed up to his bedroom, slammed the door and put on his latest Pink Floyd album

Atom Heart Mother ... loudly ... he knew it would annoy his parents. He lay on the bed sobbing his heart out, thinking about how awful his parents were to him, how unfair his life was, and how much he would like to be anyone else but Charlie Rogers. His mind was in turmoil and a cycle of negative and anxious thought was whirling round his head. He kept returning to a sick knowledge, an inner discomfort and a great fear. Over the last few years, as he had started to understand sex, he had begun to realise that he was attracted to men and he was initially totally appalled by the idea. Gradually he had come to understand that this was what he was, but also that would put him in direct conflict with his family.

Charlie felt that his life was getting out of control and he had no idea how to sort it out. In his turmoil he decided that the only way he could handle this would be to run away. He had run away many times before, usually just for a few hours. This time would be different though, he wouldn't run away today. He would make plans. He needed to save a bit of money from his job helping out at the local newsagents. But he would do it soon. Get away from his family. They must never know what he was turning into. Never.

The gruff voice of Charlie's father shouted up the stairs, 'Turn that bloody racket down.'

A few weeks later Charlie had managed to save up 10 pounds and he decided he was ready to leave. It was a warm August day and the rest of the family was on an outing. Charlie had declined to go. His father just thought he was sulking again and was actually quite pleased that the truculent teenager wouldn't be with them to spoil the day with another outburst.

Charlie packed his rucksack with a couple of t-shirts and a pair of jeans, his cassette player and some favourite tapes, with the ten pounds carefully concealed in the bottom. He knew that the rest of the family would be out for a few hours so he didn't rush. He briefly contemplated taking his favourite teddy bear but decided against it. He might get lost; he thought that would be too much to cope with. He made a mental note that once he had settled down somewhere he would get his mother to send him on.

Charlie was ready. He briefly checked his image in the mirror.

He was now over six feet tall and had grown into a lean, handsome teenager. His fair hair was fashionably long and hung round his shoulders; gleaming out from his fringes were his wonderful blue-green eyes. Charlie walked down the stairs of the house that he had lived in all his life. He went out the front door, slammed it and strode down the garden path with his head held high, although in truth a little nervous.

The walk to the station in the warm summer sunshine took only 20 minutes and as Charlie got further away from home he felt more and more confident. He knew he had done the right thing. His family must never know his secret. At the station he bought a single ticket for London (he had no intention of coming back). Sitting on the train a few minutes later, for some reason he thought of the first time that he had ever taken the train to London, with his Uncle Frederick all those years ago. He would miss his uncle and also his Aunty Iris he thought. Whilst Uncle Frederick was a little dull and very proper, he had managed to encourage Charlie to start painting watercolours and Charlie was actually quite talented. Charlie's father had never been able to engage with him about anything and Charlie enjoyed having someone who showed an interest in him and encouraged him to excel in what he was good at. 'Not bloody cricket,' thought Charlie ruefully.

The train soon reached Charing Cross and Charlie excitedly threw the door open and jumped off whilst the train was still moving. He was on the platform with several hundred other people when with a sinking feeling in his stomach he suddenly realised that he had no idea what he was going to do next.

Charlie had very carefully planned how he was going to get to London and had saved up for his trip but had never for a moment really considered what would happen when he got there. It wasn't that Charlie was stupid, he wasn't, but he had got so wrapped up in the need to run away and how he was going to do it that he hadn't really thought it through to the next part. Now he was standing on the concourse of a bustling London Terminus feeling very, very lonely. He also noticed something else: he was extremely hungry. He had skipped breakfast that morning with excitement.

Looking around he spotted a Wimpy Bar. He decided to go and

get a burger and that it would also be a chance for him to have a think about what he would do next. He found a spare table and ordered a cheeseburger from the grubby and disinterested looking waitress. It came fairly quickly along with the Pepsi he had also asked for. He fell on the burger hungrily and it was devoured in a few moments.

As he was swilling the remains of it down with the Pepsi he noticed a man on the next table was smiling at him. The man was very attractive and Charlie felt a flush of sexual excitement. He put him around his mid 20's, dark and well built. His bare arms revealed a myriad of tattoos; Charlie found this very exciting. He managed a shy half smile back and given that signal the man immediately came over to Charlie and introduced himself.

'Hi mate I'm Wayne. What are you doing here looking so lonely?' Wayne spoke with a strong London accent and Charlie found that even more exciting. Charlie almost smiled when the thought flashed through his mind that his mother would think that Wayne was 'rather rough.' 'Good,' he thought.

Now Charlie was very shy but now, made doubly shy by the fact that he fancied the man, he blushed and, although barely able to speak, managed to blurt out, 'Run away from home.'

Wayne smiled, 'Oh I see, and why did you decide to do that young man?'

'My parents don't understand me, I've been having an awful time and I need to get away from them, it's so square and boring there.'

'And did you leave your girlfriend behind as well?' Charlie thought this was a bit of an odd question, not realising that Wayne was probing for more information.

'I don't have a girlfriend, I, ummmm, I .... well .... you know,' and Charlie's response tailed off into an embarrassed silence. He went even redder and looked at Wayne who smiled and said, 'I understand.' And actually Charlie knew that he did.

'Hey fella, you haven't told me your name?' Wayne enquired.

'It's Charlie, Charlie Rogers.'

'Well Charlie boy, how about this. This is your lucky day. Not only have you arrived in big and exciting London town but also you've met me. Do you know what I'm going to do?' Charlie dumbly shook his head.

'Not only am I going to find you somewhere to live but I'm going to get you work as well. Now I think it's your red letter day.'

'Wow! that's amazing Wayne, that's fantastic. When do I start? Where am I going to live? Wow!'

Charlie had, in a flash, created a story in his mind where he had a rather good job, probably working in an art gallery, living in a nice house and where Wayne was deeply in love with him for ever after. That was the kind of boy that Charlie was: naïve, inexperienced and truly romantic. Apart from the need to get away from his parents there had been another thing driving him and that was his need to love and to be loved by a man and he felt instinctively he would find that in London. And now amazingly he had met a man he fancied straight away who wanted to help him and would be his lover. Charlie couldn't believe his luck.

'Come on Charlie boy, let's go back to my flat so I can get you ready for work tonight.' And they walked off together across Charing Cross station towards the Strand. What occurred next happened so quickly that Charlie found it hard to comprehend. Just as they reached the exit of the station a man ran over towards the pair shouting, 'Leave him alone Wayne, haven't you had enough recruits for one week?'

'Fuck off Michael, it's none of your business,' Wayne shouted aggressively back. 'C'mon Charlie, let's leave this old tosser to interfere with someone else.' At that Michael, who was a foot shorter than Wayne and looked considerably weaker, drew his arm back and landed a thudding punch to Wayne's stomach, who collapsed, doubled over on the tarmac, gasping for air.

Charlie was frightened, confused and had no idea whatsoever what was happening apart from the fact that a complete stranger had come between him and the man he fancied, a man who was going to help him so much.

'Why did you do that?' he blurted out, tears streaking down his face. 'He was going to get me a job and I was going to live with him, what business is it of yours, who the fuck do you think you are?'

'Listen,' Michael started gently, 'I need you to be very grown up and understand what I'm telling you. Wayne is a very bad sort and you were in danger. Please believe me.'

Charlie was still very tearful and angry with Michael for having interfered with his fantasy that Wayne was going to be his dashing lover but there was something in Michael's face and voice that made Charlie trust him.

'What do you mean I was in danger? I don't understand. I know I'm only 15 but I'm not stupid.' Michael, very gently and carefully, explained to Charlie that Wayne ran a house where young men were coerced into selling their bodies for sex, that they were encouraged to take drugs and become addicts and were totally dependent on Wayne who took most of their earnings. 'Now do you understand? Please believe me. I became aware of Wayne's disgusting "business" when I was working with some drug addicts a couple of years ago. It was purely by chance I saw you both walking across the station but seeing how young you are, I knew you could be in danger.'

Charlie had stopped crying and was in a slight state of shock, realising what a narrow escape he had had and feeling foolish for having been taken in so easily. He had never heard of people selling their bodies for sex, but the thought of that and having to have sex with men he didn't like appalled him.

'But what am I going to do now? I can't go home, I've got nowhere to go. I don't know what to do,' and though he didn't want to, he promptly started crying again.

'Well,' said Michael, 'you have a number of choices. You can go home to your parents, you can go to the police or you can come back with me and I will take care of you.'

Charlie had had one close escape today; whilst he was very naïve, he was a quick learner and didn't want to run from one trap straight into another.

'How do I know you're any better than Wayne is, you could just be telling me these things so that you can get me back to your house and do … well … I don't know … all those bad things to me you just said he would.'

'You're a very sensible young man. Yes of course you're right, you don't know me from Adam. Firstly, my name is Michael Lewis. What I will do to reassure you is to take you to the drug rehabilitation centre where I work and they will vouch for me. Would that make you happier?'

Charlie thought for a moment; he really wasn't very experienced with anything apart from life in the suburbs and was totally out of his depth. Momentarily he considered running and going back to his parents. Then again, perhaps this was a chance to find some help and friends in London. 'Okay Michael, I think that's alright, can we go there now?'

'Yes of course, and by the way I still don't know your name.'

'It's Charlie, Charlie Rogers.'

'Well I'm very pleased to meet you Charlie Rogers. Let's go, I think we've dealt with Wayne don't you.' At that he gestured to the station entrance where they saw him skulking out.

Charlie and Michael walked together through the bustling Strand and then up Charing Cross Road and into Soho. They eventually reached a blue front door, which simply had the name 'The Haven' written on it. Michael rang the bell and the door was opened and a tall, tough looking middle-aged woman with badly dyed blond hair let the pair in.

She welcomed them in a gruff voice with a strong accent and took them into an office where she sat them down. The office was dingy and tatty and the walls were covered with large travel posters of sunny places as if to cheer the visitors up. If anything, they made the surroundings seem worse. However, the woman seemed very kindly, if a little strange (Charlie noticed she had very large, hairy hands) and she sat them down and made them as comfortable as possible in the office surroundings.

In the next hour or so Charlie was given tea and hot buttered toast by the woman who was called Olga. She told him she was a Polish countess. Olga, in spite of her tough looks, was very gentle with Charlie and he quickly liked her. She listened attentively to Michael as he explained the situation and then reassured Charlie that Michael was known to the Centre and the police as someone who offered a safe house to 'waifs and strays' and that she would call him every day to check he was okay. Charlie was still a little nervous and overwhelmed by everything that had happened that day but his instincts and logic told him that this was all fine.

'So darling,' said Olga, 'you going to be alright. You going to let Michael look after you?'

'I think so, yes I'm sure I'll be alright,' said Charlie, still only partly sure himself. The two men thanked Olga who duly kissed both of them on the cheeks leaving a stain of cheap red lipstick. 'Bye bye darlings, take care, remember I will call you every day.'

Charlie and Michael walked out into the Soho afternoon; it was now raining.

'Michael, why does Olga have such big hairy hands?' enquired Charlie in total innocence. At that point Michael started laughing until tears were running down his face. When he could speak he finally said, 'Dear Charlie you have much to learn, so much. I shall tell you Olga's story when we get home.'

Michael explained that he lived quite a way away on the Isle of Dogs and getting there would involve a long bus journey. As they left the West End and then the City Charlie noticed that the buildings got tattier and everything looked rather dirty. Michael explained that this was the East End, a very poor part of London that was still being re-developed after being bombed heavily during the war. Indeed during the journey Charlie saw many building sites with blocks of new flats rising into the sky.

After changing buses Charlie noticed that the scenery altered again and they were now travelling through an area of grimy industrial buildings. Sometimes Charlie would get a glimpse of a piece of water and once or twice he spied a ship through a gap in a wall. 'These are the docks Charlie, where all the ships come and go into London.' Charlie thought that this was very exciting but also that everything had an air of dereliction about it. He spotted many parts that looked like they were still undeveloped bombsites and also numerous boarded up buildings and empty shops.

Eventually they arrived at their destination in somewhere called Millwall and after a short walk arrived at Michael's flat which was in a large red brick block with open balconies running along the front and what seemed like hundreds of children running around playing noisily. Michael undid the four locks that secured the front door and it swung open to reveal the most amazing hallway Charlie had ever seen.

He suppressed a gasp and was too polite to say anything but as they entered he noticed that every surface was covered in religious images. Crucifixes (many of them plastic); little plastic statues of the Virgin Mary (one of them was a lamp and had eyes that lit up); very bad prints of the crucifixion and a large mural of The Last Supper to name a few. Every single surface was covered, not one square inch of actual wall was visible.

'Olga didn't tell me you were ... um ... religious Michael.'

Michael started laughing again.

'Why do you keep laughing at me?' said Charlie, rather wounded.

'I'm sorry love, but you're just so sweet, I haven't got a religious bone in my body, it's just my little collection. Do you like it?' Charlie was speechless and all he could do was to nod his head vigorously.

'Oh good.' beamed Michael. 'There's more. I shall show you all of my collection.'

Charlie was introduced to every piece of plastic, kitsch, religious iconography in the hall. Moving onto the sitting room the theme was Hollywood with a huge picture of Marilyn Monroe and Clark Gable dominating the wall and a big, glitter HOLLYWOOD sign down one side of the room. The kitchen had more religious kitsch including a particularly gruesome crucifixion painting and intriguingly a Jesus whose head flipped open and could be used as a bottle opener. The bathroom appropriately had an underwater theme and was covered in pictures of fish and mermaids and had seashells hanging from the ceiling. Charlie found the bedroom very embarrassing as it was covered with pictures of naked men, some of them engaged in sexual acts, and in the corner was a large plastic model of the statue of David with an oversized penis.

Having completed the little tour Michael offered tea and Charlie collapsed gratefully into an armchair with cushions with pictures of Betty Grable on them, and sighed, 'Thank you ... it's been a hell of a day. In fact I don't think I have ever had a day like it.'

'No,' Charlie Rogers then reflected to himself, 'I have most certainly never had a day like this before,' as he cast his gaze around the bizarrely decorated room.

★ ★ ★

Chapter Five: A Sojourn in Docklands

August 1970

Michael and Charlie spent the rest of the day and evening in long and deep conversation. Much of the time Charlie talked and spilled out his woes like he never had before whilst Michael patiently listened. They sat in armchairs on opposite sides of the sitting room so as he spoke he could see the reactions on Michael's face. He sensed a great empathy with him.

Charlie also noticed, which he hadn't had time to do before, that Michael was an attractive man. Dark, almost black hair, cut very short in the mod manner. Piercing, dark brown eyes and thick sensuous lips. One ear was pierced with a large gold hoop. He was, however, rather old, and had revealed to Charlie that he was 36, which to the young Mister Rogers seemed truly ancient.

Michael told him a little of his life. He had been brought up in a Manchester orphanage by some particularly vicious nuns who used to beat him regularly and when he was caught in bed with another boy aged 14 he was thrown out on the streets. Charlie began to understand why Michael wanted to care for people and also that his hideous collection of religious kitsch had a point to it … it was an act of sticking his fingers up to the Church.

Charlie's fantasies had gone into overdrive again and he had replaced his earlier vision of happy domestic bliss with Wayne to one of happy domestic bliss with Michael. Yes, he might be a bit old but he was very kind and anyway Charlie expected that Michael would make a move on him at any moment. That's what men do, don't they?

The evening drew on and Charlie was getting tired and Michael could see that the boy was having trouble keeping his eyes open.

'Charlie I think it's bed time, you can either kip on the sofa or you can come and snuggle up with me, it's up to you'. Charlie took this as a signal that Michael was ready to start having sex with him and immediately stood up and walked over to his chair, leaned over and clumsily tried to kiss him. Michael pulled away.

'What the fuck do you think you're doing Charlie?'

'Don't you fancy me, don't you want to love me, isn't this what men do? Am I so ugly? No one is ever going to love me.' And he started crying again.

'Now,' said Michael, in a gentler voice, 'let's get a few things straight. You are a very attractive young man. Who wouldn't fall for those wonderful blue-green eyes? But there is no way that I am going to betray your trust. You came here in need of love and care and that I will give to you but sex is not going to happen. Do I make myself clear? You also have to understand Charlie that it is illegal; men can't have sex with each other until they are 21 years old. I could lose my job or go to prison. You wouldn't want that would you?'

'I have so much to learn,' said Charlie, still feeling a little rejected but understanding what Michael was saying.

'Yes you do have much to learn. Now what I suggest is that we go to bed. I will hold you in bed but that is all and any more advances from you and you will be on the sofa. I am taking a risk by even sharing a bed with you but I am prepared to do that.'

'That would be wonderful,' said Charlie.

And that's how they slept, every night for almost a month, in the double bed in Michael's bedroom, his strong arms holding Charlie. Comforting him when his regular nightmares kept coming back. Michael never once made any advance on Charlie who found lying in his arms at night made him feel safe, secure and loved. He had never been held in a man's arms before and it was a very special feeling, the strength of his arms and the smell of him in his nostrils as he went to sleep. Michael would sometimes lie awake in the night cursing himself for his honour and decency for of course he had fallen hook, line and sinker for the boy, and not being able to express that physically hurt him badly. But he never told Charlie.

Life with Michael was one of constant surprises and paradoxes. Sometimes Charlie would see him go out for the night looking very hard and handsome covered head to toe in leather. He would come back in the early hours, clearly tired but with a glow in his eyes. He would never tell Charlie what exactly he had been doing but Charlie had a pretty good idea. Other times Charlie would find Michael in the kitchen up to his elbows in flour making a fruitcake. On another occasion when he invited some friends round he did a hilarious impression of Ena Sharples including donning a hair net that he found when rummaging around in a box in the sitting room. 'It's my dressing up box love,' he said.

Charlie spent much of his days walking around the decaying London docks, which he loved. At this time much of them were being closed down and the area had an atmosphere of neglect and dereliction. He would sometimes find a quiet spot, get his sketch book out and draw a quick picture of a rusty crane or a lonely looking ship. It would give him lots of inspiration for water colours later he thought. One afternoon Charlie walked through the old Victorian foot tunnel under the Thames that linked North Woolwich to its sister on the other side. He thought it very spooky and atmospheric and was a little concerned that in the middle there seemed to be a significant drip of water coming through the ceiling. He quickly put the thought of tidal waves and drowning out of his mind (he could be such an over imaginative boy). On many of these walks Michael accompanied him and they talked, talked and talked.

Michael knew that although he had a huge soft spot for the young lad that it would be totally wrong to take their relationship any further, and he therefore decided that the best way to love the boy was to give him the gift of an education into the gay world. He knew from experiences of coming to London as a young man 20 years earlier that some men could be very cruel, could use youngsters for their own satisfaction and chuck them away without a thought. He was determined that when Charlie was ready to start meeting men he would do so with confidence and not fall into the claws of manipulative people. So on one of their long walks, this one through the Royal Docks where there were still a number of ships loading and unloading, Michael decided to explain all this to Charlie.

'Charlie, you're very young, and forgive me for saying this, very naïve. Please don't be cross with me. I know that you want to meet a man and fall in love, but trust me, I think you are too young. In our world, the gay world, there is much love, of course there is, but there are also many men who just want more and more sex with as many partners as possible and a pretty young thing like you would soon fall victim to the more predatory creatures. So I want you to wait. The law says that you should wait until you are 21. That is clearly ridiculous, you can die for your country at 16, but I think that you should wait until you are 18, then you will be old and wise enough to make good decisions and wise judgments.'

'But I'm so horny all the time,' blurted out Charlie.

'Yes of course, you're 15... but that's why wanking was invented dear Charlie.'

As they continued to walk through the Royal Docks Michael explained many other things about being gay. He explained to Charlie this was not always an easy path but if that's what he knew he was inside, then he would always be there to help and guide Charlie along it. 'That is my firm commitment to you Charlie boy. I will be your guardian angel for life.'

'I do love you Michael,' replied Charlie, as he had realised over the weeks that he very truly did. Michael said nothing in reply.

They walked silently for a while, and then Charlie opened up again. 'I think it's about time I went home to my parents, don't you?'

'Yes Charlie, I think you're ready.'

It was decided that Charlie would have another few days on the Isle of Dogs so that he could prepare for what was going to be a very difficult journey home. On the last day Michael arranged a little tea party. This time he made fairy cakes and he invited a few friends around to bid Charlie on his way. Olga came, who had, as promised, called every day to check that Charlie was okay. There was also a very camp but rather creepy older couple called Andrew & Andrew (Charlie thought it was most odd that a couple could have the same name). They were on a visit from 'The North' and lived near Saddleworth Moor, not far from Manchester.

Michael, with his black northern humour, always insisted on referring to them as 'The Moors Sisters' hinting darkly that they had something to do with the Moors Murders. This was of course totally groundless and they were just a couple of rather odd old queens.

Olga clucked over Charlie and made lots of fuss of him and kept saying, 'You will be okay darling won't you? And you must promise to call Aunty Olga if you are worried about anything.' Andrew & Andrew were more practical and had advised Charlie about 'coming out' to his parents.

Charlie knew that they would have be told one day and Andrew & Andrew gave him lots of tips how to do it and they reassured him that they would be there for him too when he needed it. Charlie politely accepted their offer of help but was damn sure that he would never visit them on the moors!

'So you see,' said the older, somewhat fatter Andrew, 'you're a very lucky boy. Most people have no fairy godmothers and you have four.' The whole room collapsed into giggles at this and Charlie was duly hugged and kissed by Olga and the two Andrews as they bade their farewells.

Michael and Charlie were left together surrounded by dirty plates and a few uneaten fairy cakes. They had had a wonderful afternoon. 'So, tomorrow, I am going to take you back to Charing Cross and put you on the train home. It's going to be very difficult with your parents Charlie, they must have been going through hell (Michael had wanted to contact them but Charlie had absolutely refused) and you are going to have to be very strong. At a time that is right you are going to have to tell them that you are gay and that will be the beginning of you growing up.

You are 15 years old now. In three years time when you are 18, if you still want to, come back to me and I will introduce you to the gay world. I do love you Charlie and I will always be there as your guardian angel. Love takes many shapes and forms Charlie, you will learn that as you grow up. The love that I have felt for you is very special. I will never forget you. I do hope you will come back to me.'

'I will come back Michael, I promise. And I will call you every week until then.'

'One more thing Charlie you must promise me. You remember I said that I was taking a risk sharing a bed with you? Well please don't tell your parents who you were staying with. There is no way that they would believe that I hadn't taken advantage of you and I could go to prison … don't forget.'

'Yes of course, you have my promise on both counts, I will come back to the Isle of Dogs shortly after my eighteenth birthday and I will make up some story about staying in a hostel. You have my word.'

The following morning Charlie packed his rucksack and they went back on the bus together into the centre of the city and then onto the station. Michael checked when Charlie's train was leaving and which platform it was.

At the barrier they hugged and Charlie strode off down the platform trying to look confident. Michael was struggling to hold back the tears and thought that Charlie wasn't going to turn around and wave, then at the last moment before getting on the train Charlie faced back and blew Michael a kiss.

Michael smiled, turned away and set off for the long journey home, with a heavy heart but knowing that he had done the *right* thing. Not everyone in life can be proud of having done the *right* thing, but this was one of those moments when Michael knew with certainty that he had.

Charlie wanted the train journey to go on forever as he was dreading being reunited with his parents, but of course it seemed to pass particularly quickly on this occasion. He walked slowly back up the hill from the station and reaching his road saw his house in the distance.

Walking up the front path he took a big deep breath and went up to the front door and knocked. Although there would be some tears, he was sure his parents would be pleased to see him. The door swung open. His father stood there. For a moment he didn't seem to recognise Charlie. 'I'm home Dad.'

Charlie's father's face broke into a dark and angry expression. 'Where the hell have you been? Do you know the trouble you've caused? Your mother's on Valium, we thought you were dead. Now get upstairs to your room before I throw you up there. Frankly I'm not sure I really want you back you're in such a lot of trouble.' Charlie burst into tears and pushed past his father and ran up to his room where he immediately grasped his favourite bear, who was still on the bed, and held him very tightly to his chest.

Over the next few hours a number of things happened. The police were called and told that Charlie had come home. They had been working on the theory that he had been abducted. His father came and went from his room several times, each time shouting and angry. Perhaps if he had told Charlie he had loved him at this point, it might have helped. His mother tearfully tried to keep the peace but was clearly so zoned out on Valium that she couldn't contribute much to the discussion, too zoned out to tell him she loved him.

Charlie started regretting coming home but at the same time knew that Michael was right, he was too young to be in the flesh pots of London by himself and for the moment he should make the best of it, live with his family for the next few years and try and keep the peace. Charlie kept his promise to Michael and never mentioned his name or where he had been but concocted a tale of a hostel in Soho for rough sleepers. His parents had no reason not to believe him.

It was decided that Charlie should resume his schooling even though he had missed so much and the following Monday morning Charlie was squeezed into his uniform complete with cap. His father had insisted he had his hair cut and he could feel the heavy weight of suburban conformity pressing down on him. 'Bide your time,' he thought, 'it's only a few years and I will be ready and I have my wonderful fairy godmothers looking after me.'

Dreamland

A long way away over the water a woman wakes from a dream. She has dreamed that her husband loves her fully as a woman, but awake she turns over, sees his handsome profile and knows that this will never be the case. Her love is empty and unfulfilled and as she grows into middle age she is becoming bitter. Yes it had been her choice, she had walked into the situation with her eyes open but in her young naïvety she thought she could change him.

In the docks where few ships now make land, the man awakes from his dream where he has been making love with the boy with the wonderful blue-green eyes. He feels hot and guilty about his dreams. He turns over and tries to sleep again feeling a great loss that the boy has gone.

In the South London suburbs the boy wakes screaming and sweating. His old nightmare has come back again. Every time he has it, more and more detail has been added until in the latest ghastly and bone chilling version he can see a man standing over him with an electric flex stretched between his hands and he knows he is going to be strangled. The number 80 is daubed on every surface around him searing into the boy's mind. As he goes back to sleep he enters the space where he is a bird and is loved. It always helps at these times. He doesn't know why. It is such a strange image. Why a bird?

Not far away a woman in her dreams is conscious of all the dreams that are being dreamed and sees that she is like a conductor making sure that the notes that have been written are played and make the right tune. Sometimes in her dream events start to get out of control, as if the orchestra no longer obeys her orders and she sees the boy that she cares about so much threatened and killed by an unseen man and she wakes frightened and shaken.

So many dreams. So much as yet untold, so many lives to be lived and loves to be had and for one man so much planning, control and killing to do.

★ ★ ★

Chapter Six: Peckham Depravity, a Warning and Tea with Olga

May 1971

The twisted and dark man paces up and down the cellar of the shabby and dank house in Peckham. He reflects on the enjoyment, fulfilment and *ecstasy* he reached when he had killed the third boy the week before.

It had been far too long since he killed the previous one, a lad called Peter Brand in 1963. On that occasion he remembered with satisfaction he had perfected his plans down to the last detail.

So very long and now it had been time again, everything was planned. Yes everything had been perfect. He had lured the boy back to his house with the promise of money for sexual favours. He had found him hanging around the public toilets on Peckham Rye common and suspected that the right amount of money would entice him. Oh yes he had seen the corrupted look in the boy's eyes. It wouldn't take much. Initially the boy refused but as the man raised his price to ten pounds his resistance faltered and he agreed to go back with him. As he cut the boy's picture out of the newspaper afterwards for his little gallery he saw that the boy was called Andrew Whitehead and he was 16 years old.

Yes, everything was very satisfactory. The moment of climax had been reached just as he had tightened the flex round the boy's neck. Very satisfactory, in fact almost perfect. The dirty little bastard wouldn't be free to engage in his sordid acts any longer. He had removed a menace from society.

But now, reflecting on his achievements, he becomes briefly impatient. In his loins he feels a great heat, a burning, he knows that he is going to have to act again. But he also knows that his destiny has been decided already. He knows the next boy he is going to save. He has dreamed of him often, the boy with those wonderful blue-green eyes. But he knows from his dreams that he is going to have to bide his time and wait. The time is not yet quite right. 'I shall be patient,' he thinks, 'I will plan it all so carefully. I want it to be so perfect for you Charlie Rogers. I love you so much.'

June 1971

Charlie lay on his bed, and as was so often the case was feeling sorry for himself. It had been almost a year since he had spent the month with Michael. He missed him a great deal and kept his promise and they spoke on the phone weekly.

It was often a little brief as he didn't want his parents to get suspicious. Charlie had moved in and out of depression as the need to get out of the 'bloody suburbs' and to meet a man for love overwhelmed him.

And also of course, being almost 16 he was bloody horny. All the time. He needed sex, but he had carefully taken Michael's advice and he was going to wait.

Relations with his parents were strained. His mother did her best and tried to make a fuss of him but didn't understand what troubled her son so much. His father had given up and just barked at him a lot. His parents weren't bad people and Charlie wasn't a bad person but they belonged to an orderly suburban world where everything was 'proper' and Charlie increasingly had the sense that this was not going to be his world. His stay in Michael's weird and wonderful flat had excited him, he had met interesting and colourful people and that was what he wanted. Not this. Several times he had considered telling them that he was gay but he had held back, remembering much of Andrew & Andrew's advice, and he knew it should wait until he was a little older.

'I just want to be 18 years old now so I can go and find a man to love me,' he would repeatedly say to himself.

Later that day Charlie decided to go round to Uncle Frederick's to do some painting. Charlie had very sensibly realised that Frederick lived in the same orderly and suburban world as his parents so he would never discuss his feelings with him. However he did enjoy the encouragement that his uncle gave him with his watercolours and being able to express himself this way was a great release.

Charlie got the bus over to his uncle's house, which wasn't very far away, and was welcomed in by Frederick. 'Good to see you Charlie,' he said and shook his hand. That's what Uncle Frederick did; he would shake your hand, never a hug and certainly never a kiss. No that would never do.

Frederick showed Charlie up to his study where he had his easel and watercolours arranged and he duly showed Charlie his latest work of a flower arrangement; Charlie made all the appropriate noises. Frederick was pleased with his nephew's compliments.

His wife Violet showed no interest in his paintings and he suspected that she thought they weren't very good (which actually they weren't). It was Charlie's turn to show his uncle the portfolio he had brought with him. The pictures that Charlie had painted were mainly ones that he had developed from sketches that he had made when he stayed in Docklands. Frederick was full of praise about Charlie's work and he glowed with pride as his uncle assured him how good the paintings were.

Charlie did have to suppress a slight giggle when his uncle, seeing a picture of Olga, commented, 'What a beautiful looking woman.' Charlie was sure that Frederick would not approve *at all* of Olga.

'Charlie, there is something I wanted to talk to you about,' started Frederick in a tone that Charlie took to mean that the subject was serious.

He looked up from the portfolio with an enquiring expression on his face but said nothing, waiting for his uncle to continue.

'You've never said much to your parents about the time you spent in London. You know of course that they were desperate whilst you were away thinking you had been abducted or worse. When you came back they were hugely relieved but then over the months you've refused to add anything about where you were or what you were doing and they have become concerned again. They've talked to me about it and they really don't know what to do.'

'I don't understand Uncle Frederick, I'm back home, isn't that enough?'

'Well yes, of course Charlie, but you must understand that mothers are always concerned about their children. Yours is worried that something bad may have happened to you or you might have been mixing with the wrong type of people.'

An image of Michael in his hairnet doing Ena Sharples, the creepy Moors Sisters and Olga camping it up drawling over Charlie with her faux Eastern European accent flashed through Charlie's mind. Yes he had definitely been mixing with the 'wrong type of people'. He could barely suppress a giggle.

Having composed himself Charlie carefully reassured Frederick that he had been well cared for whilst he was away and that there was nothing for anyone to worry about. Frederick seemed satisfied with the answer. 'Oh and by the way,' added Frederick, 'that uncle of yours, you know Harry that lives in Peckham. Keep away from him. Your mother has never liked him and there's been rumours you know about boys being seen going into his house.'

'I haven't seen him for years and Mum and Dad barely mention him so it's very unlikely I would see him anyway,' replied Charlie honestly.

Charlie and Frederick spent the rest of the afternoon painting together and talking about safe subjects like the weather and what there was likely to be for tea tonight. At 5pm Charlie said goodbye to Frederick and thanked him for the afternoon. He had genuinely enjoyed it and although his uncle was a bit dull it was nice to get away from his parents for a bit. He got the bus back home and sat there with a heavy heart dreading the inevitable rows that would follow his return.

July 1971

Olga had called Charlie the week before his birthday. His mother had answered the phone and passed it to him, her hand over the mouthpiece. She whispered, 'It's someone called 'Countess Olga, she sounds Russian…how exciting …you didn't tell me you had met aristocracy, how wonderful.' Charlie cringed at his mother's snobbery and then barely suppressed a giggle as he thought about Olga being upper class.

No, Olga's roots were as a lorry driver from Canvey Island. Very good woman but most certainly not blue blooded.

'Mum please can I have some privacy,' and he shooed her away.

'Hi Olga, how are you? How's Michael? When can I come to The Isle of Dogs again? When am I going to see you all?'

'Charlie darling,' drawled Olga, 'so many questions, you're making my little head spin. Now sweetie it's your birthday next week and I would love to take you out for tea. Would you do Aunty Olga a huge favour and come up to London?'

Charlie had hoped for a slightly more exciting outing than afternoon tea, but he would like to see Olga and also expected that Michael would join them as well. He so wanted to see Michael. He missed him very much. 'That would be lovely Olga. Where shall I meet you and Michael?'

'No darling it's just me. Michael, well let's just say Michael can't make it. I will tell you more next week. Meet me at High Street Kensington Underground station at 2pm next Wednesday.'

Charlie's heart sank at the news Michael wouldn't be there, but was genuinely pleased to be meeting Olga. They chatted a little more and then finalised their plans and he hung up the phone after Olga had blown him a lot of wet-sounding kisses.

So that was how Charlie and Olga came to be having tea at Barkers department store on his sixteenth birthday. They met at the Underground station and Olga enveloped him in a huge muscular hug. He barely recognised her; her hair previously blond was now hennaed, badly, and was a very lurid red. It hung fashionably long. She was dressed in a pair of bright orange hot pants (which clashed with her hair), and platform boots. Olga was a tall woman at six foot two and the platform boots now made her tower over Charlie.

The effect was truly horrible, but Charlie politely complimented Olga on her outfit and she blushed and giggled like a teenage girl. Charlie did love Olga; he thought she was just so unique, so colourful, so different from the cloying repressed suburban world that he was forced to live in. He also loved Olga because she had a large and open heart and she cared for Charlie a great deal.

As Olga and Charlie walked into the café at Barkers heads turned at the sight of this very strange looking woman and the young boy together. To his shame, Charlie felt slightly embarrassed but seeing that Olga didn't care a damn decided to ignore the stares and glared back at one woman who seemed to be muttering something unpleasant to her sour looking friend. The pair sat at a table by the window and ordered afternoon tea, including one of Charlie's favourites: scones and jam and cream.

'Now tell me Charlie,' Olga enquired, 'how have you been? Tell your Aunty Olga everything.' Charlie spent the next 10 minutes going through his various tales of woe. How his parents still did not understand him and how he was having such a miserable time at school. How he had few real friends, how he desperately wanted to come back to London, how no one loved him. Then finally he blurted out, 'And I'm really upset Michael wouldn't come for my birthday, I thought he cared about me, I think it's really unfair that he wouldn't come. Does he not think about me at all?'

'Charlie, my little darling, you are so innocent and also so self-centred. I suppose I should not be harsh on you, you are so young but one thing that you must start to learn is that everything isn't about Charlie Roger's feelings. Other people have feelings and emotions as well.' Charlie had been expecting some reassurance and was a little stung by Olga's response and his face fell.

'Do you not understand Charlie quite how Michael felt when you went home?' Charlie looked confused. 'I can see that I am a very stupid woman expecting you to grasp much ... my god you really are so selfish.'

He went to stand up and leave, fed up with the criticism from Olga who he had taken to be his friend. Why was she being like this? Olga grabbed his arm with one strong hand and pulled him back down onto the seat. 'Now shut up, sit still and listen. If you try and move again I will break your fucking arm.' Charlie was fully aware that Olga could break his arm if she wanted so meekly sat down and said nothing.

'Michael has very strong feelings for you Charlie. He knows it's wrong, you are almost still a child in his eyes. From the moment he met you he was determined to protect you and do the right thing. But do you know how much that tortured him? Have you for one moment in your ignorant self-obsession thought of his feelings? No. I thought not,' she went on without waiting for a reply to her question. 'Michael had a very tough time when he came to London all those years ago. He ended up on the Dilly because of someone like Wayne…you remember Wayne? He was used by men and then spat out when they were bored with him. When he saw you with Wayne he realised the danger that you were in and after rescuing you, swore to himself that you would not end up as he did and that he would never take advantage of you. Little did he know that the price he would pay for doing this would be a broken heart.'

'Olga I …'

'Shut up Charlie I haven't finished' she commanded.

Olga went on, 'After you went home he was terribly depressed and he dealt with this by going on a sexual rampage. My god darling I have never seen anything like it. I lost track of the number of men he told me about that year. He looked tired and ill, and I knew that what he was doing was to try and blot you out of his mind. Then last week he went out cruising on Hampstead Heath and a gang of boys attacked him. He's okay now but was quite badly hurt. He's still in hospital but should be home in the next day or so.'

'I'm sorry Olga, I'm so sorry.'

'Charlie, you have nothing to be sorry about, none of this is your doing but all I am trying to teach you is that we must always think of other people's feelings. However troubled we are we must think about the effect that we are having on others. Do you understand?'

'Yes I think so … but I must go and see him … where is he?'

'No Charlie,' Olga said firmly, 'that is the last thing that Michael needs now. Leave him alone to heal his body and his heart.'

'But he said that I could come back to the Isle of Dogs.'

'Yes you can. When you are 18. Then, Michael would treat you as an adult and if there is still something between you … well who knows … there would be such a large age difference but who knows …' she trailed off.

Starting up again in a kindly tone. 'Charlie, be good to yourself, be kind to Michael. Oh my darling you have so much to learn, but will you at least always listen to a little advice from your Aunty Olga?'

'Olga I can see I've been so blinkered that I hadn't considered what Michael has been going though. I know that I have much to learn, I am so stupid and naïve. I hate being 16 years old and so much want to be as old as you.'

At that Olga laughed. 'I'm sure when you are my ripe old age of 30 you'll want only to be 16 again.' Charlie knew Olga was at least 45; Michael had told him but he politely said nothing.

'Now let's shop darling,' and Olga and Charlie went off arm in arm to explore Kensington High Street. Olga bought herself a new purple feather boa in Biba and in Kensington Market she bought Charlie a pair of bell-bottom jeans with an embroidered pocket for his birthday.

He thought they were fab. Leaving Olga at the underground station he said: 'Thanks for my jeans Olga, they are wonderful and oh, thanks for teaching me a few things today. Thank you so much. Please send Michael my love.' Olga turned and walked off and then swung her head round and gave Charlie a great big wink.

'See you soon darling,' she shouted after him.

Dreamland

The dreamer is confused. He thinks that everything he has planned is in place. That all the steps he has taken to ensure that everything will be perfect for young Charlie are ready. That they will reach the ultimate union together and he will protect the boy.

But now he has seen a circle of people forming around Charlie. A mish-mash of people. One woman he recognises but he also dreams of a man in an RAF uniform. He doesn't know him. Also in his dream he sees a dilapidated wasteland with rusty cranes and half sunken boats, and there is a strange looking woman with lurid red hair and a dark eyed, cropped haired, tattooed man. All these people seem to form a circle of love around Charlie.

He wakes crying so frightened because he senses that the meaning of his dream is that these people may come between him and his beloved and his dreams and plans for the future will be shattered.

★ ★ ★

Chapter Seven: Reasons Why You Shouldn't Write a Diary

June 1973

When the storm came it was larger and more terrifying than Charlie had ever imagined. He had thought for some time that he should finally tell his parents that he was gay. He went over and over the conversation in his head and pictured his mother being rather tearful and fretting about the loss of grandchildren. He felt she would conveniently forget that Susan would probably have some for the sake of drama, but then hug him affectionately and say, 'I will always love you Charlie.' His father would be rather gruff and embarrassed but would assure Charlie of his love too.

He had never predicted this though. Sitting with his parents in a panelled doctor's waiting room in Harley Street. On one side his mother grey faced, on the other side his father stony faced. Nothing was being said. An uncomfortable silence lay heavily on the family. Rose had, the previous week, completely forgotten the maxim that reading someone's diaries invariably leads to finding out things you don't want to know.

Charlie unfortunately was about to learn the lesson that if you do commit your inner secrets to diaries you should take very careful steps to hide them from prying eyes. Rose had been cleaning Charlie's bedroom and spied the little exercise book in which he had written his thoughts. She couldn't stop herself; she felt a little guilty as she flicked through the dog eared pages but had a sense that her son was troubled or in trouble and maybe she could help. Most of the pages were covered in various scrawls about quite how unfair life was and how miserable Charlie Rogers was. Probably not much different from most teenagers. Then Rose got to the entry dated 15th January 1973 in which Charlie, with graphic detail, described exactly what he would like a man to do to him. She felt nauseated but forced herself to read the whole entry.

Later that day Charlie returned from school and she confronted him. 'Charlie, I think we need to have a serious conversation.' He didn't like her tone.

'What about Mum?' he replied gingerly.

'Your diaries!'

Charlie immediately knew what his mother was alluding to and his defence was to fly into a tearful rage. 'What fucking right have you got to read my diaries? How dare you. You cow.' At this Rose struck her son across the face.

'Sit down, shut up and stop crying Charlie. Please act like a man. I'm very pleased that I read this, as I was sure that when you were away someone did something awful to you and now I know. You've been corrupted and perverted by someone. No one in my family has ever been a, a ... *homosexual*. And I don't intend that you will become one now. What would your grandmother think? Do you not know how you would be used and corrupted by older men? It's disgusting and I won't tolerate it. Not in my family. What would the neighbours think for god's sake?'

Charlie's face smarted from where his mother had struck him but he was shocked into silence by her reaction. Her cold, loveless diatribe hurt with every word more than any physical blow could.

'And what I want to know is who corrupted you Charlie? I know now you stayed in the East End. I want names and an address and I will be calling the police.' At this Charlie stopped crying, this had gone beyond emotion, her cruelty had shocked him out of this. His mother had turned into a cold and dangerous bitch whose main concern was what the fucking neighbours thought.

'There is no way that I will ever tell you who I was with Mum, they did nothing wrong to me. All they did was care for me and love me but I can see that you will never believe that.' As he was saying this he was mentally thanking God (who he didn't believe in) that Michael had insisted that Charlie didn't write his address details down anywhere. He must have had an inkling of what could happen.

'I thought that you would love and support me but I was so wrong, all you care about is what other people think.'

'Too damn right Charlie, this family has a reputation to

maintain. When your father comes home he will deal with this and we will get the truth out of you about your sordid little escapades in London.'

Predictably his father had taken the news badly. He didn't say much apart from muttering about 'unnatural acts'. He didn't speak to Charlie at all. Charlie suspected this came from embarrassment as much as anger.

As Charlie lay in bed that night, sometimes crying, sometimes quite calm, he could hear his parents downstairs talking long into the evening. He wanted to know what they were saying so very quietly opened his bedroom door and went to the top of the stairs where he could just hear the conversation.

'Well that's finalised then Rose. We will make an appointment and take the boy to see Dr Masters next week. I remember reading that he has a very good reputation in the area of sexual perversion.' Charlie felt a cold claw of fear grip his stomach.

He now sat miserably in Dr Masters' waiting room, his parents either side of him like prison guards. He looked around the dingy room, dark wood panelling and a green carpet. The effect made him feel even more depressed than when he had arrived. He glanced at the receptionist. A harsh faced woman with a hairdo that looked like it had been set in place with cement.

'I wouldn't want to tangle with her,' he thought.

He had wanted to run away, but he had no money. His parents had taken every last penny away from him. He felt like an animal with its leg in a trap. He would have turned to his Aunty Iris who always helped him, particularly when there were difficulties with his parents, but she was off on a Mediterranean cruise and couldn't be contacted.

So here he was, scared, trapped and lonely and feeling completely unloved by anyone in the world. He was just putting together a scenario in his head where he would make a dash for the door when the sour faced woman picked up the ringing phone on her desk and said, 'Right away Dr Masters, I will send him in. Please go through now Charles, the doctor is ready for you.'

Charlie got up reluctantly and headed towards the door of the doctor's office. Rose tried to follow but the receptionist stopped her, saying, 'Dr Masters will see your son alone.' It was a command not a request and Rose meekly obeyed.

Charlie walked into the large office; it was panelled in the same foreboding dark wood as the reception and had only a small window overlooking the street, making it altogether a gloomy place. The doctor sat at a big leather-topped desk and didn't glance up from his paper work as Charlie timidly walked up to the chair the other side.

'Sit down boy, I will be with you in a moment.' Charlie lowered himself into the leather chair and sat there uncomfortably for several minutes whilst Dr Masters made notes with a fountain pen on a large sheet of paper on his desk.

Eventually he looked up. He was a middle-aged man, heavily bearded with small squinty eyes and not the slightest hint of a smile on his face. Charlie thought he detected a vague smell coming from the other side of the desk and he suddenly placed it as mothballs. Clearly Dr Masters had a problem with moths and his clothes had absorbed the distinctive smell. It was not pleasant.

'Now Charles, your mother phoned me last week and told me that you think you are a homosexual. She is very concerned and wants me to treat you. Are you a homosexual?'

Charlie blushed vividly, and unable to speak nodded his head.

'So are you active or passive?'

Charlie said nothing; he felt too embarrassed.

'Well, boys of your age often have an unnatural interest in other boys' bodies. You will grow out of it. I know it's fashionable at the moment but homosexuality is not normal, and the best thing you can do is to find a girlfriend, get married and have children. You will soon forget about this.'

Charlie said nothing. He knew in his heart, with every fibre of his soul that this was not true. He wasn't very sure of anything in life but one thing he never doubted was that he wanted to be loved by a man.

'I'm going to arrange for you to have a course of Aversion Therapy which will help to get these ideas out of your mind.'

Charlie said nothing. He didn't know what Aversion Therapy was and wasn't in a position to argue.

'Send in your mother and father when you leave please.'

That was it. That was the sum total of the support that Charlie got when he was at the most troubled in his life, when he needed someone to gently guide him and to counsel his parents how to love him best.

Although he would later grow to forgive his parents their conservative ignorance, the medical profession should have known better and he always hated them for it.

The journey back from London was conducted in total silence. Charlie was scared and at a complete loss of knowing what to do. His parents were acting in a completely tyrannical manner and seemed determined to make Charles Rogers in their image rather than allow him to be himself. Even though he didn't know what Aversion Therapy entailed, it sounded horrifying and the thought of having the capacity to love another man taken away from him was equally horrifying. He felt that the only person in the world that could help him was his Aunty Iris; he wondered desperately when she would be back in England. He couldn't run, he didn't have a penny.

The following day Charlie's question was answered as he heard his mother pick up the phone and say, 'Iris, lovely to hear from you, how was your cruise? We've been having terrible problems with Charlie.' At that point Rose must have realised that there was a chance that she could be overheard and stretching the telephone cord she went into the sitting room and shut the door behind her. Charlie could no longer hear the conversation from the landing where he was listening. It was probably for the best.

'What do you mean problems with Charlie?' Iris immediately replied, the cruise and her fling with the sexy purser on the liner held for another day.

'I really don't know where to start and I'm not even sure I should mention this. I have to ask for your complete confidentiality. David and I have reason to suspect that Charlie is ... you know, oh for god's sake ... one of those.'

'One of those what?' replied Iris, knowing exactly what her sister meant but determined to get her to say it.

'You know, one of those, oh for goodness sake. *Homosexuals!*' She said the word as if it would leave a very unpleasant taste in her mouth.

'Of course it's totally unacceptable and we are dealing with it.'

'What do you mean dealing with it?' Iris enquired, now deeply concerned.

'Well dear, we heard of a wonderful doctor in Harley Street who deals with sexual perversion. It's a very up-market area you know for doctors. He's going to give Charlie something called Aversion Therapy which cures this in 99 per cent of cases and he only charges a hundred guineas for the full treatment. I think that's very good value don't you?'

Iris was, for once in her life, stunned into silence. Within one short sentence Rose had demonstrated her petty snobbery, her prejudice and had discussed the price of sorting out her son's supposed 'problem' as if it was a special offer on a settee.

'Rose dear,' Iris started very carefully, knowing that she had to handle this situation with great delicacy if she was not to alienate her sister, 'I have read a little of this Aversion Therapy, and I'm not sure that this is what you would want for your son. Do you know what it involves exactly?'

'No dear, but I'm told that it is very effective. Dr Masters sent me copies of several thank you letters from grateful parents.'

'It will involve your 17-year-old son having electric shocks passed through his genitals whilst looking at pictures of naked men. Do you think that's a good thing?'

Without a pause, Rose replied, 'Iris, if it means that Charlie is cured and made normal I would accept any treatment for him.'

Iris was completely horrified by Rose's cold tone but suspected any argument was futile. She would have to act but battling with her sister was not going to be the best plan. She said little else and finished the call. After reflecting for a while she went to her bureau and got out a pad of Basildon Bond paper.

30th June 1973

Dear Charlie,

I have something very important to tell you. I don't want to frighten you but I think you probably suspect that what the doctor has got planned for you is not good. I know, and have always known that you will be happy being loved by a man. Don't ask me how I know but I do. So I am now, as your loving aunt telling you something that I never thought I would, and that is that you must leave home. It is your birthday in a few weeks time and you will be 18 years old and legally an adult. Wait until then and then your parents can do little to force you to take any treatment or to make you come home again. Trust me, this is the best way. Here's £100 for you, which will keep you going until you can find a job in London. I know you have friends there. Go to them and I'm sure they will look after you.

Your mother said that she intended to find out whom you had been with in London so she could get the police to investigate. You must make sure that they have no way of knowing where you are. I will also tell your parents that you had confided in me that you might want to go to Amsterdam one day, which will throw them off the scent. Just remember that although you will legally be an adult you cannot legally have sex until you are 21 so your friends must be protected at all costs. Whatever the truth, the police and your parents would make incorrect assumptions about your relationship with your friends.

Be happy and strong Charlie, I will always be there for you.
With all my love

Iris XXXX

Charlie wept copiously when he opened the letter the next day, and smiled when he saw the money Iris had given him. It was his passport to freedom.

22nd July 1973

'So Michael, that's how I came to leave home and come back to you so we can be together.'

Michael looked grave. 'This is a hell of a risk for me. Your mother sounds like she's on a mission and I could get into a great deal of trouble if they think I've even touched you'. Charlie sat saying nothing, giving Michael one of his biggest, saddest looks with his big blue-green eyes.

'I will go if you want me to; I will find somewhere else to stay.'

'How can I resist you Charlie Rogers? You know I love you. We will have to take great care to cover your tracks. Come here and give me a hug,' and at that Charlie fell sobbing into Michael's strong, masculine arms.

Over the next few days Charlie settled into his new life at the Isle of Dogs flat. He of course shared a bed with Michael but nothing happened between them. He was desperate for the feeling of Michael making love to him but he didn't know how to make a move. Michael insisted that he should write to his parents to let them know that he was okay. He really didn't want to do this but Michael told him that he was sure that they loved him and were finding everything very difficult to deal with. 'Please be kind to them,' he said.

'But they were so cruel to me.'

'I know love, but they didn't know they were being cruel, they really thought they were helping. One day you will understand. Please write to them.'

This is what Charlie wrote, with Michael's help (in fact Michael wrote most of it).

24th July 1973

Dear Mum and Dad,

I am writing to you to let you know that I am safe and have somewhere to live. I am planning to go to Amsterdam soon. (Charlie put this bit in to concur with Iris's lie.) *I know that you have found the idea of me being gay very tough to deal with but I'm not going to apologise. That is who I am and I hope that in time you will come to understand that I have no choice in this and that you will learn to love me in spite of this. I'm sure I will see you one day again soon, remember I am an adult now and I will make my own decisions.*

I love you both very much and I appreciate everything that you have done for Susan and me.

Charlie xx

★ ★ ★

Chapter Eight: Docklands Tales: Part One

September 1973

Charlie and Michael had been living together for 2 months and were in many respects like an old married couple. They went everywhere together. They bickered about the division of household duties, particularly as Charlie was used to having his mother running around after him and initially expected Michael to do the same. Michael would have none of this and insisted that he shared the responsibilities.

He taught him how to make some basic meals like pasta or his favourite, Shepherd's Pie. His mother had never thought it would be necessary for a boy to do this as 'There will be a very nice girl from a good family one day to look after him'. Thus Charlie arrived at Michael's totally useless but when shown how to do things proved himself to be rather capable around the kitchen.

There was such closeness between the couple that many who knew them thought that they were ideal for each other. They would spend long nights cuddled up on the settee in the little sitting room watching Coronation Street or the Generation Game and there was a calm and blissful happiness between them in most respects, but they were yet to have sex, although both of them wanted to. Now that Charlie was an adult in Michael's eyes he no longer thought it wrong. However, he still felt troubled that Charlie was far too young for him and because of this found it very difficult to make a move. Charlie was so horny that he thought he was going to explode but was far too shy to instigate anything. He feared he would never lose his virginity.

Eventually one Saturday evening Michael, his confidence reinforced by several gin and tonics, summoned up all the courage he could and putting his arm round Charlie's neck said, 'I do think you're very hot and I know I'm an old man in your eyes but I was wondering … if …'

'I thought you'd never ask,' replied Charlie who leaned over and kissed him deeply and passionately. When he finally came up for air Michael said, a little out of breath, 'I love you very much, shall we go to the bedroom?'

'That is what I want, you do know that I have never done this before don't you? You will have to be very patient with me'.

'Yes of course, it will be my honour,' and at that the two went hand in hand off to the bedroom.

Now of course in the average fairy-tale romance it would be lovely to be able to write that Charlie lost his virginity to Michael in a massive tide of lust and love and that the two spent the night holding each other and repeatedly making love until the sun came up.

Sadly that was not to be. Suffice to say, that in the world of gay sex there are some men that like to be totally dominated by other men and it quickly transpired to the pair that both of them fell into this category.

Charlie had fantasised about his dark handsome lover being rough, yet tender and gradually succumbing to his will and Michael thought the idea of being thrown round the bedroom by this gorgeous young lad was his idea of heaven.

In years to come they would be reduced to tears of laughter remembering the night that they tried to have sex and were totally incompatible but on that night Charlie felt rejected and slept on the couch having sobbed so much there were no more tears left. He only consoled himself by thinking of the old dream where he was a bird and he was loved. He thought sex hadn't worked because he was unattractive and had failed.

Michael felt terribly guilty, he had known his own sexual predilections for a long time and was angry with himself for not explaining all of this before their failed bedroom session.

The next day Michael woke Charlie with a cup of tea saying, 'We need to talk love.' Charlie rolled over and buried his face in the pillow saying nothing. He was still so hurt. Over the next couple of hours Michael gradually coaxed him out of bed (scrambled eggs on toast helped) and eventually he managed to get Charlie to respond to him.

'I am so sorry about last night. What you must understand is that I find you very attractive but I think we are both going to have to recognise that sex between us is never going to work properly. Do you understand?'

'It's me isn't it?' cried Charlie and burst into tears again.

'Please listen to what I'm saying. I fancy you, who wouldn't? You are gorgeous, but surely you must understand that men take different roles in gay sex ... surely you know?' Charlie looked completely blank, which was a sufficient answer for Michael.

Michael very slowly, carefully and tenderly explained how some men are sexually active, some are passive and some like both and that further than that some men liked being completely dominated and some liked being in control. It was just very unfortunate that both of them wanted nothing better than to be dominated, controlled and being the passive partner for a big butch man.

Charlie gradually stopped crying as Michael hugged him and continually reassured him that he loved him.

'I think I understand; when do you want me to leave?'

'I still love you, you silly sod, just because things are never going to work out in the bedroom doesn't mean we can't love each other. I want us to live together and see how things go. I will need to have sex with other men sometimes, as I'm sure you will. How does that sound? Do you reckon we can make it work?'

Charlie's response was to burst into even bigger fits of sobbing than he had before but eventually he managed to blurt out, 'Yes, please can we try?'

It wasn't quite happy ever after for Michael and Charlie; they were, in many respects an odd couple, in love but not sharing sexual love. But they were to live together for over 2 years. It was one of the happiest times of Charlie's life.

October 1973

Charlie and Michael soon settled back to their normal routine. They still slept together and held each other tightly at night, particularly after Charlie had his recurring nightmares, but the subject of sex was never discussed again. Michael would go out once a week dressed in leather and Charlie knew full well what he was up to. He would crawl back in the early hours looking tired and sometimes physically bruised. He never discussed what he had been doing, he didn't want to hurt Charlie's feelings and would spend the next day giving him huge amounts of assurance of how much he loved him. He did.

Charlie still had not lost his virginity and had been entertaining himself for hours in the bedroom with Michael's extensive collection of porn. It helped. A little.

Michael had taken it upon himself to share as much of his life experience as he could with Charlie. He felt that this was a way of expressing his love, giving him a good start in life as a young gay man, rather than expressing it through his body. Night after night they would talk into the early hours. Michael explained everything he could about how to have sex but more importantly how to know when to say *No* and when to say *Yes* and how to negotiate the type of sex Charlie wanted.

He told him how he had to be careful of the police as they were still treating gay men as criminals even though homosexuality had been decriminalised a few years before. All of this and much more came out in a series of long intense conversations over a couple of weeks, by the end of which Charlie felt that he had grown up 10 years. He wouldn't ever forget what Michael said, for the rest of his life.

With some of the money Iris had given Charlie, Michael took him shopping and they bought some new outfits suitable for gay London. Several pairs of over-tight jeans and some very revealing t-shirts. He felt that he would be dressed for a night out on the town.

One Friday night they smoked several joints together and Michael made Charlie stand in front of the mirror in the bedroom and taught him how to dance.

He explained that the dance floor was a great way for him to show himself off and attract men but that he had to dance sexily and not like his parents. It took all night. There was a lot of giggling, but after hours of Donna Summer and Diana Ross Michael said, 'Yes, you've got it, they will be all over you.'

So, on an unseasonably cold Saturday night in October, Charlie got dressed up in one of his very tight pairs of jeans and a small white t-shirt. He put on a brown leather bomber jacket for warmth and went into the sitting room to show Michael the effect. 'Stunning. You just watch how many guys are after you love. Let's go. The pub should be getting busy now.'

'Where are we off to?' enquired Charlie.

'The King's Arms in Rotherhithe, you will like it, it's very friendly. They have great drag acts and Olga will be there. I'm sure we can find a hot guy for you.' Charlie was very eager and he felt a warm flush of sexual excitement through his loins at the thought of meeting a man.

They drove off into the night and after having meandered through the Rotherhithe Tunnel they arrived at the pub. Charlie felt a little nervous and sensing this, Michael put his arm round him and said, 'Come on, you'll be fine. I will see to that.'

The King's Arms was an old-fashioned Victorian pub. It looked run down but as they walked through the door Charlie could see it was very busy. His mouth dropped open as he saw several hundred men of all shapes, sizes and ages together; he felt he had walked into heaven, he had no idea there were so many gay men in London. They quickly found Olga. On this occasion her hair was blond and she was wearing, for her, a rather discreet off the shoulder blue lamé evening dress. She kissed Charlie noisily on both cheeks.

'Daaaaarling it's so good to see you and my god you look so sexy. You will get eaten up tonight.'

They ordered drinks from the very camp barman, all blond curly hair and Charlie thought a hint of make-up. He lisped, 'Who's that gorgeous boy with you Michael, you dirty old bastard?' Charlie went red realising the comment was aimed at him. But Michael retorted, 'He's too good for you. Keep your hands off.'

'Get her,' spat back the barman spitefully.

It transpired that Olga was part of a drag ensemble called 'Sally and the Sluts'. They were to do a show that night and Olga was very over-excited, and kept saying gushingly to Charlie, 'This is going to be my big moment,' or 'This will be my breakthrough,' and similar comments.

Charlie, whilst naïve, realised that this shabby pub in Rotherhithe was not very likely to launch Olga into a major glittering career, but he was too polite to say anything.

Much of the evening went in a blur. Various men would come and chat to Michael, he was clearly popular, and some would try and chat to Charlie, who was so shy that he would clam up and could not say anything so the men soon gave up, feeling they were not getting anywhere. Michael had consumed a fair few gin and tonics and probably was not at the best level of his judgment. He hadn't noticed that Charlie, as well as consuming the drinks that he had bought for him, had also sneaked in some more from the barman. By about 9pm he had drunk five vodka oranges and was, to put it mildly, fairly drunk. He thought that doing this would build up his confidence.

Olga at this stage had gone to the ladies' toilet, which doubled as a dressing room, and Michael was chatting to a moustachioed leather queen that he clearly fancied and for a while took his eye off Charlie.

Some badly amplified music started blaring out of the PA, it was the intro to Shirley Bassey's 'Big Spender'. The curtains drew back and there standing proudly on stage were Sally and the Sluts. They were fabulous; all with heavy makeup, over-bouffed hair and the most glamorous evening dresses Charlie had ever seen.

Even though Charlie hadn't spoken to anyone, he was rather enjoying the atmosphere and through his drunken blur decided that the Sluts were terribly exciting and sophisticated. He couldn't see Michael who had disappeared somewhere with the leather queen, but was quite happy swaying by the bar and watching the show. The Sluts mimed through 'Big Spender' then 'Goldfinger' then started telling some dirty stories that he didn't fully understand. Just as they finished and were about to launch into their next number, he felt an arm tugging at his waist.

'Hello gorgeous and who are you? I haven't seen you in here before.'

'Charlie,' was all he could say. Even though he was now drunk it had not increased his confidence.

The man was probably in his mid 40's, wearing jeans that were far too tight and displaying the full outline of his genitals. On his top half a leather waistcoat, nothing underneath it, displaying a body that carried several pounds too many. He had olive skin, a greasy saggy face that looked like it suffered from a lack of sleep and small, piggy brown eyes. It was not a particularly pleasant appearance.

'So Charlie. How's about we go back to my house for some fun. Would you like that?'

Now Charlie was drunk, his guard was down and he totally forgot everything Michael had told him about how to say *Yes* and, more importantly, *No* to sex. He was also desperate to lose his virginity and whilst he found the man sexually repulsive, thought that it would be a reasonable way to do it.

'Yes, what's your name?' was all he could say.

'Teddy,' replied the stranger. The man looked slightly surprised at Charlie's positive reply, then pleased and he quickly shuffled Charlie out of the pub before he could have any second thoughts.

The Sluts were now halfway through a mime of 'Over the Rainbow' and the crowd obviously loved this number as they were singing along raucously with the girls.

Outside, Charlie swayed quite a lot, the ground didn't feel very steady and everything was blurred but he was damn sure that he would lose his virginity tonight and didn't care a fuck what Michael thought. He soon found himself in the passenger seat of a bright orange Marina driving off through the dereliction of London Docklands to somewhere unknown for the night.

Inside the pub Michael returned a few minutes later, looked around and became instantly concerned that he couldn't see Charlie. 'Jesus,' he thought, 'this lot would eat Charlie for breakfast.' He asked three men who were standing near to where he had been, 'Where's the guy I was with?' They looked back blankly. It was the camp blond barman who leaned over the bar and shouted over the music to Michael with what looked like venomous glee.

'Your friend went off with Teddy the Tongue. Didn't you know?'

At this Michael paled visibly as he knew that Charlie was

horribly out of his depth. He pushed his way through the crowd to the ladies' lavatory where the Sluts had just come off the stage.

'Olga please, you've got to help me, help Charlie. He's gone off with Teddy the Tongue.'

'Oh fuck, what the hell did he have to do that for? Weren't you watching him?'

'I'm sorry Olga I was, um busy in the toilets.' Olga gave him a long, hard, withering look.

She turned to the troupe. 'Right girls, we have to go and rescue Charlie. Michael do you have your car here?'

'Yes it's outside.'

'Okay, Doris, Maisy and Molly, follow us.' Molly, who had a bright orange beehive and was wearing a pink Lurex dress, piped up, 'What's all the fucking fuss about? He's only going off for a shag.'

'Molly dear, you are so naïve, Teddy is an evil man and Charlie is a virgin and will be in way over his head.'

'Why is he called Teddy the Tongue?' enquired Molly.

'Because every time he kisses you he tries to stick his tongue so far down your throat he can taste what you had for supper you silly cow.'

'Ooooooo, yuk.'

Michael and the four girls drove off into the night. Michael knew where Teddy the Tongue lived in Stepney and was determined to get Charlie out of his grasp. Whilst they drove through the deserted streets of Docklands, littered with rusty cars, Olga told Molly a little about Teddy.

'He's bad through and through. I honestly think he's evil; a user and a manipulator and not terribly good looking. Would you shag him dear? He can't get decent looking men to go to bed with him. He's too mean to pay for it, so what he does is to arrange sex parties, procure young naïve boys to be present and then allow them to be used by all his friends and cronies. It gives him a kind of status. It gives him power. They all think he is wonderful. "Teddy can get you anything," they say. And he can. He keeps an album with a picture of all his victims. When any of his cronies want a shag, they flick through the album until they find the one they want, then Teddy arranges it.'

'But why do the boys go along with it?' enquired Molly. 'If there is no money why do they do it?'

'He is very persuasive. He makes them believe that they will be porn stars or have a modelling career or whatever he finds out they want, all lies of course. God help them there is no way I'm going to let Charlie fall into his web.'

As the eclectic party dived through the entrance of the Rotherhithe Tunnel, a policeman caught a glimpse of the car, driven by a leather queen with four over-made-up women in evening dresses in the back, one of whose wig had slipped and revealed she was a man. 'Country's going to the fucking dogs,' he muttered to himself.

Charlie meanwhile had arrived at a shabby Georgian house in Stepney with Teddy and had been hurried through the front door before the neighbours could see. Charlie felt excited and was quite aroused at the thought of sex. Yes, the guy was foul, but he had to start somewhere. Poor Charlie had so little confidence in himself that he had no idea that anyone decent would ever find him attractive. 'This will do,' he thought.

He was led down some narrow stairs into a cellar. Dimly lit. Walls painted black. In spite of his drunken state he suddenly felt very unsure of what he was doing. Apart from anything else this place reminded him of his bad dreams.

The cellar smelt musty, of leather and various odours he couldn't place, but in future he would know were associated with sex. In the middle of the room was a contraption that Charlie didn't recognise. Made of leather and metal and looking a bit like a climbing frame (he thought).

'Get undressed Charlie and get yourself in the sling. The boys are upstairs and they will so enjoy meeting you.' At that Teddy walked off up the creaking wooden stairs. Charlie didn't pick up on the fact that Teddy had mentioned other men and despite the rather unpleasant surroundings, a little bit of him thought that there was in some way still a small amount of romance involved.

He meekly undressed and then went and sat on the edge of the sling. He had no idea how it was meant to be used. He was cold and felt rather silly and a bit vulnerable sitting alone, naked in the middle of the dark cellar.

He heard the door open above and then to his surprise and growing consternation he heard several gruff voices and the sound of more than one pair of feet coming down the stairs. He felt sick and began to realise he had no idea what he was doing and that the situation was getting out of control.

'Charlie boy, I told you to get into the sling, the boys are ready.'

Charlie looked up and Teddy was standing there with two other men. They were in various states of nakedness and arousal. None of them were very young, none of them were very pretty.

'Get in the sling, there's a good boy,' and Teddy started to guide the now petrified boy's feet into the footrests of the contraption. After a bit of fiddling around, the still very drunk Charlie found himself lying horizontally, legs spread and raised in the straps. Although naïve, young and innocent, he now realised the purpose of the contraption. The three men stood by his feet leering at him. They all had various leather accessories. Waistcoats, chaps, harnesses. The outfits did nothing to make them look any sexier, their sagging stomachs and wrinkled skin only too obvious.

'Let me have him first,' one of the guys mouthed breathlessly through his aroused state and lurched towards Charlie, grasping at his crotch. He now fully realised his fate and was petrified. He did the only thing he could think to do and screamed at the top of his voice.

At that very moment there was a massive bang from above the cellar as the front door was kicked down, followed by the sound of running.

'What the fuck!' shouted one of the leathermen. 'I thought you said there was just the three of us.' The cellar door burst open. Charlie could just see the top of the stairs and he saw to his complete surprise Michael followed by Olga still in her Lurex dress, followed by the other three 'Sluts', all in their show outfits and teetering down the stairs in their high heels.

'Get out of my fucking house Michael and take these creatures with you. Charlie is here of his own free will and we are having a little party, perhaps you want to join in?'

'Well Teddy, I think you have a choice here. Yes I am happy to leave him here with you but I think the police will be rather interested in your activities don't you? He is only 18 you know.'

'Take him then you sad old bastard, I'm sure we can find someone else much better. Perhaps you two can spend the night together, I heard that you are sooooo close. Take the stupid little idiot. We'll find someone much more interesting for our party.'

'Perhaps they should all stay and we could make a big night of it,' breathed one of the moustachioed leather queens. 'I'm sure these girls will fuck like bitches.'

At that Doris, in a rather fetching black cocktail number and with long dark ringlets, hit the leather queen full in the face with her clenched fist. All hell let loose. Charlie, still trussed up in the sling watched mesmerized as the half naked leather queens and the girls proceeded to enter into a full on fight. There was a lot of swearing, thumping and squealing and a blur of Lurex, dyed hair and leather and Charlie couldn't really make out who was getting the upper hand.

But eventually Teddy and the two other men were lying face down, tied up with their own leather straps with a stiletto heel in each of their backs. 'Good work girls,' said Michael with some relief.

He tenderly unravelled Charlie from the sling and wrapped him in a blanket that he had found on a mattress on the cellar floor.

'You all right Charlie? Hope we got here in time.'

'You fucking bastard, you're just so jealous aren't you? You never want me to meet a man.' He burst into tears and moments later vomited noisily all over Michael. The girls released the pressure of their stilettos from the leather guys' backs slightly.

'I think we will leave you trussed up down here for the weekend Teddy, have fun,' laughed Olga.

'One day Michael I will get you for this,' spat Teddy, 'I will take my time but you will live to regret this night.'

'Come on, let's take him home.' And at that Michael and the girls helped the still snivelling Charlie up the stairs and into the car and drove off into the East End night.

So it was that night Charlie still didn't lose his virginity, he was saved from Teddy the Tongue and his mates and everyone involved learned not to judge people by appearances – when it came down to it the butchest-looking leather guys were camp as Christmas and totally incapable of defending themselves and could be beaten in a fight by a bunch of glammed-up Drag Queens!

Dreamland

A long, long way away the woman has dreamed again. She has been shown this is a foretelling and she now begins to understand exactly what she has to do. She understands what 80 means and she knows that one day she will need every ounce of her powers, every last vestige of her energy to reach out a long, long way and write the word:

BELOW

When it's needed. When the time is right. It has to be done. 'Please no more dreams, enough, I understand now,' she shouts into the air at she knows not who.

But shortly she is asleep again and is propelled into a strange dark smoky place where missiles are falling from the sky and dirty tired-looking people are hiding under the ground from explosions.

Of this she has no understanding.

★ ★ ★

Interlude 1973

Iris reflects

Poros, Greece, September 1973

Iris lay on the white sun bed staring out to the calm, turquoise Aegean Sea, sipping on her third Ouzo of the afternoon. She found the spirit very strong and a pleasant numbness would soon spread though her. 'Good,' she thought, she fancied an afternoon's sleep.

She was tired, she had spent the night with a very vigorous young Greek called Michaelis, around 28 and darkly handsome with a trim, defined body. She felt very self-satisfied that although she was 48 years old she could still pull gorgeous young men. She had made a further date with him for the next night and she relished the anticipation of his hard young flesh thrust into her again.

She closed her eyes. Not asleep but pleasantly hazy, she started to drift off into deep thought. Last night's gymnastics were uppermost in her mind but then gradually her attention shifted. Her thoughts turned to the recent grim events and she cast her mind back to when they had begun the previous year.

Sometimes when there is a thunderstorm it starts with a few plops of rain, so infrequent that you're not sure if it's raining or not. Then the heavens open, there is a massive downpour and huge crashes fill the sky. It was a lot like that with Harry. A few clues, a slight disturbance, then all hell letting loose as the truth came out.

The first splashes of the storm had come in a call from her sister Rose. After running though the normal pleasantries, chat about the weather, what she had been speaking about at the Townswomen's Guild that week Rose said conversationally, 'Oh by the way did you know that they have still not caught anyone for murdering those boys in Peckham?'

'I know it's terrible isn't it. We don't want a monster like that on the loose.'

Iris's dreams over the years had never abated and she had lived in fear that her beloved Charlie was at risk from such a man and she knew that it was up to her to protect him and allow his story to be told.

'I still think that Harry is bloody peculiar, you remember what happened that Christmas with Charlie. I wonder why the police have not interviewed him? It's terrible. Frederick is always going on about him. He does *live* in Peckham you know dear. I was round at Violet's the other day and Frederick is convinced Harry has something to do with it.'

After finishing the call Iris tried to put the thoughts of the murders out of her head. It wasn't going to achieve anything dwelling on this now. But for some indefinable reason she had niggling doubts. Maybe it was a flicker of sight, nothing more. Apart from anything she didn't know until Rose had told her that Harry lived in Peckham.

She couldn't leave it alone in her mind, something was bothering her. She didn't know what. A little niggle. Something. Iris still wasn't sure what to do or indeed if she would do anything, her sight was so limited it was frustrating.

A few days later she decided to call her sister Violet to see what her thoughts were on the matter. Whilst Violet was most prim and proper she was also very practical. She would mention nothing of her dream–driven fears about Charlie. Purely concerns about Harry living in the area and being so odd.

She dialled Violet's number and after a few rings the phone was answered.

'Badgers End, Partington speaking.'

Iris had to stifle a giggle at the pretentious way that Frederick chose to greet callers. 'Hello dear,' she started, 'how are you? I was expecting to get Violet.'

'I'm off work with a bad back at the moment and Violet is out shopping, can I help you?'

Iris hesitated for a moment having expected to discuss the matter with Violet but then thought, 'Frederick's a sensible soul too. Let's see what he has to say.'

'Frederick, you know about the Peckham murders, I know this sounds stupid but I've got this awful sick suspicion that Harry Rogers is involved. You know, David's uncle. I have no idea why apart from the fact that he lives in Peckham and his odd behaviour in the past but I just have a feeling. What should I do? Am I just being stupid?'

'Well Iris, I think sometimes intuition is a very underestimated thing. If you have concerns it is important that you talk to the police about them.'

She continued, 'I can't see how that would help, I have nothing to go on. Just a feeling.'

'Well perhaps you should go and see Harry and have a chat with him. See what you think after that.'

'Maybe, well let me think it through and thank you, I do appreciate your advice.'

'Alright dear, well lots of love and let me know how you get on won't you?'

'Yes of course, and send my love to Violet.'

'Bye dear,' and Frederick put down the phone.

Iris continued to mull things over for the next few days and really wasn't quite sure what she would do. But eventually, Iris being Iris, she determined to take matters into her own hands. She would go and see Harry. She called David, her brother-in-law, the next day. 'David, good morning, how are you?'

'All the better for hearing you dear.' Iris chatted briefly about the weather, which was particularly damp for the time of year, and then dropped in, 'Oh! by the way, do you have your Uncle Harry's address, there's something I want to talk to him about?'

David was slightly mystified. No one had had much to do with Harry since the Christmas when Charlie had been so upset and Rose had suspected him of some wrong doing. 'What do you want to see him for Iris?'

'David, can you do me a great favour and not ask me that question?'

David was fond of Iris and agreed, he had no reason to press it. He found Harry's address in the little leather bound book that he and Rose kept by the phone and read it out to her. 'Be careful if you go there, it's not a very safe part of London for a woman to be wandering around by herself.' Iris thanked him and brought the conversation to a close.

The following day she drove to Peckham to speak to Harry. He wasn't on the telephone so she'd have to take the risk he was at home. As she got closer to the house which was in Victoria Street, she could see that the area had been heavily bombed during the war and was only now being cleared to make way for new housing. It didn't look like much of an improvement to Iris; huge concrete apartment blocks were being built as far as the eye could see. Here and there a few streets of dishevelled Victorian terraces still showing wartime scars remained, but mostly the new prevailed and the new was large, ugly and grey. She hated it.

Iris turned the car into Victoria Street and quickly pulled up outside the house. She knocked on the door, not sure of whether she wanted Harry to answer or not, or what she was going to say to him if he did. She wasn't even sure why she was here. It was just an inkling, a slight glimmer of sight.

She was about to turn away when she heard a shuffling in the hall. The door opened and the faded figure of Harry stared at her blankly. 'Do you remember me Harry, it's Iris, Rose's sister?'

He clearly did because he smiled, revealing one single tooth left in his upper jaw. He gestured her into the dingy hallway saying nothing. He was dressed in an old, baggy pair of trousers and a string vest. Iris could smell the stale odour of unwashed body and her stomach turned slightly.

She followed him into the tiny kitchen, which was in complete disarray and covered in grease and cobwebs. Mountains of unwashed plates were on the drainer, some sprouting green and black mould.

The place smelt. A combination of damp, rot, rats and something indefinable that Iris didn't want to think about. Afterwards she would often come back to the thought that if evil has a smell, it was this: Harry's kitchen.

'Why you here?' Harry asked.

'I wondered if you knew any of the boys who have been murdered here over the last few years.'

Harry shook his head, looking confused. Why was Iris there asking him questions?

'Can you tell me anything about them?'

Harry stared blankly. Iris recalled now that Rose had always maintained that Harry was quite simple and this was confirmed by the limited conversation he was able to have with her. He smelt like his house, old and rotten and she felt discomforted by the seedy look in his eyes. His clothes were ancient, faded and threadbare in places and he hadn't shaved for days.

'Do you know who killed the boys?' Harry shook his head again.

Iris began to feel that her trip was futile and she was going to find out little, so she got up to leave. 'If you think of anything Harry, call me. Here's my number,' she said, handing him a piece of paper with the number scrawled on it in pencil. 'If you think of anything can you call me please?'

'Don't go yet … have tea,' he managed to say. He clearly had little company. Who would want to spend time in this dreadful place? Iris very much wanted to leave. Harry was not a pleasant man to be with and the house was revolting. She felt that the stench emanating from him and from the vile surroundings was starting to permeate her skin. She felt slightly nauseous. But the extra time with him may still just give her the opportunity to glean some information if indeed there was anything to discover.

Harry put the kettle on the gas stove and lit the ring with a match. 'Going to toilet,' he said and disappeared upstairs.

Iris sat for a few moments taking in the decay and rot of the kitchen then suddenly her eye fell on a narrow door. A cellar door. A cellar. Cellars featured heavily in her dreams. She had to have a look. She went over to the door. It was locked.

She went back to the sink, withdrew a knife with a sharp point and went back to the cellar door and wiggled the inadequate lock until she heard something click. She pulled the door ajar.

There were some stairs. At the top was an old fashioned light switch, which she flicked to turn on a low wattage bare bulb that barely illuminated the dank, odorous space. She took a couple of steps down the creaking stairs. What she saw next stopped her in her tracks and she felt a twist of nausea going through her stomach.

On the wall below, written in huge red letters that looked like blood but may also have been red paint was one single word. A name. Shocked, Iris brought her hand to her mouth to stop herself screaming. The word scrawled in 3 feet high, red letters was:

CHARLIE

She had to get out of the house. She had to run before Harry got back. She couldn't confront him. She walked backwards out of the cellar door and picked up her handbag from beside the kitchen table. As she did she heard Harry flush the toilet upstairs. She swiftly walked down the hall and out of the front door, half expecting him to grab her from behind.

It is an awful feeling when you think that someone is behind you and is going to grab you. It's a little bit like when you were a child and had to jump into bed in case a monster hiding underneath grabbed your foot. That's what it felt like now but the monster was real and he was called Harry and if she didn't get out of the house damn quick he might grab her and she might end up dead in the cellar.

She opened the front door and gratefully ran out into the street, fully expecting Harry to chase after her. He didn't and she drove off, back towards home, shaking, crying and nauseous.

The matter was brought quickly to a head. She arranged a meeting with the police, told them of her fears and what she had seen. They arranged a search warrant and the next morning went to Harry's house and found, apart from the word CHARLIE, some damming and conclusive evidence. Several pieces of clothing that belonged to the boys including underwear, school trousers and a long piece of black electric flex which was hanging on a hook in the cellar. Harry was promptly arrested and charged.

As the story came out, Iris felt a massive sense of relief. A great weight falling from her shoulders. She now knew that Harry had Charlie in his sights and that fitted in with her dreams. She knew that he had been stopped in his tracks. Iris had made the right connection, the monster had been defeated and she thanked God (who she didn't believe in) for the sight she had been given to be able to do this.

Harry's trial was brief, the evidence was so damning, and Iris took the stand herself to describe how she had found the scrawled word 'Charlie' and also Harry's way of looking at the boy and what had happened all those Christmases ago. He was found guilty of all three murders and was sentenced to three consecutive life imprisonments. In actuality he served little of these as he hanged himself in Wandsworth a few weeks later.

'Yes,' Iris thought, 'it was the right thing, Harry was stopped and I protected Charlie,' but it didn't stop her finding the whole series of events shocking and sickening. The monster had been stopped but three boys had suffered terribly as they died and their families would live in torment for the rest of their lives.

Dreamland

Iris had drifted off to sleep, eased into a dream state by the rough strong spirit she had been consuming. It was not the first time that this strange variation of her dreams came to her, 80 80 80 80, the number seemed to grow organically in her vision. The number had first come to her in her dreams a few days after Harry's death. Now it never left them. She had no idea what it meant.

80

She could see, hear, feel, taste and smell the number in her dream, it filled every molecule of herself, she was confused and she felt dream-fear.

Suddenly, with a start, she snapped awake as she became aware of a male presence by her side. She smelt strong Greek cigarettes and thick sensuous lips kissed her briefly and she felt the brush of stubble against her skin. She opened her eyes to see Michaelis smiling at her.

'Shall we go and have some more fun now, I need you so much?'

She smiled and said nothing but got up from the sun bed and followed him into the hotel.

Iris spent several more wild and passionate days and nights with the gorgeous Greek youth. By the end of the week he was declaring undying love for her and meant it and she was thinking it was about time she left. He told her that he would give up his job and come to London and he asked her to marry him. She said she would think about it but knew full well that she would not. He promised to fly to London the following month to be with her but before he could, Iris sent him a letter saying untruthfully, that she was still married and that he must not come as her husband was a very violent man.

We so often read of holiday romances where someone goes off to a sunny resort and falls in love with a waiter or a pool boy. Invariably the man has had a stream of willing women (or men) falling into his arms that summer and on their return to England the holidaymaker is broken hearted when they hear nothing from their lover. But for Iris and Michaelis the story was different. He genuinely loved her in spite of the age difference (perhaps because of) and he would have been a wonderful lover and considerate husband. But Iris was incapable of seeing this, she didn't want to let anyone into her life, however young and vigorous because there was a special love that she had once had and would always have, yet that could never be fulfilled.

★ ★ ★

Chapter Nine: Docklands Tales: Part Two

31st December 1979

Michael was very pleased with his new home. He had spent the last two years converting the derelict Victorian pump house in Lime House into a stunning apartment. He thought that this part of London would do very well so he was sure it would be a good investment. There were so many plans for the derelict dock areas and one day he would sell at a handsome profit. But that was for the future. For now this was going to be one showpiece of a home. This is where he would show off his collection and this is where he was going to throw legendary parties

The centrepiece of the apartment was a massive double height reception area with a vaulted Gothic ceiling, where the pumps had been. Next door was what had been the machine room and he had divided it into three bedrooms and two bathrooms. He had furnished it with sleek modern furniture and as he looked at the effect he sighed with contentment.

Perhaps what some people would find less tasteful was that Michael had brought his collection of religious kitsch from Millwall and it had been massively expanded so the new home, whilst furnished with the latest contemporary look, still had every surface covered with plastic Virgin Marys, crucifixion scenes, even in one place a little model of the manger at Bethlehem. He didn't give a hoot what anyone else thought. He loved it. 'It's my collection love,' he would say with a camp wave. As well as the religious kitsch, he brought all his other 'Art' so there was still a Marilyn Monroe themed room and now, amongst other things, a Judy Garland bedroom (the spare) and a Dusty Springfield bathroom

Michael was looking forward to the party he was planning for that evening. It was New Year's Eve and he wanted to make sure that the New Year was welcomed with a bang. He had invited about 50 friends. All gay men. He knew how the party would end up. His parties always did. Lots of hot men having sex all over his apartment. Yes that would be good. The most important person on his guest list was Charlie, his best friend and in some ways the love of his life, although they had never made love. Michael sometimes regretted this, they could have made such a perfect couple but that's how it was and in spite of that their love was solid. No one could ever separate the two friends and many who knew them still thought that they were a couple.

Later that evening Michael showered and got into his best leather gear for the party. Firstly he slipped on a pair of Levi 501's, and then these were complimented by his chaps that he had bought a few weeks before. On his top half he wore just a leather waistcoat. He was 42 years old but kept himself in good shape swimming four times a week so he could still get away with showing off a bit of body.

He checked round the apartment to ensure that everything was set up. Ashtrays out, drinks ready. He had turned the heating up; it was a very cold night and he suspected that many of his guests would end up naked. He didn't want them to get a chill he sniggered to himself.

Michael jumped as the sound of a roaring lion was amplified across the echoing reception room. It was what he had set up instead of a doorbell. It still caught him by surprise and gave him a little pleasured shock each time it went off. He went to the huge arched doorway and pulled the door open to find Charlie standing there shivering with the cold in spite of the flying jacket, scarf and heavy leather gloves he was wearing. 'Come in, I'm glad you're first, I always get so anxious when I have a party worrying if people are going to come.'

'You silly sod, people always come, your parties are wild and you invite the sexiest men in town. Why wouldn't people want to be here?'

Charlie walked into the apartment and hugged Michael hard and kissed him on the lips. 'You all right mister?' he enquired.

'Yes, great thank you, I'm so excited about tonight. I have some really hot guys coming; we are going to have a ball. I've got one or two lined up that I think you might be keen on.'

Over the next hour the lion roared numerous times. Firstly the DJ, Calvin, a small, blonde and rather lovely 23 year old that Charlie had briefly dated. He struggled in with his box of records and dumped them by the DJ decks that the equipment hire company had set up earlier that day.

Next, the guests gradually arrived until, by about 11pm, the apartment was packed with about 50 men gyrating to the latest disco sounds being pumped out by Calvin on his decks. When he dropped one of the latest hits there was appreciative whooping from the men.

Charlie was having a thoroughly wonderful time, dancing, a little drunk and enjoying snogging some stranger. He felt a hand on his arm, it was Michael.

'Come over here Charlie, I've got something for you,' and he beckoned him over to the open plan kitchen. Michael pulled something out of his pocket, a little tin, and he put it on the marble breakfast bar. He then gestured to Charlie. 'Go on, open it, and try one.' Charlie had no idea what Michael was offering, so opened the tin. In it were about 30 very small, orange tablets. Just bigger than a pin head.

'What are they? Is this drugs? You must be mad. I don't take drugs.'

'Don't be so boring Charlie, they're Microdots ... you know, LSD. Try one. I haven't done it before but a guy I have been seeing got them for me and says they are great for sex.'

Charlie was slightly drunk and for a moment his resistance lowered and he started to reach towards the tin to take one of the little orange tablets. Then suddenly he withdrew his hand, he was still sufficiently in control of his faculties to know that he didn't want to take LSD.

'No Michael, I don't want to take drugs and I'm not sure you should either.'

'You're such a party pooper. Andy, who sold them to me told me they're really strong. I haven't had one before but tonight, mmmm, I reckon I'm going to have some great horny fun.'

Charlie was a little wounded at being called a party pooper by Michael and flounced off whilst Michael went round the dance floor dispensing the little orange pills to anyone who wanted them. Charlie thought nothing more of it for the moment. He had his eye on a very sexy guy who was dancing near him. Maybe 40 years old, tall, muscular and covered in tattoos. He set him in his sights and went in for the kill. Within minutes he was snogging the sexy stranger and he gradually manoeuvred him towards one of the bedrooms.

Michael meanwhile, having dispensed his wares, decided to take one of the Microdots himself. He had never taken LSD before and had no idea what to expect. He went back to dancing in the melee of men as they threw their arms around to 'Disco Star Wars', a huge hit from a couple of years before.

Michael thought he had picked the DJ well this time, the guy clearly knew what his guests enjoyed and was piling on hit after hit. About half an hour later he suddenly noticed that the disco lights he had set up seemed to be more colourful, the music was even more wonderful and the men looked even sexier than they had earlier in the evening. He realised the drug was starting to do something to him. He danced on and on, now fuelled by the chemical and everything was becoming a blurred but very pleasurable haze. Lights, dancing and men.

After what seemed like days of dancing (it was probably a couple of hours) he started to feel very horny and decided to go and explore the various bedrooms where he suspected that many of his guests would already be engaged in various sexual acts. He was right. In the main bedroom a heap of heaving leather and flesh seemed to fill the entire room. His vision was filled with blurred images and seeing the men having sex made him feel even hornier than he had done before.

The other two bedrooms contained much the same scene and through Michael's drugged haze he was able to feel a sense of satisfaction that he had been able to arrange another good party. 'I have a reputation to maintain,' he thought to himself. Many of the guys looked in a similar state to Michael, their pupils dilated and their eyes staring as they concentrated on getting the best enhanced sexual experience that they could.

Maybe all would have been well if Michael had engaged with one of the men and started to have sex himself and had lost himself to passion. However, in spite of the fact the he felt very horny, he wasn't able to get it together to start sex with anyone. His head was far too all over the place. He couldn't settle, couldn't find someone that was just right. His head was spinning, his mind was a myriad of tunnels of bizarre thoughts and he was surrounded by over the top religious iconography.

This now took on a new dimension, the crosses glowed, the Virgin Mary shot laser beams from her hands and more disturbingly one of the Crucifixion scenes had real blood pouring from Jesus' wounded hands.

He kept wandering around trying to find somewhere to settle and as he did he started to feel more and more edgy. The men no longer looked as attractive as they had before, and he started to feel irritated by them. God they were ugly he thought. As he walked around, actually by this time swaying around, he was so out of it, he saw the faces of the men changing. One turned into a cat, another into an elephant and another, the spitting image of Marilyn Monroe. Yes, it was all rather disturbing and he was now finding the whole experience a bit much. He wanted to feel normal again, wanted all these peculiar people out of his apartment and actually wanted to sleep.

It still could have been okay if Michael had found a quiet corner, or a vacant bed, taken a sleeping pill and crashed out, but he was tripping so much he didn't know what to do. He didn't really know where he was any longer and more and more of the men around him were turning into bizarre animals. One looked like a rhino and another had whiskers like a mouse.

He lurched out from the main bedroom where much of this ghastly menagerie was nesting and as he did so, came face to face with a large gold (actually plastic but covered in gold paint) crucifix. Maybe three feet high and hanging on the wall. It had been one of his prized souvenirs on his latest visit to Lourdes to source items for his collection. This was the final straw, the one that broke the proverbial camel's back. Something in his head finally snapped, some of what those ghastly nuns had beaten into him at that dreadful children's home bubbled up in his mind. With the LSD still coursing through his brain cells, he was suddenly convulsed with a religious fervour and a hatred for everything homosexual.

Michael grabbed the crucifix from the wall, tearing it from the screw that held it and ran back into the main bedroom, holding it in front of him as if to ward off vampires.

'Repent Ye Sodomites!' he shrieked at the top of his voice.

Now you have to remember that many of the guys at the party had also taken one of the orange Microdots and were in a similar state. One in particular, a man called Phillip who was one of Michael's leather scene buddies, was completely gone. Seeing this leather clad man, waving the cross around for some twisted, acid-fuelled delusion, he decided it was the Devil and started screaming in mortal fear for his soul.

There was mayhem. Naked and half naked men started running around. Michael kept waving the cross shouting, 'Repent Ye Sodomites,' ever louder and louder. One couple was so engrossed with each other that they looked up, saw him and thinking he was the Angel Gabriel, went into religious ecstasy and then got back down to having sex again, the best either of them had ever had.

By now there was the sound of glasses being broken and the disco music suddenly ceased as dazed and confused men, many of them aroused and naked, ran around like a herd of half anaesthetised elephants bumping crazily into each other. Furniture was knocked over and some of Michael's precious ornaments and collection were broken.

'REPENT YE SODOMITES!' shrieked Michael now running up and down, the cross held high and proudly over his head. Like an avenging angel he ranged up and down the huge reception room, shouting ever louder and more messianically, 'REPENT YE SODOMITES!'

At that point, as if it couldn't get any worse there was the roar of a lion; someone was at the front door. Charlie who was still relatively sober and trying to get things under control opened it. Before he could say anything ten uniformed police burst in and started pinning shouting, naked and very dazed men to the ground. One by one the men were restrained and encouraged to put some clothes on and were handcuffed. This in itself was an ordeal for the

30 men that had taken acid, as getting a t-shirt or a pair of jeans on was like getting an octopus into a string bag.

'Come on you fucking queer boy perverts, we are going to sort you out down at the station.'

The police were becoming quite aggressive with the men who were still trying to find something to cover their nakedness with and Charlie heard several crunches and thumps as a policeman's booted foot connected with one of the partygoers.

Eventually all of Michael's guests had been herded into a number of police wagons which were parked outside the pump house. The last person to be pushed in quite roughly was Charlie.

At that moment he turned around and saw, to his shock, a fat and unpleasant figure that he hadn't seen for years. Teddy the Tongue hadn't improved with age. He was leaning against Michael's front doorway, smoking a cigarette and smiling a large, unpleasant and self-satisfied smile.

'Hello Charlie and hello Michael. Happy New Year. I heard about your little party and I thought that the police would just love to get an invitation. They are just so intolerant.' Teddy had clearly finally got his revenge.

The group of men were taken to Lime House police station, many of them in a complete state of shock as their acid trip went from bad to worse. One minute they had been having a great time at the party having sex with each other, then some religious maniac started shouting at them, waving a cross, and now they were incarcerated in damp, graffiti covered and uncomfortable police cells. Some of them were groaning and some crying. The guy Phillip, who had thought that Michael was Satan, had his trip degenerate to the point that he thought he had actually been taken by Satan and was going to be tossed into the Fires of Hell for eternity.

There were a number of results of this disastrous night. Michael was charged with running a disorderly house. He was bailed and then 6 months later brought to trial at the Crown Court. He got a 2 years suspended sentence and was put on probation. He was also sacked from the job he loved as a counsellor working with young offenders. That was the part of it that hurt most. He had genuinely felt that he was making a difference to these troubled youths and helping society with some of its vagaries. But society was not able to deal with him because he was a little different.

He was never a bitter man and he soon brushed himself down and got a new and better job working with an organisation counselling gay men. But he never took drugs again and never had another party. His reputation as London's best party host was gone forever. Quite often when he went into gay pubs, even amongst complete strangers, he would hear someone sniggering, 'Repent ye Sodomites.'

The other guests were charged with gross indecency and they received fines or suspended sentences depending on the particular sexual act that the police claimed they were engaged in. Much of it complete fabrication of course.

As for Phillip the leather queen, the acid trip in the police cells was too much; his mind snapped and he had a religious conversion himself. In his permanently confused state he knew that his only salvation and indeed the salvation of the whole of humanity would to be to go off and fight Satan. He knew it was his duty. He was last heard of in a little monastery on a remote Scottish island. He lived out his days as a beekeeper, with a reputation for making the most beautiful honey from bees which had supped on the heather clad slopes. He would be heard rambling as he tended the hives mumbling to himself, 'Away from me Satan.' But then occasionally, in his more lucid moments, 'It was a fucking good party, best I've ever been to,' and there would be a little twinkle in his eye.

Dreamland

So, so many dreams. Charlie has stopped having the dreadful dream of the man that was going to kill him in the cellar but he still dreams often of the awful place and the cellar walls scrawled with the number 80. He doesn't know why his dreams have changed or what they mean. He has no awareness of what has been done to protect him, and neither should he. He still has his good dream too of being the soaring bird in a sun filled sky; it has never left him.

Iris often dreams of what she has done. She repeatedly re-visits the cellar where she saw the word CHARLIE, but now, surrounding the word she too sees the number 80 in chalk white letters on every single surface.

The difference for Iris is that she now knows the true meaning of the number 80, and this dream is no longer a foretelling but a memory, a reflection. She awakes shuddering and sickened as her mind keeps revisiting what she has carried out. She knows that the secret that she carries will gnaw at her for the rest of her life but is determined that no one, particularly Charlie, will ever know the full truth.

A long, long, long way away and a long time ago a dark handsome man dreams again, and he dreams the whole story. He knows everything. Every twist and turn of fate. Every detail. He awakes from his dream, there is still a big hole in his soul and it hurts, the most terrible and deep hurt like a knife twisting in his heart.

★ ★ ★

Chapter Ten: A Night out at the Theatre and Luke the Psychic Bear

September 1981

Life was grand. Charlie was happily enjoying being single He had grown into an extremely handsome young man, tall, lean with sensuous lips and of course those wonderful blue-green eyes.

He had lots of guys chasing him and was happy to have one night stands, sometimes a date or two, but he had no intention of getting bogged down in a relationship. He was having far too much fun. He also had a great group of friends. His best friend was Michael and they still loved each other very dearly, although they no longer lived together.

Their unusual relationship had lasted two years before Charlie fell in lust with yet another man (it happened on an almost weekly basis) and this time he moved out, all the way to Crawley, against Michael's advice where the affair lasted 2 months. He really wanted to go back to Michael but by this time Michael was also dating so he rented a flat in Crystal Palace, later on being able to buy one of his own.

Michael would always be there and Charlie knew that although other men would come and go and there would be loves found and lost, Michael would give him the continuity and support he needed.

He reflected again on how lucky he was. His parents, whilst having dealt with his sexuality in an appalling manner, had eventually realised that if they wanted their son, they would have to cope with this aberration. Actually, it was two of Charlie's godparents, Iris and Frederick, who had engineered this.

Iris had always been open minded whereas Frederick had struggled with the concept of a homosexual nephew, but he was ultimately a man that cared about the family and cared deeply that his nephew should have a good relationship with his parents. Charlie's mood clouded slightly as he thought of the meeting that

Iris and Frederick had arranged with his parents, after his departure to London. It was over lunch at Frederick's house. Iris was her normally loving, extrovert and wonderful self but it was actually Frederick who helped most by saying, 'Rose, David. I don't begin to understand how Charlie is feeling and what he has gone through, I'm not sure I totally approve of the life style he wants to live, but I do know that we must stick together as a family and show our love for him. Life is too short and precious for us to fall out with each other.'

Rose, who had been stony faced, burst into tears and threw her arms around Charlie and asked for his forgiveness. His father made a few herrrumphing sounds, which Charlie took to mean that he agreed. The lunch hadn't been easy, he didn't often like to think about that afternoon, but it had enabled him to have some type of relationship with his parents and he thanked Iris and Frederick deeply for that.

Later that week Charlie had arranged to meet Michael in the West End. They were going to see the musical Evita for the 23rd time. They both loved the show and had become thoroughly addicted since they had first seen it together a couple of years before. They met at Leicester Square tube station. Michael was accompanied by his friend Elizabeth Hodgson. Charlie had met her a few times before and liked her. She was in her sixties, terribly glamorous and still rather gorgeous. She had her greying hair swept up into a big bouffed arrangement on her head, which showed off her fine, rather aristocratic features well. She spoke with the accent of the well-to-do from the Home Counties and one could imagine her owning a race horse stable or being the Lady of the Manor, in a rather grand Georgian house in the Cotswolds.

In fact, Elizabeth was a high-class hooker. She worked from a small but immaculate apartment in Mayfair and her specialty was fetishes. Once Elizabeth knew that Charlie was to be trusted she had said to him over a large gin and tonic, 'Darling I have to do very little; I have regular clients most of whom are rich Arabs or English judges and MPs. They book me into the best hotels in London for the night, I get dressed up in my leather fetish gear and mostly all I have to do is walk all over them in my stiletto heels. They pay me a thousand pounds for that.'

Charlie loved her and hoped that in the future they would become firm friends. Elizabeth had also said, 'Now Charlie, darling, if you're ever hard up I can put you in touch with the right people and get you some work. Only high class of course sweetie, you're a nice looking boy and you could earn good money.'

Charlie was genuinely touched and stored this information for a rainy day. Tonight Elizabeth was dressed in ankle-length emerald green satin for the theatre, her hair was bouffed up even more than normal and she had a discreet string of pearls around her neck.

They loved the musical as ever and in spite of having seen it so many times Charlie still cried once or twice. Later on, as they came out of the theatre, Elizabeth said, 'So did you enjoy the show again tonight boys?'

'It was wonderful,' replied Michael, 'but we always do. Of course if it wasn't for you we wouldn't have seen it in the first place. Oh please tell us the story of why you got to be interested in Evita again, please.'

'Oh darling, I must have told you that tale a hundred times.' She feigned a slight resistance, but this was her party piece and she would of course oblige.

'Pleeeease tell the story for me,' chipped in Charlie.

'Okay, if I must. Well darlings, it was in the 1940's and I was an air hostess. I was of course *terribly* young. In those days it was such a glamorous job we thought we were like film stars, it was so exciting. I used to work for an airline that had a weekly flight to Buenos Aires. It took over 24 hours you know.

Well, on one of those flights I started chatting to a passenger. If truth were told dears I fancied him. He was rather gorgeous. For some reason I can't recall we started talking about Eva Peron. I knew a little about her but wasn't really interested. He told me that he thought that one day she was going to be extremely famous and that if I got the opportunity I should go and see her speaking from the Casa Rosada, the presidential palace, as it was such an amazing spectacle.

Well darlings, I wasn't really that bothered and I had heard that some thought she and her husband were fascists. But I was on a long stopover in the city and I had nothing else to do that day. Well dears, I went and all I can say is that it was the most amazing spectacle I have ever seen in my life. The colour, the passion that she spoke with. Her clothes and jewels! Amazing. Over the years the memory dimmed somewhat, then suddenly, 30 years later they are making a musical about her. Well, I had to go and see it and I had to persuade you too.'

'That is fabulous, thank you so much for telling it again,' said Michael. 'I so much wish I could have been there. But at least we can get to see the musical!'

The men said their farewells to Elizabeth and swayed off down the Charing Cross Road singing loudly and badly, 'Don't Cry for me Argentina'.

When they got back to Michael's apartment they smoked several joints, were in helpless giggles and had their usual post show conversation about the frocks, the jewels and the glamour, pontificating long and hard about what it would be like to have tea with Eva Peron.

The following weekend Charlie got in just before 6pm after the short walk from the office and switched on the TV for the BBC news. Thatcher was ranting on again. He couldn't stand the woman, her awful grating voice and mad staring eyes. He turned the sound down so he didn't have to listen to the bloody woman any more. He made himself supper of baked beans on toast and sat down, the TV still playing silently, and began to make his calls for the evening. First he dialled Iris's number. She answered the phone quickly and as always sounded delighted to hear from him.

'Charlie darling, how are you?' she enquired.

'I'm great thanks Iris, bit of a long week at work but looking forward to the weekend. I'm going out dancing tonight.'

'Now I'm not sure that's all you will be doing dear,' Iris replied naughtily. He went red. Although he had a very open and honest relationship with Iris he didn't always want her to know exactly what he had been doing.

'I may just go home by myself this time, who knows.'

'Yes dear,' she continued sounding unconvinced. Iris went on to tell Charlie about her latest fling with an estate agent, '25 years old and very fit.'

'So you and I are not entirely different,' he joked gently.

In truth Iris worried about Charlie, he never seemed to settle down for long. Three or four dates then the guy was dumped. She thought that he should find someone to love him. He could be such a vulnerable and fragile boy, but this is what he chose and she wasn't going to interfere.

They chatted on for another 10 minutes talking about fashion, how much they both hated 'that awful woman' Thatcher and then of course talked about boys in general.

His next call was to Michael; they spoke on the phone almost every day and were as close as ever. 'Hi Michael, it's Charlie. Where have you been since Wednesday, I've been trying to call you?'

'I was staying with the Moors Sisters for a couple of days. Needed a bit of fresh air and some time away from London.'

'How are they?'

'Creepy as ever but very good hosts. I did get worried at one point because I saw a hole in the garden and thought they were digging it for me but it turned out it was just a new pond.'

'Don't be so wicked Michael,' and they both dissolved into giggles.

They then reminisced, as they so often did, firstly about the time they had failed to have sex with each other.

'You said, 'Manhandle me you brute!' Charlie reminded Michael. They both were now in tears of laughter as for the umteempth time they recalled the disastrous night.

'Oh I do love you Charlie you know that don't you?'

'Of course, and I love you too, always, who couldn't? And of course I have you to thank for launching me on this life of gay madness.'

They then reminisced about how Michael, bored with the subject of Charlie not losing his virginity, had eventually paid a rent boy to seduce him. It was over a year before he found out what Michael had done and he initially was hurt and furious but now, 8 years later, it was another source of amusement between the two of them. 'And he cost me twenty fucking quid love. That shows how much I love you,' Michael jibbed at Charlie. They finished their conversation by blowing loud kisses to each other over the phone and Charlie felt happy and loved as he always did with Michael.

At 10pm Charlie left the flat and walked down the hill to the station where he got the train for the short journey into the centre of town. After arriving at Victoria, Charlie caught a Circle Line train to Embankment. As he got closer to his final destination, he noticed that there were more and more gay men on the train, clearly heading for the same night out that he was, the huge gay club, Heaven, that lay under the railway arches at Charing Cross. Many of them were heavily moustachioed with cropped hair so it was very easy to spot them as gay. At Embankment the doors of the train opened with a hiss and Charlie briskly walked up the stairs towards the station entrance. Walking up Villiers Street he saw that the queue for the club already snaked around the corner.

After half an hour he was at the head of the queue and soon found himself in the cavernous interior where he made for the toilets so that he could change out of his jeans and into his disco shorts. This done and his clothes in the coat check he moved to the dance floor. It was only eleven so not full yet but already a few men were dancing to the latest tunes. Charlie loved to dance and he was soon gyrating away, gradually noticing that the dance floor was filling up with more and more men.

By midnight Heaven was a sea of moustache, satin shorts and bottles of poppers and he was having a wonderful time. He never tired of dancing and loved the atmosphere of the place, and was particularly excited when the laser show started. Around 12.30 the DJ dropped 'Lay All Your Love On Me', one of Abba's latest hits; the dance floor went wild and his dance moves progressed to excited new highs.

Halfway through the tune he noticed that a guy dancing opposite him was smiling. He smiled back. The man was sexy. Charlie and the stranger gyrated around each other for 15 minutes without speaking. Disco dancing is often a gay mating ritual and this was clearly what was on the stranger's mind, his eyes revealing what he thought. Charlie in return noticed how attractive and sexy the guy was. Maybe 35 years old, dark haired and bearded, tall, very broad and heavyset. Not fat but beefy, and very hairy. He was what gay men in later years would call a Bear. Eventually the guy leaned over and spoke to Charlie. 'Hi Mate, my name's Luke. How are you? Are you having a good time?'

'I'm Charlie, I'm good thank you, having a great time.' This limited dialogue was conducted against the background of highly amplified disco music so both involved had to strain to hear.

Conversation was not essential and the men spent an hour dancing with each other and giving each other smiles and winks. After what seemed an eternity, Luke leaned over and kissed Charlie on the lips. He was immediately aroused as he felt the beefy man's tongue probe the inside of his mouth. They kissed and danced and for a while it was if there was no one else on the dance floor as they became so engrossed with each other. Eventually Luke whispered in Charlie's ear. 'Do you want to come home with me?'

'I thought you would never ask.'

The pair got their jackets and Charlie's jeans from the coat check and quickly found a taxi outside. Luke lived in the Barbican and the taxi ride only took 20 minutes. Charlie soon found himself in a small and functional studio flat on the 20th storey of one of the Barbican towers with an amazing view over London.

Luke was a good host. Charlie was offered a beer, a joint, cigarettes and cocaine (which he declined). He felt comfortable in the older man's company and was now looking forward very much to falling into the hairy, beefy stranger's arms and having great sex. After chatting for half an hour or so Luke gestured to the bedroom and Charlie followed. They were soon pulling each other's clothes off and falling into a passionate, sweaty, hairy embrace where they had vigorous, exhausting and exciting sex. It was good. He was pleased.

When they had finished they lay in bed smoking another joint and chatting. 'So Charlie boy, tell me a bit about yourself, you haven't said much.'

'I've been too busy to talk,' Charlie smiled. 'Not a great deal to tell. I live in Crystal Palace, I've got parents who don't really approve of me and I work for a travel company. Nothing much really, I'm pretty boring.' As he spoke he glanced over to a table which was near the bed, and to his surprise he saw a deck of Tarot cards spread out.

'Wow, can you read the Tarot? I would love to have my cards read, can you do that for me?'

'It's late and I'm tired. Can we do it another time?' Charlie knew full well that there probably wouldn't be another time; he rarely let that happen, so became a bit more insistent.

'Oh pleeease Luke…. I so much want to know my future,' and he gave him one of his pleading looks with his wonderful blue-green eyes.

'Oh okay, you win, you did ask very nicely,' and at that Luke reached over to the table and with a sweep of his hand brushed the cards together and picked them up. Still naked, they sat on the bed, whilst Luke spread out the cards.

'Mmmmm, I see a big hairy stranger who will put a smile on your face.'

'Oh right,' giggled Charlie, 'now tell me something I don't know'.

Luke closed his eyes, inhaled deeply and centred himself. He began to scan the cards. He had a genuine gift and was able to see things about people's lives, little hints, small clues, and titbits of advice. He generally kept it to things about the latest men in their lives, that's what most of them wanted to hear. That's what he planned to do with Charlie now. He never lied about what he saw in the Tarot but he could steer the reading in the way that someone wanted.

Charlie saw Luke close his eyes, and could see that he was breathing deeply and slowly. He knew what to expect, he had had his cards read before. Sometimes the reader picked up his childhood dreams involving the number 80, the cellar or being a soaring loved bird and questioned him as to the meaning. He of course didn't know. He kind of expected that this was what Luke would see and tell him about now.

He wasn't prepared for what happened next. Luke's face changed. It was only slight, a blink and you would not notice it but it was as if a dark cloud had briefly come over the sun. Charlie felt a little chill go through him. Luke's breathing got deeper and deeper and he realised that the man had gone into some kind of trance.

'Are you okay?' he enquired, touching the man gently on the arm.

Luke clearly could not hear and said nothing, but after a few moments began to speak in a strange, rather distant sounding tone.

'So far, far away, so lost. I see a huge distance, a great chasm, across which you are unable to reach. So far away from home. But I see something else, and that is a great love, a love the type of which few have ever experienced. It is a love of great ecstasy, a bonding of two souls. But Charlie, you are so lost, such a lost boy. And there is more, I see a great loss that has been and is also to come; I see a huge and complex paradox, it is a story that has already been told and a prophecy for the future. A great and terrible loss. But you are lost, so sad, the lost boy. So, so far away from home.'

Charlie now was completely freaked and slapped Luke hard across the face. He immediately snapped out of his trance going, 'What the fuck?'

'What did all that mean, you've scared me?'

'What did what mean? I haven't started reading yet,' replied Luke, confused.

Charlie actually now didn't want to know what he had meant, so they both agreed it was best to put the Tarot away and they had sex again and then slept.

In the morning Charlie left early, and thanked Luke for a great time, promising to call him soon. He wouldn't of course. He rarely did, there were so many more men to meet and there was no way he would get trapped into a relationship. He thought about the Tarot reading and it still bothered him ...the 'lost boy', what the hell did that mean? Actually even if he had wanted to see the guy again he certainly didn't want to know anything else about this.

This scared him and one of Charlie Rogers' ways of dealing with things that scared him was to stick his head in the sand and pretend that they didn't exist.

★ ★ ★

Chapter Eleven: Stitches in the Quilt

September 1986

Charlie sobbed in huge racking gasps. He felt frightened, lonely and vulnerable. During the last few years a very dark shadow had fallen over gay London and a terrible bird of prey was circling ever closer, plucking off his friends one by one. He wasn't sure how much more he could deal with and life, which had seemed so fresh and exciting only a few years before, was now laden with illness and death.

It was probably at the end of 1982 that Charlie had answered the phone to Michael; they chatted a bit about men. 'All bastards,' concluded Charlie. 'You know me, pick 'em up, shag 'em a couple of times if they're lucky, and move on. It's the best way, no complications.'

Michael didn't argue, that's how Charlie was. He would of course have loved to have complications with him but that was never going to happen. He did worry about Charlie though; he seemed to have developed a veneer of hardness over the years. He wished that he would meet someone and settle down. He needed to be loved Michael felt. He was a wonderful man, so attractive, sensitive, kind and loving. He was sure that there would be someone for Charlie one day soon. He just needed to let himself open up and be loved.

'Charlie, by the way, have you seen some of the news reports from San Francisco, this new illness that they have been going on about? It seems to be getting worse. And now there have been cases in Europe as well. So it's not just an American issue as we had all thought.'

'Oh come on, you know the press, I expect that they are making a big fuss out of nothing and it will all blow over soon.'

'I hope you're right Charlie, but there was something else I wanted to tell you. I have an American friend who is a doctor. He has told me that there is a suspicion by some medical people that this illness may be sexually transmitted. He has advised me to either stop sleeping around or to use condoms. Please think about it, for me.'

'Well I'm certainly not going to stop having sex Michael … it's my hobby,' Charlie sniggered. 'And as for condoms: you've got to be kidding.'

'I'm not Charlie.' He sounded deadly serious.

Charlie changed the subject; he didn't want his hedonistic sex-fuelled lifestyle to be spoilt by some imperceptible and undefined risk from America. 'You going to Sitges this year?' and the dark shadow from across the Atlantic was forgotten for the moment as they chatted on.

Now sitting on the bed in his Crystal Palace flat, crying his eyes out, Charlie reflected on that conversation he had had with Michael when he thought the press were over-dramatising the situation. 'My God, I couldn't have been so wrong,' he thought. The illness, now called AIDS, was far worse and far more widespread than had ever been predicted a few years before. He closed his eyes and reflected on the dreadful culling of his friends that had started shortly afterwards.

The first of Charlie's friends to be taken was sweet gorgeous little Calvin who had DJ'd at Michael's party all those years ago. He died at the end of 1983. Just 27 years old. He had noticed some strange dark patches on his legs earlier that year and he was dead in 9 months. Then the Moors Sisters, both of them gone within 6 months of each other. Michael joked rather cruelly, 'My God I didn't know they still had sex,' but this time neither he nor Charlie laughed.

One by one so many of the people around Charlie were picked off. Most of his friends from the 1970's were taken in four years. He was even saddened when he heard that evil old Teddy the Tongue had died.

It was in July that year that the phone rang one rainy Wednesday evening. He had started to dread the telephone. So much bad news. He wasn't sure he could bear any more.

'Charlie, it's Michael.'

'Michael, hi, how are you?' His mood lifted. He was genuinely pleased to hear him, he always was. They had been friends now for 13 years and as close as ever.

'Charlie I'm so sorry, I'm so, so sorry, I've let you down so badly. I've got KS.'

Charlie was silenced for a moment knowing exactly what a KS diagnosis meant, Kaposi's Sarcoma, a common cancer in AIDS patients. It took a few moments for the shock of what he was hearing to kick in and when it did he felt like he had been punched in the stomach.

'I'll be around as soon as I can. Try not to worry. I'll be right there.'

It was hardly going to help telling him not to worry as he had been given a death sentence, but these are the futile things that we say at such times. Little platitudes, desperately hoping that our words will make the situation better.

Charlie packed an overnight bag and called a cab to take him to Lime House. The taxi arrived in 10 minutes, honking its horn, and he left the flat still in shock. He had been in massive denial since the beginning of the AIDS crisis that Michael would be okay and anyway he was the one that had suggested using condoms. Surely he was okay? Perhaps it was all a mistake.

The taxi ride through South London seemed to take an eternity and Charlie felt quite car sick as the large saloon lurched around the residential streets.

Eventually the taxi dropped him off outside Michael's apartment and he rang the doorbell, still a lion's roar. Michael opened the door, ushered Charlie in quickly and collapsed tearfully into his arms.

'I'm so sorry, I'm so sorry,' Michael kept repeating this over and over, 'I've let you down so much.'

'What do you mean, you're ill, you haven't let me down, I'm going to take care of you, don't worry.'

'But I promised to always look after you and I'm not going to be able to do that now, I've let you down.'

'Well now it's my turn to look after you. It's about time.'

He couldn't be comforted and Charlie eventually called a friend who always had some Valium on standby for various dramas (usually man related). He asked him to put some in a taxi. Charlie held Michael tightly trying to calm his huge sobs until the Valium arrived. When it did Michael washed it down with a couple of gin and tonics and finally drifted into a drugged sleep.

Michael was taken from Charlie 2 months later by PCP, a vicious and untreatable pneumonia. Gone. That's what AIDS did in those days. It could be brutal, quick. Gone. Barely time to say goodbye.

Now lying on his bed crying, Charlie felt a huge loss, a great chunk taken out of him. His dearest friend and the only man he had ever loved. His grief was huge. He had been with Michael in St Bart's hospital when he had died the day before. That much Charlie had been able to do. He held his hand and kept telling him how much he loved him as he slipped away. Charlie had no idea how he was going to be able to cope without him, he felt desolate and alone but he also knew that there were things that he needed to do to send Michael on his final journey.

There were few friends left to mourn Michael. Most of them were dead. Those that were still alive had seen so many funerals in the last few years they couldn't cope with another, so his cremation would just be attended by Charlie and Olga. She had survived too.

Early October 1986

The following week, Charlie and Olga waited in Michael's flat. Charlie was dressed as he always was. Jeans, t-shirt, flying jacket. Michael had been very specific in his instructions that there was to be no mourning garb at his funeral. Olga was wearing a bright scarlet floor length dress with a huge matching hat and a veil half-concealing her face.

At 12 noon on the dot the doorbell rang and the undertakers stood grim faced at the door. Charlie immediately noticed with horror that the four men wore rubber gloves and pointed them out to Olga.

'What the fuck are you wearing those gloves for? He's dead, he's not going to harm you,' she remonstrated.

The head undertaker squirmed and replied obsequiously, 'We have the right to protect ourselves … Sir.'

'If you call me Sir again I will knock your fucking head off.'

The head undertaker took a step back as if physically assaulted by the words.

'Wait here,' Olga barked at the now troubled looking men. Not only were they having to deal with AIDS which they had read all about in the newspapers as a 'Gay Plague', but they were being confronted by this bizarre woman in a hideous red dress, who had clearly only recently been a man. 'Charlie come back into the apartment, we'll sort this out.'

'But we have to get to the crematorium, they won't wait, we'll never get there now.'

'We will see about that darling, I'm not letting these shits insult Michael.'

Olga made a telephone call. Very brief. But Charlie could hear the sense of urgency in her voice. 'Don't worry I've sorted it.' Charlie said nothing but looked at Olga with tears in his questioning blue-green eyes.

Five minutes later a large flat-bed truck driven by a big, hairy, burly man covered in tattoos came round the corner. In the passenger seat a younger man who looked like his work mate. Heavily tattooed as well and good looking. On the side of the cab 'Lime House Scaffolding' in bright blue letters.

'Now boys, I need you to help Aunty Olga,' and the two men compliantly got out of the cab of the truck and Olga started to whisper to both of them in an urgent tone whilst occasionally giving frosty glances to the undertakers.

Eventually Charlie heard the older one say, 'Of course Olga, it would be our honour and pleasure.'

'You can fuck off now you miserable bastards and don't think you've heard the last of this. Give us the coffin,' Olga spat at the now completely bemused undertakers.

Frank and Steve, the scaffolders, went respectfully to the back of the hearse and started to withdraw Michael's coffin. Olga and Charlie went over to help them and soon they had secured it on the back of the truck. 'Come on boys or we're going to be late,' shouted Olga.

Charlie and Olga sat on top of the coffin, Frank and Steve got back in the cab and they started the engine, ready for the drive to the crematorium.

'Fucking diseased perverts!' shouted one of the undertakers behind them, 'Maggie's going to sort you lot out, you wait and see.'

So it came to pass that Michael's coffin was taken to West Ham Crematorium on the back of a scaffolder's truck, driven by two burly men, with his best friend and a transvestite in a scarlet dress sitting on top of him. He would have loved it.

After 45 minutes full of startled, bemused looks from shoppers in West Ham High Street, they arrived at the crematorium. There was to be no funeral service, Michael didn't want that, but he had asked that two songs be played. Firstly his favourite Dusty Springfield song, 'You don't have to say you love me' and then of course, 'Don't Cry for me Argentina'. Michael's last words to Charlie had been, 'I may finally get to have tea with Evita now,' so the song was more than fitting. That was it … that was all he wanted.

On the way back Charlie, who, lost in his grief had said little all day, leaned over to Olga in the back of the truck and kissed her. 'Thank you for giving Michael his dignity when those fucking undertakers tried to take it away. One thing I want to know though. Frank and Steve, why did they do this for you? They look just the kind of men who would hate us.'

'Oh Charlie, you have so much to learn in life. One lesson is that some men who look very straight and actually are married, like to get dressed up as women sometimes. Frank has a huge soft spot for me. He loves his wife and children dearly but every month or so, we have a special night together, dress up and have some fun. Oh yes, and Steve is his son. He knows all about his father and me, as does his wife, and they support him in this expression of his personality. The other lesson Charlie is that sometimes we will find prejudice when we are least expecting it, and sometimes we will find an open mind when we most expect prejudice. Never judge a book by its cover.'

Charlie kissed Olga again and they held hands, frequently lapsing into tears on the journey back to Lime House.

A week later, and the final act of Michael's wishes was to be carried out.

Charlie and Olga arrived by taxi at the run down wharf in Wapping where they knew that a boat would be waiting for them. Charlie was carrying an urn holding Michael's ashes; Olga carried a portable tape recorder. She was dressed in a long flowing silver gown with a massive blonde wig, which hung down in pigtails either side of her head.

Frank, the scaffolder, was in the boat, a 60-foot Thames barge. On the prow he had erected the rainbow flag, down each side were sprays of white flowers. Olga got precariously into the barge, almost tripping over her dress, followed by Charlie, and the boat set off down the river. It was a mild October morning and a little mist came off the water. As the boat passed Greenwich, Olga stood on the prow with her arms up to the sky, as if in some invocation to the Gods. Charlie switched on the little tape recorder that had been hitched up to powerful speakers and it was thus that this bizarre crew was seen, cruising around the Thames Barrier construction site 10 minutes later. On the back, Olga stood majestically, arms high, commanding the heavens to take Michaels' spirit, the embodiment of Brunehilda. From the music system at top volume emanated Wagner's 'Ride of the Valkyries' whilst from the side, Charlie sprinkled Michael's ashes into the Thames.

On one of the half built pontoons of the Thames Barrier, Bill and Dave were having a break from their painting. They looked up from their morning cup of tea as they heard the music approaching through the mists. They stood wide eyed as the bizarre little tableau was played out beneath them.

'You know what Bill,' started Dave, 'I reckon we should keep off the whiskey.'

'Mmmm,' agreed Bill sagely reaching for the kettle.

Late October 1986

Two days after committing Michael's ashes to the Thames, Charlie sat in his flat, still in a complete state of grief, trauma and loss. He read and re-read the letter that Michael had left for him.

St Barts Hospital

September 1986

My dearest Charlie, not long to go now and I think time to say goodbye. I'm not going to go on too much about how wonderful you are and how much I love you. You know that already and you will become conceited.

I think that our friendship and love has been the most wonderful thing for the last 13 years. It has meant everything to me. Seeing you growing from a boy; being there with you as you learned how to be a gay man. It has been my privilege.

One thing that has always concerned me though, is that whilst we were friends sharing a special and unique type of love I wonder if there was room for anyone else? I hope I am not being arrogant, but I suspect that whilst you had the security of me in your life there was never going to be anyone special. I think being single and having lots of sex is great but I wonder now, now that I am gone, if it's time for you to think about what it means for me NOT to be there any longer. Perhaps it is time for you to have a man that will love you, as I have, but completely. You need to be loved with a man's body, his heart and his soul. My god Charlie, can you imagine if we had been more compatible, perhaps we would be lovers still, but we shall never know. We are never told what would have happened. We only know what did happen. But none of that changes what you have meant to me and I believe what I have meant to you.

Please now Charlie Rogers, open your heart and be ready to be loved. I know with every fibre of my tired body that there is someone special out there for you.

Thank you for being the best and most wonderful friend a man could ever have.

With fondest and everlasting love.

Michael XXXX

PS Oooops! I went on much more about how much I love you than I meant to !!!!

PS. PS for goodness sake can you tell Olga to stop wearing red…it really isn't her colour!

PS. PS. PS and it cost me 20 fucking quid love!!!

Charlie smiled a wry smile, as he remembered how Michael had paid the rent boy to seduce him. 'He had to make a joke even now didn't he?' And the tears flowed again.

★ ★ ★

Chapter Twelve: At the Eye of the Storm

16th October 1987

Charlie lay in bed, still sleep hazy and unsure as to what he was hearing. The windows of his flat were rattling hard and there was a weird rushing noise that he couldn't pinpoint, punctuated by crashes and bangs coming from outside.

Jumping out of bed naked he went to the window and pulled back one of the curtains to see a huge, raging storm blowing litter, debris and leaves down the street. Outside the flat a large London plane tree had been felled and was lying across a car whose alarm was valiantly trying to join in the mayhem. It was an ear splitting counterpoint to the roaring wind.

Charlie was now a little apprehensive; he could see what the tree outside had done to the car. He could hear the wind lifting roof tiles up from above him then dropping them down into the street. He decided that it would not be wise to go out so he went back to bed, pulled the duvet over his head and hid. It seemed like the best possible strategy at the time and actually was probably a very good idea.

There was no way that he could sleep and soon his mind was whirring and he was thinking deeply about Michael and his awful death the year before. Charlie thought about this constantly, his sense of loss for his friend was enormous and he was still depressed and feeling isolated. To lose this handsome, loving, wonderful man at the peak of his life, yes, that was wrong and he was not really sure how he was ever going to get over it.

In the first few months he had been numb. Death had come quickly. AIDS was so savage that Charlie had barely time to adjust to the fact that Michael was ill. After numbness came anger and he would berate the universe selfishly, 'Why me, why my best friend, how could you leave me so alone?' And he would punch the wall of his bedroom until his knuckles were bleeding and then he would lie, in a foetal position, sobbing for hours on his bed.

After the anger came numbness again and it was a big, dark, empty space, a cold arid nightmare loneliness that Charlie now inhabited.

The storm seemed to be blowing ever louder outside. Once there was a huge crash as a chimney from an adjacent property came thundering down into the street. He could hear this, even from under the duvet and a ball of fear gnawed at his guts. He really wanted someone with him, someone to hold him and someone to assure him that everything was going to be okay.

'Fuck you Michael,' he shouted into the mattress, 'fuck you, why did you have to go and die on me? I need you now.'

If you had been in his room that night, you wouldn't have been sure what was louder, Charlie Rogers' crying or the sound of the great storm. Both of them went in waves, reaching crescendos and then sometimes subsiding slightly, but never stopping.

Charlie eventually found the peace of sleep in the small hours. It wasn't deep and it was constantly interrupted by crashes and bangs, but it was rest of a sort. As he went in and out of this sleep, his mind was achingly active and it whirled around through dark tortured thoughts. He thought about what Michael had said to him in his final letter about finding love. He had gradually understood over the months that he had been a de-facto boyfriend. He had provided all the warmth, love and security that Charlie needed without any of the commitment. He sometimes had a glimmer, a fragment of insight, that this might have taken its toll on Michael, but in actuality, in his self-centred, self-obsessed manner, he had never really grasped it fully.

In the depths of Charlie's bereavement he would not have been capable of letting anyone into his dark world. It was a private place of grief and one that he needed to work through for himself. He wanted to feel the loneliness; he wanted to feel the depth of sadness. He felt that if he let that go, in some way he would be letting Michael go from his heart. He drifted in and out of sleep, the storm was still blasting outside … but through the night it gradually started to quieten down and as it did Charlie's sleep got deeper and he was able to finally enter a level in which he could dream.

On this storm-ravaged night Charlie's dream was very simple. The old nightmare of the number 80 was not revisited. It had rarely come to him in recent years. On this night, which saw England being blasted by the most violent storm in her history, Charlie saw Michael in his dream, Michael, handsome, strong and re-assuring. No longer ravaged by illness and looking happy and calm. He was standing on top of a high cliff overlooking the sea. The sunshine golden as it is late in the day or in the autumn. Overhead a white bird circled noiselessly on the swirling air currents and Charlie could feel love pouring from it in great, palpable waves. Normally Charlie was the bird in his dreams but on this night he was watching the bird. It was good too. Michael was quite a long way away from him but he could see that he was smiling. As the dream continued he turned and started to walk away with a camp wave of his hand and as he did Charlie wanted to chase after him but was restrained from moving as those in dreams often are. He wanted to cry out and talk to him and get him to come back but when he tried to speak no words would come out of his mouth.

Michael continued to walk away, along the grass covered cliff top, into the mellow sunlight. Finally he turned and gave Charlie a huge wave, blew a kiss and then the image faded and disappeared.

That was it. Often when we dream things are shown to us very clearly but they fade as we wake and we try to remember what we have seen, heard or experienced. But from this dream, on this night, Charlie awoke with Michael's smiling face clearly in his mind and he was left wondering what it had all meant.

The following morning Charlie pulled on his boxer shorts and his Levi 501's. He selected a clean white t-shirt from his wardrobe and then completed the outfit with one of his favourite leather jackets. Now that the storm had stopped he was keen to go and see what had been happening outside. He had briefly watched the BBC news and was shocked at the pictures of devastation that were coming in from across the country.

After having his breakfast of toast and marmalade and a cup of tea, Charlie went off walking around Crystal Palace. He walked through streets that were littered with debris, fallen trees and occasionally a crushed car. At the corner of one road a whole section of scaffolding had been ripped off the side of a block of flats and was piled up in a metal mish-mash. As he walked, Charlie thought long and deeply about his dream, and how he had seen Michael waving goodbye to him. 'What does it mean?' he thought to himself.

Now Charlie was a bright man but sometimes he could be amazingly slow to understand things that were glaringly obvious, particularly when they were things about himself. So it took a lot longer to sink in than it should have done. Half an hour later, whilst sitting in Crystal Palace Park near the tall skeletal BBC transmitter, surrounded by fallen trees and branches, he suddenly shouted out loud, 'I'm such a fool, why am I such a fucking fool? He was trying to tell me it's time to let him go.'

Two drunken tramps were sitting on the next bench to Charlie and one muttered to the other, 'Bloody weirdo, you get some really dodgy types here now.'

And it was time to let Michael go. So it transpired that on this night when nature wreaked her terrible force on England causing huge amounts of damage with her wind, that something else was blown away. That was Charlie hanging onto his grief for Michael.

In the months and years after the Great Storm fresh new young life would sprout in the ravaged woodlands. Firstly tiny shoots thrusting up out of the devastation and much later saplings would reach up to the sky and grow steadily into strong, broad tree trunks. Thus it was with Charlie's life now. The old and the familiar blown away, leaving devastation and a terrible sadness, but now he was ready for a new life to start its heady growth.

December 1987

Charlie had started going out again. On this Friday night he had arranged to meet Elizabeth at the private view of a new art exhibition in Brixton. He met her outside the tube station at 7pm as arranged. As ever she was elegantly dressed, this time in a classic pink Chanel suit; the contrast with the streets of Brixton, still edgy after riots several years before, was striking.

'Sweetie, hello,' said Elizabeth, greeting Charlie affectionately with a big hug, 'it's so lovely to see you, it's been so long. How have you been?'

Actually she knew full well how Charlie had been, she heard enough through mutual friends and was determined to get him out and meeting people again.

'I'm okay,' he replied, 'I think I'm getting there. You do understand don't you Elizabeth?'

'Yes of course sweetie, I miss him terribly too you know.'

At that they walked off arm in arm down Atlantic Road, weaving in and out of the drug dealers hawking their wares, to the little art gallery that had just been opened.

'Now Charlie I know you're a bit of an art enthusiast, so I thought you might enjoy this, and there is someone terribly nice that I would like you to meet.'

He didn't notice the emphasis that she put on the word 'terribly' so in his usual unaware self-absorbed way he had no idea of what she had planned.

They arrived at the gallery; the building and its surroundings were covered with graffiti and Charlie was a little surprised that anyone had chosen to open an art gallery in such a place. As if to answer his thoughts Elizabeth squeezed his arm and said: 'It's just so deliciously urban isn't it dear?'

They gave their invitation cards to the surly looking doorman who looked like a tattooed bulldog, and entered the building, which clearly had been a shop at some point. Instantly the atmosphere changed and Charlie could see that the room was full of young, colourful fashionable people chatting and drinking, in stark contrast to the drug dealers and urban grit outside.

Elizabeth scanned the room and Charlie sensed that she was looking for someone. He felt a pressure on his arm as she propelled him towards her target. 'Tiago, this is Charlie who I told you about. Charlie this is Tiago.'

Charlie, for all his experience with men could actually be quite shy and seeing Tiago he immediately went weak at the knees and blushed, for Tiago was gorgeous.

'Tiago is the artist dear, he is Brazilian and very successful. Let me leave you to chat,' Elizabeth chirped. 'Oh there is Maurizio, I must go and say hello to him. Can I leave you to talk to each other?' Charlie started to protest; meeting this handsome stranger found him at his shyest.

'Ummmm, have you been in London very long?' he managed to stutter out.

'No only a few days, I have been travelling with my exhibition all over Europe. Come, let's go and get a drink from the bar.' And he gently steered Charlie to the other side of the room where the drinks were being served.

Charlie could feel himself becoming aroused by Tiago's presence. He had seen enough of the man to realise that he was devastatingly sexy. Probably in his early 40's, a little shorter than Charlie with a very fit and lithe body, dark skin and the most cheeky and sparkling pair of brown eyes that he had ever seen. Tiago spoke English with a soft Brazilian accent, it sounded so sexy.

'So Charlie, do you like my pictures?'

Charlie had of course taken absolutely no notice of the art whatsoever since he had arrived. 'Ummmmm, yes they are wonderful,' he lied.

The pair chatted on and shared a few drinks; the artist sometimes introduced Charlie to other people but he paid little attention to them. He only had interest for this man and he was determined that he would get him into bed. And he did. Tiago and Charlie spent a fierce night of passion at Charlie's flat later that evening. Rough, very masculine and hard sex. It was wonderful. They alternated sex with long, deep conversations about the meaning of life. Then late in the morning, both exhausted from their exertions, Charlie went to sleep surrounded by Tiago's strong arms and with his head on his firm, hairy chest.

Charlie waved Tiago goodbye the following morning, having in the space of a few hours, fallen head over heels in love (well at least in lust).

It would be great that it could be written that Charlie and Tiago lived happily ever after, but they didn't; they had 3 months with each other in an incredibly intense and fiery relationship. Tiago cancelled the rest of his tour to stay with him. It was a highly sexually charged but stormy few months. Tiago had huge amounts of energy and was incredibly demanding so there was a lot of love, but also many fights and tears. Eventually though he had to leave, his visa had expired and there was no way he could stay in England. Charlie was devastated ... but he learned something, he had begun to open up, just a little, to being loved.

March 1988

Something else happened shortly after the Great Storm. A few months before, Charlie's mother had called and told him that his godfather Stephen had died in New Zealand. Charlie had never quite forgiven him for going off when he was a child. There had been Christmas and birthday cards but that was about it. But Charlie was sad to hear that he had died. Not long afterwards he had received a letter from a solicitor advising him that he was a beneficiary of his godfather's Will. Charlie hadn't really expected very much and thought that there may be small cheque coming his way so it was a huge shock when he received a further letter.

Johnson, Johnson and Maitland
1011 Auckland Street
Napier
New Zealand

Dear Mr Rogers

I refer to our letter of 1ˢᵗ July 1987, in which I advised you that you were a beneficiary of the late Stephen Foster's will. I apologise that this matter has taken so long to discharge due to complications with the estate but we are now in a position to advise you of the legacy your godfather has left. I am pleased to be able to tell you that we will shortly be finalising the estate accounts and will be sending you a cheque for £250,119.32.

Yours sincerely

W.F. Johnson

★ ★ ★

Chapter Thirteen: The Second Summer of Love

July 1989

Everything in the universe is a cycle. After life comes death, which is followed with new life. After dark comes light. The 1980's had been a terrible time for gay men who lost a large proportion of their friends and the survivors were often racked with guilt. 'Why me? Why did I survive?' It was against this backdrop of dark tragedy that Charlie first emerged into the light to find love. Sure it was serial and not enduring love but it was love and he was prepared to let another man into his life and to inhabit that part of his soul.

Something else had been happening in the last few years of the 1980's as well. A counterpoint and a reaction to the horror story of AIDS. That was the explosion of gay clubbing, fuelled by the drug Ecstasy. Charlie was now part of this wave of euphoria that stuck its fingers up to death and illness and he was determined to be able to enjoy himself again.

There had been a number of boyfriends since Tiago had left for Brazil in 1988. There had been Ray, Irish and very left wing, Stephan, French and deeply complicated, Al who was also Irish and broke Charlie's heart several times and another Charles, twenty years older. This Charles had a little sports car and Charlie thought he was very glamorous. He was totally besotted with him but Charles already had another boyfriend. And so the list went on.

He was happy; he of course still missed Michael most terribly but was now able to think about the great times that they had shared rather than the awful way that he had died.

Charlie had moved to Kennington the previous year. He had sold the flat in Crystal Palace as he could now afford to live more centrally thanks to his inheritance. Living near Central London suited him much better as that was where gay life was more likely to be found. Charlie had actually been very sensible with his inheritance. As well as buying the flat in Kennington he had treated himself to some new clothes, and then had bought a house in Dulwich, which Iris had assured him would be a good investment because of the well known private schools in the area. Maybe at some point he would sell it for a profit but first he had quickly let it out for a good rent.

'Yes,' Charlie thought, inhaling on his 20th cigarette that day, 'life is good, I'm having a grand time.'

He was single again. Al had broken his heart a little 3 months before by finally telling him that there was no way their relationship was going anywhere. Actually the heartbreak lasted only a few days and then Al was history. Yes, life was good.

And so it was, on this Friday in July 1989, Charlie anticipated his Saturday night out. It was his birthday and he was surrounded by cards that he had been sent by friends and family. He was going to celebrate properly by going to Heaven, for a night of Ecstasy fuelled dancing with his friends. He had only taken the drug twice before but he loved the way it made him feel. He was confident, happy and my God did he dance. The atmosphere in London gay clubs since the previous year had been electric as Hi NRG music had morphed into House and increasingly the dance floors were sent to heights of excitement by the new drug that was sweeping the scene. Initially he had resisted taking it. After Michael's awful experience with acid at his New Year's Eve party all those years before, Charlie was quite moral on the subject of drugs. Eventually though, seeing how much his friends were enjoying themselves, he had given in and was washed away on the hazy loved up wave that was to become known as the 'Second Summer of Love'. He loved the new music; everywhere you went you would hear 'Ride on Time' or 'Numero Uno' and it seemed so fresh and to promise a new dawn after the savage early years of the AIDS crisis.

It was all planned. He was going out for his birthday with three of his close friends. A couple called Phil and Richard (who usually procured the drugs) and another guy called Matt who he'd had sex with a couple of times but then it had tailed off and they'd become firm friends.

'Yes,' he thought, 'it's going to be a great night, dance myself silly and then I think it's about time I hooked myself another boyfriend.'

The following morning he got up early and missed breakfast, just having a cup of tea, as he often did. He bathed and got himself ready for his birthday shopping trip to the West End. Just as he was leaving the flat, the phone rang. He almost didn't answer it. 'Oh! bugger, it might be important,' he said out loud. He picked up the phone; it was his Aunt Iris.

'Hello Charlie, just calling to wish you Happy Birthday, I'm sorry I missed you yesterday but I was mmmm, busy.' He knew exactly what 'busy' meant for his aunt... yet another man, so having this interest in common he instantly forgave her.

'Don't worry Iris. I do understand, was he hot?' She didn't reply but smiled to herself at her nephew's cheekiness.

'What are you doing this morning Charlie?'

'I'm off out to the West End to buy myself a new outfit for tonight.'

'Oh that's lovely dear, well enjoy your shopping trip.'

'Must go Iris, I have shopping to do. Love you.'

Charlie left the flat and travelled on the short tube ride to Oxford Circus where he browsed round the shops and bought himself a new outfit for the evening. A fresh pair of Levi 501's. He never varied with those, but now everyone was wearing t-shirts or hoodies with fluorescent designs and smiley faces and Charlie decided that he should join the latest trend, so he found a t-shirt that he liked with a big yellow cheesy grin on the front at a little shop he frequented in Soho.

Happy with his purchases he caught the Northern Line back from Leicester Square to Kennington and walked out of the tube, whistling 'Ride on Time' and getting a wave of excitement about his club night out later that evening.

He pulled his keys out of his jeans and put them into the front door. As he opened it he heard an odd sound and it took a few seconds for him to work out what he was hearing and seeing. Charlie's flat was on two floors and now, through what was left of the sitting room ceiling, streamed large volumes of water. Plaster lay around in chunks on his furniture, splattered all over the carpet, and there was water pouring all over the CD player he'd bought himself the month before. Charlie did a typical Charlie thing and burst into tears.

A few minutes later he sat in the middle of the sitting room floor surveying the ruins of his flat. Much of the ceiling had come down due to, he'd discovered, a leaking joint under the bath. He was still tearful and had no idea what to do. He had never been very practical but had just about worked out how to switch the water mains off. The carpet was sodden, everything was covered in plaster and he started to realise with horror that he was not going to be spending a relaxing night at his flat after coming back from Heaven with a man in tow.

'My weekend's ruined,' he wailed out loud. Right now the thought that he wasn't going to go out for the night and meet some hot guy was even more devastating than the state of his flat. He was still pondering the wreckage of his home and weekend a few minutes later when the phone rang. He managed to retrieve it from under a piece of plaster. It was Iris, for the second time that day.

'Charlie, are you okay? I had a funny feeling something was wrong, you know me, is everything all right?'

'No it's not,' he blurted out tearfully, 'my flat's flooded, my ceiling has collapsed and my weekend is in ruins.'

'I'll come right round, give me half an hour.'

As promised, Iris arrived shortly afterwards and surveyed the wreckage with Charlie.

'How awful dear and on your birthday weekend,' she commiserated. 'I know a man who's very good with these kind of things. Why don't I get him around tomorrow and he can clear up and start fixing the ceiling, how would that be?' She knew how useless Charlie was and that he would need some help sorting this out.

'That's great Iris but it doesn't salvage my birthday weekend, I've got nowhere to sleep and anyway I'm not in the mood to go out now. I'm so upset.'

'Where will you stay tonight darling? I would offer but I have a friend coming round for dinner and I think he may be with me all night.'

'Iris do you ever stop?' And he finally managed to laugh.

'Why don't you go and stay in Dulwich for a few days? You'll be comfortable and you can still get a cab up to town if you decide to go out.'

Charlie thought about this briefly. He still hadn't got around to re-letting the house since the last batch of tenants had moved out the previous month. Iris had always helped him with this and she had been busy and away on holiday. 'Good thinking Iris, can you run me over there?'

'Yes of course dear. Pack a few things in a bag for a couple of days and we can be there in half an hour.'

'I do love you Iris.'

'Cupboard love dear, when I do something for you,' but she smiled as she said it.

An hour later Charlie was installed in the house in Dulwich. Iris had driven him down through South London as promised, arriving at the house in Hurst Court Road after stopping on the way to get some basic provisions. They were soon sharing a cup of tea in the little kitchen overlooking the rather overgrown garden.

'It is rather grim dear, isn't it?' said Iris with a disapproving expression on her face as she glanced around the kitchen. The decor was distinctly early 1960's and now looking dirty, battered and tired. The kitchen still had its original 1920's fittings, a deep china sink, some very inadequate looking cupboards and a hideously greasy old gas stove.

'It's just all so old fashioned dear, I'm really surprised that you didn't do anything about it.'

'I've been procrastinating for 2 years about what to do and haven't been able to decide. I think before I let it out again I may get it sorted out. I can get a better rent then. It is rather shabby isn't it?' For the first time he'd noticed quite how bad the house had got and felt rather ashamed.

'Yes dear, I know, well you will have to do something about it soon before it all falls apart. Anyway, I must away, Peter's coming round in an hour. He's very sexy and I need to make myself look gorgeous for him.'

'Tell me more, who is he, how old is he, is he another of your toy boys?'

'Don't be so rude. I met him when he was doing some building work on my house recently and I think he's at least 30 so there isn't really much of an age difference, and my goodness he is so gorgeous, fit and vigorous.'

Charlie knew full well that Iris was in her 60's and thought, 'Good on her! I hope I can still pull them like that when I'm her age.'

Shortly afterwards, he let Iris out of the front door, kissed her and waved her off. He had calmed down from the shock of seeing his ruined flat earlier that day and was now determined to go out for his birthday celebration. Having bathed he would relax for an hour and then get dressed, before calling a cab to take him out to Heaven. 'Yes, I will still have fun tonight and I'm going to get myself a man,' he smiled to himself.

9pm came and he noticed that he was out of cigarettes. 'Damn, I'm gasping,' he thought and then remembered that there was a shop 5 minutes walk round the corner. He pulled on his clothes quickly and went to find his wallet that was in his jeans that he had packed earlier. Putting his hands in the various pockets he could feel no wallet. 'Fuck I'm sure I put it in there.'

Charlie then spent the next half hour going through everything repeatedly, every item of clothing, every room, but to no avail. He started getting angry and frustrated as each search of a room revealed nothing. He was now tearful again, 'I don't fucking believe it.' He knew he had left Kennington with the wallet and remembered paying for the provisions in a corner shop. 'Oh bugger, I must have dropped it there, that's all I need.'

He knew that the shop would be closed now. Thinking on his feet he dialled Iris's number, perhaps she would be able to lend him some money. There was no answer. He then mentally went through a list of various people he could ask for a loan. Having identified who would probably be able to help him he picked up the phone again. The line was dead. So that was it. A flooded flat, a collapsed ceiling, no money, no phone, no way of getting any money until Monday. 'And it's my birthday. It's not fair.' wailed Charlie. By this stage he was so angry, tense and upset with the whole day that he decided it wasn't meant to be for him to go out, that he would cut his losses and go to bed. He would go out the following weekend. 'I can get everything sorted out by then, my flat will be fixed and I can enjoy myself as I had planned to, I suppose it's not the end of the world.' Actually inside he really felt that it was the end of the world. He was trying to cheer himself up.

But Charlie had ultimately remembered that sometimes in life one needs to know how to keep going and keep trying, but equally one also needs to know when to stop. Clearly everything was stacked against him on this Saturday night and he had finally decided to give up.

And so it was that on the 22nd July, 1989 when he had been expecting to be out with his friends and falling into the arms of a delicious stranger, Charlie Rogers ended up going to bed early and by himself in his house in Dulwich. It wasn't what he had wanted but sometimes we cannot do the things we want even when we have planned them so carefully.

What Charlie didn't know as he struggled to get to sleep in the musty and dingy bedroom, surrounded by tatty old furniture and nestling under the duvet he had bought from Kennington, was that this night would change his life, for the rest of his life, in the most amazing way that he would never have thought possible, would never have even dreamed of.

★ ★ ★

Interlude 1944

Doodlebug Summer

The Air Ministry, Aldwych, London, 22nd July, 1944

Robert Harrison sat at the mahogany desk in his office at the Air Ministry pondering what he was going to do with his life after the war. 'That is if this bloody war is ever going be over.'

He was 29 years old but with knowledge, wisdom and weariness forged through battle that exceeded his years. In 1940 he had joined the RAF and had fought with the Few over the fields of England during the Battle of Britain. He seemed to live a charmed life and although he flew hundreds of sorties before and after the battle he was never injured. That was until early in 1944, when flying his Spitfire protecting a Lancaster Bomber stream that was attacking a Flying Bomb site in Normandy, he was shot through the leg. It wasn't life threatening and after a couple of weeks in hospital he was able to walk again with crutches, but he wasn't able to fly.

Robert was frustrated and angry that he could no longer do the job he was trained to do to defend his country. He was offered a job in the Air Ministry in London. He didn't know much about what he would be doing but at least in some manner he would be part of the war effort. That was a limited compensation.

Now 6 months later he had just about recovered although was still walking with a limp. He had begged to be able to go back on active service again, but the Air Ministry seemed determined to stand in his way. What he didn't quite appreciate was that he was so damn good at his job, and now the Ministry needed people with brains to help with the intelligence that would fight the latest round in the battle against the Nazis.

For over a year the intelligence services had known that London was under threat from Hitler's secret weapon programme. Bombing raids had been carried out to try and destroy the sites from which the missiles would be launched, with some success, but now London was under attack and since June countless Flying Bombs, known to Londoners as Doodlebugs, had hurtled into the capital killing and maiming thousands and destroying large swathes of buildings. Robert was part of an intelligence team which analysed the attacks. He was very good at the job.

Now, reflecting on this, he felt a mixture of frustration and achievement. He had so desperately wanted to keep flying, that was his passion, but he also knew that his detailed intelligence work was paying off and because of his efforts the people of London would ultimately benefit.

For some reason on this day Robert's thoughts went very deep; they started to stray to the inner emptiness that he barely felt able to confront. He knew that inside there was a deep, guilty secret. It was something that he had never been able to talk to anyone about and he was not even sure that he understood himself. His thoughts travelled to the cold empty place that lay within, and he promptly pulled them back again. He had no right to indulge himself in this way. People were dying all over London and it was his job to try and help stop this. Robert was a very self-disciplined man, he always had been even before his military training and he considered that his emotions and personal happiness were not priorities. The expression of his emotions in any way was something that he struggled with.

He had been brought up in a comfortable home and his parents had made sure he had a good education, but it was a childhood devoid of any expression of emotion. His mother was a cold, aloof woman, lost in some inner turmoil. The face that she showed to the world seemed stony and uncaring. Her marriage to Robert's father was leaden, conventional and weighed down with suburban duty. They didn't fight, his father didn't treat her badly but there was an air of resigned disinterest between them. They certainly didn't seem like they were in love.

Once she had started mentioning a man she'd met before she'd married his father and he had noticed that a hint of colour came to her cheeks as she spoke, but she quickly caught herself and changed the subject. His father was an accountant; a dull and stolid man whose main excitement for the week was to get the Sunday Telegraph and check the cricket results. Sometimes Robert would see a glint in his eye as if he was thinking about something a long way away.

There were times when Robert wondered why they were actually together. It was in this home that Robert's emotions had no avenue to express themselves, no opportunity to come to the surface and thus they turned inwards and were buried in his soul to make him cold and withdrawn.

Robert was shaken out of his thoughts as he heard the engine of yet another Flying Bomb overhead. The missiles' jet engines made a distinctive noise that some compared to a rusty motorbike going up a hill. Once heard, never forgotten. Almost immediately he heard the engine cut out and he knew that one ton of high explosive would shortly be diving into another London street. He counted 10 seconds and in the distance there was the sound of a massive explosion accompanied by a slight vibration in his feet. The surface of the glass of water that stood on his desk shimmered.

There was a knock on the door and a WAAF carrying a tea tray came into the office beaming: 'I know you must be ready for a cuppa Sir,' the pretty girl smiled.

'You must have read my mind, I am rather thirsty.' He suddenly felt lonely and putting convention aside he thought that sharing tea with the girl would take him away from his thoughts. 'Stay and have tea with me.'

The girl was a little taken aback. She wasn't used to officers being so familiar but in truth she found the handsome young man very attractive so was pleased and agreed.

'London is still getting a terrible pasting isn't it Sir? I'm so frightened. My friend Daisy was killed the other week when the Doodlebug fell in the street outside. She was working in her office on the first floor on the other side of this building and she was blown out of the window.'

The girl's voice had a slight tremor as she spoke; Robert knew she was keeping a lid on her emotions. That's what they had to do.

'It is terrible, but we will win this battle and we will win the war, I'm sure of that.'

The girl immediately felt better, not so much that she necessarily believed Robert but hearing his steady, masculine and confident voice made her feel a bit safer. Now feeling a little bolder she felt she could be more forward. 'I'm planning to go for a walk down by the Thames tomorrow lunchtime, perhaps we could have our lunch together down there?'

Robert immediately froze at this apparent attempt at intimacy. He was happy to talk about the war or safe things such as the weather but the suggestion that he and the girl should spend some time alone together was really too much. 'That is not possible, you know that officers are not allowed to fraternise with subordinates.' Whilst this was true Robert also knew that the rule was flouted on a daily basis and he could if he wanted to but it was a convenient excuse.

The girl blushed heavily, realising that she had overstepped the mark. Muttering her excuses she left the office backwards, tripped over a waste paper bin and had to retrieve the contents of the tea tray from the floor in a hurried and embarrassed manner. Robert said nothing, and turned his attention to the paper work on his desk.

It would be easy to say that Robert was unhappy, but the truth was a little more complex than that. He actually didn't know if he was happy or not. Happiness wasn't a concept that he really entertained. He thought much about his duty, about what he had to do to help win the war and mostly thought little about himself. Today had been an exception and he thought harshly, 'I need to get a grip, there isn't time for self indulgence.'

At 5.30pm Robert packed up his desk and pushed the leather office chair back in place. He pulled on his uniform cap and strode out of the office and downstairs into the street below.

The Aldwych was still showing its scars from the Doodlebug that had exploded a few weeks before, windows were boarded up and pieces of debris were still being cleared away. In the distance there was the dubdubdubdubdub sound of another missile, then the silence and a massive crash. As Robert glanced up he could see a pall of smoke rising from streets a mile or so away.

He quickly caught a tram and settled down for the journey home. He had bought a paper that morning and he read this on the journey to take his mind off his work, his empty life that he didn't even really know was empty and the occasional distant explosions. Not long afterwards he got off the tram at his stop in Dulwich and walked around the corner to his house in Hurst Court Road.

Later that evening Robert sat in his favourite armchair smoking a pipe with his feet up on a little footstool. The house, as always, seemed large and empty. His eyes flicked up to the wooden mantelpiece where there were two framed pictures of his parents. One was on their wedding day and the other was his mother holding him as a baby in her arms. He missed them greatly since they had been killed in the Blitz. He hadn't lived in a family that was exactly overflowing with love but my God he missed their presence and reassurance.

Robert, being a young man, had strong sexual urges and no outlet for them. Most of his colleagues in the RAF and the Air Ministry had a string of pretty young WAAFs on their arms and he was sure that the pre-war sexual prudery was not being observed. Robert feigned shyness and avoided the advances of the girls that he found rather pushy.

Now feeling sexually frustrated his thoughts turned with embarrassment to something that had happened years before when he had been at school. There was a boy called Trevor, the same age as Robert, tall, lanky and dark who had befriended him. It had become apparent that Trevor had an interest in him beyond immediate friendship and once, up in Dulwich Woods, he had encouraged Robert to touch him intimately. He had initially hesitated, feeling sick and tight in his stomach, but with pent up sexual arousal he had relented.

The boys ended up having rudimentary sex with each other. When finished, Robert felt disgusted with himself and ran off into the woods. When he saw Trevor the next day at school he couldn't look him in the face let alone speak to him. He pushed past him rudely in the corridor leaving the hurt boy confused and crying at the rejection.

Now years later, he reflected on this single moment of intimacy with embarrassment. On the one hand the thought of Trevor's hands on his body still filled him with excitement. On the other, he felt deep inside that it was wrong, a basic and terrible wrong. There was no way he would give in to that kind of temptation again. There had never been any further moment of sexual intimacy for him either at school or in the RAF and his only relief was privately by himself.

At these times his thoughts would always stray to Trevor and the moment they had shared in the woods, and sometimes he would think about what would have happened if they had taken their sexual exploration a step further. But once he had finished the act he would again be racked by guilt at these thoughts and be consumed by waves of self-loathing.

Robert heard the wail of the air-raid sirens, indicating that another salvo of Doodlebugs had been picked up on the English radar somewhere across the Channel and would soon be hurtling into London. He knew he should probably be in the shelter but he climbed the stairs to bed and heard the first clattering of a Doodlebug overhead as he tucked himself under the eiderdown.

Dreamland

Tonight Robert dreamed, and he dreamed the dream that he had been having ever since he was a little boy. It rarely changed. It was simple, it made him feel good, and it was a counterpoint to his cold and empty life. The dream was no different tonight. He was on top of a weird high conical hill, looking out across flat marshlands towards a glistening river estuary in the distance. He suddenly became aware that by the side of him was a man, a handsome man. When he looked into his eyes he could see that they flashed with an amazing blue-green colour. He had never seen eyes like it before; he was holding hands with the man. The man turned to him and kissed him on the lips. He enjoyed the sensation very much. In his dream state he felt a rush of sexual excitement but more importantly a sense of being protected, warm and safe. He knows that the man and he share a deep bond, he doesn't know how. He cannot define it because he has never experienced it but in his dream he is feeling love. Sometimes he will awake with a start feeling hot, guilty and ashamed for what has come to him in his sleep. He knows nothing of the meaning of dreams.

On this night though, his dreams are to be interrupted by a turn of events that will change Robert's future forever, in a way he never could have considered possible.

★ ★ ★

Part Two: The Transformation of Charlie

Chapter One: The Zero Hour

22nd July 1944

In a clearing of dense woodland in the Pas De Calais, a region of Normandy not far from the coast, the Doodlebug sat on its concrete launch pad, primed, fuelled and ready for its deadly flight to London. The launch pad had already fired ten missiles towards the English capital in the last few days and now the team was preparing the eleventh.

The order was given to fire the weapon and there was a thudding roar as its primitive jet engine spurted into action and a huge fan of orange flame came out of the rear. The missile was released; it started to move, slowly at first then with rapidly increasing speed it accelerated up the launch pad. It was soon airborne. It wobbled slightly and the Luftwaffe officers briefly worried that it may misfire and turn on them. Many did. But on this occasion the Flying Bomb steadied and lumbered into the air. Soon all that could be seen was the flame in the night sky. The dubdubdubdub noise of the engine, gradually clattering away into the distance.

Not long after, the crude missile was crossing the French coast, its nose pointing in a seemingly determined manner towards England. It crossed the English coast near Hastings in East Sussex and flew onwards at 1000 feet across the Weald. The people of Southern England had got used to the Flying Bombs trundling overhead to deliver their warheads onto London, so few looked up or even noticed this particular bomb. It was now 11.00pm and most were in bed or in air raid shelters. The missile started to nose into the outer London suburbs and then, as it was programmed to do, the jet engine abruptly cut out. This happened as the missile was crossing Upper Norwood at exactly 11.05pm and the sound of the engine stopping startled people under its path, as they knew that it would soon fall to the ground and explode. The little unmanned aircraft started to glide down now that its engine had been silenced; the air whooshed over its stubby wings, over Crystal Palace and onwards towards Dulwich. Now at only a hundred feet or so it skimmed over Dulwich Park and it was clear that its final trajectory was aiming it at the houses which lined Hurst Court Road.

The deadly Doodlebug just missed the chimney of Robert's house and made its final dive just beyond the bottom of his garden, falling in the grounds of the big brick church. It was only 300 feet from where Robert lay drifting in and out of sleep. As it passed over the house he was snapped awake by a loud swooshing noise. Even though he was used to the Doodlebugs because they'd been raining down on London for weeks, he couldn't work out what the noise was. Just as he was starting to get out of bed to investigate, a massive pressure, like a punch to the chest, pushed him to the floor.

He still had his eyes open and he could see the blackout curtains that hung at the window were now streaming inwards, horizontally. At the same time he realised that he was being showered with massive jagged chunks of glass. He felt a warm wind rushing over his body and he could feel his eyeballs bulging with the pressure. Next the wind seemed to be rushing in the other direction and things from the room were being sucked out of the shattered windows. He covered his head with his hands but could feel himself being struck by flying objects, shards of glass and plaster falling from the ceiling. While it seemed at the time to take forever, it was probably only a few seconds.

As more and more chunks of the heavy plaster ceiling tumbled down, some hitting Robert on the head, he realised he was starting to lose consciousness. He had time to wonder if he was going to die but he could feel himself drifting away. Then nothing. Black. He could feel no more.

Hurst Court Road, Dulwich, 22nd July 1989

Charlie, lying in bed under his duvet in the same house, separated by exactly 45 years, suddenly became aware of a weird pressure in his eardrums. He shook his head, it still didn't go and now, almost instantaneously, there was a massive roaring and his mind summoned up the picture of a jet crashing overhead. It was only a few months since Lockerbie and he started to become very scared. Fearing some terrible disaster he pulled the duvet further over him. There was a huge bang, the house shook, then as quickly as they had started, the noises and sensations stopped.

Charlie, now completely confused and very worried, gingerly emerged from the security of his bedding. 'What the hell's happened?' he wondered out loud. 'I reckon a plane has crashed.' He reached for the switch of the bedside lamp and flicked it on. The room was totally intact, no signs of damage. He pulled himself out of bed, swung his feet to the floor and stood up. As he did he noticed something very odd; there was a pile of bedding in the corner he didn't recognise, then with shock he saw a hairy foot sticking out of it. 'What the fuck?'

He went over to the pile, and pulled off what looked like an old fashioned pink satin eiderdown. Under the pile of bedding, curled up in a foetal position with his hands over his head was a man. 'Who are you, how the hell did you get in here?' Charlie shouted out in shock and confusion, and actually stumbled backwards and almost fell over the bed at the bizarre scene that confronted him. The man said nothing; Charlie now saw that he was unconsciousness. His eyes were closed, he had no signs of injury on him, but clearly he could not hear him. There was no reaction at all.

Charlie was in a state of complete confusion at how this man had come to be in his bedroom. He briefly wondered if there had been a plane crash and the man had been blown out into the room, but no, all the windows were intact. There was no way that had happened. He also realised that the man might need some kind of medical attention.

Charlie bent over him and started to check him over to see if he was injured. He was wearing striped pyjamas; the thin fabric would not have protected him from any kind of crash, but he could not see any blood. The man was, however, covered in what looked like plaster dust.

Charlie now moved from being in a state of shock to thinking that he was in a dream. One moment he had been lying in bed, the next there had been a weird sensation and noise and now he had found a man in pyjamas wrapped up in a pink eiderdown on the bedroom floor. It was really too much to take in. 'This must be a dream, surely this must be a dream?'

Normally you would expect someone to pinch themselves to ensure that they were not asleep but Charlie's awareness that he was not in a sleep fantasy world came gradually. He started to realise quite how normal everything looked, apart from the stranger on the floor of course. Time ran normally, no other weird events occurred. In dreams time is usually jumpy, you move round from place to place, time to time, event to event with no notice. No, this was real life and yes there was a man unconscious in his bedroom and there was no logical explanation how he had got there.

Having worked out that this was not a dream Charlie then began to worry that this was some nutter that had broken in, had concealed himself and now lay, feigning injury and ready to pounce on him. 'Jesus, not only is my night out ruined but now a fucking psycho has broken into my house.'

He reached gingerly for the extension phone on the bedside table and started to dial 999. He would get the guy out of his house as soon as possible. Cursing, he realised that there was no dial tone, the line was still dead. As he put down the phone he heard a groaning come from the pink eiderdown. In surprise, and getting ready to protect himself, he dropped the phone and picked up a large bronze bust that was on a table by the window. It was of a half naked woman. It had been a gift from Michael who called her Bertha and had always described her as 'That Fallen Woman'. Charlie hated it and thought it crude but could not bear to part with it so consigned it to the Dulwich house. Now he was determined that she would fall on the stranger's head.

'Doodlebug, call the ARP,' the stranger whispered weakly.

'What did you say?'

'Doodlebug, please call the ARP.' The effort of saying these few words seemed to be massive and Charlie could barely hear him. His eyes closed again.

'I have no idea at all what you are talking about,' replied Charlie. However, he began to think that the man was not feigning the state he was in; he seemed genuinely weak. Charlie let down his guard a notch but still held Bertha tightly in case he had to use her as a weapon.

There was something else that he noticed as he looked at the man: he was extremely handsome. Very dark, with his hair slicked back in an old fashioned style. He had finely defined features and high cheekbones. As he had briefly spoken he had caught a glimpse of his dark brown eyes and even in the state that the man was in, they sparkled. Charlie was a sucker for sparkly brown eyes.

Although the man lay prone on the floor Charlie got a sense of the size of him, tall and broad and even though he was wearing pyjamas he could see that his body was muscular and well put together. Charlie was used to sizing up men in an instant and deciding if he found them sexually attractive and it took only a few seconds for him to realise that this was probably the most handsome man he'd ever seen. He could see the man's eyelids fluttering and saw that he was sinking back into some kind of unconscious state. He began to feel that this man was not going to hurt him and needed his care and attention. Even in these moments though his thoughts turned to sex. 'Just my bloody luck, the sexiest man I have ever seen is in my bedroom and he is unconscious.'

Charlie went to the bathroom and ran a flannel under the cold tap. He went back into the bedroom and to the man on the floor and tenderly bathed his face. After a few moments the cooling water seemed to have some effect and the man opened his eyes again. He looked at Charlie directly and Charlie saw for a moment a flicker of something in those brown sparkly eyes. A lost, almost little boy look and for a moment he thought that there was something familiar about the man. He went through a quick mental search of the people he knew; the men he'd had sex with. No, he couldn't place him. The man had the looks of a film star. 'That's it; he reminds me of some film star,' he thought.

'Thank you,' the man whispered, 'you are very kind.'

'That's okay, but you need to do some explaining Mister. Firstly how did you get into my house, secondly what do you want and thirdly convince me that I shouldn't either call the police or knock you out with Bertha.' At this Charlie's eyes flicked to the bronze bust that was now on the floor next to the man as if to emphasise the deadly nature of his weapon.

'I'm sorry I don't understand, I told you it was a Doodlebug, it must have exploded very near here.'

'What the hell is a Doodlebug?'

'You know, a Flying Bomb. There's been hundreds dropping round here in the last few weeks.'

Charlie suddenly recalled that his grandmother used to tell him stories about the bombs that everyone called 'Doodlebugs' which the Nazis had fired at London at the end of World War II. He started to worry that the man, the very handsome man, was, sadly, deranged or, then again, maybe this was some kind of elaborate joke one of his so-called friends was playing on him.

He decided the best strategy was to humour the man. 'Oh right, Doodlebugs, yes … of course. Lots of them. Oooo, those Germans are right bastards aren't they.'

'Yes! Quite! So will you please call the ARP and they'll call the ambulance and take me to the nearest hospital taking air-raid casualties. Please, I don't understand what the problem is.'

Charlie felt the conversation was going nowhere fast. He reached for the phone, deciding it was unfortunately time to call an ambulance and have this beautiful loony taken away. Sexy he might be but he could well have escaped from the local psychiatric hospital or something. At that point he remembered again that the phone wasn't working but he feigned a conversation with the 'ARP' and decided it was best to keep the stranger engaged and pretend there must be some hold up with the ambulance. He didn't know what else to do.

'So where are you from, where do you live?' It was Charlie's standard chat-up line.

'What do you mean? I live here; this is my house.'

'Don't be ridiculous. This is my house.'

'Look Sir, I have no idea who you are or how you got in to help me. Thank you though, but as I said, this is my house, I've lived here since I was a child. It was my parents' house.'

'Right,' Charlie replied still feeling that humouring the man was the best strategy. 'So when did you move here do you reckon?'

'Oh I can't exactly remember, I was very young but I suppose it must have been around 1924. Why do you ask?'

'Great,' thought Charlie, 'the escaped loony thinks he's a ghost or something.' Handsome though he was, Charlie was getting worried now. The man obviously really believed it was his house and he was scared he would get violent about it. Charlie was just about to run out of the room, and actually probably run out of the house, when the man's eyes closed again, his head slumped to one side and it was clear that he had entered a further state of unconsciousness.

'Well once again,' Charlie thought grimly to himself, 'this isn't turning out to be the Saturday night I had in mind.' Although still very confused and actually a little frightened he was a very compassionate man and decided the best thing to do was to make the stranger comfortable and then sort the situation out in the morning. He managed to drag him up onto the bed. He was heavy and a dead weight and in spite of Charlie's natural strength it was several minutes before he had managed to manoeuvre the unconscious man onto the bed by which time he was sweating profusely.

It was a hot night; it had not rained for weeks and he was exhausted with his exertions. He made sure the man's head was comfortable on the pillow and pulled a single sheet over him.

He looked so serene and so very, very handsome. Charlie checked his breathing; his breaths were deep and steady. He could have stayed there all night looking at him but remembered the man was quite possibly a stark raving lunatic. He went to the door of the bedroom, took the key out of the inside of the door, closed it behind him and locked the man inside.

'I'll deal with this in the morning. I'm sure Iris can give me some advice. She always has an answer for everything.'

★ ★ ★

Chapter Two: Breakfast in Dulwich

23rd July 1989

Robert had not had a good night.

'No it was most definitely not a good night,' he thought ruefully to himself as he tossed and turned, awakened by the raucous morning chorus. He could remember little, only jagged fragments. He woke around 4.30am not really recalling clearly what had happened. He first of all thought that he had been having a nightmare. He was hot and sweaty and he could smell the sour odour of his own body. A massive thumping headache seared though his temples. Then, slivers of memory started to come back to him. He was pretty sure that his house had been bombed, he could remember being pushed over by the blast.

'I suppose I'm in hospital now,' he thought to himself, but then looking around the room it didn't look like a hospital room. Actually for a moment he thought he was still in the bedroom of his own house. The room was the same shape, the bay window was the same, but no, this couldn't be his house. The wallpaper was different, like nothing he'd ever seen, a brightly coloured orange pattern. This certainly was not his house but surely not a hospital either. Robert's mind whirled round and round as he struggled to take in his surroundings. 'Perhaps one of the neighbours has taken me in,' he thought: that would account for the room being the same shape, all the houses on that stretch of the street were similar. 'My goodness they have strange taste though.' He looked around at the wallpaper and furniture, all of which was unfamiliar and in a style that he had never seen before.

He swung himself off the bed, carefully placed his bare feet on the ground and gingerly put the weight onto his legs to test that they were working. Yes they seemed to be fine, although, as he straightened up to a standing position his head thumped even harder and a wave of dizziness almost made him sit down again.

He steadied himself with one hand on a table by the window and looked out. The curtain hadn't been drawn the night before and he could see straight out into the garden. To his shock he could see sixty feet away the very same oak tree he'd climbed and frequently fallen down as a little boy. Behind it, and framed by it, was the church at the bottom of the garden that he saw every day of his life when he woke up. Now completely thrown by seeing that he was indeed in his own house, but somehow not his house, he threw himself back on the bed and closed his eyes desperately wishing for some more sleep. 'I must have had a bang to the head, that's why everything looks so weird.'

It seemed like Robert had only had his head on the pillow for a couple of seconds when there was a click and the door of the room swung inwards. He opened his eyes and looked at the strange man who had been asking him odd questions the night before. He said nothing. Actually he did not know what to say. He had rather thought the man had been part of a dream, but it was now clear that he was real.

'Right,' Charlie started. 'I have no idea who you are, I have no idea how you got here, and I may be taking a serious risk by not calling the police but you seem like you are in need of some care and attention. Would you like to have a hot bath and then some breakfast?' Robert was pleased by the offer. In spite of his sleep he felt grimy and tired and the thought of a warm soothing bath was very agreeable to him. At the mention of food he also realised that he was very hungry.

'Thank you so much, that would be very much appreciated and by the way I have not introduced myself, I have been so rude. I am Squadron Leader Harrison.'

Charlie's weekend was getting more and more bizarre by the minute, not only did he have the sexiest man that he had ever seen in his house, although he had no idea how he had got there, the man was now claiming he was an RAF pilot!

'My name is Charlie Rogers, and ummmmm what's your first name, I don't think we need titles here do you?'

'It's Robert, Mr Rogers, Robert Harrison.'

'For goodness sake call me Charlie, everyone does. Can I call you Robert?'

Robert was rather thrown by this lack of formality but was too flustered by the situation to disagree.

'Let's get you in the bath,' and he showed Robert the bathroom where he had already run a steaming hot bath full of water. He was used to seeing men naked and started to follow him in so that they could continue their conversation. 'And I will get to see him without his clothes on,' he thought naughtily. But Robert shut the door pointedly in his face and Charlie heard the click of the bolt being slid across.

After about half an hour Robert came down the stairs to the cramped kitchen where he could hear Charlie preparing breakfast. Walking around the house was very strange for him. On one hand it seemed exactly like his house but then everything just seemed so wrong. The paintwork, which had previously been dark brown, was now all white, the walls were covered in various garish wallpapers and everything looked old and dirty. It was his house; it must be because of the oak tree and the church outside. It looked though as if someone had painted a picture of something and got it slightly wrong. 'Yes it is like a bad painting,' he thought.

Charlie was busy frying eggs and bacon and there were already four pieces of toast waiting in the toast rack. On the small Formica table he had laid out the cutlery, the plates and two glasses of orange juice. Charlie gestured to Robert, 'Sit down, make yourself comfortable.'

He was still very wary of the man but the thought of sharing some time with him was becoming increasingly appealing. Much of last night's fear of him being a psychopath had gone, although he was still a little unsure and added, 'A friend of mine will be around soon. He's doing a Karate course at the moment. Perhaps we should start again with the conversation we had last night. Tell me a bit more about you and how you have managed to end up in my house?'

'There is not a great deal to tell Mister, sorry I mean Charlie. As you know I am Squadron Leader Robert Harrison, I live in Dulwich in South London in a house remarkably similar to this at

125 Hurst Court Road. I joined the RAF in the summer of 1940, flew Spitfires and was invalided out earlier this year after I was shot through the leg over France. I now work in the Air Ministry. I can't tell you the nature of my work as it is secret. Yesterday I came home, went to bed early and shortly afterwards I think a Flying Bomb exploded at the bottom of the garden and I don't remember much more. The next thing you are standing over me with a large bronze bust in your hands asking me lots of strange questions. Please can you explain what is going on, perhaps I have had a knock to the head but everything seems so confusing. Oh and by the way where did you get the oranges from to make the juice? I haven't seen any in the shops for months.'

As Robert told his story Charlie sat with growing amazement and waves of bewilderment pouring over him but had started to feel rather sorry for this handsome man who seemed so lost and who clearly had had a knock to the head. The man seemed to genuinely believe that he was still in World War II. Charlie briefly thought about calling the police or a doctor again but decided instead to go on humouring him. 'Well we are indeed at 125 Hurst Court Road but it's my house, I bought it a few years ago. You mentioned the war and being in the RAF so what date is it then?'

Robert thought it was a very odd question and had to think for a moment to get the answer. 'It's, I think the 23rd, yes 23rd of July.'

'Yes it is,' replied Charlie, 'two days after my birthday,' but then continuing to humour him, 'what year is it?'

'It's 1944 of course.'

Charlie now had no doubts at all. Clearly this man, however handsome he was, was not in possession of his faculties. He felt terribly sorry for him and wondered how he had come to lose his memory and live in such a deluded state. 'Well I can assure you it's not 1944,' he stated. 'It's 1989 and I'm very concerned about you. It would seem you've had a blow to the head or something. Would you like me to call a doctor for you?'

Robert looked angry. 'I can assure you that there is nothing wrong with me. My house was bombed last night and I suffered some trauma I'm sure, but my mind is clear. I think it is you that is deluded and what have you done to my house? Perhaps it's me that should be calling the police.'

Charlie felt the situation was getting out of control again. 'Hey, hold on please, don't get angry with me. Look, I can prove it's 1989, here's yesterday's newspaper.' And at that Charlie handed Robert Saturday's Guardian. His eyes flicked to the date on the heading.

'I don't understand,' he said turning decidedly pale, 'there must be a mistake.' Robert's head was spinning and he felt like a drunken man that tries to keep a grip of reality as it slips through his fingers.

'This is 1989 you tell me. So is the war over, did we win? Please tell me. I'm not sure I'm coping with this and how come you are in my house and how can it be 1989?'

'It most definitely is. The war's been over since 1945 and we won but this doesn't explain anything to me. Who you are, how you got here and why we both think that this house is our own.'

'I don't know Charlie but you seem kind. Many people would have called the police by now. I can promise that you can trust me, and everything I tell you is the truth. I would like to find some way of proving to you that I do live or have lived in this house at some time. Perhaps I am a ghost. Have you considered that possibility? Perhaps I'm dead. Oh my god I'm dead and I am haunting your house. That must be it!'

These concerns echoed Charlie's from the previous night but he decided not to feed the man's fears further. 'Do you know what, I have an idea,' he said. 'Why don't we go and have a look at the electoral registers for the area. They are in a library in Borough High Street. That might show us something. I can show you my name on the register and the date. Would that prove to you what I am saying?'

'Not dressed like this,' replied Robert. 'Do you have any clothes I can wear, perhaps a spare suit?'

Charlie giggled inside, 'A suit, what is the guy on about?' Charlie only ever wore suits for weddings and funerals and certainly did not have one here. 'I'm sure I can find you something.' He had bought a few changes of clothes the day before and he recognised he'd be a very similar size, apart from his much broader chest. So

Charlie found a pair of jeans and a white t-shirt, which for him was very baggy, but when Robert pulled it over his muscular frame it stretched tight over his hard firm body. Charlie's feet were also a similar size to Robert's and he gave him a spare pair of trainers. 'Let's go up to town, are you ready?'

Robert was distinctly uncomfortable in the very casual outfit he was now wearing but decided to agree anyway. They left the house and walked the few hundred yards round the corner to the bus stop. As they walked down the road Robert was totally mesmerised. Clearly this was still the Hurst Court Road he knew, all the houses were the same, it was definitely the same place, but then again everything was different. Firstly, there were large amounts of cars, and these were cars like he had never seen before. Instead of being black, the oddly shaped vehicles were in all possible colours – red, yellow, blue, orange. He found it very noisy with the constant hum of car engines in his ears. Overhead he heard a roaring noise and he flinched out of instinct as he was used to dodging Flying Bombs. Instead he saw a plane, larger than he had ever seen before with bright colourful markings all down the side. The engines were making a totally unfamiliar noise. They walked round the corner. He noticed that the gardens of the houses were not as neat as he remembered, whilst all the houses themselves were in a much better state of repair.

Lining the streets on both sides were more and more parked cars. It all looked so odd. 'So are we going to get the tram?'

'There haven't been trams for …' and Charlie stopped. He knew the man must be mad, but he was so convinced by his own delusion, there seemed to be no point in trying to get Robert to understand. Instead they stood at the bus stop. Robert was wide eyed at the traffic and the aircraft noise and how colourful everything looked.

The drab, decrepit wartime grey of London was replaced by something so much more vibrant. All the front doors were different bright colours, as were the clothes of the bizarrely dressed people they saw. Robert noticed something else as well; many of the people in the street clearly were not English. Some were black and some looked Indian.

'Why are there so many foreigners in London today? Is there an exhibition of the Empire on at the moment?' Charlie said nothing but thought, 'I'm really going to have to teach this guy a history lesson or two,' and then, 'for fuck's sake, I'm starting to believe his delusion, the guy is clearly deranged.'

The bus came 5 minutes later and the pair sat, Charlie saying nothing and Robert staring wide-eyed at a London that was not the London he knew. Many of the buildings were familiar, but then there were whole areas which looked like nothing he had seen before. When the bus reached Elephant and Castle he didn't recognise anything at all. Instead of the familiar high street and market all he could see were hideous concrete buildings as far as the eye could see. 'What happened here, why is it all so different? I don't understand.'

'Well I think that Hitler's bombs had quite a lot to do with it.' And then Robert remembered how much the area had been damaged.

'But why did they make it look like this after the war? It's so ugly.' To that Charlie had no answer.

Eventually they arrived in Borough High Street and found their way to the library where the electoral records were held. They entered the building and were greeted by a rather cute young gay boy, aged about 25 who Charlie thought he recognised from the scene. He glanced up from his desk and looked at Robert and blushed….. he clearly fancied him.

'Can you tell me where I can find the electoral records for Hurst Court Road in Dulwich please? I'm interested in the period around 1944 and also the one from last year,' Charlie asked politely.

The boy switched into professional mode and was pleased to be able to assist with the query and directed them to a set of large wooden shelves that held rows and rows of oversized, bound leather books. 'You will find what you want there.' Charlie hurried Robert away from the desk quickly feeling a stab of jealousy going through him.

The pair found seats at the long table that ran down the middle of the room and Charlie went over to the shelves and ran his finger up and down the row. Shortly he removed a volume marked

'Dulwich 1988' and placed it on the table. He opened the book and turned the pages until he found Hurst Court Road. He ran his finger down the page until he reached the entry for number 125.

There was going to be no surprise for him that his name would be there but he needed to prove to Robert that this was indeed his house. Perhaps the man would finally start to get a grip on reality, perhaps not, but this seemed like a good starting point. The entry boldly stated:

125 HURST COURT ROAD. CHARLES STEPHEN ROGERS

'There,' said Charlie quite gently, 'does that prove to you that this is my house?' A shadow of anxiety and confusion crossed Robert's face.

'Well yes, I can see that but it explains nothing else. Am I dreaming, have I gone mad or am I a ghost?'

For the first time Charlie heard a slight shake of emotion in Robert's voice and he thought he saw the glint of a tear in his eyes. He instinctively reached over and put his hand over Robert's, which was resting on the table. He felt the hand stiffen, it was swiftly withdrawn and Robert coughed as if to cover embarrassment. Charlie decided to keep talking to cover his *faux pas* in touching this man's hand and said, 'Don't worry it'll be okay, I'm sure we'll get to the bottom of this. Let's have a look at the 1940's records and see if that helps.'

The nearest register that they could find to 1944 was 1939; they presumed this was due to the war and they thumped the volume down onto the table. This one smelt musty and its pages showed their age. They quickly found the page for Hurst Court Road and their eyes flicked down the page together. It was Robert who spotted the entry first:

125 HURST COURT ROAD. ARTHUR R HARRISON, DOROTHY M HARRISON, ROBERT S HARRISON

'There, I told you, it was my house too, I told you, and I must have been killed by that bomb. I am dead!' At that a squirrel-faced woman with a grey bun looked up from her studies with a venomous looking expression.

'Schhhh. Please ...I'm trying to work.'

They left quickly. 'Just wait until I tell Iris about this,' Charlie thought. They went back to the house where he made them some lunch. He went to the phone and was pleased to hear that the telephone line had been restored. He dialled Iris's number. He really needed some advice.

'Ola,' it was Consuela, Iris's Spanish housekeeper.

'Hello Consuela, can I speak to Iris please?'

'Señora Wilson, she has gone to New York, on Concord.'

'When will she be back do you know Consuela?'

'She will be gone one year.'

As Consuela had been speaking, Charlie suddenly vaguely remembered that Iris had told him a while back about going to New York, but he was still irritated. He needed some advice from her. Damn. He was actually quite cross. He relied on Iris a lot and would miss her not being around. He thanked Consuela and put down the phone.

He went back to the kitchen table where Robert sat eating the ham and egg salad he'd prepared.

'So Mister, you certainly don't have the appetite of a ghost. Let's try and work out a bit more about what's going on here.'

'That would be good,' replied Robert, still with the lost look on his face. 'Well I shall begin by telling you everything I know.'

★ ★ ★

Chapter Three: A Conversation with a Ghost?

23rd July 1989

'So Charlie, that's about it. That's everything I can tell you about my life.'

For the last few hours Charlie had sat more or less silently as Robert told him his story. He told him most things about his life (although of course nothing of his deepest inner secret). Actually he had never talked like this before to anyone. In 1944 it wasn't so normal to open up to people emotionally and certainly not to a stranger. But sitting looking at Charlie, constantly noticing his wonderful blue-green eyes, Charlie occasionally encouraging him or prompting him, he felt that he wanted to confide in this man. He felt a strange sense of familiarity with him although he knew that they had never met before. There was something about Charlie that made him feel that he could trust him.

He told him of his childhood in Dulwich, spent in the very house in which they were now both sitting. Charlie had a sense of Robert's loneliness as an only child, and although he did not directly criticise his parents, Charlie correctly felt that his upbringing had lacked any real emotional warmth.

When Robert told him of his parents' death in an air-raid shelter in Kennington, Charlie could see him struggle to keep his composure. It was still clearly a raw wound. He knew from his own experience that just because one's parents are not perfect does not stop you loving them and when they are gone they are still sorely missed.

He talked at length about how he had fought in the war as a Spitfire pilot and Charlie was moved to tears by hearing of his bravery and determination to do the job he had been trained to do. By this stage he was totally entranced by Robert, but realised that he was never going to get this man into bed, but for once he was with a handsome man and his thoughts were not turning to sex.

He sat for hours listening to him talking, looking at his dark, finely cut features and wickedly twinkling brown eyes and was happy to hear him speaking from the depths of his soul. He had a deep masculine voice which only very rarely betrayed any emotion. This was one of the few times of his life that Charlie was not thinking about himself, and being in the position of allowing someone to open up and divulge their inner feelings felt like a great privilege.

Eventually, Robert seemed to run out of steam and it was clear that he had said as much as he needed to for the moment. Charlie wanted to continue the conversation though; he was enjoying the experience of supporting someone else.

'So is there a Mrs Harrison?' he asked.

'No, I've been far too busy with the war for anything like that.'

'And do you have a wife?' Robert enquired in return.

Now Charlie had been an out gay man for years, he was confident with his sexuality and as far as he was concerned had nothing to hide. But for once he felt shy and embarrassed. 'For goodness sake what will this guy think about my life?' So he lied vaguely, 'There is no one special at the moment.'

A slight awkwardness fell between the pair. Neither of them really knew why. After a few moments, which seemed to drag on for ages, Charlie said, 'Well we still need to get to the bottom of why you are here.'

'Indeed I think you're right, in some manner we need to understand and explain my presence. This morning I was convinced that I had been killed by a Flying Bomb and that for some reason I was appearing to you as a ghost. Now I am not quite so sure. Today I have spent many hours talking to you about me, about my life, about my emotions. Do you know that this is the first time that I have ever done that with anyone? In my time this is not considered normal, I was brought up in a family where the expression of emotion was considered slightly indecent. But there is something about you, something about your face, which seems so familiar, and something about your eyes that makes me trust you. When I talk you are never judgemental, you just listen and seem to understand.

But what I am trying to say, is that whilst I have been talking to you today and reflecting on my emotions I have felt deeply that my emotions are very real. I still feel happiness and sadness, I still feel the loss of my parents, I still feel lonely and I am still bitter that I cannot fight in the war any longer. Now tell me ….are these the emotions of a ghost? If this is death it is a very strange death as today I feel more alive than I have ever done before.'

Charlie was moved by this speech. Clearly his careful handling of the man was paying off and the man felt comfortable. He was pleased.

'It seems much the same to me Robert. Today, I have felt privileged to listen to your life story, and similarly, I have a sense of familiarity with you, it is like I have known you a long time. Listening to you, hearing your story, feeling your physical presence in this room, I tend to reach the same conclusion. I have dealt with death; my dearest friend Michael died a few years ago, so I know what death looks and feels like. I cried myself to sleep every night begging that he would come back to me as a ghost so at least I could have a little more of him, but there was nothing, no sign, no apparition. For me, after that experience there is no after life, there can be none. Michael has gone and there has never been a trace of him.

You, you are vibrant and emotional and, I am absolutely totally convinced, alive. So what we have to consider is, if you are not a ghost, the only other possibility is that you have somehow travelled through time. Yes I can only assume that this is the case, you have travelled through time. I have no way of knowing how, most would say that this is impossible but what other explanation is there?'

At that Robert's composure finally cracked and he started crying in big, deep, racking sobs. Charlie knew not to express any physical intimacy, he had been rebuffed before, and so he decided to re-assure Robert with words instead.

'Robert, whilst this seems so improbable, so unlikely and so beyond our imagination, I cannot think of any other explanation. You are most certainly not dead. I think we are both clear about that, so how else did you get here? Don't worry, I will look after you, you have nothing to worry about. I know that this is unimaginable but together we will get through this…is that a deal?'

Robert was still crying but less strongly now, his eyes were reddened and his face was wet with tears. He managed to respond, 'Thank you Charlie, you are such a kind man. How I came here may well remain a mystery to us both but one thing I am pleased about is that I have met you.'

Charlie thought to himself slightly sadly, 'If only we had met under other circumstances, by God we could be good together,' but out loud said, 'It is a pleasure to meet you too.'

'So now we have decided that I am not a ghost, and we know that I am a man who is in the wrong time, then I am going to have to decide what is going to become of me. I have no money. I don't know how I will earn a living. How can I? I don't exist, or rather I do exist and I should be 74 years old. How the hell am I ever going to fit in with this strange world of yours?'

Charlie had realised from quite early in the encounter that he had no alternative but to offer him somewhere to live. Sometime in the last 24 hours he had lost all suspicion of this enigmatic man. As he had become more and more fascinated and enthralled by his presence and his story he had totally put aside his fears. He no longer worried that he was going to harm him and had totally started to believe that somehow for this man, time travel was possible.

'So what we are going to do Robert is to make you comfortable here. You will have everything you need but at the same time we need to find out about how you travelled here through time and how we can get you home again.

Is there anything else that you have not told me, any clue or slight detail that you have overlooked?' Robert furrowed his brow and clearly was thinking hard to try and find something that he could tell Charlie.

'I'm sorry, there is nothing more I can tell you. Is there no one who we can talk to who could help?'

'Well who do you suggest, the police? What would they make of it? They would probably have you locked up as a dangerous fantasist. Or should we try a doctor…he would just make you see a shrink…. I really don't know. I am as frustrated as you. I think we have to deal with this alone, just you and me. I know nothing of time travel apart from what I have read in H.G.Wells books and what I have seen on television, but those are just fantasies.

I believe that there are many strange things in the universe that we do not fully understand. A few years ago who would have thought that putting a man on the moon would be possible?'

Charlie saw Robert's expression change to one of surprise.

'Oh yes that hasn't happened in your time yet. Bloody hell I am going to have to teach you a lot about history aren't I?'

Robert shook his head and smiled. 'If you have somehow managed to time travel once maybe you can time travel again, maybe we can get you back to 1944. There must be some way.'

Actually Charlie was beginning to realise that he really didn't want Robert to leave. He liked his company and the smell and presence of him made him feel excited and alive.

'Or maybe we could go time travelling together,' added Robert, 'now wouldn't that be amazing?' And at that the pair spent the next half hour debating the finer points of which parts of history they would visit, from Ancient Rome to King Arthur and to some strange and unknown future.

It was the first time that the conversation had lightened and as they pondered various parts of history and what they would do there, Charlie noticed that Robert was smiling and laughing for the first time. As he did his brown eyes glinted cheekily like two dark jewels and his smile seemed to light up the room.

Eventually both of them realised that they were fatigued. It had been a long and very strange day and Charlie showed Robert to the front bedroom where he had made up the bed for him. 'Well I had better say good night, sleep well,' and he shut the door behind him. He went and tucked himself up in the back bedroom where he had met Robert the night before.

Both men lay in bed struggling to get to sleep; both men had streams of complex and conflicting thoughts going though their heads. Charlie lay thinking hard about Robert with a sense of frustration. He was so sexy, so handsome and so much the man that he had always wanted to meet yet he was so out of his grasp. There was no way that this very conservative man from 1944 was ever going to succumb to his sexual desires so he felt that he had to close off those thoughts in his head. It was so damn frustrating. Yet at the same time there was something that he liked very much about him. There was solidity, a sense of honesty and trustworthiness that he had rarely encountered with the numerous dates and affairs he had had. He wanted to know more and more about Robert and kept saying to himself, 'It's as if I have known him all my life.'

Robert in the other bedroom couldn't stop thinking about Charlie. His handsome face and beautiful eyes filled his thoughts. Since the boy at school he had closed off all thoughts of sex or fancying men and now he had allowed himself to think for a moment what it would be like to feel Charlie's body and lips against his. Moments later he was consumed with pain and guilt at having allowed himself to stray into this tortured part of his mind.

Charlie in the other bedroom lost in his own thoughts was startled when he heard deep racking sobs. For a moment his instinct was to go and comfort Robert. He stopped himself and buried his head under the pillow so that he couldn't hear the anguished crying any longer.

The following morning Robert seemed to have composed himself, or at least said nothing to Charlie of his emotions. After they had had breakfast Robert said, 'Come upstairs: I have something to show you.' Charlie looked intrigued and followed him up onto the landing where the loft hatch was gaping open and Robert had rested the ladder against the aperture. 'Come on,' and at that Robert started to climb into the attic. Charlie followed and Robert leaned through the loft opening and extended a strong muscular arm to help him up. Charlie felt quite sick with lust as his hand touched his arm.

Robert had already switched the loft light on and he was pointing to one of the roof beams at the back of the house. 'Look, look here.' Charlie could see there was a name carved into the beam.

ROBERT HARRISON 1925

'There! I did it when I was about 10 years old and it's still here. Isn't that amazing! I remembered it when I woke up this morning.'

Charlie felt very touched that he had wanted to share this with him, and now had further confirmation that this had been Robert's house all those years before.

'Well you may not be a ghost but it does make you bloody old,' he joked.

Robert looked rather lost again for a moment and then continued, 'I suppose everyone that I know must be very old or dead. It is a very frightening thought. I am totally alone in the world.'

'Robert, whilst you are here you will never be alone, I will be with you,' and Charlie gave him a big meaningful look. Robert blushed deeply and said nothing.

After an awkward pause Robert said, 'Come on let's go and get cleaned up, I'm covered in soot.' It was now Charlie's turn to feel sad, but he said nothing. He would be a friend, nothing more, and Charlie knew that that was likely to hurt him but he had made a commitment to the man and he intended to fulfil it.

★ ★ ★

Chapter Four: A Very English Summer Outing

July 1989

Charlie had done the most rash thing that he had ever done. He had always been a bit prone to impetuousness but this took the biscuit. On the Monday after Robert had arrived mysteriously in his bedroom he had phoned in sick to work. He was bored with his job managing a bunch of stroppy telesales operators at the travel company he worked for. He had more important things to focus on. So on Wednesday he took the final act and called his boss, a gorgon of a woman with nasty bleached hair and an attitude problem, who he generally referred to as 'Mussolini'. He told her where to stick her job. Yes that was satisfying. He could not stand her bullying any longer and now having a convenient excuse in his head, he had acted.

It probably wasn't wise, but there was plenty of money in the bank and this was something new. He liked Robert, he liked him a lot. Charlie had very firmly pigeon-holed him as 'friend' rather than 'shag'. That's what he did with men, but that didn't stop him feeling hot and excited when he was close to him and feeling a wave of sensuality rush through him each time Robert caught his eye. He would quickly look away, feeling that he had overstepped the mark, and be embarrassed. But for the first time in his life, Charlie was experiencing something new, getting to know a man he fancied without considering him as a potential sexual conquest.

He would have given his right arm to fall into this handsome man's embraces but for now, he actually felt rather happy. He didn't know why, but a feeling of contentment and at the same time giggly excitement filled him. He couldn't really identify the feeling, he totally failed to appreciate that he was falling in love with Robert. Love for Charlie followed sex, this was uncharted territory. All the signs were there for anyone to see. He hung on Robert's every word and they spent days together in Dulwich talking, sharing ideas and jokes and laughing more and more as the days progressed.

For Robert the experience was different. Strangely, almost bizarrely, it was he that thought more readily about sex with Charlie. He was no fool and he had gradually worked out that Charlie was as he termed it '*homosexual*'. There were lots of clues: never any mention of girlfriends and then a certain sense that he was being defensive if Robert's conversation strayed too far into intimate areas of his life. Charlie had opened up to some extent to him, had told him much about his parents and also about the loss of his dearest friend. He made no mention of his sexuality, his numerous lovers and the sometimes chaotic life that he had had. No, Charlie gave Robert a very sanitized version. In spite of this, over the last few days, Robert had worked out what he was about.

Ultimately we know when people are flirting with us and although Charlie thought he was putting on the butchest possible act, and pretending not to be interested in Robert, he was flirting big time. He couldn't help it. His eyes gave him away.

So it was, that the conventional, conservative RAF officer from a very cold and repressed family went to bed each night fantasising about sex with this wonderful man. As human beings we cannot change suddenly, our habits and attitudes are too ingrained in our souls and Robert would lurch in and out of sexual fantasies into self-loathing and back again. Perhaps the programming he had had at the hands of repressive English society would stay with him forever. Perhaps he could forget it but now it was being challenged. A number of things were driving this for him. Firstly the raw, guttural sexual attraction that he felt for Charlie. This was so huge and all encompassing that like a tsunami it washed away all resistance in its path and the inbuilt walls of his personal guilt started to crumble. The other things that were driving it were to do with Charlie's personality, his openness, his honesty, and his decency. Despite Robert's resistance there was a voice inside his head which seemed to be saying, 'He is a good man, perhaps it is not so bad.'

Then of course what was really driving Robert to strip layers of negativity away was that he was falling head over heels in love with the man. He had never been in love before but he suspected what this strange feeling in his heart and stomach meant and it was good.

So this is where we find the men on the Thursday after Robert arrived. The weather was gorgeous, the sky blue, they had time on their hands to enjoy, and unbeknown to each other, in their own individual way, were falling madly in love. It was not an easy ascendancy into the elevated state of union for either man and they were like cars without headlights creeping at 10 mph along a foggy road.

Charlie had hired a car and the two men drove from Dulwich down through Bromley and then onto the A21 out towards the coast. The weather forecast had promised another perfect summer's day and the temperature was likely to be 29 degrees so they had decided that a trip to the seaside would be fun. Charlie immediately remembered his childhood outings to Camber Sands and suggested that they head off down there. Robert also remembered going to Camber as a child and added, 'We went on a steam train.'

Charlie was a skilful driver and he steered the car through the light traffic on the dual carriageway with a deft hand. There were points of the journey where the men said little, comfortable with the silence. At other points they would chat away like two old friends who hadn't seen each other for ten years and then collapse into fits of laughter at some silly joke. After Tonbridge the road narrowed and Charlie drove a little slower round the curves of the serpentine route that cut through the Kentish Weald.

'Shall we have some music?' he said.

'Yes that would be nice, might get bored talking to you otherwise,' replied Robert, but smiled as he said it.

Charlie laughed and, reaching over into the glove compartment, got out a couple of tapes whilst steering with the other hand. Without looking he inserted one into the cassette player and the car was suddenly filled with banging House music. The number was 'French Kiss' which was huge on the club dance floors that summer. Charlie smiled, he loved the tune, and then looked over to Robert who had the most horrified look on his face. He suddenly remembered that there was no way that Robert had heard anything remotely like this before and seeing that from his perspective realised how bizarre it must sound. He pressed the eject button and the cassette glided smoothly out.

'Sorry about that, I don't think you're quite ready for House music,' Charlie laughed.

'Was that music? I thought something was wrong with the machine.'

Charlie laughed again and slid the other tape into the player. This time it was more suitable and soon the honey, gravel tones of Billie Holiday were soothing the pair. Tiago the Brazilian artist had introduced him to Billie Holiday during their brief affair and he still loved her music.

'Now that's more like it,' said Robert and they both sang along to 'The Way You Look Tonight' as they motored on through Kent into East Sussex.

The day was still sunny and there was barely a whisper of cloud in the searing blue sky. The weather seemed to accentuate both men's moods and they felt like they were being washed away on a wave of elation.

Deep in the Sussex Weald at Flimwell Charlie swung the car to the left and took the road to Rye. Robert had been this way before, all those years ago, but actually only a few years ago for him. He noticed that outside London little had changed; the English countryside still spread out seductively before them in the same glorious and beautiful way that it always had. He was still thrown by the amount of traffic on the road but was now starting to get used to it. Otherwise England was still England, her countryside and villages unchanged, and he felt a great comfort in that.

Shortly they arrived in Rye, that ancient town that was once a port and was now stranded several miles inland. Charlie quickly found a car park and they walked up the steep cobbled streets together towards the Mermaid Inn where they had reserved a table for lunch.

'Good morning,' he smiled at the receptionist. 'I have a table reservation, Mr Rogers, two people for 1pm.'

The girl checked her list and nodded, 'Come this way gentlemen,' and she showed them into the heavily beamed dining room. They had to duck to get their heads through the door.

They were shown to a table in the window overlooking the street, which was beautifully laid with white linen, silver cutlery and sparkling crystal.

'I thought I would make it a special lunch today Robert, this is one of my favourite places.'

'What are we celebrating?'

'Mmmmm. A sudden arrival from 1944 I think.' They both laughed.

The menu was duly brought to the table and they selected their meal, both having the same: cold lobster, followed by Romney Marsh lamb. Charlie ordered gin and tonics for the pair of them and a bottle of Bordeaux to go with the lamb.

'I am really having such a wonderful day Charlie, it is so good of you to bring me here. I feel awful that I have no way of paying for anything. I am in such an impossible situation.'

'That's the last thing that you need to worry about mister, my bank balance is extensive.'

'Well, I have always been used to paying my own way. It is good of you but I promise you that one day I will find a way of paying you back.' He paused for a moment then continued, 'I am so glad I met you Charlie, you are so kind. I do hope we are going to stay friends.'

At that Charlie said nothing and looked away a little wistfully.

'I'm sorry have I said something to upset you?' 'Robert gently enquired.

Pulling himself together Charlie replied, 'No of course not. My mind just wandered for a moment.'

Robert felt emboldened by the mood of the day. 'Is there something that you have not told me about yourself?'

'I, I, I don't know what you mean,' Charlie stuttered. Then finding his tongue, 'I've been very open with you,' he lied quickly. 'Why do you ask?'

Robert didn't want to spoil the meal and replied, 'Oh no reason, just me being nosy.'

At that moment the lobster conveniently came. It interrupted this slightly awkward conversation and both of them were pleased.

They hungrily devoured the lobster; it was fresh, moist and good and tasted of the sea.

For the remainder of the meal the conversation ebbed and flowed naturally with no awkward moments. Charlie spoke much of his favourite places in England, which included where they were going today, but also talked much of the countries he had visited across the world. Robert thought this was amazing. In his time only very wealthy people travelled and even that had of course abruptly stopped on the outbreak of war. His most exciting holiday as a child had been to the Isle of Wight.

He was amazed by the quality and quantity of the food that they enjoyed. Large juicy and pink Romney Marsh lamb chops had followed the lobsters and then they completed the meal with a sticky treacle tart with sumptuous clotted cream. Robert was used to eking out an existence on basic rations and he couldn't remember food as good as this even before the war.

Over coffee they both smoked cigarettes and were temporarily quiet before they started chatting and laughing again. 'Right Robert, I think it's time for the beach. We need to swim and work off this lunch.'

Charlie paid the bill and they walked out of the hotel and down the hill to the car park, both giggling about various inconsequential things as they went.

Twenty minutes later they arrived at Camber Sands having driven across the strange, wild and, Charlie thought, rather spooky Romney Marsh. They parked up and Robert retrieved a couple of rucksacks from the boot, which held rugs, towels, drinks and snacks. They walked off into the sand dunes and soon found a cosy spot where they would spend the afternoon. It was a little hollow on top of a dune, surrounded by tall grasses and wild flowers.

Both men stripped off to their white boxer shorts and snuggled down into the hollow, lying on the rugs that they had packed. Their heads just stuck up enough so that they could see the view down to the sea which was half a mile out across the flat golden sands. As Robert had taken his clothes off Charlie had got the first glimpse of his defined muscular body and felt sick to the stomach with restrained lust. He had to look away so that Robert would not see his interest.

Through the day Charlie's mood had been swinging from wild elation to a sick tension. Yes he was having a wonderful time with this amazing man but now, finally, on this perfect day he had started to understand with total horror that he was falling head over heels in love with Robert. To Charlie this seemed impossible and doomed and in a normal Charlie way he would think, 'Even if he was gay he certainly would not fancy me.' For all his bravado, for all his sexual conquests, he had little self-confidence, actually almost zero.

They were quiet for a while, Charlie lost deep in his thoughts but at the same time trying to enjoy the moment. The sky was still clear, and all that could be heard were the waves crashing in the distance, some children playing ball below and sometimes a jet starting its long descent into Gatwick. He could feel the hot sun roasting his body and the warm sand pressing into his mostly naked flesh.

'I can't do this,' he kept thinking to himself, 'I just can't do it. It's going to destroy me. How can I be a friend with a man that I feel like this about? It's impossible.' He wanted to reach out and touch Robert's hand and tell him exactly what he felt but knew he couldn't.

Robert was sensing more and more that Charlie was distancing himself; he had been quiet now for half an hour and had allowed him the space to think. Robert could see that there were multiple thoughts and emotions whirling though his mind. His eyes betrayed it.

Robert, the repressed, lonely man who barely knew what 'gay' meant, was also something else. He was brave. He had never faltered in his duty in the RAF and whilst sometimes feeling a rational fear, had done his job with a steely and steady determination. Now lying with Charlie, clearly seeing that the other man was going through some kind of turmoil, he reached down inside his soul, galvanized his will and decided to speak. This was the most frightening thing he had ever had to do. Yes, being shot at by the Nazis was terrible but having to confront his innermost self was worse.

For Robert this was a superhuman act, having in a moment to reject years of conditioning, but he was so brave and driven, that he finally managed to speak. 'Charlie, when you told me earlier that there was nothing else you wanted to tell me about yourself, I don't think you were telling me the truth. I can see that you are troubled now and that something is coming between us. I do wish you would open up this last layer of your soul to me.'

'How can I?' Charlie blurted out and started crying. 'I want you to be my friend yet you will hate and despise me if I tell you the truth about myself.'

'I don't quite understand what you mean. What could I possibly hate and despise about you? You are a kind and wonderful man.'

Charlie said nothing but continued crying.

Robert felt again that it was up to him to take the lead. 'Charlie, there is something that perhaps I need to tell you. In these last few days that I have got to know you, and realised what a wonderful human being you are, I have understood something about myself. I have always shied away from thinking about it; I could not cope with the thought; I couldn't cope with the shame.' Charlie's blue-green eyes stared questioningly up to Robert's. 'Charlie I am trying to tell you that I am falling in love with you and because I am falling in love with you, all my programming, everything society has ever told me, is drifting away. Sure I still feel guilty, that's going to be a tough one to challenge, but because I am falling in love with you, I think I can cope with what I am.'

Charlie being Charlie and sometimes very slow on the uptake still didn't get it.

'You mean you love me as a friend?'

'Do I have to spell out every word? Do I have to paint every brush stroke on the painting? No you wonderful man, I am telling you I want to love you with every part of my body, my mind and my soul and if you will consider being mine I will cherish you and look after you forever.' Charlie was so shocked by these revelations that all he could do was to wail louder and louder.

'I can see that I have misjudged the situation,' continued Robert sadly, 'Forgive me, I thought you were interested in me too. I thought I saw it in your eyes. Please forgive me for making such a fool of myself,' and he started to get up and pull on his jeans.

'Please, please don't go,' Charlie managed to get out through his sobs. 'I can't take this in, surely you're not gay and anyway why would a man like you be interested in me? Yes of course I fancy you for God's sake. I think I'm falling in love with you but I would never be good enough for you.'

'Charlie, would this reassure you?' At that Robert bent over and brought his face close to Charlie's and pressed his lips up against his. Charlie moaned slightly with excitement and succumbed to his deep, probing passionate kiss.

There were no bells or explosions but the seagulls and the crashing waves orchestrated their long deep, masculine kiss on this perfect English summer's day, and that was a symphony enough for them in their mutual ecstasy.

★ ★ ★

Chapter Five: Perfect Motion

Charlie and Robert drove back through the long hot, humid summer evening from Camber. Charlie's mood could best be described as one of complete and abject shock. He had never entertained the thought that Robert could be gay, or could fancy him let alone fall in love with him. This had been unthinkable, yet now this wonderful, handsome, strong man was sitting smiling by his side with his hand gently resting on his leg. Yes shock, that was what he felt but at the same time an amazing sense of elation. What most moved him was that this conservative man who clearly struggled with anything emotional, had managed to find the inner strength to overcome his fears and declare his love for Charlie and he correctly took this as a great testament of Robert's love for him.

They drove on towards Dulwich, both having a sense of urgency that there was something they had to do. Charlie had wanted the kiss to develop further on the sand dunes on Camber beach but Robert would have none of it. Having sex somewhere where they may be caught was really too much for this man with very rigid ideas to contemplate. He pushed Charlie off laughing, 'You'll have to wait mister, we've waited a week so a few hours won't make any difference.' Charlie was his normal self and feeling rejected put his big lost boy look onto Robert. The latter re-assured him wordlessly with a hug and further loving kiss.

Now coming closer towards Dulwich in the car, it was Robert's turn to feel nervous. He urgently needed to have sex with Charlie, wanted to express with his body what he felt for him, but of course he was completely inexperienced and didn't know where to start. 'Charlie, I have something to tell you.'

'You've changed your mind, you don't really fancy me.'

'Don't be silly, I don't think you've listened to what I have told you, I love you fully with my body and soul and I want to show that to you, to make love to you. But you are going to have to be very patient with me.'

'What do you mean?'

'Oh for goodness sake, do I need to spell it out? I've never had sex with a man before; in fact I've never had proper sex with anyone before. There was a boy years ago at school but that was a brief fumble, nothing more.'

Now Charlie drove even more wide-eyed and amazed. This handsome man had never, at the age of 29, had sex. In his world, one driven by sex, this was unthinkable. 'Fucking hell Robert, how have you coped?'

'I have never met anyone and fallen in love. For me I had to be in love before I could consider sex, one without the other is meaningless. Do you not understand that? You must have loved the men you slept with?' Charlie struggled with the concept and decided to remain tight-lipped on that point.

He eased the car into the drive of the house and they quickly made their way through the front door and once it was shut they were in an embrace again, a new urgency taking hold of them as the fulfilment of their overwhelming desires came closer.

'Stop, Robert, I need to wash, I'm really sweaty, give me a breather. Actually let's shower together.' A few minutes later the men were standing under the very rudimentary shower in Charlie's bath, spraying water everywhere and enjoying their nakedness, covering each other with soap and then drying off with rough towels.

'Come on Robert, let's go to the bedroom,' and at that Charlie took his hand and led him to the back bedroom where they had met a week before.

So it was that this 29-year-old man had the first proper sexual experience in his life, and a very sexually experienced man made love for the first time.

It would be nice to be able to say that there were long explosions and fireworks, but for Robert and Charlie their first union lasted only a few minutes. Normally Charlie would have been horrified and categorised this as a 'crap shag' and sulked but this was different. He wanted to please Robert rather than just get his own gratification and he knew that teaching him how to make love properly would require patience.

Charlie now lay with his head on Robert's hairy chest, smelling him and feeling his skin against his body. He had truly, in that moment, never been happier. But of course, Charlie being Charlie, even in that moment of great happiness he managed to feel insecure. He suddenly felt overtaken by a wave of emotion and burst into tears.

'Whatever is wrong Charlie? I thought that this is what you wanted, aren't you happy?'

'Yes, yes, of course I am,' blurted out Charlie, 'I want this more than anything else in the world, I'm just so worried that you will get fed up with me and won't stay.' Robert was really perplexed at his response, having no knowledge of how Charlie had treated men and therefore how Charlie expected to be treated himself.

'Charlie, I have overcome a massive obstacle, my own inner fears, to be here in this bed with you. My body has been screaming out for this, but I have been held back by the heavy weight of society's conditioning of me. Do you not understand that it is only because I love you so very much that I have been able to do this? Your love and your goodness have been beacons that have helped me out of the dark place that I have been in for so, so long.'

'Do you think having found you that I would let you go? My God do you think so little of me?'

'You really love me?'

'Charlie how many times do I have to say it, I love you, I have never loved and I am sure I will never love anyone like it again.' Charlie was satisfied with this reassurance and snuggled his head back onto Robert's chest.

They slept together, holding each other tight even though the night was hot and made them sweat, holding each other as if to protect their partner from some unnamed demon.

Dreamland

Both men dream that night, in their newly secure world where they have both found someone to share their inner secrets and soul with. Charlie only dreams his good dream, he is a bird again soaring and free and joyful and his sleep is not disturbed by any nightmares. The number 80 is forgotten in his blissful happiness. Robert too dreams of flying, but in his Spitfire, high in the sky like Charlie, but on wings of metal, rather than wings of bone and feather. It seems to him in his dream that it is war torn England that is the fantasy, and he wakes in the night with a start and it suddenly comes to him that the new reality seems more real, and that 1944 is like a story, a memory, already starting to fade.

The following week Charlie decided that they should both move back to his flat in Kennington. The Dulwich house was really basic and needed a lot of work and he knew that they would be far more comfortable in the flat. The builder that had been sorting out the damage caused by the water leak had called to let Charlie know that everything had been resolved and later the same day they packed a bag and called a cab to take them up to Kennington.

Robert looked out of the cab window, intrigued with every detail of the city that he knew, yet was so different. To his eye, seeing the city full of people of all different colours and nationalities was very strange. However Robert, whilst a conservative man, had realised that the stuffy old society which he so despised had been blown away and the London that he now saw was more vibrant and exciting than it had ever been in his era. This London was better and he loved it.

That evening Charlie and Robert made love again; they had barely been out of bed for the last few days. Robert was learning how to make love properly. Charlie was patient with him and taught him how to hold him and where to touch him, and in doing he also learned how to give of himself and make love.

There is a wonderful state that we are in when we first fall in love. Every touch, every kiss, every glance is electric and there is a symmetry to the energy that flows between the two. Perfect motion. Charlie and Robert are in a state of perfect motion with each other. It is a beautiful dance of passion, and as they physically reach heights of ecstasy they dig deeper and deeper into each other's souls.

Life for the pair began to settle down into a routine. They spent their days seeing London, their nights talking and making love and neither man had ever been happier. So this is where we find Robert and Charlie a couple of weeks after they have met. In the flat in Kennington. Charlie is making spaghetti Bolognese; Robert is watching the TV with wonder. He sits tight-lipped as he watches EastEnders and wonders if all the changes in English life have been good ones.

The phone rang and Charlie quickly answered it; it was Iris.

'Charlie darling, how are you?'

'Iris, where the hell have you been? I've been trying to call you for the last ten days, I have such exciting news.'

'Oh it's so difficult with the time difference dear, and I have been rather tied up.'

Charlie smiled to himself at the mental image this summoned up. He was sure that his beloved aunty who was very unencumbered with convention could absolutely have been tied up by one of her latest conquests.

'What is it you wanted to tell me?' Iris finished.

'Well you're not going to believe this, but I've met a man, a really wonderful man, and you know what?' He looked across to Robert smiling as he spoke, 'I think he is really the one.'

'Oh Charlie that's wonderful, I'm so happy for you, what's his name, where did you meet, where does he live?'

'Well you're not going to believe this either, he …' and he stopped himself. He had fully intended to tell Iris of how Robert had come to be with him but he stopped himself, realising how bizarre this was going to sound. No, he decided in a moment. This was a secret that he was going to keep between the two of them. It would be better like that.

'Go on dear,' prompted Iris, 'what am I not going to believe?'

'Oh, oh nothing,' stuttered Charlie, 'just that I am in love,' he covered his tracks quickly. 'His name's Robert, he's incredibly handsome and he's just arrived in England after a long overseas journey. He's very kind and, well, he makes me feel safe.'

'Oh, darling that's wonderful, I'm so very, very happy for you. When I come back to London next year I shall look forward to meeting him, perhaps I can persuade him that he likes women. He does sound rather dishy!'

Charlie completely irrationally felt a hot wave of jealousy going though him. He controlled what he said and tried to make a joke of it, but failed in his delivery. 'Now Iris, he's gay. Do you really think that is going to happen? He likes men.'

'I was only pulling your leg dear,' she replied defensively.

Charlie had recovered his composure now and changed the subject. 'So when will you be back? you're always going away and leaving me. No one ever thinks of me. It's just so unfair.'

Iris's response took Charlie completely off guard, it was so unexpected. He was expecting her normal re-assurances.

'You are so bloody self centred Charlie, you really have absolutely *no* idea what you are talking about, you have *no* idea what I have done for you. If you had, perhaps your attitude to me would be a little better.' She spoke with anger and emotion.

'What do you mean I don't know what you..........'

And at that the line was cut off.

'Damn her,' thought Charlie, 'I really wanted to get more advice from Iris.' But he quickly dispelled the notion. She may have had a constant parade of different men in her life but he wondered if she had ever been in love. She was not the person to seek advice about love from. He was also completely perplexed by her angry tirade at him.

He returned to stirring the spaghetti Bolognese and Robert switched off the TV now totally bemused with what it was showing as entertainment. They ate the meal on their laps on the sofa, accompanied by a glass of red wine, speaking little, a comfortable secure silence.

Later on they talked again. Charlie had spent much time in the last few weeks explaining to Robert how much had changed since 1944. He now spoke of what the experience had been for gay men. Charlie had never forgotten how Michael had taught him about the gay world when he first came to London and now it was his turn to pass that gift of knowledge onto Robert.

He explained to him about the repression that gay men had suffered during the post-war period, legalisation in 1967, and the heady rush of liberation in the 1970's. When he went on to explain the dreadful wave of death since the early 1980's, he struggled and found the newly revisited subject as raw as ever. He had to keep stopping and have Robert squeeze his hand to encourage him. He spoke at length about Michael, tears throughout choking him into silence.

When he had finally composed himself enough to speak again he said, 'So you see Robert, since your time we have come so far and enjoyed so much freedom, but have also had to endure unbearable loss.' After a moment or two he continued, 'I've talked about all that stuff enough Robert. It hurts so deeply, it's good to talk about it in a way but only for a while, and now I must put those awful memories away.'

They said nothing for a few minutes, then lightening the mood, 'So Robert, what are we going to do with you? You don't exist, you can't possibly get a job, I don't even know what we would do if you needed a doctor.'

'I think we will have to invent a story, maybe that I have lost my memory and don't know who I am, then eventually I can become a real legal person again. However, I am more concerned about how I will pay my way. I can't have you supporting me forever and I really have no way of working at the moment. As I said to you in Rye, I will, I promise, pay you back one day.'

'I've told you repeatedly not to worry about that Robert, but I do have an idea. How about we sell the house and we buy a bed and breakfast in Brighton or Bournemouth. There are lots of gay men who want weekend breaks and they enjoy staying in a gay hotel. I think it would be good fun, what do you think?'

'I think it's very exciting to be making plans for our future. For all I care we could run a fish and chip shop together. I thought that I would spend the whole of my life alone and now I have the privilege of sharing it with you. I keep pinching myself to see if I am still awake. But yes. I like the idea of being by the seaside with you. I love the sea and I reckon we could run a really good business.'

'I'm not so sure about the fish and chips, we would both stink of frying all the time!'

They both collapsed into laughter and then into an embrace and were soon naked and making love for the third time that day. Each act of love has been more intense than the last, perfect motion, perfect passion, perfect emotion, and tonight, as ever when they are finished they lie, holding each other tightly, and feeling secure, safe, loved and deeply content.

Dreamland

A long way away over the water Iris sleeps a deep, deep sleep. She is exhausted from her exertions with the man that is now lying by her side in her bed. Early in the night she sleeps too deeply to stray into dreamland but later he disturbs her moving around in the bed and she begins dreaming.

All she can see, all she is aware of is a huge:

80

which fills her entire vision, nothing else. She wakes, sweating, and remembers. That's what she always does; on waking just for a second she has forgotten, then the knowledge of what 80 means, of what she has done, and the sick guilt she carries washes over her once again. She gets up and walks to the window of the 35th floor apartment. Stretching out below her is the jewelled carpet of Manhattan's lights. She looks out wistfully across the Hudson River towards the east, towards London, hoping that all the plans that she has made will work.

She goes back to bed, and reaches for the comfort of the hairy Frenchman who is her lover and she is soon in the security of his large, muscular arms. She is sleeping again and quickly re-enters dreamland. Now instead of seeing the number 80 she has the word:

BELOW

emblazoned before her eyes. She is aware of its meaning. She knows its importance. She sits, seeing the word reflected in a mirror, written on the wall behind her by another hand. Then everything changes and she is the one writing the word, in reverse on the wall to be seen in the mirror and she can see herself looking in the mirror seeing the word with a startled expression on her face.

★ ★ ★

Chapter Six: More Reasons Why You Shouldn't Write a Diary

August 1989

As Robert had fallen in love with Charlie he had put aside all his conditioning and conservative nature. He was washed along on a tide of love and lust and the world that he was living in seemed so unreal and dreamlike, so far away and long ago that he had forgotten much of what had gone before.

Sometimes, when we are very happy it can take one word, one incident, one glance to send us off into a spiral of despair and sometimes, when we are unhappy the reverse can happen. Well, it was like this for Robert now, buoyed up by his love for Charlie, putting aside his conditioning and it was only going to take one little pin prick to burst that particular bubble. When that came it caused a massive explosion and threatened to de-rail the two men from their happy path together.

Charlie, whilst a very intelligent man, could sometimes do remarkably stupid things and did not always learn life's lessons. He had forgotten that keeping a diary could be very dangerous unless one makes absolutely sure that it is never going to be read by anyone else. He had for some years kept what he liked to call 'my little red book' a leather bound journal for writing thoughts in, a present from Iris. Now Charlie didn't really have anything very deep to say but he did find it necessary to record the details of all the encounters he'd had with men. There was a date, a name (when Charlie knew it) a brief description of the encounter and then a score. Men were scored from 1 to 10 depending on their performance. He thought that it was very amusing. In his head it somehow gave him some status with his friends when he was able to say, 'I had a 10 last night.' To be honest he had totally forgotten the book and its secrets and that it might be wise to hide it from Robert's eyes.

But so it was that Robert, whilst making the bed one Saturday morning, spied the book, discarded in the space beneath. Perhaps if it had said 'Diary' on it he would have known not to open it but it said nothing on the cover so he did. Immediately, he knew he was going to see something he did not want to but it was too late to stop.

On just the first page there were details of the sex Charlie had had with six different men over a period of 3 weeks. Dates, names, description, scores. He felt sick. He clasped the book to his chest and strode angrily into the kitchen where Charlie was making breakfast. Charlie looked around as he heard Robert walking in; he was smiling but as he glanced at the book in Robert's hand he froze. 'Robert, that's mine … please … please don't look at it.'

'So what score were you going to give me?' he asked in a trembling voice.

'I'm sorry you were never meant to see that, I forgot it was even there.'

'Too damn right I'm sure I wasn't meant to see it. Oh I'm sure that's the case. You wanted to keep your sordid secrets from me.'

He was flushed and Charlie could see that he was losing his temper. He had never seen Robert like this before. 'What kind of man are you Charlie? I thought that I had met a decent human being but am I wrong? It seems I've met some kind of monster. You have been working through these men as if they are just disposable things, trash that you can take what you want from and move on. For God's sake don't you see how you have used them?'

'*I've* used *them*. How dare you! *They've* used *me*. All of them. They're all fucking useless bastards! All they wanted was my body, they never cared for me.'

'And what exactly makes you different from them?' replied Robert with heavy sarcasm.

'How dare you, how dare you judge me like this. You have no idea what things are like now for gay men. We can do what we like; there isn't the repression that you had to live with.'

'I may have lived a very lonely life, but in your vile obsession, have you ever really experienced proper love? No of course not. This isn't love, you are like a warped machine. It's revolting and I'm not really sure that I want to be part of your life. From the amount of men that you seem to have had in your bed I suspect that you will get bored with me pretty quickly. How long do I get Charlie? Six weeks? Six months? You tell me Charlie Rogers because I think I've got a bloody right to know. How long? Tell me you filthy bastard.'

Robert was now shouting and there was a fat vein pulsating in his temple. Charlie did what he always did and burst into tears.

'I've seen enough of your tears and I'm really not interested in them now, stop snivelling it's not going to help. It's always about you isn't it? You're so bloody self-centred that you can never see the feelings of anyone else around you. I don't think I have ever met anyone so selfish in all my life. Stop that bloody crying now or I'm out the door.'

'And where do you think you're going to go?' Charlie managed to blurt out between his big sobs. 'You don't exist, what are you going to do?'

'I don't think that's your problem anymore. Now that I have seen your true self revealed, I no longer see the person I thought you were and with that went any right that you had to interfere with my life. I think I'm going to leave now, I would rather be alone than be with a pervert like you. You think my time was so repressed don't you? You think it is so hilarious that we were repressed gay men who lived celibately or in fear of being found out. Oh yes you think your liberated gay world is so damn wonderful don't you?

But can't you see that you have lost so much. Where is the self-respect in all of this? Where is the love? Tell me that because from where I am standing I can't see any at all. I'll tell you what, I'm going Charlie. I'm leaving, I don't want to be with you anymore. You have ruined and broken the love that I felt for you.'

Charlie was by now hysterical, his moment of happiness was in ruins; the man he loved so deeply was now seeing his true self and hating what he saw. 'But I've changed, I love you, don't you understand that?'

'Love!' spat Robert, 'you don't know the meaning of the word.' And at that he made for the front door.

'Please don't go, please, I can make it better, please don't leave me,' and Charlie grabbed hold of Robert's arm in an attempt to restrain him. Robert pushed him roughly away. 'Don't touch me. You sicken me.' He left the flat, with Charlie lying on the floor crying his heart out.

Robert walked and walked and walked. He had nowhere to go but that fact wasn't going to keep him with Charlie. No, he just needed to get away. What Charlie didn't realise was that this incident had awoken all of Robert's own guilty feelings about being gay. The guilt he'd thought he'd walled away was now surging back inside him and he felt sick to the core as he thought about what he had been doing with Charlie. It was wrong, all wrong and it was going to have to stop.

He walked round the streets of Kennington; he didn't know where he was going, but an hour later after having meandered around in endless circles he found himself at the entrance to Kennington Park. He walked in and realised that without planning it he was at the site where his parents had been killed.

They had been returning from visiting an aunt in Battersea one October evening in the Blitz. The air raid siren had gone off and the passengers were turned off the bus at Kennington as the raid intensified. His parents ran for an air-raid shelter just inside the park but shortly afterwards a German bomb penetrated the trench and they were killed. Robert had never had the dignity of having their bodies to bury. They were buried with many others where they died. As he approached the site he saw that a rose garden now grew on the area and there was a small brass and concrete plaque commemorating the tragedy.

He sat on a wooden bench by the rose garden, and thought about his parents. He thought about the disgust he felt with himself at having strayed into this new life of depravity and he thought about Charlie. Then he wept. His misery was complete.

Charlie had just about recovered a modicum of composure and did what he so often did at times of crisis. He called Iris. It was only nine in the morning and therefore the middle of the night in New York. 'Who is it?' asked Iris sleepily as she grabbed the phone from the side of her bed.

'It's Charlie,' he said in tears. 'I've done something awful,

Robert's left me, I don't know what I'm going to do. I love him so much.'

'Now calm down, there must be something we can do. You two sounded like you were getting on so well. What's happened, what have you done?'

'He found my little red book.'

'Oh Charlie you fool, can't you see how that looks? It looks bad enough in 1989 but just imagine how it seems to someone from 1944.'

'I know, he thinks I'm a vile monster, I am a vile monster, what am I going to do? I've ruined everything. He's left and I don't know where he's gone.'

'Well dear, well I'm sure you can find him, you're in Kennington aren't you? Call it my sight or intuition but I think you'll find him on a seat in a place that's very special to him in the Rose Garden in the park.'

'How could you possibly know that Iris? I've never known your intuition to be that good. How can you possibly know that, you're not a fortune teller or something?'

'Please don't ask me how I know but trust me, I can assure you that you'll find him there.'

Charlie was still confused but did trust Iris so now went off on another tack. 'But Iris, I don't know how that is going to help, he hates me. He's seen the real me and hates it. How am I ever going to get his trust back?'

'Well you're going to have to use every ounce of your resolve, every argument that you have to convince him. You need to assure him that you have changed and have done it for him. I expect there is something else dear and that is that he's probably jealous. Jealousy is a very powerful emotion, very destructive.'

'How can he be jealous? This is in my past, not now.'

'Yes but he doesn't know that, he thinks he'll lose you back to this previous life you seemed to revel in. Maybe he's jealous in advance of losing you and don't you think that maybe he's also a bit jealous of your past?'

'How do you mean Iris?'

'Oh Charlie dear, you are so slow sometimes,' Iris chided

gently. 'When you wrote to me last week telling me all about him you told me that he was more or less a virgin at 29 years old. Don't you think he would have liked to have had some of the fun you've had? Can you imagine what it was like for him being sexually repressed all his adult life? Yes, I suspect he is jealous of that too.'

Charlie was starting to get a little glimmer of what Iris meant.

'But if this is true, how do I ever re-assure him. How do I convince him that I am prepared to change and give myself totally to him forever? I love him that much. I know that he's the man I've been looking for all my life.'

'Charlie, one of the things that upsets me so much about our society is that gay relationships are not valued in the same way as straight ones. If you were able to get married I'm sure that you two would be proposing to each other already. Perhaps a proposal would convince him.'

'Yes wouldn't that be bloody wonderful,' replied Charlie bitterly. 'But that's never going to happen whilst that bloody woman is in power and probably not in my lifetime. So let's forget about that, it's a pointless conversation.'

'Are you really prepared to commit yourself to him?'

'Yes, haven't I told you enough times?'

'Don't get touchy with me dear. Well there is a way, it is a completely bizarre idea but it would marry you in a way, in the eyes of those that really matter. Are you prepared to be very open minded?'

'Go on Iris.' He was intrigued by the line of conversation and desperate to find any way that he could get Robert back. Actually, at that moment he would have done anything.

Over the next ten minutes Iris explained her suggestion, very slowly and carefully. It was, as she said, completely and totally bizarre and he initially felt himself resisting the idea but she was persuasive and by the end of the call Charlie was excited and ready to run off to Robert to talk to him.

'Okay Iris, I understand. Yes I will try, give me the woman's number.' Iris read out a London telephone number which he scribbled down with a little pencil he kept by the phone. 'Thank you so much Iris, I'm going to go and try and find him now, I will talk to you soon,' and put the phone down before his aunt could say anything else.

Half an hour later Charlie was sitting next to Robert on the bench in Kennington Park by the rose garden. He was exactly where Iris had said he would be. It was an overcast and humid August day; the metallic grey colour of the sky did nothing to lighten the men's moods.

They said nothing for maybe 20 minutes. Robert's anger had subsided but he was still consumed with waves of guilt and self-doubt as well as an emotion, which was indeed jealousy. It hurt. Physically. Charlie on the other hand had become much calmer. He knew that for once in his life, he was going have to be the strong one, he was going to have to take the lead, he was going to help this man come to terms with the situation. Eventually he spoke. 'Robert I am so sorry that you found out about my past in that way. It was wrong and I can see that I have hurt you greatly.' Robert said nothing and looked away. He didn't know how to respond.

After a few moments Charlie continued, 'I'm not going to make any excuse for my past, but equally I'm not going to apologise for it either, that is the person that I was, there are lots of reasons for that.'

Robert finally spoke bitterly. 'Yes the reason is that you're an animal.' Charlie breathed deeply; he knew he had to be calm if he was going to salvage the situation.

'Robert, what I want you to consider is that I'm a product of now. I'm not saying it's right or wrong but that's how it is. I have had lots of sexual experiences, just like most of the people I know. It's what we do and we love it. We could debate forever if this is good or bad but that is how it has been for me. What I am prepared to do is to be someone totally different for you. I am prepared to reject everything that has been me and that has meant so much to me, so that I can be with you.'

'And what if I don't want you anymore, what if I don't want this life? What if I can't cope with the thought of what I have become?'

'Well Robert, I'm a product of my time, you're a product of your time. In your time everyone who ever talked about being gay said it was wrong. In my time they still do but less so. What I am asking of you is in the same way that I am going to be a different person and leave my past behind, I want you to be a different person too.'

For the first time Robert looked up and his eyes opened wider as if to ask a question. 'Charlie I don't know if I can do that, I think I'm forever consigned to a life of being alone because I have been taught that this life is wrong. How can I forget what I have been taught? Tell me that. My heart still beats more strongly when I see you, you know what I feel for you, but my head is telling me this is all wrong.'

'Don't you think that sometimes our hearts are right? Our heads are so full of crap that we have been told and taught. What we really feel is in our heart, true love, true emotion, there are some times that we must absolutely follow what it is telling us.'

'Maybe, yes maybe you're right, but tell me Charlie why does it all hurt so much, why is there this pain in my chest, why do I feel sick? Is that my heart or is what is whizzing around my head ripping me apart?'

Charlie actually couldn't believe how calm and controlled he was being. He felt that in the last hour he had suddenly grown up. He had always placed himself in the role of needy, in need of looking after and in need of support and now suddenly someone else needed him. It made him feel good. He felt taller, stronger, more masculine somehow. 'Well Robert what I am going to ask of you is to follow your heart, forget everything you have ever been taught, forget the Robert Harrison that was. I too will be following my heart. I will be putting aside everything I was and will be a new person too. The two new people that we will become will be blending the good from each other.' At that Charlie got down on one knee in front of Robert, clasped both of his hands tightly and looked him directly in the eyes.

'Robert, the laws of this retarded society don't allow me to marry you but I want to give myself to you, to you alone, to no other man, in mind, body and soul for ever more. If you will still have me. I would be very honoured if you would be mine.'

'But...' Robert started.

'Shhh!' and Charlie put a finger to Robert's lips to silence him.

'There is a way that we can make a commitment to those that matter, the stars, the planets, the solar system, the spirits of those who have gone and are yet to come. There is a way Robert. Are you prepared to trust me?'

Robert felt his heart melting just a little at Charlie's dignified words. 'Yes, maybe, I think I am. Please tell me what you mean, how can we make such a commitment?'

'I spoke to Iris, I asked for her advice and she has told me what we should do. This is going to require a superhuman leap of faith by both of us.'

Over the next 10 minutes Charlie explained Iris's plan to Robert whose eyes widened with amazement and whose jaw dropped with shock.

★ ★ ★

Chapter Seven: Madam Morgana and the Mists of Brockley

'I can't believe we're doing this,' giggled Robert as they walked up the street from Brockley station, lined with London plane trees and tall, grand, Victorian houses.

Charlie replied enthusiastically, 'I know it is just completely mad, but it feels so right at the same time. Oh, I think Madam Morgana's is just around the corner from the directions she gave me on the phone.'

After the conversation they had in Kennington Park, the two men had gone back to the flat. They were both feeling sick, tired and stressed from the argument and the awful feeling that they were going to lose each other. However, they now felt they'd reached a common ground and that they had a plan that would divest them of everything they had ever been and they would become changed people. In their union they would share a little of each other, losing the negative things that had held each of them back in very different ways. Having heard Charlie's proposal, Robert's heart had melted and he began to believe, just a little, that he was not just another conquest. In the next few days they gradually re-assured and comforted each other that everything was going to be okay and that they would indeed reach mutual understanding. Charlie knew that he had Iris very much to thank for this.

Iris's plan was outlandish, bizarre and Robert suspected probably illegal but something in him had changed. The edifice of English conservatism was starting to crumble, just a little, and he was beginning to see that it had its own limitations. In spite of everything, his feelings for Charlie were undiminished and this was driving him to be bold and to think the impossible. To do something so ridiculous might just be the answer to their conundrum, two men from such different backgrounds forgetting their pasts and forging a union for the future.

Iris had explained very carefully to Charlie what he was to do and that was to seek the help of a woman who called herself Madam Morgana. According to her publicity she was a 'Wise Woman' who hailed from Brockley. In fact her name was Hilda Shrubshore and she had worked on the deli counter in Woolworths for years but she didn't tell people that. She maintained she came from a long line of travelling Romany gypsies and fortune-tellers: it sounded more suitable for her role than the truth – her father had been a plumber and she had been brought up in a semi in Slough.

The men stood rather nervously at the front door of Madam Morgana's house. It was decorated with little gold and silver stars and moons. Robert felt he'd never done anything so bizarre in all his life. In fact, this man who in his time stream had just a short period before been flying a Spitfire over France *had* never done anything so bizarre. Charlie's life had been a little more, should we say, eclectic, but he was still unsure of what to expect when they went in.

The door opened and a very small dark woman, no more than four feet tall smiled up at them. 'Greetings, I am Madam Morgana, welcome to my house. You must be Charlie and Robert. Come in, welcome. Please take your shoes off and leave them by the door.'

She was probably in her early 60's. She had a wrinkled, dark complexion and her hair was covered in a rather elaborate turban which had the repeated motif of stars and moons all over it. As she moved, her long black gown released a slight fragrance which Robert recognised from his childhood church days as incense, and also a spark of static (it was clearly made of nylon). A large black cat purred around her ankles.

Robert started to giggle, he couldn't stop himself, and hearing this Charlie gave him a withering glance and a whispered, 'Stop it!'

Madame Morgana, ignoring Robert's rudeness, led them into the small sitting room that lay at the front of her house. It was quite dark, the tall wooden shutters were closed and the only light came from candles that were randomly placed around the room. In the middle was a low, ornately carved table around which lay a number of large comfortable-looking cushions covered in an Indian fabric. She gestured to them and the pair meekly obeyed and sat cross-legged on adjacent cushions.

Now that Charlie's eyes were adjusting to the candlelight he could pick out some of the things that lined the walls of the room. There was a long-dead stuffed owl in a glass case. There were hundreds of candles, some ancient-looking, like they hadn't been lit for years, dripping long stalactites of wax and dust. There were rows of shelves with books, most of them large leather bound volumes. The nearest shelf was just by Charlie's left shoulder and he was able to pick out a few titles, 'The Spiral Dance', 'Avalon of the Heart' and 'Modern Witchcraft'. In the middle of the table was a large crystal which clearly was used for telling the future.

Robert was first to speak. 'I'm not sure that we should really be here. I don't wish to offend Madam Morgana but I really don't want my fortune told. I think it's nonsense and I am beginning to doubt why it was suggested we should come here at all.'

Charlie looked most uncomfortable at his comments.

'Young man,' Madam Morgana began, 'I take no offence, and I shall ignore the fact that you giggled when you saw me. I would tend to agree that fortune telling is nonsense. Please don't tell any of my clients that. They pay me 10 pounds and I tell them what they want to hear. I have to earn a living you know. I tell them of a lover that is to come in the near future, I tell them of a message from someone departed. Most of it is rubbish but it makes them happy.'

'That does nothing to reassure me,' said Robert stiffly.

'Please let me continue, I understand your scepticism. What most of my clients do not know is that I am also a priestess of what some call the Old Religion. Some people call me a Witch.'

At that Robert started to get up saying, 'I've heard enough of this nonsense.'

'Sit down and shut up,' commanded Madam Morgana in a quiet but authoritarian tone that no one could disobey; Robert compliantly did. He felt like he was a little boy and had been told off by a particularly fearsome schoolteacher.

'I expect from your response and your arrogance that you know little of the ways of the Old Religion but I understand from Iris that you wish to have an inseparable bond, to partake in an act which will bind you together in the eyes of the universe so that you may share in each other's love for eternity. I am able to offer you a hand fasting ceremony. This is a simple pagan way of binding two people together but one of the deepest spiritual significance.' Robert could feel himself fiercely resisting, whereas Charlie sat with large eyes hanging on to everything that Madam Morgana said.

'Tell me this, what other alternative do you have? Let me pose that one simple question to you, what alternative is there? Clearly your love for each other is beyond most people's imagination, I can see that in your eyes. You have to strip away the layers of the people that you have been in your lives up to this point. Iris has told me a little. I understand that you Charlie, in your fragility, in your quest for real love, ended up on a shallow and loveless path. Robert, as for you, I know nothing of your background but I have been told that you have been brought up in such a way that contemplating a relationship like this is very difficult. Your Christian church holds nothing for either of you; in fact many Christians would condemn you. So I ask you again, what alternatives do you have?'

If you walk away from me now it is of no concern to me, I shall see another client later today and I shall tell them of their love life … but you will be stuck in the place that you are now. Are you prepared to lose each other and not take the risk that what I am proposing may just be the right thing?'

Charlie needed no further persuasion; he knew what he wanted to do. He didn't care that the only thing he knew about witches was what he had read in the Narnia books. He didn't care that this woman seemed to be part of some bizarre religious cult, but he did care that it offered him hope.

Robert was still shocked and resisting the woman's arguments. 'I was brought up as a Methodist, Madam Morgana, and you are right that the Church would be horrified at this relationship and also this witchcraft that you practise. I was taught to believe that witches are evil and do great wrong to people. How do I square that with what you are trying to tell me? I was taught that people like you are in league with Satan. I really don't want to be any part of this.'

Charlie felt that this was going nowhere and looked at Robert with pleading eyes but said nothing.

Madam Morgana continued, 'I know that people of your faith are taught that we are wrong, that we are evil, but ours is a simple creed. We worship nature, the cycles of the moon and the earth going around the sun and we believe that Satan is a Christian invention. We are nothing but people who believe that the universe is the most beautiful thing and that if we cherish and act with it then it can show us all the wonders it has. I just ask you Robert that you suspend all your scepticism and fears and put your trust in me. I only want to help you, I am not allowed in my faith to do any harm. It is against our beliefs. Why don't I explain a little more of what the hand fasting would involve, what it would mean and also a little more of my religion? If at any stage you hear anything that sounds evil or wrong you can stop me, question me or you can leave. How would that be?' Robert felt slightly reassured and he could feel Charlie's hand squeezing his to encourage him.

Madam Morgana explained very carefully more about her faith and what the simple ceremony would involve, where it would take place and what its meaning would be. She talked passionately and explained that pagan people like herself respected all religions, including his own Christian god. This took over an hour and during that period Robert began to trust the woman a little; her voice was re-assuring, her tone was soothing. She was using every ounce of her persuasiveness and skills because she knew that the hand fasting was right for the two men. She knew that in her heart.

Robert would repeatedly butt in and question her as to the meaning of something she said and the two batted ideas back and forth like a shuttlecock. Somewhere during the conversation Robert began to realise that Madam Morgana only wanted to do good and her simple faith, whilst completely alien to him, clearly was not the evil one he had been told it was. Sometime over an hour later he made a decision that he would trust the woman, that he would go along with the plan.

'Madam Morgana, you are a very persuasive woman, I am coming to understand that you are not evil and only want to help us. Whilst this faith of yours is something I have no knowledge of, I am not an ignorant man and I am prepared to learn and be open-minded. I apologise that I have questioned you so much and have been so doubtful.'

'I have no problem with your questioning; we must question in order to reinforce our ideas and faith. Questioning is what helps mankind to evolve on a spiritual path. You are a very intelligent young man, but tell me Robert what was it that made you change your mind?'

'You are a very eloquent woman Madam Morgana, but ultimately it is not your arguments that have weakened my feeling against your religion. What has swayed me is your love for us and your wanting to help us and that is a more powerful weapon than any words you can use.'

That was exactly what Madam Morgana wanted to hear. The intellectual arguments about faith and philosophy were one thing but what Robert felt inside was the most important. He had felt her goodness, her love for humanity, her love of her simple faith, her love for the two of them in their plight and her love of wanting to do the *right* thing.

Charlie had said nothing as Robert and Madam Morgana had been in deep conversation, but now he looked at him and said, 'Are you ready to hear what we are to do?'

'I'm ready,' replied Robert.

Shortly afterwards the two men left Madam Morgana's having agreed the details of the hand fasting ceremony, both of them with their own certainties and doubts, but both driven and determined that their path ahead lay together.

Dreamland

Madam Morgana had lied.

She could see the future and as soon as she met the two men she had had a sense of what they were about, had an inkling of what lay ahead for them and felt it best to remain tight lipped. So she lied, pretending that her fortune telling was only a cheap gimmick.

As she slept that night she entered a dream space more vivid than she had ever encountered before. In it she learned much about Robert and Charlie, she learned what had been before and more about what was to come. She could see great paths and patterns of destiny mapped out like glowing lines of lights before her eyes. She could see much of what was written, of what was pre-destined and of what was fixed. She also saw that there were those whose own paths were heavily intertwined with the two men's. She saw that often like herself, they were trying to do good, although there had been a terrible evil but it had been dealt with.

What disturbed her, and made her toss and turn and at one point cry out, was when she began to understand that all the actions people took in this story had a cause and effect. She had a picture in her head of the powerful winter waves tearing at the English coastline. Sometimes part of it would crumble and would then be carried along in powerful currents only to be deposited miles away to form a new bit of young land. Sometimes mankind would try and interfere with that natural process and build sea defences. Sure this stopped a cliff crumbling in one place, but it also stopped a new piece of land growing somewhere else.

It was like that with Robert and Charlie's lives; people with their best intentions carrying out a set of actions that they thought were in the men's best interests, but not understanding that every action has an effect.

Madam Morgana's dream now turned back to the vision of the radiant interwoven lines of destiny; these were now tangled into a complex knot and she could no longer see which was fate and which was the result of something someone had done.

In her dream she sensed something else as well. She could see aspects of the couple's lives like layers of an onion. She had seen many of the layers, she had understood what each different level of skin meant, but now she was frustrated. There was a layer of onion skin so thick that she was unable to penetrate it. It was resistant to her and however much she picked at it she could not see what lay below. What she did sense was that a further, deeper, amazing and wonderful level of meaning lay beneath the men's lives, but she could see no more than that. Her powers had found their limit.

★ ★ ★

Chapter Eight: The Glass Isle

Charlie and Robert came to Glastonbury in the morning. There were heavy summer mists swirling across the Somerset levels and as they drove towards the little town they could see the cone shaped Tor sticking its head up like an island in a milky sea. Indeed many centuries before, Glastonbury had been an island for much of the year when the sea flooded the marshland that surrounded it.

Madam Morgana had explained much about the place to the men. She had told them that some called it Ynis Witrin or the Glass Isle and that some called it Avalon, but whatever you called it, it was the beating spiritual heart of England. She had explained gently to Robert that it didn't matter what your faith was, but here you would feel deeply in touch with it and also with that of others. She had told them how, in the times of the Old Religion, Glastonbury had been sacred and that Druids and priestesses had worshipped among the apple trees on her slopes. She explained that many believe that this is where King Arthur was taken after his death and that the site of his grave could still be seen. Most importantly for Robert she told him of the Christian significance and that many people believe that Christ came there to be educated by the Druids. They also believe that later, after the crucifixion, Joseph of Arimathea brought the Holy Grail back to Glastonbury and hid it there. She explained that as well as all those layers of belief, Glastonbury was a centre of pure massive spiritual energy. She compared it to a radio transmitter sending out huge currents of magical and spiritual power across England.

The men soon found the guesthouse at the foot of the Tor which they had booked by phone the day before. A middle-aged woman, still embracing the hippie culture she'd found in the 60's, greeted them. She wore a long flowing Indian skirt and a cheesecloth blouse. Pink Floyd was playing in the background. She was cheerful and welcoming and showed them to their sparse room that had a large window with a view up the slopes of the magical hill.

'Are you two here for a holiday or have you come to find out about Glastonbury's mysteries?' the woman politely enquired.

Charlie somehow felt that he could trust her. 'No, it's something much more amazing than that, we have come to have a hand fasting ceremony on the Tor.'

Robert went bright red and started coughing to cover up his embarrassment. Seeing this, the woman smiled, 'How wonderful. All are welcome here and I know that your relationship will be celebrated in the eyes of the Goddess and the universe. I know you are often treated harshly by society but in my home you are welcome and I will come and celebrate your union on the Tor with you if I may.'

Robert was reassured and thanked the woman. 'I'm sorry if I appeared rude, I always expect people to want to say terrible things when they hear of the nature of our love. It is so refreshing to hear you talk like this. Please, yes come to the ceremony.'

'I shall, and I shall bring you a gift. Now I shall leave you. Blessed be,' and she left the room.

Robert and Charlie unpacked their bags; they had only put in a few things for their short stay. They lay on the bed in their underwear wanting to rest after their long drive from London.

'I still feel as if this is some strange dream Charlie, I really have never experienced anything quite like this. But you know what, it feels right. I feel that there is only good at play here. Madam Morgana convinced me of that. Now hearing our host being so welcoming makes me feel even better.'

'That's good, I'm glad you're feeling more comfortable. What do you think she will give us for a wedding present?'

'Goodness knows. She does seem to have some odd taste. What is that outfit she's wearing?'

'It's because she is an old hippie, that's what they used to wear.'

'What's a hippie?'

Charlie laughed and then gently explained the explosion that started in America in the 60's to an intrigued Robert.

After they had rested for an hour they went to explore the town. The ceremony was not until the evening so they would have plenty of time for sightseeing and relaxing. They had lunch in a cafe and then walked through the abbey grounds with its beautiful swards of green grass framing the ruins of the long destroyed building.

Not long afterwards Charlie looked at his watch and said, 'I think we need to be getting ready don't you?' Robert agreed and they returned to the guesthouse where they showered and dressed. There had been a long debate about what they should wear. Charlie had called Madam Morgana for advice; she'd said, 'Wear what you are comfortable in, what you feel sexy in.' So they did. They decided that they should dress very casually, it seemed right for the type of ceremony. They both put on the new jeans they'd bought for the occasion and simple white t-shirts.

Both of them were now feeling very nervous and Robert had become rather quiet. Charlie, being his normal insecure self, asked, 'What's wrong, have you changed your mind?'

'Charlie for once can you have a bit of trust in me. Do you realise what a leap of faith I have had to make to undertake the act that we are about to do? It is massive for me. But I am able to do that because I know that you love me so much. Can you now, finally trust me too?'

'I'm sorry, yes of course and by the way you look gorgeous.'

Robert smiled, 'So do you. Come on mister or we'll be late.' He slapped Charlie's bottom and they left the bedroom together, laughing.

Together they walked down the street towards the place where the first part of the ceremony would be held. This was where they would meet Madam Morgana as she was to guide them through the stages of the ritual. Shortly they arrived at the entrance to Chalice Well garden. Morgana had explained that this was one of the sacred sites in Glastonbury for both pagans and Christians. She told them of the stories that her namesake, Morgana-le-Fay, used the well as her magic mirror, but also of the story that Joseph of Arimathea had deposited the Holy Grail there when he came back to Glastonbury.

Madam Morgana was at the entrance and she embraced the two men. Today she was dressed in a flowing white robe, exactly the same shape as the flowing black robe when she had first met them. 'Welcome, welcome to Chalice Well. Are you ready for your purification?'

'Yes we are ready,' said Charlie, 'but I must be honest that I know little of what this means and what we are to do.'

'Don't worry yourself my child,' assured Madam Morgana, 'I will guide you through everything that has to be done. Are you ready?' Charlie and Robert both nodded their heads, but still looked a little nervous. 'Come on, follow me,' encouraged Madam Morgana. 'I will explain to you again what the meaning of purification is.'

The two men walked up the little winding path that weaves itself through the English garden that surrounds the well. Charlie thought that it was the most beautiful place he had ever seen. It was so quiet and peaceful. In one corner a long haired man sat on the grass gently tapping a big flat drum covered with what looked like animal skin. The drumming only accentuated the peace and quiet. The men said nothing whilst Madam Morgana explained again the nature and meaning of the purification ceremony. They were to come here, to this sacred well and in a symbolic act would take of some of the waters. Those waters, which had once held the most precious relic of Christianity, would help to cleanse the men, purify them and prepare them mentally and spiritually for the final act of union.

They reached the well head which was covered with a big circular wooden lid with an ornate metal decoration. 'This is the most sacred spot, in the most sacred town in all of England, Charlie and Robert. The symbol on the well head is the Vescia Pisces which is an ancient symbol, the two interlocking circles represent the blending of the masculine and feminine principle. Come, rest by the wellhead and contemplate.'

They sat there, in silence for half an hour. Both of them in deep thought about their lives and the various things that held them back and troubled them. Charlie thought much about his pursuit of love and realised that although he had loved he had never been prepared to commit himself to anyone. He understood that it would take that act of commitment before he could feel fully loved himself.

Chalice Well was working its magic on Robert too and he was having moments of massive clarity and understanding. He now saw that many of the values he had been brought up with were good ones in the way he had been educated to care for and respect others. He also realised he could differentiate these from the things that had been taught to him which were wrong. The hatred of anyone of a different colour, of his sexuality or anyone who was slightly different at all, he now knew this teaching was wrong.

Eventually Madam Morgana said gently, 'I think you have reflected enough my two brave souls, now let's go and cleanse you.' The three walked down the path amongst the flowers to where the waters of the well spilled out into a little channel. 'Now take the waters, let them wash your fears away,' she instructed.

They both knelt down and cupped water in their hands and drank. The sides of the channel were stained red and the water had a heavy metallic taste. It was very cold and very good and both men felt that they were drinking liquid light. They stepped back from the channel and sat down on one of the little stone seats by the water and felt the magical liquid start to flow through their veins. It was like they were being washed from inside, it was as if every negative thought, every problem, every moment of guilt, every negative thing they had ever been told was being washed away.

When they had sat by the wellhead, all they had been through in their lives before and since they had met came bubbling up in their minds, just as the well bubbles up from under the Tor. Now all that was being washed away. Both of the men felt a wonderful sense of calm and happiness flood through them. They were more privileged than many people would ever be, so much was being cleansed, much was being removed, all that was wrong and troubled was being taken from their souls. It was like they were regaining the innocence of childhood again while keeping the wisdom of grown men.

After what seemed like a long time Madam Morgana spoke. 'You're done here. Are you ready for the next stage of your journey together?'

It was Robert who replied, 'I thank you for the act that you have performed here, I've never in my life felt so happy. Today I feel at peace. Thank you and yes I am ready. All my doubts and concerns are gone. Yes I am ready for the ceremony that lies ahead.'

'I am too,' agreed Charlie. 'I too have never been at peace; I am now. Thank you Madam Morgana.'

'Good, that is as it should be. Now are you ready to climb the Tor?'

It was a hot day, and the men knew that the climb up the steep sides of the hill would be quite arduous, particularly for Robert who still had a slight limp, but they knew that this was an important part of the journey. They walked up the lane with Madam Morgana, the three in silence, pondering the enormity of what they were about to do. The narrow road was lined with hedgerows and as they brushed past the group would catch the fragrance of the wild flowers that grew there. Bumblebees dashed around busily heavy with pollen from their day's work.

As suspected the walk up the steep Tor was tiring. Although it was now early evening it was still very hot and by end of their 10 minute climb they were sweating and out of breath. But it was worth it. Neither man had been on the Tor before and the sense of awe at arriving at the top was exhilarating as they saw Somerset spread out below and the Bristol Channel glinting in the distance. Robert remembered his recurring dream and was amazed.

There was a small group of people sitting on the grass and Morgana beckoned the men towards them. 'Here are my friends who will help us to celebrate your bonding.' The group, which consisted of six men and six women, welcomed Charlie, Robert and Madam Morgana warmly.

'Welcome brothers,' said one bearded man. 'We are so honoured to be at your hand fasting.'

'Thank you,' replied Charlie, 'we are honoured to be here in this amazing place.'

'Shall we begin?' said Morgana. 'Are we all ready?'

Just as she did another woman walked over to the group. It was the landlady from the bed and breakfast, now dressed in a long orange robe. She was carrying a bundle in her arms. Clearly Madam Morgana knew the woman as she smiled and said, 'Hello Willow, we're so pleased you can join us.'

'So am I and I have a gift for Charlie and Robert.' At that she showed them what she had in her arms; it was garlands made from the wild leaves and flowers from the hedgerows. 'Come, let's prepare them.'

Willow went over and gestured to the men to remove their t-shirts. When they'd done so she draped the garlands over their naked torsos and around their heads, like crowns.

'Thank you Willow, we are deeply touched, what a wonderful gift,' said Charlie when she was finished. He realised the very special nature of her present. He felt now that they had been dressed for the ceremony. They kissed her on the cheek and she blushed slightly.

Madam Morgana raised her voice. 'Now let us cast a circle of power around Charlie and Robert.' At that, four of the guests went to the edges of a rough circle around the men. Morgana told them they were at the cardinal points: East, South, West and North. They then proceeded to ask the spirits of each point to be present at the circle.

Things were becoming a blur for the couple; the men had never experienced anything like this before. The group was chanting and singing unfamiliar songs but although the men knew little of the ritual they felt safe and loved at the heart of the circle. They heard the group singing about the Goddess and the green earth and much more; they knew little of its meaning but it gave them an inner energy and elated them as it prepared them for their union.

Eventually the chanting stopped and the men felt heady and excited with anticipation of what was to come next. Madam Morgana spoke again. 'Brothers and sisters, we have come here today to celebrate the union of Charlie and Robert. They have been on long journeys to get to this point. They have faced trials and obstacles but their love has finally brought them here and now they are ready for the hand fasting. They have been purified and their souls are ready to make this huge change and to become as one.'

She turned to the men: 'Charlie and Robert, are you now prepared to make the ultimate commitment, to put aside all others and join in a union which is so wonderful that your love will keep you together for all time?'

They both replied, 'We are.' At that Madam Morgana gestured to one of the women who immediately brought over a length of thin red rope. She took Charlie's and then Robert's hand and loosely wound the rope around each of them to bind them together.

'Charlie and Robert, in the eyes of the Great Goddess and the Great God, in the eyes of the universe itself, in the eyes of everything that has been and will be, you are now as one and will be for the remainder of your lives on this earth and for all time. So mote it be.' At that a huge cheer went up and there was much kissing and hugging. After a few minutes Madam Morgana hushed the crowds with a theatrical wave of her arms. 'Now we must celebrate, bring the wine over, let us drink.'

A couple of the group opened the bottles of wine and mead and passed around big ceramic beakers. There was more chanting and singing and gradually over the next couple of hours the group got merrier and merrier and laughed and talked about the new couple's happiness until eventually Madam Morgana spoke again.

'Hush, hush Charlie and Robert, there is something else that you must do. You must make love, in the view of the God and Goddess on top of this special magical hill. For to the God and Goddess sex is sacred and in their honour.' In spite of everything that had happened Robert blushed deeply.

The magic circle was now closed with one of the group at each of the four cardinal points thanking the spirits of East, South, West and North for having been present and at that the group started to break up and drift away, each kissing Charlie and Robert and wishing them well before they went. The last to go was Madam Morgana who said, 'Remember what you must do, my dears. Mind you, I don't expect you will need any encouragement!'

'Madam Morgana, I don't know how to begin to thank you,' replied Charlie with tears in his eyes. They both hugged and kissed the little woman and she walked off down the steep hill.

It was now totally dark, the sky was cloudless and a billion stars twinkled in the dark canopy. They had sleeping bags, blankets and refreshments that the group had left for them and they were ready for their night together. 'I'm not sure what we have just done Charlie, but I think it is something amazing and special that I have never done before. My love for you is sealed and completed and tonight I don't think there is a happier man on the planet.'

'If there is a happier man on the planet it is me,' said Charlie, for the first time in his life secure in the love of another. 'Let's make love under the stars and seal our union in the way we've been told to.' This was to be an act like neither of them had ever experienced before. It was wild yet tender, sometimes animal but always affectionate and the two felt that the very universe was powering their sacred love-making on this very special, magical and spiritual night.

Eventually after some hours they came together in an enormous orgasm, a wave of physical and emotional love; they felt complete and at one with each other. Then they were tired and they slept under the majestic canopy of stars, holding each other with huge waves of love and happiness pouring through them. They had shed every last vestige of their old selves, been bonded in a sacred union and had now consummated that act in the eyes of the Gods.

Dreamland

People dream, animals sometimes dream, trees dream. What not everyone knows is that the universe dreams as well. Sometimes these are big sweeping dreams with super novas, black holes and solar systems forming and collapsing and sometimes the dreams are of the ordinary stories of the infinite life forms that populate it.

On this special day Charlie and Robert had thrown away their old existence and come into a sacred union with each other. They had chosen to do so at an energy point that would radiate the love and happiness of the pair across the stars like an enormous transmitter. How could the universe not be aware of something so majestic, so wonderful, so beautiful that was being announced in such a way. Madam Morgana thought she had selected the site for the hand fasting well, but what she didn't realise was that like others who were acting out of good intentions, she too knew nothing of the cause and effect of her actions. When she had dreamed of the tangled webs of fate, she never saw that this message of love radiating across the stars was an amazing way to bond the two, but was also bringing attention to something that was best left unseen.

The universe celebrated their love and when it dreamed, it dreamed of the pair and dreamed of the wonderful life that the two would have together. Then suddenly there was a disturbance, something that was not quite right, and something that did not seem to fit. It was not that the universe was judging the relationship, far from it, for any love, any act of love between any two beings was sacred, but there was something wrong. It felt like an itch, or like when one piece of a jig-saw puzzle has been put in the wrong place and needs to be moved to complete the picture. Finally it realised what was awry and could see that actually according to its own natural laws of time and balance the two men should not be together, could not be together, and it was a mistake that they had come together in the first place. The universe was never malicious, never judgemental. It was not capable of being so but it was very precise. Very insistent that its natural laws, checks and balances should be followed at all times. Otherwise chaos would prevail.

★ ★ ★

Chapter Nine: Ordinary Things

After the dizzy heights of Charlie and Robert's amazing bonding on Glastonbury Tor, the next weeks and months were by contrast, very ordinary. They settled into the flat in Kennington, as one, in their sacred partnership, both having left large pieces of what had been their former selves behind. That had been Iris and Madam Morgana's plan, an act so transformational that Charlie would forget his loveless sex marathon and Robert would forget his repression. It had worked.

Now, each day passed steadily and happily and settled into ordinary routine; it was a routine they both loved. Instead of thinking about huge concepts of spiritual transformation they were now able to concentrate on the everyday things that make two people happy, making a home together, having friends together, living and laughing together.

They had discussed at length and then agreed what they would tell Charlie's friends about Robert. There was no way that they would share the truth with them. Charlie knew that he would get facetious comments about 'One too many E's love?' from various people and really couldn't handle it so they decided to concoct a cover story. This said that Robert had been in the RAF but had to run away when it was found out he was gay. He'd lived abroad for a couple of years and then came back to England under an assumed name. Of course they all believed it. Why wouldn't they and Charlie's gay friends got very overexcited about the concept of a man in uniform. Of course most of them fancied Robert so it was all a big gay fantasy for them.

The first person who Charlie introduced Robert to was Olga. He had hesitated a little as he correctly thought that Robert would never have knowingly encountered a transvestite before. Charlie talked to him about it before the meeting and Robert was charming and flirtatious with her. Charlie was proud of him. Yes, Robert really had changed. Olga giggled and went red when he kissed her farewell and called Charlie the next day saying to him, 'Oh my goodness dear, he is so delicious, I think I may get him to run away with me, I'm sure I could make him *very* happy.' For once Charlie wasn't jealous and was pleased with her appreciation of his man.

What he didn't know was that whilst he had been out of the room Olga had said to Robert, 'Darling, you will look after him won't you, he has not always had the easiest time. He is quite fragile. You seem to be just what he is looking for, you seem so, so solid.' Robert blushed slightly as he noticed that Olga inadvertently dropped her eyes to his crotch as she said 'solid'.

'Olga, I can see you care about Charlie a great deal, I think he is very fortunate to have a friend like you. I will do everything in my power to look after him, care for him and love him. If I don't, I suspect I will be answerable to you!'

She laughed, 'Yes darling you will be and you know that Aunty Olga could floor you with a punch if she wanted to don't you?' But she said it with a smile and both of them laughed. They knew that there would be no need for her to defend Charlie.

So here we find Robert and Charlie on a hot September night in Kennington. The windows of the flat have been flung open as it is humid and the noise of the traffic and sirens, which is the constant background symphony to London, pours through. Charlie sits on the floor between Robert's legs who is stroking his hair tenderly. They have just finished their meal and are enjoying chatting about the events of the week. The night before they'd been to a dinner party arranged in the new couple's honour by Charlie's old friend, the hooker, Elizabeth Hodgson. The evening was a great success and the guests were enthralled by Robert's untrue story about running away from the RAF.

They chat about the dinner now, about the extravagant food and the eclectic guest list. Elizabeth had excelled herself as ever. Business was rather good at the moment. She had confided in Charlie that she had a new client who was a very highly placed Conservative minister but refused to be drawn on who he was. She had therefore arranged for caterers and staff at her latest Mayfair apartment and the group of ten guests toasted the couple with

Bollinger champagne, paired with Beluga caviar, before tackling a six-course gourmet meal.

'It was a great evening Charlie, one thing though, I didn't know if you noticed, but when we arrived Elizabeth gave me such an odd look. First of all I thought she didn't like me or approve of me for some reason and then she said, "Do I know you dear, you look a little familiar?"

'I replied, "I'm sure I have not had that pleasure." She then said, "Please excuse me, you must remind me of someone else. Just for a moment … I thought …" and then she trailed off.'

'Perhaps you were one of her clients,' Charlie jibbed at Robert.

'Now you know that's not very likely don't you, you silly bugger. I don't like women in bed, remember? I'm hardly likely to pay for the pleasure am I, although I have to say she is rather attractive.'

Charlie laughed, 'No, I suppose you're right.'

'How long have we been together now?' Robert asked, knowing full well that Charlie would know the answer.

'Well it's 2 months, 3 days and I think about 22 hours.'

'Well happy 2 months, 3 days and 22 hour anniversary then handsome.' They both started giggling and were soon on the floor in another passionate embrace.

31st October 1989

Charlie put down the phone. He had been talking to Madam Morgana who called frequently to see how the couple were getting on. 'It's amazing, I never thought I'd meet anyone like Robert, he's so kind and loving and so good looking, just like a film star. I never thought someone like that would fancy me.'

'Have you considered Charlie that maybe he never thought someone like you would fancy him?'

'No, that never occurred to me. I never thought much of myself Morgana. I know I should perhaps be more confident.'

'Well Charlie, I think you have finally met the man who will make you more confident. Also remember this dear. Whilst some people find arrogance very sexy, it is not a very loveable quality. I think that one of the reasons that you love each other is that you are both in your own way shy and unconfident.'

'You are very wise Morgana, you've helped us so much.'

'You're welcome Charlie. I'm not sure about wise, but I have lived quite a long time and the Goddess has asked of me that I should be a healer so I try to do her work and help people when they face spiritual troubles.'

'I really don't understand your Goddess,' Charlie replied, 'and I don't really think that I believe in any Gods or Goddesses anyway, but I do know that you are a good woman. That is enough for me.'

'And you are a good man Charlie Rogers. Now, one thing that I want to tell you is that in my faith, today, 31st October it is the festival of Samhain. It is our New Year. In modern times this has been corrupted into your Halloween but to us it is a joyous time, a time of renewal. But also Charlie it is a moment when we can be very close to those who have departed. The veils between this and the next world are at their thinnest. I think you have lost someone special Charlie, I can see it in your eyes. Now is the time to be close to him.'

'I have lost many friends Morgana, AIDS has seen to that, but there was one special friend and although I don't share your faith I will make a point of being close to him tonight. Thank you.'

So it was that in tribute to Michael, Charlie and Robert drove out to the Thames barrier on the night of the pagan new year, the night which Morgana had said was the one on which the dead should be honoured. Charlie thought that this place was most fitting as this was where he and Olga had committed Michael's ashes to the Thames three years before.

Robert knew how important Michael had been to Charlie and was happy to drive out to the barrier with him to share the moment. Charlie was quiet all the way as they drove through South London to Greenwich. Robert had never seen the barrier before and was amazed at the huge structure with its strange futuristic looking pods rising out of the river. They had brought candles with them and they sat on a derelict wharf by the Thames with their legs dangling over the edge. The candles were now lit and flickered in the jars they'd brought to protect them from the autumn wind.

For a while they said little, content to feel the moment and watch the ships nosing through the gates of the massive flood barrier.

'He was such an amazing man Robert; he saved me several times from terrible fates. When I first ran away to London when I was 15 he rescued me from the clutches of someone who would have made me become a rent boy. I can't think how different my story would have been if he hadn't. These were wonderful things Robert, wonderful things he did for me, but what I loved about him too was his humour. Who else could have come up with the story of the Moors Sisters?'

'The who sisters?' Charlie spent the next 10 minutes explaining about the Moors Sisters and at the end of the story Robert understood a little about Michael's mad sense of humour.

'Why do we have to lose people Robert? It seems just so unfair. I loved him so much. Not like I love you of course, it was a different love. Why did he have to go?'

'Well Charlie, I can't answer that and I suspect that there is no answer, it is a random act of fate but reflect on this. Part of what makes you what you are is the time you spent with Michael. You should feel blessed and happy for that. He clearly was a wonderful man.'

'He was. To lose a friend like that leaves a most awful gap. I can't begin to tell you how it feels.'

'Well that's sometimes the flip side of loving Charlie, when we love we have to accept that one day we'll ultimately lose that person, it's part of life, but would we give up having any of the people that we love in our lives? No of course not.'

'To accept love is to also understand that there has to be great loss, we have to be able to feel pain as well as joy; if we did not feel the pain we would feel nothing.'

'I'm not going to lose you Robert, am I? I couldn't bear the thought. I want us to be together until we're 95 years old.'

'I'm sure we will be. I'm not intending to go anywhere anytime soon.'

'Good, having found you, I finally feel complete and happy.' And Charlie leaned over and kissed him on the ear.

The pair were silent for a few minutes. 'You know what, if Madame Morgana is right about this being the night when we can be close to those who have gone, I wish Michael would give me a sign. I wish I could see his ghost or something, I really do. I think it would help me to believe that there is something else after we die. I really struggle with the thought.'

At that very moment there was a sudden strong wind, which in spite of the jars, reached inside the containers and blew out the candles. At the same time there was a massive roaring thud as a clap of thunder broke overhead and almost immediately big, heavy blobs of rain began to fall on the pair.

'Okay Michael, I get the point,' laughed Charlie. 'I think you're trying to tell me you're there aren't you?' And they both laughed and ran for the cover of the car.

On the drive back to Kennington Charlie started, 'By the way, did I ever tell you that we saw the musical Evita 35 times and that Michael wanted to have tea with Eva Peron?'

'Who's Eva Peron?' replied Robert.

'I can see I'm going to have to give you another history lesson,' Charlie laughed.

25th December 1989

'Happy Christmas,' beamed Olga as she opened the door of her house, a huge Georgian property overlooking Blackheath in south London. Olga had settled down with a man a couple of years before and it transpired that he was very, very wealthy. She hadn't been attracted to him for his money; he was very discreet about his wealth and she was already in love before she saw his bank balance. She had met him when she was working in a drag cabaret in Vauxhall. They had dated for a while and just gelled. She fell in love and gradually found out that he was a multi-millionaire. He had made his money from scrap metal. They couldn't marry as Olga was still technically a man and would always legally be a man, but they looked and acted like a married couple. She had never been able to enjoy expensive clothes or have a nice home and had scrimped all her life, but now in her 50's she was finally dressing elegantly and was sporting a large emerald ring. She had found the man of her dreams.

George, her partner, had never been gay or interested in cross dressing and had previously been married to someone called Jean, a ferocious, weasel-like woman who had given him 30 years of mental hell. Jean, much to George's relief, had finally run off with someone who had more money than him.

He'd been reluctantly taken to a pub in Vauxhall one night by a friend and he met Olga over a gin and tonic at the bar. He immediately knew what Olga was about but didn't care. For whatever reason, it was love at first sight. It was probably that he looked into Olga's eyes and saw the goodness within her.

Now, George and Jean had two children and one of them, Andrew, never spoke to his father again after first meeting Olga. He had left the house spitting venom and snarling, 'I bet that pervert is just after your money, just you wait and see. I will see a solicitor about this. I will make damn sure she, I mean *It* doesn't get a fucking penny out of you.' George had said nothing and promptly saw his own solicitor the following day and wrote Andrew out of his will.

His daughter Felicity was initially taken aback at her new step mother but then saw how much her father loved Olga and how much that love was returned. She gradually came to appreciate her goodness and decency and understood that this was what her father had fallen in love with.

Most of the neighbours in Blackheath cut George off socially and would not speak to him and he was barred from the golf club. He didn't care a hoot, it was never really his thing anyway. For the first time in his life he had a partner who didn't whine at him all the time and clearly adored him. He was in heaven. He had to be open minded and flexible about sex but actually he had found it all rather enjoyable.

So on Christmas Day 1989 we find George and Olga, Robert and Charlie and George's daughter Felicity enjoying a very traditional family Christmas. Felicity was recently divorced but had brought her two young children, Jane and Tom, to the celebration. They adored Olga who clucked around them like a mother hen and was always showering them with presents.

Olga had made an extravagant and huge turkey lunch with all the trimmings. She was an accomplished cook and the group hungrily attacked the succulent bird and its accompaniments followed by the most luscious, richest Christmas pudding that anyone had ever tasted. Towards the end of the meal George stood up and said, 'I have something to say.'

'Oh gawd it's not a toast to the Queen or us queens is it?' laughed Olga.

'No Olga, it isn't, but I've something very important to tell you all. Jane and Tom would you go and play in the drawing room please.'

Olga now stopped laughing and looked rather concerned; what was her partner going to say, was it bad news? As if he had heard her fears he leaned over and squeezed her hand. 'Don't worry my love it's nothing bad.' Then he continued, 'I'm sure that some of you must know that I am a man from a very conventional background. I was brought up by religious parents in Bexleyheath and thought that everyone would be married and have children. That was the way of things. I was also brought up to be prejudiced and to believe that anyone different was wrong or evil. Now, I have something to get off my chest. To tell you of something very bad I did a long time ago.'

The entire group sat wide-eyed waiting for whatever was to come next.

There was a deathly silence. 'When I was 16 I was knocking around with a group of boys from school. One night, we took the train up to London. We'd been drinking. One of the boys had stolen a bottle of wine from his father's cellar. We found our way to Soho; we knew what we were going to do. We went and stood outside a bar where gay men met. There were a few bars like that even in those days and after we had been there for about 15 minutes one of the men came out alone. We followed him and beat him up.

'I remember hitting him and kicking him so hard. I wanted to kill him for what he was. I remember so vividly his pleading eyes looking up to me from the pavement seeming to ask the question, "why?"'

Olga was tearful and started to get up from the table. 'I'm not sure I can listen to this George,' she quivered.

'Please hear me out Olga,' and he gently encouraged her to sit down again.

'I know now how deeply wrong that act was. I can never forgive myself for it and shall make no excuses. I'm not sure that there can be any atonement for it; however what I am going to do is this. As I have now written Andrew out of my will, the money that would have one day been his I am going to use to set up a refuge for gay men, women and transsexuals in Soho. Somewhere to go if they are young and have run away from home or are troubled in any way. They will shortly be getting a cheque for two million pounds. I know I can't ever change what I did, but I want you to know how sorry I am. Having met Olga and then all of you, I have learned how wrong prejudice is and how human life benefits from different characters and types of people. I have also learned that we must only ever judge people for what their actions are, not what the colour of their skin is or who they choose to have relationships with.'

There was now not a dry eye around the table. Finally it was Olga who spoke. 'George, I cannot begin to understand what you did, and I'm not sure it should be forgiven, but I do know this. To grow up without prejudice is an amazing thing and one that should be applauded. To be taught to be prejudiced but to then learn through your life that it is wrong and to be prepared to let your conditioning go, well, I think that's an even more amazing thing. To forget how you've been programmed and learn that there is a better way. Now that takes a very big man to do that.' Olga stood up and embraced George and kissed him.

This raised a huge round of applause and Olga gave George a further big hug and kiss. 'Come on, let's have presents now,' beamed Olga; clearly she wanted to lighten the moment. She called the children in and went over to the huge spruce Christmas tree dripping with gold decorations and at least 10 feet tall, reached down and started retrieving the various presents, which she had carefully wrapped and left beneath its branches. Each of the group, in turn opened their immaculately wrapped gift.

Firstly the children, a new Barbie for Jane and an Action Man for Tom. Next Felicity loved the silk Liberty scarf that Olga had picked out for her. George got a set of books on English song birds, one of his passions. Lastly, Charlie and Robert were left to unwrap their gifts. Charlie could hardly hold back the tears as he saw that his present was another teddy for his collection. He still loved his teddies.

'I really didn't know what to get you Robert,' said Olga. 'I don't know much about what you like but as you used to be in the RAF I thought you might like the book I picked out.' Robert tore away the glittered paper from the gift. It was a large hardback book. On the front was a big picture of a World War II Spitfire. The book was titled:

'The Battle of Britain. The Story of the Few'

Robert was not generally an emotional man but could feel tears welling up behind his eyes. He blinked them back not wishing to cry in front of everyone.

'Olga you are a remarkable woman. You have absolutely no idea how perfect this gift is. You really don't.'

He went over and gave her a big hug and kiss.

'Well dear, the other reason that I bought it, is when I looked at the picture on the front cover I noticed that one of the group of pilots standing around the Spitfire looks just like you.' Robert said nothing, but glanced down again to the picture. Charlie had heard what Olga said and looked at him with the obvious question in his eyes. Robert just nodded his head and smiled.

'Come on, carols,' said George and he led the group to the piano where they sang 'Hark the Herald Angels Sing' rather badly due to having drunk a lot. Charlie looked over at Robert. 'I don't think I could have wished for a more perfect first Christmas with you.'

Robert smiled and blew Charlie a kiss. 'Love you,' he mouthed.

★ ★ ★

Chapter Ten: Dinner at Mario's

25th January 1990

Since Christmas Charlie and Robert had started to work on their plans to open a gay bed and breakfast in Brighton. They knew it was going to be difficult for Robert to work and this seemed like the ideal plan. 'You are legally 75 years old you know, you should be retired,' Charlie would joke with him. They made a few trips down to Brighton to look at properties and were excited at making these plans for their future together. It was decided they'd sell the house in Dulwich to fund the project but keep the Kennington flat so they had a London base when needed. They'd driven down to Brighton again the day before and now had a couple of likely properties lined up. It all now depended on selling the house quickly.

'It's going to be so wonderful Robert, working and living with you.'

'You might get on my nerves,' laughed Robert. Before Charlie could reply the phone rang. It was Iris calling from New York.

'Charlie, how are you?'

'I'm very well Iris, very happy and still madly in love.'

'I'm very pleased to hear it. Are you still in Kennington with Robert?'

'Yes, we prefer to be in the centre of town and the Dulwich house really is so decrepit.'

'Oh that's good dear.'

The rest of the conversation was taken up with Iris enthusing about Maurice, her new French boyfriend. 'Such wonderful strong arms dear.'

'Glad you're having fun Iris.'

'I am. Must go, the bill will be enormous. Love you.'

'Love you too,' replied Charlie and put the phone down.

'God my aunt is unstoppable, yet another toy boy,' and Charlie went on to tell Robert about Iris's latest conquest. Just as he finished, the phone rang again. It was Elizabeth. 'Charlie how are you darling?'

'All the better for hearing you,' he replied.

'How do you and Robert fancy trying this Italian restaurant I've discovered? It's called Mario's and it's near Crystal Palace. It's run by one of my clients, would you like to go tonight?'

Charlie put his hand over the mouthpiece and mouthed to Robert, 'Dinner: Elizabeth: tonight?' Robert nodded his head enthusiastically. 'That would be charming Elizabeth.'

'I'll pick you up at seven then dears.'

The pair both got themselves showered and smartened up. Elizabeth was one of those people who you always looked your best for. She picked them up as planned and drove them off into south London to her favourite Italian restaurant. The owner, Mario, was clearly fond of her and made a great fuss of the group including offering a number of complimentary drinks. They talked a lot at dinner about Robert and Charlie's plans and how they were going to set up the business together.

'One thing that worries me Charlie,' Elizabeth cut in, 'I've never seen you as someone who does hard physical work, are you really going to make all those beds and clean all those bathrooms? I am rather struggling with the thought.'

'Don't be silly, you know I have quite a lot of money already, so the project will be well funded. Do you really think I'm going to do the cleaning? No we'll have staff.'

'I have to say that is a great relief to me,' replied Elizabeth. 'You barely know one end of a vacuum cleaner from the other.'

'Don't be so rude, I'm not that bad,' and the group all laughed.

The dinner was completed by tiramisus followed by coffee and amarettos. Elizabeth paid the bill with her American Express card; she had always treated Charlie when they went out. The pair protested politely.

'I insist dears, I'm flush with cash at the moment. My government minister is so generous. My goodness he is such a dreary man, but get this. I never have to have sex with him. His particular fetish is that he gets dressed up in a maid's outfit, you know, black dress,

211

apron, feather duster, and I have to give him commands to clean my flat. For me dears it's a win-win situation, he pays me a thousand pounds for the privilege and my flat is immaculate.'

'I do wish you would tell us who he is,' pleaded Charlie.

'Now that is asking too much. All I will say is he is very famous and one of Mrs Thatcher's right hand men.'

'Oh you are such a tease,' Charlie replied, disappointed that he wasn't going to get this bit of tittle-tattle.

By the time they left both Elizabeth and Charlie were a little tipsy. Only Robert was sober as he had agreed to drive back. He thought it best not to mention that his driving licence was probably a little out of date.

'That was lovely Elizabeth, thank you and what wonderful food.'

'Yes it's rather a find isn't it? Mario is so crap in bed dear but by goodness does he run a good restaurant.' They all laughed.

'Why is he so crap in bed?' asked Robert.

'Let's just say dear that his intentions and generosity are bigger than his cock.' Robert and Charlie laughed loudly again.

She went on, 'Oh by the way Charlie, you mentioned you might sell your house in Dulwich. I've been thinking of moving out here when I retire. I wonder, as we are so close by, could we take a look?'

'Yes of course, it's just down the road from here. Robert, can we make a quick detour via Hurst Court Road?'

Shortly they arrived at the house and they got out of the car and walked up the path. It was somewhat overgrown with weeds and Charlie felt embarrassed that Elizabeth was going to see the state of the place.

'Hang on a moment,' said Elizabeth, 'I've left my bag in the car. I won't be a minute,' and she went back down the path to the car to retrieve it.

Charlie had his keys in the front door and continued to open it and he and Robert entered the dingy hall. They hadn't been there for some weeks and they stepped through a deep pile of junk mail. Charlie flicked on the light and the hall was lit up from the rather grubby floral lampshade that hung over their heads. 'I'm just going up to the bedroom, I think I left the t-shirt you bought me up there Charlie,' and at that Robert headed upstairs.

He shouted down, 'I can't find it, can you remember where …'

Roberts's words were abruptly cut off and at the same moment the hall was plunged into darkness. Almost immediately there was a bone crunching, ear splitting roar, like a double thunderclap. The noise was huge and overwhelming. Then a split second later a massive roaring whoosh, like an express train letting off steam. Charlie tried to shout Robert's name but the noise was so loud that it was lost in the terrible cacophony.

It all happened in seconds but to Charlie it was like a slow motion film. He knew that sound, that feeling, It was the same he had experienced when Robert was delivered to him from 1944. 'Robert! Robert! Robert!' He ran upstairs and into the back bedroom. It was empty. He ran round all the other rooms on the first floor; nothing. Robert was gone.

Charlie ran back downstairs, hysterically shouting Robert's name. The door of the house, which he had left ajar, pushed open and Elizabeth came brightly in, flicking on the light switch. 'Got my bag dear, why were you in the dark?' She saw Charlie crying and looking shocked. Her tone changed immediately to one of concern. 'Charlie dear, what's happened?'

'He's gone, he's just disappeared!' cried Charlie, 'He's been taken away from me Elizabeth. I don't know what to do, please help me. Please.'

Elizabeth was now highly concerned, clearly something bad had happened here. 'Who's gone dear?'

'Robert of course. Robert's gone Elizabeth.'

'Who's Robert dear? A friend of yours who was staying here?'

'Elizabeth! We just had dinner with him.'

'Charlie darling, there wasn't anyone with us at dinner; it was just our own little date.'

Charlie's cries of anguish now reached a new peak and Elizabeth rushed over and cradled the broken man's head in her arms.

25th January, 1945

Robert was completely dazed and slowly opened his eyes. With a growing horror he started to notice he was no longer in the 1989 version of his house. The décor that had been so familiar to him in 1944 stared him in the face. The dingy brown woodwork, the blackout curtains at the window. He immediately understood what had happened and screamed and sobbed. With his head buried in his hands he curled up on the bedroom floor.

What Charlie and Robert had no way of knowing was just before they entered the hall of the house, but also 44 years ago, a tall red and white Nazi V2 Rocket was launched from its pad in the Netherlands. After rising up vertically in a huge cloud of exhaust fumes it started its ascent into the stratosphere. A couple of minutes later its short flight was complete and it was nosing towards Dulwich. It plummeted to earth and there was an ear splitting double thunderclap as it broke the sound barrier and then a huge swooshing noise as the sound of the rocket engines followed. It collided with earth a quarter of a mile from Robert's house. Not close enough to damage it badly but the blast wave broke more windows and took yet more tiles off the roof. Somehow, the blast not only ripped across the south London streets but penetrated through the very fabric of time, opening up the weak spot that Robert had been propelled through only 6 months before, and then sent him back to where he had come from.

Dreamland

On this terrible night it is not surprising that Charlie and Robert had terrible dreams. Elizabeth finally got Charlie home; he had categorically refused to see a doctor and she held him for hours as he ranted on about Robert. She had no idea what he was talking about. Eventually in the small hours she gave him a Valium and a sherry and he was soon knocked out. He shouldn't have been able to dream, the sedative was so strong, but he did dream.

He dreamed repeatedly of the number 80. That old strange nightmare came back. He was scared seeing the number and in his sleep state felt tense and fearful. He then dreamed of Robert, he kept seeing him in the distance, far, far away, sometimes so small he was just a speck on the horizon. He would try and cry out his name and each time he did no sound came out of his mouth.

Once he awoke in the night and reached over instinctively for Robert's comforting arms and then started crying again as all he felt was a cold empty bed. Eventually he found sleep again and was blessed with visiting his happy childhood state where he was a bird soaring in the sky and feeling very, very loved.

A long, long time ago, in the same room, Robert had finally managed to get to sleep. He had found a bottle of malt whisky that his father had bought just before the war and was saving for a special occasion. After half the bottle his mind and flesh were anaesthetised and he fell into semi-consciousness. It was a blessed relief. Even though his brain was fogged with alcohol he dreamed of a time when he had been with a wonderful loving man with blue-green eyes; a time when he had been content and complete, where he had once stood on top of a strange cone shaped hill, deeply in love and looking out to the twinkling river estuary in the distance.

★ ★ ★

Interlude 1948

1: Star Girls

October 1948

Robert's taxi drew up at the entrance of a huge canvas marquee that served as the terminal of the new Heathrow airport. He had to navigate narrow wooden planks across an expanse of muddy grass to get into the entrance. He heard that there were great plans to build a modern terminal but he wondered when that would ever happen. It was freezing cold and he was pleased that he had wrapped up warmly with his thick overcoat and gloves.

He quickly found the British South American Airlines check-in desk. As he approached, a trim, immaculately coiffed girl in a navy-blue uniform beckoned. 'Good morning sir, are you travelling on the flight to Buenos Aires?'

'Yes, good morning, it's Robert Harrison.' The girl quickly scanned her eye down a large sheet of paper on the desk and ticked his name. After having tagged his baggage which was then taken off by porters, she directed him to the waiting area.

'Would you like a tea whilst you wait sir? When your flight is ready for boarding one of our Star Girls will show you to the aircraft.' He walked over to the crude departure area; it looked most unwelcoming with little more than hard wooden chairs. It was cold. He sat alone, drinking the watery tea a tired-looking waitress brought him and got lost in his memories as he so often did.

His thoughts turned to Charlie; there were few times that he wasn't present in Robert's mind. His crude arrival back in 1945 in the wake of the V2 Rocket explosion had ripped the heart and soul out of him. Those 6 months with Charlie, the love, the intimacy, the companionship. So brief, so intense. He had thought that his stay in the future was going to be forever. He had no sense, no foreboding and no fear. He was with Charlie deeply, passionately and wildly in love and nothing else mattered.

Perhaps, if either of them had ever had time to reflect, they might have thought that as they had been blasted together they could be blasted apart again. But they were too in love to think of anything. And actually, it would have been inconceivable for them to think this thought, too dreadful, too frightening. So, Robert and Charlie went through their 6 months together at the eye of the hurricane, where calm prevailed and nothing could touch them, and in massive denial about what might come to be.

'Another tea sir?' the waitress enquired, and from her tone it was clear she was hoping he would refuse.

Robert grimaced at the thought, 'No, one will be enough thank you,' and returned to his recollections.

In the first few days and weeks after his return to 1945 Robert had been shocked and dazed, he didn't understand what had happened, he started to question his own sanity and sometimes he even doubted that Charlie had ever existed. His grief and loss were so enormous that he felt as if a rabid animal had taken a bite out of him. He now understood what the romantics meant by a broken heart.

Weeks turned into months and months turned into years. There would never be another Charlie, probably never another human being that he would love in the same way, and he really didn't know how he would cope, but somehow he did.

In the spring of 1948 he got a very good job with J. Millbank & Kleinstein, a big pharmaceutical company based in Marylebone. He threw himself into the new role wholeheartedly. It was a way of blotting out the inner pain and torment. He spoke of Charlie to no one, how could he?

He made no friends in the office and in the evening would get the train home and spend long periods, staring at the walls, drinking, lost and in mortal pain. His job was his way of functioning; it hid his real self. At work he was efficient and extrovert, he didn't have to talk of emotions or himself, just the product and how to sell it.

It was because of Robert's job that he had the opportunity to make a trip to Argentina and he jumped at the chance. The night that he and Charlie spent talking about Michael at the Thames barrier, Charlie had told him all about Eva Peron and how later Michael became fascinated with her history through the tales of his friend Elizabeth. Eventually Charlie took Robert to see the musical and when they left he laughed, 'Now do you understand why we wanted to have tea with Evita?' The trip to Argentina was something that had to be done; it was an act of completion, a pilgrimage, something that had to be done for Charlie and Michael.

Robert felt a hand on his arm. 'Mr Harrison, we've been calling the flight, you're the last passenger, please hurry.' He was so engrossed in his thoughts that he hadn't heard the Star Girl calling his name over the crackly tannoy system. He followed her out over the tarmac towards the big four-engine aircraft and up the steps into the front entrance. He noticed the name of the aircraft was 'Star Leopard'; it sounded very glamorous.

Robert was tall and he had to bend his head to get into the narrow cabin. He found his seat and he saw that it would recline and turn into a small bed for the night part of his lengthy trip that lay ahead. Soon afterwards the cabin doors were closed. The four Star Girls went up and down the aisle making sure everything was secure in preparation for take-off.

It was dark outside and as the engines started up one by one a big spurt of flame poured from the exhausts, briefly startling Robert who was sitting by the window. After running the various engine and equipment checks the pilot pushed the throttle levers forward and the huge Avro Tudor airliner started to move slowly across the tarmac. Within five minutes it was on the end of the runway and the captain was opening the throttles to full to accelerate the Tudor to take-off speed.

In the cabin Robert noticed how much everything vibrated and the noise from the propellers seemed to beat in waves at the cabin walls. He grimaced realising that this was going to be a long and tiring flight. The aircraft took off over London and Robert took great pleasure in seeing the city he loved spread out before him. The lines of streetlights looked like strings of jewels cut only by the dark ribbon of the Thames through its middle.

Later, after finishing the meagre cold chicken meal, he rang the bell to get the attention of the Star Girl. She came over promptly.

'Yes Mr Harrison, what can I do for you?'

'Could you get me a blanket please?'

'Yes of course sir,' and she came back with it from the wardrobe by the galley a few moments later. Robert gratefully spread the thick woollen blanket out over his knees and thanked the hostess.

She replied, 'You're welcome sir. Is it your first time with us?'

'Yes,' he replied, 'I haven't been to Argentina or South America before.'

'Are you on holiday sir?'

'No, I work for a pharmaceutical company selling new medicines. I'm sure you have heard of President Peron and his wife Eva? Well she has started some kind of charity called the Eva Peron Foundation that's in charge of dispensing welfare to the poor, and they are also responsible for procuring most of the medicines. We're going to try and strike a deal with them to sell them our new antibiotic.'

'I'm not sure I would want to deal with her,' the woman replied a little haughtily. 'You know she went to Spain last year to visit Franco and he's a fascist. I think we've had enough of fascists in Europe don't you?' Robert was fully aware that Eva Peron's reputation was, and would forever be, controversial, so felt it best not to get into a debate.

The Star Girl went on, 'I'm sure she's a very important person in Argentina but I doubt that anyone outside that country will ever hear of her.'

Robert flicked his eyes up to the nametag, which stated boldly in gold letters: 'Elizabeth Hodgson.' For the first time in a long, long while he smiled a broad smile; 30 years in her future this woman would inspire Charlie and Michael to see the musical version of Eva Peron's story time and time again.

You know when you've seen a play or a film several times, or you've read a favourite book on umpteen occasions? You know much of the dialogue and when a character says something you know the line that's coming next. It was like that for Robert now, but instead of a play or a film or a book the lines he knew were about to be spoken were real.

'Now I don't know how but I think you're wrong, one day everyone will know her name all over the world. If you get the chance go and see her speaking from the balcony of the Casa Rosada, the presidential palace. The spectacle is meant to be amazing.'

'I may well follow your suggestion,' Elizabeth Hodgson replied. 'I have a few days layover in Buenos Aires. You have intrigued me.'

Robert said nothing else, knowing he'd said what he needed to. Elizabeth went off and busied herself in the little galley quite bemused by the man's comments but determined to find out what he was talking about.

Shortly, Elizabeth helped prepare her passengers for the long night crossing. Over a day later, having landed to re-fuel twice, the Tudor airliner finally touched down in Buenos Aires. Robert was exhausted. The flight had been draining and he was very pleased to put his feet on terra firma again. As he walked across the tarmac the first things he noticed were two huge billboards, one with the image of Juan Peron and the other of his wife: idealised, thirty feet high Hollywood style images, Peron's hearty smile and Eva's radiance shining down on Argentina's people. The taxi ride to central Buenos Aires took over an hour and along the route Robert would frequently see posters and billboards with the same giant images of Juan and Eva Peron, Eva's red lips pursed in an almost erotic smile. These were interspersed with thousands of Argentinian flags, the dazzling yellow sun radiating down from countless lampposts.

He soon arrived at the very grand looking Alvear Palace hotel. He had been getting increasingly excited on his taxi drive into the city centre. He was struck with the beauty of the city with its wonderful ornate buildings and how bright and cheerful everything looked after grey, war-damaged London.

He could feel a vibrant pulse about the place, and enthusiastically anticipated getting to know Buenos Aires a little. After checking in he was shown up to his suite by a very old-fashioned-looking footman in tails and quickly went to bed. He needed sleep and he wanted to feel refreshed for seeing the city the following day.

The next morning he awoke and had breakfast with two cups of strong coffee. He had never tasted coffee like it; it made the coffee he was used to drinking in England seem like dishwater. Robert wanted to see as much as he could of Buenos Aires so he decided to get a guide for the day. The hotel concierge made a call and he soon found himself in a little black and yellow cab that skilfully negotiated the city's famous traffic.

The taxi driver was called Arturo and was young, maybe 25, and Robert blushed when he saw how attractive he was, dark, swarthy and lithe with flashing dark brown, almost black eyes.

'Where do wish you go Señor?' Arturo enquired.

'Show me the city, show me everything,' said Robert excitedly.

'I'm sure I could show you *many* things.'

Robert blushed again noticing the emphasis that he put on 'many'. 'I think he is flirting with me.'

Arturo proved to be an excellent guide, showing Robert the sights of the buzzing Argentinian capital. They shopped in the Cala Florida and he was intrigued to see a shop maintaining it was a Harrods! He was awestruck at the massive, broad Avenue Neuvo De Julio that dissects the heart of the city, and loved the vibrancy of the place, its people rushing about their busy lives and the huge ornate buildings. Arturo took Robert for lunch at a Parilla Grill off Florida where they ate the best steak Robert had ever had.

During the meal the conversation inevitably turned to Evita. She was the name that was on everyone's lips. He asked Arturo what he thought of her. 'She is wonderful. My mother, she is a widow and she has ten children, I am the oldest and she has had to bring us up alone. She asked Evita for a little help and she gave her a sewing machine so she could mend clothes and earn a few pesos. She is a saint, like the Madonna.' As Arturo spoke of Evita his eyes came alive. Robert could see the love, almost religious fervour, that he felt for the President's wife.

It was so strange to be sitting here, talking to this handsome stranger about Eva Peron, who years in the future would be the subject of a musical he would go and see with the man he loved so much. After lunch they visited the Recoletta cemetery with its ornate tombs where Robert knew that Evita would one day be buried.

As they walked around the empty cemetery together, amongst the huge ornate tombs, silently, enjoying the peace, he felt Arturo's hand brush against his almost imperceptibly and a thrill of sexual arousal shot through him. Arturo gave him a big wink. 'Perhaps I can show you some things more interesting than sightseeing?'

'That would be wonderful,' Robert replied. He surprised himself. He was normally so reserved but this man was very attractive and he felt deeply in need of intimacy. He hoped Charlie would understand, it had been 3 years now, but still a pang of guilt went through him. He then thought to himself with a smile, 'I suppose I must have become a little like Charlie if I can consider doing this.'

Arturo drove Robert to the dingy little apartment that he rented near the Retiro station. After chatting a little he leaned towards Robert and kissed him and they were soon frantically pulling at each other's clothes.

They had sex. Fierce and passionate sex. It was the first time that Robert had been in a man's arms since Charlie and it was good. He knew he would never see the man again but it made him feel just a little bit alive, being kissed, being appreciated, being held.

'Please, you must be very discreet,' Arturo said when they had finished, 'things are not easy for men like us here.'

'I understand.' replied Robert, 'it's much the same in England, you can trust me.'

They had sex again. When they'd finished they lay in bed smoking rough cigarettes with Arturo's head resting on Robert's firm chest. Arturo suddenly jumped up with a cry and grabbed his watch from the bedside table. 'Quick Robert,' Arturo shouted excitedly, 'get dressed, I have something wonderful to show you.'

Robert looked slightly bemused but meekly obeyed. When he had finished dressing he withdrew his wallet from his pocket and handed Arturo a large wodge of peso notes.

'What is this Robert? I cannot accept your money. I did not do this for money, please, you will insult the memory of the day we spent together.'

'Arturo, I know you were not after money, but you've told me of your mother's plight. Please. Accept this so that she can give a little extra to her children. I would be honoured if you let me help.'

Arturo burst into tears, 'I have never known such kindness; I think you are blessed by Santa Evita herself. Thank you so very much.'

'What is it you're going to show me, as if I have not had enough fun today?'

'Tonight Sir, we will see Evita on the balcony of the Casa Rosada.'

★ ★ ★

Interlude 1948

2: Tea with Evita

17th October 1948

Robert and Arturo hurried through the streets of Buenos Aires on foot. The thoroughfares were now too crowded with people eager to see Evita to consider taking the taxi. Hanging from buildings, everywhere the eye could see, there were hundreds and thousands of images of Juan and Eva, interspersed with Argentine flags.

Huge crowds of workers from the docks, factories and slaughterhouses had packed into the city to see their beloved Goddess speaking from her temple. As they got closer and closer to the Plaza De Mayo the crowd got denser. Arturo and Robert were being pushed and shoved from all directions as the crowd frantically surged to get a glimpse of Evita.

Finally, they managed to get into the huge square and they could see ahead of them that every inch was packed with excited people. Robert felt a stab of disappointment, as there didn't seem to be any way they were going to be able to see much.

'Come Robert, I have a friend who can get us a better view.'

Shortly Arturo was knocking on an ornately decorated doorway. It was opened after a few moments and a man, perhaps a little older than Arturo but broader and with a big Roman nose, welcomed him warmly. 'Robert this is my friend Raul.'

The three men climbed up a winding staircase with Art Nouveau metal banisters to the fourth floor. As they did Arturo explained that Raul was the night watchman. One of the offices would have the most spectacular grandstand view of the Casa Rosada. Raul opened a long pair of wooden shutters and Arturo was right. The view was amazing and they could clearly see the palace and the balcony, Evita's stage. Below was a dense sea of people and Robert could feel the energy like electricity surging up from the square.

Big search lights had been set up so that the front of the Casa Rosada, and in particular the balcony, was illuminated. They had only been there for a few minutes when a huge roar went up, then like a sudden wind the name 'Evita' began to be chanted. It started in one corner of the square then quickly rippled through the crowd like a wave, over and over until it felt that the crowd were going to work themselves into hysteria.

Below the window of the office building Robert could see people crying and embracing with happiness at the thought their Madonna would soon appear to them. They were shortly to be rewarded.

An additional set of spotlights suddenly and theatrically lit up the front of the Presidential Palace. Out onto the balcony stepped Evita, dressed like a film star in Dior and dripping with jewels.

She silenced the frenzied crowd with a gesture of her arms and tens of thousands of faces looked up like expectant children from the Plaza Del Mayo waiting for their saint to utter some words of blessing.

She spoke harshly, passionately, sometimes with rancour but always with a sense of righteousness. She spoke at length of her love for Peron and how he would save the nation, of her love for her workers and her hatred for the wealthy landowners. At each highlight of her speech she would punctuate it by raising her arms and gesticulating to the crowd. Her speech was laden with emotion and with expressions of love and admiration for her beloved people. Robert could not understand any of what she said in Spanish so Arturo was translating it breathily into his ear.

Eventually she finished speaking and the crowd reached another peak of ecstasy and then gradually, after maybe ten minutes, realised the show was over and started to disperse. Robert and Arturo bid farewell to Raul and set off back to the Alvear Hotel where Robert said goodnight to Arturo with a promise of a meeting the following evening. He needed to sleep. He had had the most amazing day; the sightseeing, the sex and the sheer wonder of seeing Eva Peron performing on her chosen stage in front of her followers. It was something that Charlie and Michael would have loved, he reflected sadly.

The following afternoon Robert sat in the suite of the hotel. He was nervous. His office had arranged for Eva Peron to have tea with him at the hotel so that a deal could be struck with her Foundation. The phone rang; it was the concierge.

'Good afternoon sir, Señor Miller is waiting for you in reception.' David Miller worked for Millbank & Kleinstein in Argentina as their local salesman and would accompany Robert at today's very important meeting.

Robert had been brought in as he was a senior director of the company and was in the position to negotiate the contract. The lift creaked slowly down to the ground floor where a bellboy pulled the ornate brass gate open and Robert saw David Miller waiting for him by the reception desk.

Robert and he exchanged the normal pleasantries. 'So Mr Harrison tell me what you've been doing in Buenos Aires since you arrived, have you been enjoying yourself?' Robert smirked to himself as he fantasised what the man's reaction to him describing the sex session with Arturo the day before would be. He sensibly resisted saying anything. David Miller was small, grey and mousey with a little moustache. With his round glasses and shabby suit he looked the picture of English conservatism.

'Well last night I did something rather extraordinary, I went to see Evita speaking from the balcony of the Casa Rosada'.

David Miller's reactions took Robert completely by surprise. First of all he coughed and looked uncomfortable and then blurted out, 'I'm not sure why you would want to go and see that dreadful woman. You know she used to be a prostitute don't you? She's cheap and common and decent people are appalled at the influence she has on the President.'

Robert was genuinely startled.

'My family has been in Argentina for three generations and that woman has damaged our wealth and standing so that she can buy jewels for herself. Why in heaven's name would you want to go and see the whore on her stage? I have to deal with that woman's Foundation because of my job and that's bad enough.' David Miller, suddenly remembering his standing with Robert, coughed, embarrassed by his outburst, and started talking about the cricket results from England. The pair walked awkwardly into the tall, cool, marbled hall that was the Alvear Palace's lounge.

Robert waited anxiously in the ornate reception room with a stony faced David Miller and Evita arrived, theatrically 15 minutes late. He suspected it was deliberate.

She walked in, flanked by two suited bodyguards with guns bulging in their pockets and a petite female secretary who was the interpreter. Robert and David Miller stood up to greet her. She was dressed simply, a black Dior suit accentuating her slender figure. Her hair, dyed blond, was pulled back sharply into a bun at the nape of her neck. Hanging from each ear were some very expensive looking diamonds and on her lapel an extravagant diamond spray. She looked elegant, crisp and business-like and gave Robert a steely gaze. She sat down at the table and beckoned Robert and David Miller to do so too.

'Good afternoon Señora Peron. I have heard much of your work and understand that you are doing a great deal to help the poor people of your country.' Robert then went on to explain about his company's new antibiotic and how effective it was. This was all carried out through the interpreter.

At this Evita banged her hands down on the table and Robert could see her cheeks flash with small dots of red as she became passionate and enraged.

'I have to see thousands of my poor people die, they have so many illnesses, they often have no way of being treated, they die from T.B., they die from pneumonia, it makes me so angry. Why is it that only the wealthy in Argentina can afford these drugs? No!' she shouted, banging her hands down again on the desk, 'My Foundation will ensure that medicines are available to all, rich and poor, old and young. This is my mission.'

Robert could see the woman was absolutely passionate about her cause but he suspected something else. He realised he was being softened up for a good deal. Eva Peron was, as was to be expected, a tough negotiator; she yielded little, but then again neither did Robert.

She screwed the price down to the last peso. Robert was prepared for this and although he strategically seemed to yield to the Señora at the appropriate moment, in fact he ended up with the price he had anticipated at the outset.

At that point tea was served, with sandwiches, scones and cakes in English style. As the waiter poured Evita's tea the cup rattled as his hand shook so much. She smiled a little to reassure him as she took the tea with a still elegantly gloved hand but the man looked even more petrified.

Having dispensed with the negotiations Eva Peron and Robert chatted on for a while and he saw from her eyes that she was frequently flirting so he did too. She talked to Robert about her 'Rainbow Tour to Europe' and how she had loved Spain, Italy and France. 'I did it for my people,' she said rather dramatically, 'I wanted the old countries in Europe to know Argentina is rising up and will be South America's shining star. '

She asked him about his life in England and if there was a 'Señora' Harrison. He felt she was probing and simply said, 'There was someone special once, but not any longer.' She didn't continue the line of questioning seeing the pain in Robert's eyes that he was unable to conceal.

They chatted on and spent another half hour together, mainly making small talk and avoiding difficult subjects. Throughout the meeting Evita was charming and polite and clearly enjoying the company of a handsome man.

When they had finished and Evita gestured to her bodyguards that it was time to leave, she said, 'Thank you Mr Harrison for a most charming afternoon, I do hope you will be returning to Argentina soon and that we can continue our acquaintance.'

'That would be charming Señora Peron.'

Robert realised that David Miller had said almost nothing throughout the meeting; he had been so engrossed with the conversation and flirting with Evita that he had totally ignored the grey looking man. Now, seeing that the meeting was over, Miller made his excuses and left. Robert saw a flicker of contempt on Evita's face as he did so. Clearly she had taken a dislike to the man.

There was something else that he wanted her to do. He took a large manila envelope from his briefcase, opened it and passed its contents to Evita. Putting on his best gleaming and rather flirtatious smile Robert asked one final request. She seemed flattered and agreed and reached over to take the envelope's contents from him. He gave her some very detailed instructions via the interpreter. When she had finished they rather formally bade farewell to each other.

The two people that history had never intended should meet went their separate ways. 'Tea with Evita, oh my God, Charlie and Michael would have loved it,' laughed Robert to himself later.

Robert stayed in Buenos Aires for another three days. Each night he saw Arturo and they had long, wild, passionate sex. He knew that nothing would ever come of this.

He wasn't Charlie, he liked the man but that was all. He hardly knew him and they lived in separate countries on the other side of the world from each other, but what they had shared was good and satisfied his sexual hunger.

Arturo lay in Robert's arms on their final evening together. Arturo was very sad; they had promised to keep in touch, saying perhaps they would visit each other one day but he knew that probably would not happen.

'Robert, you have been so kind to me, you are such a good man, I will always remember this time that we have spent together. Thank you. I must ask you, is there something I can do for you in return? I feel I have taken so much of your generosity.'

'Well Arturo, there is something that would mean very much to me.' He spent the next half-an-hour explaining a very important task he had to carry out.

Arturo was completely bemused by Robert's request. He felt strongly for the man and wished that they could have spent more time with each other. In truth, in the short time he had known Robert he had started to fall in love with him. He was also a very honourable man and he promised himself that one day he would carry out his handsome lover's request.

Robert left Buenos Aires the next morning, never to return. He arrived back in London, exhausted from the long flight, to chilly, grey autumn weather and as his taxi drove back from the airport to south London he pondered on what life there would be for him here. There had been a brief moment, a spark with Arturo but there was no one else, and whilst the loss of Charlie still gnawed deeply at him he wasn't sure that there ever could be. He had liked Arturo, enjoyed the moment but it had also re-emphasised to him how alone he was in London. He had been able to have this brief respite, perhaps because he was in another country, far away but he knew that in London he would drift back into his loneliness and he wanted no man if it was not Charlie. It felt like he was falling into a deep, deep pit, the ground was being pulled from beneath his feet. The future was bleak, loveless, grey and empty. He had no idea what the coming years would hold for him apart from loneliness and unhappiness. The brief moment with Arturo had only been a temporary halt in his downward spiral of despair.

His only redemption at that moment was that he felt with satisfaction that he had done what he needed to do for Charlie; there was nothing else. Only emptiness.

★ ★ ★

Interlude 1974

1. Below

South London Suburbs, June 1974

Iris looked at herself in the dressing table mirror. She was pleased with the reflection; 48 years old, very attractive, few wrinkles; she smiled smugly. She was getting ready for a date with her latest fling, Miguel, a Spanish flight attendant who she had been seeing for a few weeks. She wasn't sure whether her looks or her bank balance attracted him but actually she wasn't too bothered.

She had needed to keep busy; it was a way of blocking out the horror of Harry's trial and the awful dreams that had followed. Her sight had shown her nothing more, but she had an inner knowledge that something would come to pass. She was completely perplexed by the number 80 she had seen chalked up on the cellar wall in the dream, but it had to mean something, she was sure of that.

The little green trimphone on her bedside table rang; she answered it. It was Rose. 'Hello Iris, how are you?' she enquired.

'Very well, thank you darling, just getting ready to go out for dinner.' She thought that she wouldn't mention who with, Rose was so very disapproving.

Rose went into a long diatribe about David's latest promotion and how wonderful it was and how excited she would be to be able to move to a 'nicer' suburb. Ever the social climber thought Iris. She then moved seamlessly into a rant about Harold Wilson and how he was going to tax all their hard earned money and wondered when we would have a 'proper' government back in power.

'Now Iris, I'm calling to ask you a favour. Do you remember that Violet and Frederick are going off on some dreadful package holiday to Sorrento? He's so tight dear, they could afford far better. Well, anyway, I said I would take them to Gatwick and the bloody

Marina has broken down again. I wonder if you wouldn't mind doing it for me.' Iris mentally sighed. She was always happy to help people out and her sister and brother-in-law had always been good to her, but she didn't want to be stuck in rush hour traffic for hours.

'When is it Rose?' asked Iris, hoping that it would be a time when she could truthfully say she was busy.

'Tomorrow evening. They have to be there at 10pm, it's one of those ghastly charter flights so it flies at night. Would you help me out dear?'

Not being able to come up with an excuse Iris reluctantly agreed. She called Violet and made arrangements to pick them up. She was very grateful and most apologetic that Frederick 'couldn't afford a taxi'. Iris smiled to herself: 'Too bloody tight more like.'

That night Iris enjoyed herself and forgot about her task. She met Miguel outside their favourite Italian restaurant and they dined then went home and had sex, oiled by wine and joints.

At 8pm the following evening she got into her Mercedes and drove the 10 minutes to Violet and Frederick's house. Iris eased the Merc up their drive and applied the brakes so it came to a halt just by the heavy oak front door. It was already open and Iris could see the couple starting to bring their numerous suitcases out onto the step. Frederick waved. 'Hello dear thanks very much for this, a taxi would have been so expensive.' She decided not to respond.

Iris was actually rather fond of her brother-in-law. He was tight and like his wife a snob but they had always been supportive to Iris, particularly during her divorce from Roger a few years before. She didn't forget kindnesses and was always pleased to do a little something in return for the couple.

They both hugged Iris and kissed her on the cheek. Frederick busied himself making sure all the suitcases and holdalls were safely in the boot of the Merc. He got back in the car saying, 'Off we go then, I would go down the A23 from Croydon.' Iris took no notice; she hated back seat drivers and she knew her way to Gatwick.

As she switched the engine on Violet said suddenly, 'Oh stop dear, can I just check my passport's in my bag?' Iris, slightly irritated, switched off the engine and Violet got out of the car, opened the boot and fiddled around in one of the holdalls for a moment. 'All here Iris, I just had to check, you know how nervous I am about travelling.' She got back in the car and Iris started the engine and moved gently off down the drive.

The traffic was light and the trip to Gatwick airport took an hour. Ignoring Frederick's instructions she had taken her favourite route over the North Downs. She pulled up at the passenger drop-off area, wished them both a happy holiday, kissed them and then drove off into the night.

Iris went off to sleep quickly that night. She'd drifted off making plans for her next romantic fling. She was getting bored with Miguel and had noticed that the sexy tattooed youth who had been coming to clean her windows had been flirting with her.

In the early hours she woke trembling, sweating and frightened. Her dream had come to her again. Exactly the same dream as the last time she had it, the same dream she had been having since Harry's death in Wandsworth.

The terrible dank cellar, the chalk scrawled number 80 on the wall. 80, 80 what the hell does it mean?

She kept turning it over and over in her head for an hour before blessed sleep returned, but neither rational thought nor her sight were able to help her.

She decided in the morning she'd do a run to the supermarket for her week's shop. She got up early, still feeling tired from her interrupted night's sleep. She skipped breakfast, just having a strong cup of coffee instead to get her going and left the house, picking up a pile of old clothes for the charity shop as she went. She opened the boot of the car to put the clothes in and as she did she noticed a book towards the back of the boot.

It was a paperback, Arthur Hailey's 'Airport', and she quickly appreciated that it was meant for Violet or Frederick to read on holiday. 'It must have fallen out of their baggage, not to worry, he can always buy something else if he will part with the money,' she laughed to herself.

She picked up the book to take it back into the house to look after for their return. As she did a sheet of paper slipped out and fell onto the gravel drive. She picked it up; it was folded and as she opened it she could see that it was covered in Frederick's scrawly handwriting. She struggled to read it, but as she focused she realised it was a list:

Tommy David Dawson 1959
Peter Eric Brand 1963
Andrew Whitehead 1971
Charles Stephen Rogers?

Understanding, processing and accepting information that we don't want to take on board can sometimes take longer than it should, and Iris stood for a few minutes totally bemused. But then, with a sensation moving through her bowels like an icy claw, a hideous sickening knowledge came to her. Not the sight, just a memory. Andrew Whitehead. His beaming boyish face staring up from the grainy black and white image on the front of the Evening Standard several years before, dressed in his school uniform with his scruffy grey pullover and trousers patched at the knees. Iris's legs seemed to buckle beneath her and she had to steady herself on the wing of the Mercedes as she thought she was going to faint.

Iris barely slept that night. There was no sleep deep enough to allow for dreams; she had a constant spiral of images and words in her head which she still didn't understand. But she knew fully what the names of the boys from the list meant. Earlier that evening she had sorted though old newspapers that were kept under the stairs, eventually finding the copy of the paper she wanted, the Evening Standard dated 21st April, 1972.

It was headlined 'Peckham Monster Jailed'. It went into salacious detail about Harry's trial and what he'd supposedly done to the boys. Tommy Dawson disappeared in 1959, Peter Brand in 1963 and Andrew Whitehead in 1971. Iris had recognised Andrew Whitehead's name and was pretty sure that the other names on the list were going to be of the other boys. The old newspaper confirmed it.

Iris's limited sight had come fleetingly to her and continued to show her the number 80, over and over again. Apart from that and the list of the boys' names in Frederick's handwriting she had nothing to go on. There certainly wasn't any indication that Frederick could possibly be involved with the dreadful killings. In any case he was a nice, kind, gentle and decent man. Dull and mean and very conservative yes, but not a killer.

What she was sure of was that she couldn't let the matter rest, she felt that the list was of importance. She was determined to get to the truth and to protect her beloved Charlie. Iris dwelled for several days on what to do next, deeply troubled but unsure of what she could do. All she had was a list; the police would hardly be interested in that. She needed more.

One week later, having reflected long and hard, she decided on her next move. She was going to go to her sister's house and have a look around, see if there were any other clues. She rather felt as if she wanted to do this to exclude any possibility of Frederick being involved. Then she could rest content.

Violet had given her a spare door key so that she could check things whilst they were away on holiday. Iris drove over, parked the car outside and unlocked the heavy oak front door and stepped into the hall. The house was modest; Violet was always stressing what a 'nice' area it was in, whatever that means, Iris smirked to herself. The hall was small and mean and like the rest of the house felt old fashioned. Violet and Frederick hadn't yet gone for the trend of fitted carpets and there was a little runner down the middle, maroon with a pattern. Iris thought it was horrid.

She didn't really know what she was looking for but planned to work though the ground floor first. At the front on the left was the sitting room and this is where she entered first. It was immaculately tidy, nothing out of place. A small brick fireplace contained a display of fir cones and horse brasses hung on the wall around it. Everything was drab, dull and out of date and Iris knew that the couple had kept all their furniture since their marriage in the 1940's. Nothing was ever changed. Frederick was far too careful with money for that.

She looked around the room carefully. Nothing, not even any books. Just the sitting room furniture, a large old-fashioned TV and a few ornaments. She left the room and then repeated the process in the dining room and kitchen. It was all very orderly, very proper and very dull. She went through all the kitchen cupboards and drawers; everything was very clean. Not a crumb to be seen. So tidy, so organised. Iris wished ruefully that she could run her life like this then reflected, 'Yes but it's too tidy, it's soulless.' She had been in her sister's house on many occasions but never by herself so had not had the chance to look around. She had never quite appreciated how *cold* it was. Cold, soulless, loveless. She shivered.

She didn't think she was going to find anything and really didn't want to but she just wanted to be sure that there were no further clues or evidence. She was increasingly confident that there wouldn't be. She climbed the stairs to the first floor with the same horrid patterned red carpet as the hall. She firstly went into the bathroom at the back. Frederick had actually splashed out on having this modernised recently. 'It's Avocado,' Violet had said, 'it's so stylish.'

She carefully went through everything in the two big bedrooms. One was a study in Boudoir Pink. 'Really naff,' thought Iris. This was clearly the main bedroom as there was a dressing table with Violet's brushes and hand mirror. She noted the twin beds. The front bedroom had the air of being seldom used and was furnished with old walnut furniture.

There was only one room remaining to look around and that was the small third bedroom that Frederick used as a study. As with the rest of the house the room was sparse and immaculate. An easel held a half-finished oil painting, one of Frederick's latest works. It was a still life of flowers. Badly executed and completely devoid of any soul or passion. *Cold,* like the house. Also a Victorian drop-leaf bureau, closed, a dining room chair and, over the bureau, a large oval mirror.

Iris pulled the chair towards the bureau, sat down and dropped the leaf. Everything was tidy and ordered. To the left a few of the pigeonholes had been reserved for paint brushes and oils. To the right there was paper work. She began the task of going through the various bills, bank statements and correspondence. It was all very correct. Very organised. She raised an eyebrow when she saw the balance on Frederick's bank statement. It was in excess of £10,000. Iris recalled the constant complaints he made about lack of money and how difficult things were, so she was flabbergasted to discover quite how solvent he actually was.

Nothing. She felt satisfied she'd been through the house thoroughly. There was nothing here and her confidence that the list of names was meaningless increased. Perhaps Frederick had only ever added Charlie's name to it because he was a concerned godfather. She pushed the leaf of the bureau back up, it clicked into place and as it did she saw something in the mirror.

A slight movement, a shimmer, a shifting, a nuance, as if someone had briefly moved behind her but was now out of sight. Iris felt a cold shiver go through her. She was sure she was alone in the house and had double locked the front door behind her when she came in. She wasn't even sure that she had seen anything, just a fleeting movement, then it was gone. She looked into the mirror again and with a shock realised that she could now see something else.

In the reflection the dark green wall behind her was visible and on the wall in large white chalked letters one word :

BELOW

Her stomach cramped up into a ball and she swung round to look for the writing on the wall which she was sure hadn't been there before. Nothing. The wall was empty. Just the drab green wall. Nothing. She turned round and looked in the mirror again and there was the word BELOW still glaring from the wall behind her.

'What the hell does that mean? How has it come to be here?' she thought and began to try and think what the mysterious message was about and if it had been written for her. She looked around the little room as if trying to find a clue and her eyes fixed back on the bureau. There was nothing on the floor below the bureau so that wasn't it.

She had looked though the drawers below the drop down and had only found stationery. BELOW. It had to be something. Iris then ran her hand under the bottom of the bureau. Below the bureau, perhaps that was it. Nothing. She then pushed her arm forward a little more and swung it from left to right. A small splinter pricked her and she withdrew her hand and pulled a thin sliver of wood from her finger. She pushed her arm under the desk again, stretching right to the back, and as she swung it from side to side she felt something as her hand reached the furthest right extremity. A lump. She pulled at it and the object came away in her hand. It was small, lumpy and metallic with something loose attached to it.

Bringing it from under the bureau Iris saw the strip of sellotape that had held whatever it was to the bottom of the bureau and at the same moment saw that the object was a Yale key with a little plastic key fob attached to it. She pulled the sellotape off and let it drop to the floor and looked at the fob. It was one of those little plastic fobs that have a strip of paper in it to write an address on. Her eyes focused on the paper and she could see a number. It was very small but after a few seconds it sunk unwillingly into her now panicking mind. She let out a huge gasp and clasped her hand to her mouth as if to silence herself and dropped the key.

Written on the paper was: 80

★ ★ ★

Interlude 1974

2. : Number 80

There are those times when denial is no longer an option and it was now one of those moments for Iris. Since she had seen the list with the boys' names on it she had a horrible sick feeling that Frederick was involved with the killings. Now finding the house key with '80' on it, the number she had seen so often in her dreams, in that moment she knew the truth. It hit her like a punch to the gut. There was now no escape, no possible alternative answer. She had helped send an innocent man to his death and Charlie was in terrible danger.

Her first reaction was to run, get out of the house. She felt as if the house with its black secrets made her dirty and she was frightened. Rationally she knew Frederick was in Italy but she half expected him to appear at any moment and find her with the key in her hand.

Her head swam and she steadied herself against the wall, but over the next few minutes she began to think a little more rationally. She knew that she had no idea where the key belonged but she had a week before Violet and Frederick flew back from Italy and therefore time to investigate further. She went round the house and made sure that everything was left as she found it and put the key in her pocket, determined to discover which house the key belonged to.

Iris was relieved to leave the house and drove home where she poured herself a large gin and tonic. Twice. Her shattered nerves were eventually calmed and she focused her mind to try and work out where the key belonged. She knew the key didn't belong to Violet and Frederick's house as she had tried the lock. Did Frederick have another property? Nothing had ever been mentioned. He was a very discreet man and Iris knew little of his past or where he'd come from. How was she going to find out where the key would fit? She had no doubt the key would unlock secrets, but she wasn't sure that she was ready for what she would find. She had no choice though, it had to be done.

After an hour or so, Iris decided to go through the old newspapers about Harry's trial. She didn't know why but had nothing else to go on. Perhaps that would be a starting point. She flicked her eyes down the musty Evening Standard with its gruesome headline. Nothing. She read through it again.

Then her eyes stopped on the bold letters at the top of the article, just below the headline. She had read it probably three times before without noticing anything.

'Harry Rogers of 78 Victoria Street, Peckham was yesterday sentenced to three life sentences for the Peckham murders.' Something clicked. It took Iris much longer to work it out than it should have done really.

Then thudding into her consciousness she suddenly realised what was in some ways obvious. The next house to that was 80. The number 80 which had puzzled her so much was the house next to Harry's and she had the key for it.

'No, it couldn't possibly be that simple, surely not.' But in her gut she knew that's where she would probably find the final truth.

She had no knowledge of Frederick ever having had a property in Peckham. She also realised with a start that she knew nothing of his life before his marriage to Violet. All Violet ever told him was that he came from 'a good family'.

Iris knew that she must visit number 80 Victoria Street. Maybe she would find some evidence, maybe enough to ensure Frederick was prosecuted and Harry posthumously pardoned. Whatever happened, what was paramount was stopping Frederick before he got to Charlie.

Iris mulled over the fact that Frederick and Harry had been neighbours. Was this a coincidence or was it part of Frederick's terrible plans? She cast her mind back and tried to recall if she had ever seen them together. She thought that coincidences usually have a deeper meaning and was sure there was one here.

Iris began to lay careful plans. The following morning she drove to the High Street and had a copy made of the key. She then went over to Violet and Frederick's house and re-taped the original key to the bottom of the bureau in his study. She didn't want him to know he'd been found out.

She steeled herself for the next part of her plan, which was going to involve another trip to Peckham. Frederick's return was still several days away so she knew she was safe. She decided to get the train to Peckham Rye not wanting her car seen in the area. She got off the train; it was chilly and raining, even though it was mid June, and she started the 10 minute walk to Victoria Street.

As she finally turned into the street she saw that the row of Victorian terraces was mainly boarded up. In the middle was a gaping hole where some of the houses had been demolished by a bomb in the war, the site still surrounded by corrugated iron. One house half way down the terrace still looked like it was occupied and she momentarily felt sympathy for its occupants surrounded by this decaying urban squalor. She suspected that the Council would be demolishing the street soon and building yet more of the grey concrete flats that were already covering much of the area.

The street was strewn with litter and two burnt out cars. Reaching the end of the terrace she first walked past number 78. Harry's house. The house where she had descended into the cellar and seen the word 'Charlie' on the wall. Its windows and doors were boarded up and someone had sprayed 'SCUM – ROT IN HELL' in big red letters across the boarding.

Next door was number 80. Her destination. The windows and door were still accessible. Very decrepit, mouldering net curtains at the window. Tight lipped about the secrets within. Nothing had been painted for years and years.

She stood outside for a few minutes quite frozen. The rain had turned to drizzle but she noticed it little. She was chilled to her stomach but that had little to do with the weather. She dreaded what would come next.

She put the key into the door half hoping she was wrong about where the key belonged but it opened stiffly. Her nostrils were immediately assailed by the acrid smell of damp, rot and rats. She had put a torch in her pocket but flicking the ancient light switch was relieved that the electricity was still on. A bare bulb swung from a flex in the hall, the cracked and broken tiled floor was covered with piles of junk mail.

She briefly stuck her head round the door of the front and back rooms and kitchen. Nothing, bare, stripped. But she was delaying the inevitable, knowing she must look in the cellar beneath her feet. Her dreams had driven her there, had signposted her to this place and now she was at her final destination. Reluctantly she found the cellar door that was underneath the stairs and wiggled it open. The smell got even worse and it crept into her nose and mouth in spite of her quickly putting her hand over her face.

There was another light switch at the top of the little narrow staircase and she switched it on. A thin grey light percolated up from below. Gingerly she walked down the stairs, which creaked and shifted slightly, filled with dread about what she would find. As she finally stepped onto the cellar floor she could see that it was long and very narrow but that on the long wall were a number of pieces of paper. The light from the dim light bulb was too inadequate to make them out so she got the little battery torch out of her pocket and felt for the knob. The thin beam clicked on and she focused on each of the pieces of paper in turn.

A row of pictures. Three of them grainy black and white images of the boys clearly cut from a newspaper. Each of them neatly labelled with a little white sticker with Frederick's handwriting in red ink.

Tommy Dawson
Peter Brand
Andrew Whitehead

Their faces seemed to stare out of the pictures and out of time, begging for a salvation that would never come, their innocent and naïve eyes holding no knowledge of the horrors that awaited them. Below each one a small photo, each one a picture of the boy, clearly dead, bound up and gagged. Iris quickly looked away then she saw that there was one more picture in the ghastly gallery, a recent colour picture. Not labelled but it was of course of Charlie. She knew it would be.

It was the simplicity of the ghastly collage that Iris found so awful. She hadn't known what she would find, dreading the worst, but this simple proof thudded into her mind like leaden weights.

She knew she had to get out of the house, could no longer cope with the smell and horror and quickly went back up stairs. Locking the front door, and gratefully finding herself on the street in the damp London air, she took a great gulping lungful to purge herself of the evil miasma of the house.

Her mind was in turmoil. She knew without doubt what the truth was but what was troubling her was if she had enough evidence to see Frederick put away. She wondered if the police would be prepared to re-open the case. But she had to stop Frederick; she had to save Charlie, whatever it took.

As she sat on the train home thinking hard about what she would do, she came to an irrevocable decision. She couldn't risk the police not taking her seriously, not believing her story and putting Charlie at risk. She would have to deal with Frederick herself.

Three days later Violet and Frederick returned from Sorrento. Iris had managed to ensure that Rose would meet them at the airport. There was no way that she could smilingly greet her brother-in-law with the terrible knowledge that she had grinding inside her. She made the next part of the plan. She wrote a letter on her typewriter, apparently from the Council arranging to meet Frederick at Victoria Street the day after his return from holiday. The letter indicated that there may have been some mistake about the compensation level he had been given for the compulsory purchase of the property and that he was to meet a council official to 're-assess the size of the house' at 9 o'clock on 25th June. She hoped he would fall for it, knowing the whiff of money would probably get him into the trap that she was laying for him.

The morning of the 25th came and Iris once again got the train to Peckham Rye and walked slowly and deliberately with a searing tension headache between her eyes, to her destination. She knew what she had to do. Turning into Victoria Street she saw bulldozers and workmen and realised that the Council had already started to demolish one end of the street. It wouldn't be long before Number 80 and its horrible secrets were gone forever. She got there just before nine, wanting to make sure that she was ready to greet Frederick. Once again she let herself into the house but this time waited in the hall not able to bear to go down into that terrible hell of a place again.

She waited, pacing up and down. Frederick was late damn him. Then finally at 9.15pm she froze hearing a key click in the door and it swung open.

The expression on Frederick's face as he came into the hall was firstly one of confusion, then of recognition, then lastly, a sick attempt at a smile. He quickly composed himself and greeted Iris cordially.

'Hello dear, what are you doing here? I must tell you all about our holiday, it was lovely. Sorrento was so charming.' The situation was surreal, so uncharted, that for a moment Iris began to make polite enquires about the trip, but she stopped herself before issuing any further banalities.

'Frederick,' she started slowly and evenly, 'you know why I'm here. I know about the boys, I know what you've done.'

His face switched from the forced welcoming smile he had put on to something grimmer and darker. This was a new, different and evil looking man. 'Oh you were always so clever weren't you? So much brighter than that fucking stupid snob bitch of a sister of yours I married.'

In spite of everything she had learned Iris was shocked to hear the careful, always kind and prim Frederick speak like this. This was a new man, someone starting to show his black, hard soul to her.

'Tell me something Iris dear, how did you find out about my special place? My place where I have loved my wonderful boys so very dearly and where I will soon love my very special Charlie?'

Iris didn't want to start talking to Frederick about her dreams and visions, so instead of replying to his question she responded: 'Frederick, you know you're going to be stopped now don't you? I'll protect Charlie to my grave, there's no way you're touching him. There's nothing I can do for the poor boys you killed but Charlie will not become another of your victims. If you are not prepared to turn yourself in to the police then I'm going to have to do it myself. I think it would be better for you if you were to confess. I have no desire for vengeance Frederick. I just want to protect Charlie.'

As Iris spoke, Frederick's face developed a more and more malignant expression and she saw a look of contempt cross his face.

'Do you really think you can stop me Iris? I've made my plans so carefully, in so much detail. You have to understand that everything I've done, I've done for Charlie. You know how important planning is, getting every last detail right. I had to make sure everything was perfect for Charlie.'

Iris was slightly thrown by this response and started to interject, 'But wha ...'

Frederick continued without allowing her to speak. 'You have to understand that although I loved the other boys, they were only like steps along a path. I had to make sure that when I came to protect Charlie then everything would be perfect. Each time I did the *thing* to the boy and then put him out of his misery, I perfected my approach. I perfected the details, I got better and better. I love Charlie that much. I wanted it to be just right you see dear.'

'What the hell do you mean protect Charlie? You intend to kill him,' Iris managed to butt in.

'Yes of course dear, of course I was going to kill him but don't you understand that the whole point was to protect him from himself? I had seen in my dreams what he would become, with that abomination he called love he would be entangled with. How could I allow that to happen? I did it all for him, all those years of careful planning. I wanted everything just so.'

Iris, whilst horrified at Frederick's sick logic, now knew that she was talking to someone who had little normal rationale left, if he had ever had any at the outset. She deliberately moderated her tone, wanting to coax more information out of him.

'So tell me, what I don't understand is how you ended up with a house next door to Harry's. Was that just a coincidence?'

'No of course not, don't you remember, everything was planned. It's been planned from the beginning. From before Charlie's birth, from when I started having the dreams. I met

Harry, the poor pathetic sod, at Charlie's christening. He was having to move out of his bed-sit in Bermondsey at the time and I made him the offer of being caretaker of one of my houses. I was brought up by my parents in Victoria Street, useless fuckers they were. After the war I bought up two more houses in the street and let them out. Harry was my tenant. I never told your stupid fuck of a sister where I came from. She was far too much of a snob to admit that she had a husband from Peckham, so I made up a tale of parents in a nice country village who had sadly died of TB. Poor bitch, she believed every word. I had had so many dreams by then you see Iris, I knew what would become of Charlie if I didn't save him and I also saw that Harry might be useful one day.

I decided that when all my plans were made and perfected then I would get Harry to take the blame. Then there was no risk that I would be stopped before I could save Charlie, you do see that dear don't you? I know of your sight as I have dreams of my own and I used it, I manipulated it, I helped you make the connection to Harry, but it was the wrong connection. Don't you think that's rather clever? Once I knew that you had made the connection I encouraged you to go and visit Harry and planted all the evidence in his cellar. You fell for it hook, line and sinker.'

'One more question Frederick. Where are the three boys' bodies? Can you not give their parents some kind of redemption? Can you imagine their torment at never having been able to bury their sons? If you have any humanity please do this, give those families some peace.'

'Well dear that's not going to happen now is it? What was left of them went into the Thames a long time ago.'

Iris never really knew whether her next action was because she snapped at this further cold throwaway comment or whether it was a deliberate act. It didn't matter. She swiftly withdrew the little pistol she had been carrying in her coat pocket, took aim and shot Frederick squarely between the eyes.

★ ★ ★

Interlude 1986

A Present

St. Bartholomew's Hospital, August 1986

Michael was very weak and he knew he had only a short time left. Charlie had been with him every day in these last few weeks. He'd held his hand, reassured him, hugged his emaciated body and brought him titbits of tasty food and fresh flowers.

There was a knock on the door of the room, it was one of the agency nurses. A diminutive and rather cute young gay boy called Tim. 'Michael, you have a visitor, he says you don't know him but it's very important that you see him. He says he has come a long way and has something very important and special to give you and that he must see you alone.'

Michael was intrigued; he felt so weak and ill, could barely speak or move and normally limited the visitors to a few chosen special friends; he almost told the nurse to send the man away. But then thinking about the tone of urgency and importance that the nurse had conveyed he decided to agree. 'Okay show him in … is he sexy?' He spoke in rasps, struggling with his tortured lungs. When he had finished the few words he pulled an oxygen mask to his face and took a few welcome deep breaths.

'He is a bit old for my tastes but quite handsome.'

Tim left the room briefly and returned with a tall, slim dark-skinned stranger. He was probably in his early 60's, but still lean and handsome. In spite of Michael's condition he could still appreciate an attractive man and felt himself blush slightly. 'Who are you? Why have you come?'

'My name is Arturo.'

He spoke with a heavy accent that Michael took to be Spanish. 'I can't tell you too much. I don't really understand myself but many years ago I made a promise that I would come, on this day, to this place to see you and to give you a present.'

Michael had no idea what Arturo was talking about. 'I think I must be losing my bloody marbles,' he thought.

Arturo said nothing more but withdrew a large manila envelope from his pocket. It looked very old. 'Open it, please Michael.'

'I'm too weak, please do it for me.' Arturo carefully opened the envelope and withdrew the contents and laid them on the bed by Michael so he could easily see what it was.

It was a large colour photograph, clearly old as it was starting to fade. It took a few moments to take it in then he gasped as he could not quite believe what he was seeing. It was a picture of the woman that fascinated him so much, smiling, her bright red lips like a 1940's film star and on the bottom was scrawled,

For Michael with fond regards
Evita
18th October 1948

Michael didn't know what to think, his head was spinning. 'Is this some type of joke?'

'Michael, it was almost 40 years ago that I was given this envelope to give to you. The man who gave it to me anticipated that you would question its provenance, but trust me it is real and Evita dedicated it to you. The man said to mention a name that would confirm the validity of his gift to you.'

'Who, what name?'

'Charlie.'

Michael now had tears running down his face. Receiving this amazing gift of love from across time had moved him immensely and he totally forgot to concern himself any further how it had come to be sent to him. Hearing Charlie's name from the lips of this handsome stranger was enough for him. Clearly he knew that he was never going to have tea with Eva Peron but, 'This is a bloody good compensation for that,' he thought with a smile.

'Please tell Charlie nothing of this, it would be far too confusing for him,' added Arturo. 'I was also told to tell you something else and that is that he has not met the man who gave me this picture … yet.'

Arturo left shortly afterwards; he knew that he could not explain how this picture had been sent across the years for Michael but he was pleased and satisfied that he had finally, almost 40 years later, kept his promise and returned Robert's kindness and generosity,

Michael lay in his hospital bed that night, his head whizzing round, trying to work out how this had come to be. He knew in his guts that this was real, but had no concept of how it had happened. What he did know and didn't question for one moment was that he felt deeply, deeply loved.

★ ★ ★

Interlude 1997

Flowers in the Park

Dulwich, South London, 31st August 1997

Charlie showered, washing away the grime of another long night out in the fleshpots of London. He had been out to a bar in Soho and had drinks with a couple of friends. It hadn't been the best night by his standards; he was single again having just come out of a 6 month relationship that hadn't been going anywhere. The guy wasn't prepared to make any commitment and had started being evasive and unavailable, so Charlie, much as he liked him, had finished it.

Aged 42, he was really wishing he could meet someone and start dating again but on that particular night no one had taken his fancy. He came home by himself feeling lonely and dejected.

He dried himself and went to his bedroom and lay down lost in his thoughts. He loved the room, it was where he met Robert eight years before; that wonderful handsome man who he thought was going to be with him forever. Then he had been snatched away as quickly as he arrived.

What had made it even worse, if worse was possible, was none of Charlie's friends could remember Robert. It had started when Elizabeth walked into the hall of the house finding Charlie hysterical. When he cried, 'He's gone, he's disappeared,' Elizabeth thought she knew who he meant for a moment, as a fleeting memory touched her mind, like a fading ghost, then nothing.

He had introduced Robert to many of the people that he knew, and then after he disappeared, one by one, they denied all knowledge of him. At that point Charlie thought he was losing his mind and if truth were known, he was on the verge of a breakdown. Iris of course was ever reassuring and remembered everything Charlie had told her about Robert. In Charlie's mind though this wasn't enough, she had never met him in person, had only heard

Charlie talk about him in his calls to New York. In his frantic brain he pictured himself describing this wonderful man to Iris on the phone from an empty room, some kind of fantasy lover.

For weeks Charlie skulked around, barely washing and eating little; he lost a stone, he looked gaunt and drawn and communicated with no one. The following month he had decided to visit the house in Dulwich again; perhaps it would hold some answers. Walking around the shabby and run down property he felt more and more dejected, the parlous state of the place only emphasising his mood.

As he was walking around the top floor his eyes flicked up to the loft hatch above. He remembered what Robert had shown him: his name carved into the beam in the attic. He realised with a start that this would provide him with the evidence he needed to re-assure himself Robert hadn't been a delusion. He felt sick with the thought that he may find nothing written up there, but he had to know. He was desperate to either find out that Robert had not been a fantasy or that he actually needed to seek professional help.

Frantically he prodded open the loft hatch and pulled down the ladder and then scrambled up the metal steps into the cold, sooty smelling void. He fumbled around and found the switch that controlled the single little bulb hanging forlornly from the rafters. Carefully navigating each beam so as not to put his foot through the floor he went to the back of the house and ran his hand over the long angled rafter where he'd seen Robert's name written. Charlie's heart stopped a beat. A wave of joy and then deep sadness poured through him as he spied the words he had first seen when he was in the attic with Robert.

ROBERT HARRISON 1925

But there was something else. There was more writing carved into the wood to the right of where Robert's name was. Charlie was sure it hadn't been there before. He read it, and his heart missed a beat as he did.

C + R 1944-1989

Charlie gasped, slipped and put his foot through the bedroom ceiling. His jeans were torn by the ragged plaster board and he felt warm blood running from a gash in his leg. He didn't care; he knew he was not going insane. Robert had got back to 1944 and left this message for him. It was the beginning of his recovery. His loss was still enormous, but now he no longer doubted his sanity.

Gradually Charlie started to put his life back together. He tried to comfort himself by thinking that perhaps Robert would find his way back to him but eventually realised that this probably would not happen. Eventually he began dating again, initially with disastrous results and he never again found the deep love that he had felt with Robert, but there were men, and there were relationships.

Six months after Robert disappeared Charlie decided to sell his flat in Kennington and move to the house in Dulwich. He felt he had to do this, it was Robert's house too albeit in a different time, and it was a way that he could feel close to him. He threw himself into restoring the house, turning it into a home that everyone admired; beautifully and tastefully furnished and with the loveliest English cottage garden.

He did it all for Robert; he thought he would like it. Every time he picked the colours or the fabrics for a room he would talk to Robert out loud: 'What do you think about this? Do you like the colour?'

Once he visited the library again where he had looked at the electoral records with Robert. He found Robert's name at the address up to 1954 but then he disappeared. Charlie tried to find out if he'd died but was never able to come up with anything. It was a comfort knowing that he had gone back to his own time and not been killed in the process. Charlie being Charlie would then start to feel intense jealousy about who Robert might be meeting and would hurt desperately at the thought that he may fall in love again with another man.

Charlie was snatched out of thoughts of his lost love by the sound of a fox yowling in the garden. He finally decided it was time to sleep. As always when he put the lights out he spoke to Robert: 'Wherever you are, I still love you, and one day we will be together again. Please wait for me. Wherever you are, I love you very much. Sweet dreams.'

He gradually drifted off into welcome sleep thinking about his lost lover's strong arms around him and then for further comfort revisited the memory of the old dream of being a bird soaring in the sky and being loved and special.

He had probably been asleep for no more than 30 minutes when the phone ringing rudely awakened him. As he reached for it he glanced at the digital alarm clock which glowed a green 5.30am at him.

'Who is it?' he demanded gruffly.

'It's Iris, switch on the TV now. Just do it.'

'What the fuck Iris, what are you going on about?'

'Just do it, you won't believe what's happened,' and at that the line went dead.

Charlie reached for the remote control and flicked the 'on' button. The BBC news came on and Charlie watched with a dropped jaw as the ashen faced news reader, with trembling emotion in his voice broke the awful news from Paris. It was one of those moments that Charlie would remember where he was when it happened for the rest of his life.

September 1997

Anyone who lived through Diana week in London can remember the quiet sense of mourning that befell the city. It was a strange heavy atmosphere and the entire bustle seemed to have gone out of the capital. It was if everyone had gasped together, in one collective expression of shock, and then held their breath. They will also remember the enormous floral tribute bouquets piled up in huge banks that appeared in Kensington Palace gardens in the days following the Princess's death.

Charlie decided he would like to pay his respects to Diana and arranged to meet Olga there at 6 o'clock on the Friday evening. He met her outside High Street Kensington underground station as he had once before, when he was just 15. He saw her coming in the distance and waved frantically to attract her attention. Olga was a commanding woman, towering over most of the people milling outside the station. Charlie had never really known her true age but suspected she must now be in her early seventies. She greeted Charlie warmly with a huge, almost crushing bear hug and kissed him on both cheeks. 'Charlie darling, you look great, it's been too long.'

They had not seen each other for about 6 months and Charlie felt slightly guilty. He cared deeply for Olga, she was a connection with Michael and they would always remain firm friends, but sometimes the pursuit of men got in the way of maintaining friendship in Charlie's life. 'Thank you Olga, you look lovely too.'

Actually for once Charlie wasn't lying. Olga had learned over the years how to dress in a sophisticated and stylish manner and she was turned out just as any other English middle class woman would be. Today she wore tweed, as if from the Home Counties, and looked rather good in it. She had dropped the Eastern European accent and not wanting to revert to her native Estuary English had taken elocution lessons and now spoke with a twang to match her tweed. She had her beloved George who she still lived with in Blackheath to thank for all of this.

'I'm not so sure about looking great. I had my 42nd birthday not long ago and I'm feeling very old Olga.'

'Don't be silly, you are still a boy in my eyes and you're still as gorgeous as ever.' Charlie blushed, but appreciated the compliment.

'I still haven't quite taken in what happened to Diana.'

'It's just so terrible to see a woman so beautiful taken at such a young age. It just doesn't seem right. I thought it was very important to come here to see the floral tributes and to pay our respects.'

'I agree Charlie, she was such a wonderful woman. We must never forget that when no one else would touch people with AIDS, Diana did. Come, let's walk up to the garden.'

She put her arm through Charlie's and they walked slowly and silently up to the gates of Kensington Palace Gardens. As they strolled up the pathways they both understood what a unique moment this was; neither had ever seen anything like it before, they doubted they would again. Bunches of flowers piled several feet high and tens of feet deep, candle shrines, cards, and teddy bears. Everywhere they could see was covered in this extraordinary tribute to the dead Princess. Frequently they would stop and bend down and read one of the messages pouring out its heartfelt grief at this awful and untimely death.

'What it must be like for those poor boys of hers, I can't begin to imagine the grief they must be going through,' said Charlie.

'You're right, but let's not forget that we have both experienced great loss in our lives, we do know what it's like to lose people we love.'

'Yes, I still miss Michael, he was so special, so real, so alive, and I know that you must miss him sorely too.'

'Gosh, how many years is it now? To lose a friend such as he, well, does one ever really get over that? I think not. I think all you can do is to accommodate the loss, live with it that is all. But my dear, when I mentioned loss I was also in your case thinking of someone else, someone I think you loved once. I'm so sorry, I don't know why but I can't recall his name or how long you were together, I think just a few months, but since that time, you've always had a sad look in your eyes. I know you've thrown yourself into having a life and having fun, but that sad look in your eyes, it's never gone away. He must have meant a lot to you.'

'He was everything to me Olga. He was and is the only man I was ever prepared to give my whole soul to. But I don't understand, no one else remembers him. Why do you?'

'It's not really that I remember him Charlie, but I've known you longer than any of your other friends, I know you well. I remember you before your love, and after your love. I remember the effect it had on you.'

'Olga, he was called Robert but trust me, some things are best left unexplained. I think he's probably dead. You did meet him, several times, but like everyone else somehow you forgot him once he was gone.'

'You are still being mysterious Charlie, but I won't press you if this is not something that you want to talk about. Just remember, if you ever want to tell me everything I'm always here to listen.'

'Thank you Olga, that is very much appreciated. One day I may talk to you about it. Sometimes I have wondered if it was worth it. Oh yes, I loved him, but I've never been able to find anyone else to compare with him. So was it really worth it, just having him for 6 months?'

'Charlie, sometimes you are so remarkably unable to see things about yourself. I shall tell you why it was worth it. Do you remember all those years ago when we had tea in Barkers and I told you off for being self-centred and not thinking about Michael's feelings? Well that's because you were always self-centred and thinking about how much everyone should do for you. Please forgive me for my harsh words but that is how it was.' Charlie said nothing, but felt uncomfortable; he always did when anyone expressed anything negative about him. The sky was darkening now and the thousands of candles amongst the floral tributes were starting to look like little glow-worms; every now and then he noticed the heavy smell of burning incense as they continued to walk around the garden.

'Do you not also realise how much you changed after you lost this love? Oh yes sure you were devastated, you clearly had lost the man of your life, but there was a massive change in you and that was one for the better. Everyone noticed it, you started being much more caring and considerate to other people. Instead of constantly hearing about your woes, your friends started to feel supported by you.

Do you understand that we are all a product of the people that we meet and the experiences that we have? They all leave their mark on us and mould the way we behave and what we believe in. There is no question Charlie that he changed you from being a selfish but gorgeous lost little boy into a caring and loving man. I always used to think of you as 'The Lost Boy', did you know that?'

With a sudden flash Charlie remembered Luke the Bear's Tarot reading from years before. Perhaps that's what he'd meant. He had never found out. He replied, 'No, I didn't know you thought of me like that but what you're saying Olga is that I had to lose Robert to become a better man, that's pretty harsh isn't it?'

'I'm not saying that is what had to happen but it is what did happen and you should value what he left you. Sometimes we can only be truly compassionate and caring when we have been through pain ourselves. It certainly worked for you. I think you finally let someone love you and in that process you loved yourself a little more and became a much better person to be around.'

'I can't say that I find your words easy to listen to Olga, I wonder why if I was so selfish and self-centred that you or anyone else wanted to be my friend.'

'Charlie, you really are terribly thick. What people could also see in you was great goodness, and somewhere under the rather confused person that you were, a very kind and lovely soul. Goodness knows why you got so buried but you did.'

'Well maybe I have my parents to thank for that.'

'We so often do dear, but don't be too harsh on them. As I said, we are all a product of everything that we have experienced, for better or worse. Your parents were a product of their times. They didn't have the knowledge or emotional language to know how to deal with you properly. It doesn't make it right, but be a big man Charlie and find some forgiveness for them.'

Charlie said nothing but by now he was crying. His discomfort at Olga's words had flowed away and he was feeling a deep and raw emotion.

'Yes, I think I have been able to do that Olga, in their late life before they died they both became a lot mellower and I spent a lot of time talking to my mother. I think we found some kind of peace with each other. In spite of what they tried to do to me, I miss them, and yes I loved them. It's better that way. If we hold bitterness inside it just eats us up.'

'Sometimes Charlie you are wiser than I have given you credit for. Come on, dry your eyes,' and Olga reached into her pocket and withdraw a perfumed lace hanky, which Charlie dutifully dabbed his eyes with.

For a few minutes they walked silently, taking in the atmosphere and reading some of the messages of sympathy. One of them said: 'Blessed Diana, People's Princess, a star in heaven forever'.

'Do you believe in an afterlife Olga? Do you believe that Diana is up there watching over her boys, making sure they're guided through their lives from beyond the stars? Do you think that Michael comforts us still and do you think that Robert is out there somewhere looking after me?' Charlie sounded deeply cynical as he said this.

'Now that is a very deep question. I'm an old woman and even though I've lived a long time I don't have the answers for everything. But yes, I don't believe this life is the end. I believe, Charlie Rogers, that one day, when you eventually reach the end of your time on this earth, you'll be with Michael and Robert, and if you want you'll be able to have a chat with Diana as well.'

'And what about tea with Eva Peron?' said Charlie lightening the moment.

'I think in the next world anything will be possible,' replied Olga sagely.

'I so wish you're right Olga, but try as hard as I may, this is not something I believe in. I'm not religious and I think that when we're gone, that's it. I so want what you're saying to be right but I just don't believe it. Sorry.'

'You may well be right Charlie,' Olga sighed, 'but thinking there is something better afterwards perhaps is what keeps us going through the trials and pains and troubles of this life.'

'False dreams Olga, that's all it is for me.'

Olga sighed again, 'Yes, probably just an old woman's dreams, but they are comforting ones.'

They spent another 10 minutes walking quietly around the park. Eventually they decided it was time to go home and they made their way back to the Underground station where they said their goodbyes. As Olga hugged Charlie, she suddenly said, 'Was he a pilot or something dear?' for she had started to remember, not much, just little fragments of what had been Robert.

They flashed through her mind and she struggled to remember more, a little like we do when we wake up from a vivid dream and the details gradually drift away from us. Charlie gave her one of his biggest smiles. 'Yes Olga, he was, I think that something about today, in this amazing place, something about the raw emotion of what we have seen and felt, has touched us and opened us up, and in that process somehow you've started to remember him again. I don't know how but knowing you can remember just a little is enough for me. Thank you.'

As Olga sat on the Circle Line train on the way home she muttered under her breath, 'But how did I ever forget him? What a stupid old woman I am.'

★ ★ ★

Part Three: Discussing the Causal Nexus

Chapter One: Iris's Story

King's College Hospital, Camberwell, August 2010

Charlie lay on the uncomfortable and narrow hospital bed. The doctors had been in to see him the previous day to break the news. The latest round of chemo hadn't worked and that was the last line of attack. He was only 55 and probably had only a few weeks to live. He wasn't entirely sure what his emotions were; sometimes numb, the morphine didn't really help with that, but sometimes he was very scared.

He had found out he had lung cancer the year before, caused by years of smoking. It was widespread when it was discovered and in truth there was probably little that could be done, but he tried to keep a cheerful optimism and focus on getting better. He never admitted to his family and friends that he had been told that there was only a small chance of recovery. He would just keep talking about plans for the future and what he was going to do when he got better. He thought that was what they wanted to hear and sometimes a little bit of him slightly believed it as well.

He was fortunate enough to have a small private room. He had paid for that himself; he hated sharing a hospital ward with strangers. He couldn't sleep and didn't really want to talk with anyone. He was too lost in his thoughts.

On this occasion, his reminiscing firstly turned to his family. His parents had been dead for some years. His love for and relationship with them had been complex and sometimes difficult, but he mourned them deeply and now wished they were there to hold his hand and reassure him.

Olga had been a tower of strength in her loving and practical way. His sister Susan, who now lived in Australia, called every day. He thought also of his beloved Aunty Iris. She was now eighty-five years old and the person he loved most in the world. They had always been close and she had been a constant and unwavering good influence in his life. She was the person that knew more about him than anyone else and he trusted her completely.

Lastly, he thought about his lovers. There had been so many. But he had only ever truly and deeply loved once. The love that he still felt for Robert was huge, deep, and unmatched. That strange and wonderful 6 months had been 20 years ago, 20 years since the handsome airman from 1944 suddenly came to him one night, 20 years since he was savagely snatched back.

As Charlie thought of him he started crying with big sobbing gasps. As he did the door of his room opened and the harassed looking nurse, callously ignoring his tears, told him he had a visitor. He quickly tried to calm himself but was still crying a little as his beloved Aunty Iris came into the room carrying a large bunch of white flowers, his favourite colour. On seeing her, and the extravagant bouquet, his crying got louder again.

Iris rushed to the bedside and put her arms round his fragile body and hugged him. She said nothing but kept holding him gently until very gradually his crying subsided as he felt the warmth and love pouring from her.

She released him from her arms, and he lay back on the pillow finally managing a smile for her. He looked into her still beautiful face and felt a sense of tranquillity. He was, as ever on seeing her, amazed that she was 85 years old and did not have a grey hair on her head. She was as immaculately made up and dressed as she always had been.

'Is that a little better Charlie?' she gently enquired. Then she spoke slowly and tenderly enquiring about his treatment and how he was being looked after. He had not spoken to her about the graveness of his illness, but she knew anyway. His appearance and the morphine pump would have given that away even if she hadn't instinctively known.

'Thank you Aunty Iris. You always manage to calm me don't you? You always did. Do you remember when I was 4 years old and I had run away from home, how you comforted me?'

She replied smiling, 'Yes of course I do, and please don't call me Aunty. It's so ageing.'

They laughed together for a moment.

'Charlie,' Iris said quietly but with a tone of gravity. 'I have come to talk to you about something very important, something that you now need to know, something I have known much of my life but have not been able to tell you.' Charlie felt a slight shiver at her tone and wondered what awful secret she was about to reveal; some skeleton in the family closet perhaps? Had his father been having an affair with her? He had wondered sometimes.

Sensing his concern, she quickly whispered, 'It's nothing to worry about Charlie, it's not bad news, it's something which is very important and that now that you are dying you have a right to know.' That was the first time that anyone had acknowledged he was terminally ill and he was pleased that it was Iris. She paused for a moment as she steadied herself mentally.

'Charlie I want to talk to you about Robert, I do know his story and that he came across time from 1944 dear.'

Charlie's eyes widened and tears started to flow again at the sound of his lost lover's name. 'But Iris, how did you know? I never told anyone. Iris how did you know?' he demanded.

'I will now at the end of your life tell you my story,' she gently replied. 'I can't explain everything and certainly don't understand how some of these events have come to pass, but what I do know with all my heart and soul is their reality and also their importance to you.'

Holding his hand gently she relayed her tale:

'As you know I was brought up in Beckenham with your mother and Violet. When I was a little girl I always felt different from other people as I sometimes dreamed of things that came true or sometimes just knew that things would happen before they did. It made me a little lonely because I knew that other people didn't have this gift and I also thought that if I told them about it they would think I was a bit odd. So I kept it secret.

When I was 14 years old I received a mysterious present, a pack of Tarot cards. I don't know from whom, but whoever it was suggested that I had a talent that should be explored further. In 1940, during the Blitz, I was practising with the cards and I went into a trance and had a vision. I had never experienced anything like this before and can only presume that the Tarot cards acted as some kind of trigger or channel to a different mental state.

The vision was of two men deeply in love with each other (Charlie's eyes flicked up to Iris's as she said this) and two men that were torn apart and lost that love. I knew in my vision that this was the deepest and most wonderful love that anyone could ever experience and because of that the loss that they would both feel would be unimaginable. I also knew intuitively that in some way I would be involved with these events and would have to help, it was part of my destiny. The two men were, of course, you and Robert.

Although I knew instinctively that a weight of duty was on me I had no way of knowing how and when it would be played out and how I was to help. I tried using the cards again and although I saw some other trifling things, I was given no further clues about what was to happen. I bided my time wondering how the threads of the tapestry would be stitched together.

I got on with my life and although I never forgot what I had been shown, I put it to the back of my mind and there were times when I began to wonder if anything would actually happen and if I had had a false vision.

In 1953, feeling a little depressed for some reason, I decided to go out for a walk in Dulwich Park. We enjoyed simple pleasures then. I still don't really know what took me there, it was a few miles from my home in Beckenham and involved an awkward bus journey, but for some reason on that day I felt drawn to the place. Now, having seen everything that has happened I think that fate made me go there. I can't explain it any other way.

I remember it clearly as a cold February day and I met Robert there by the little lake in the park. These details still come back to me after almost 60 years. We began chatting and I quickly understood how very, very lost he was. I knew he had been contemplating suicide.

It was 8 years after he'd been torn away from you and propelled back in time to where he had originally come from. He was so very desolate.

Later that day I suddenly remembered where I had seen his

face before. I recognised him as the dark handsome man from my vision. Initially I was very attracted to him, who wouldn't be, he was so good looking, but it quickly became clear that he wasn't interested in women. I liked him though and a very strong and deep friendship began to develop. Over a period of time he began to open up and tell me his strange and wonderful story. He told, with great joy and sorrow, of how he had spent time in 1989 with you, of his deep love for you and his awful desolation at the loss of you.

You'd told him about me and Robert also knew what your parents were called, Rose and David. Given this information, and calculating the age that his Charlie was, we deduced that you were their unborn son. So the first thing I did was to ensure that he befriended them. It was easy, Robert was so charming and I think Rose fancied him as much as we all did. We knew that this would at least ensure that he could be around to guide and protect you.

Now Charlie, I have to tell you something you may not have realised. You remember your godfather Stephen who left and went to New Zealand when you were little? Well dear, Stephen and Robert are the same person. Did you know?'

At this point Charlie gasped. He hadn't worked this out but actually now he thought about it, it felt like it was a knowledge he'd always had. He now knew why Robert looked so familiar when he first met him.

'Several years after I first met Robert, you were born, and as soon as I saw your wonderful blue-green eyes I knew everything was starting to fall in place. It was me that suggested to your mother that you should be called Charles. Because, of course, I knew you would be called Charles.

Robert and I had decided that he should start using his middle name Stephen and his mother's maiden name, Foster, so that when you grew up, and then later met in 1989, you wouldn't associate the two men. It would have been far too confusing for you. He wanted to be a positive influence in your life, but then realised how deep the pain of watching you grow up would be. Can you imagine how terrible that would be for him? The man he loved, now a child, 40 years younger than him. Eventually, when you were 5 years old, he emigrated to New Zealand as he couldn't bear to be around you anymore. He married a woman called Ellen over there for the sake of companionship and although it was a relationship of convenience, he found some type of love in it. She was a good woman and she loved him deeply and accepted his distant and unaffectionate response with dignity.

We now knew we had to make plans to ensure that what had happened still happened. Firstly, Robert arranged for you to own the house in Dulwich by leaving it in trust in his will with the condition that it be sold on to you. Do you remember how hard I worked on you to buy the house with the money that he had left you?

I had to persuade you it was a good investment. As you know he died in 1987 but he had been resolutely determined that you two would meet, an event which was in his past, but your future.

We knew that a bomb had exploded near his house in 1944. This somehow, propelled him through time to meet you, on the same date, in the same place, in the same house in 1989. There must have been some kind of psychic link between you and when the bomb fell it caused a rupture in time and you were drawn together. It was clear to us that you had to be in that place, in 125 Hurst Court Road, Dulwich, for the two of you to meet, so we planned for you to be there. You see my darling you met him because we planned for you to meet, we made it happen, but we could only do that because we knew the story already.

I'm sorry I can't explain any of this any better, although I have some vague psychic powers, my understanding of things so complex is extremely limited. We also understood that a second bomb that fell in 1945 had somehow ruptured time again and propelled Robert back to his original era.

We had both hoped you would live in the house in Dulwich and we wouldn't have to interfere further, but you decided to buy the flat in Kennington. I bided my time, watched and waited and planned.

Now dear, don't be cross with me, but do you also remember why you stayed in the house on 22nd July 1989? You never usually did, as you liked to be near the centre of town. Do you remember you had a flood the day before in your flat? I'm afraid that was me. I let myself into your flat; you always had a spare key at my house. I damaged the pipes under the bath so when you came home the whole flat was pouring with water and uninhabitable.

When I called you were in tears, and I suggested staying at Hurst Court Road. You agreed quite easily dear, I was so pleased I didn't have to engage any other subterfuge to get you there. Oh but just to make sure, do you remember you couldn't find your wallet? That's because I had it. I wanted to be certain you didn't go out for the night and with no cash or cheques I knew you were stranded. Lastly, for good measure I called in a favour from a man I knew who worked at the local telephone exchange and he cut your phone off.

I had you in the right place, at the right time for you and Robert to be drawn together and I now knew that I could leave everything else to naturally fall into place. Robert and I had discussed that I should not see him in 1989, we thought it was going to be far too confusing for everyone involved. That is why I went to live in New York for a year the day after you met him. Do you remember I flew off on Concord with that rather sexy French youth I was seeing?

I also knew that when I came back the following year Robert would be gone and back in 1945. Of course dear, the rest is history. The fault in time happened, the fates drew you together, you met, loved and then terribly lost each other.

Of course whilst you were together, I was able to help and guide you when things were not going well. Do you remember after that awful row when he found your little red book I told you he would be in Kennington Park and I suggested contacting Madam Morgana about the hand fasting? Well of course Robert had told me where he went after your row, and also about Glastonbury Tor so I knew what I had to do to make these things happen.'

Iris now looked exhausted. Her story telling had emotionally drained her and she noticed that the sun outside the mean window was starting to dim. After a few minutes of silence, which they both relished, she said, 'Perhaps I should leave Charlie, I have told you everything I know, we are both tired and it's getting dark. I should get home.'

Charlie's mind was a torrent of conflicting emotions. He was elated to be talking to someone about Robert again. It made him feel real and it had been so tough trying to hang onto that reality over the last 20 years. That felt good. But what troubled him was the sense that both Robert and Iris had manipulated the meeting in the first place.

'Iris, I am finding it very difficult to comprehend the way that Robert and you planned all this. I accept that you both acted out of wanting to do what was best but do you have any idea how this fucked up my life? I had Robert for six months, yes just 6 months and then ever since I have been trying to find someone that will match up to him but I never did.' Charlie started to cry again.

'I don't think I can be angry with you because I know you love me but I do feel very confused. Also, Iris, why the hell didn't you tell me about any of this! Maybe I could have found him, maybe we could have had something together even though he was an old man by then.'

Iris was deeply troubled by her nephew's response to her story telling and had long feared that he would feel manipulated. She also knew that in his normal way he was being over dramatic. Whilst Robert had been the love of his life, there had been other men and other loves. 'Ask yourself this Charlie, even though you lost each other, would you do the same thing again? Do you regret meeting Robert?'

'No of course not, I would not give up one single second of what we shared together, not one single second. He was the most wonderful man I have ever met and I love him still.'

'Trust me Charlie, you must understand that I don't think any of us had any choice in this. Yes we planned to ensure you met, although your love had already happened, but we were only able to make those plans because it *had* happened. The dice that have been rolled for us have thrown up great joy but also at times deep tragedy.

You must also understand that other people, not just you, have been hurt by these events. Do you not have any understanding why I had a marriage that didn't last, do you not understand why I couldn't settle down with any other man?'

Charlie in his naïvety had still not worked it out. 'I loved him too. Deeply. I knew I could never have him fully, he was yours, my God I was jealous of you but I never stopped loving him. So I was spoiled for other men too. That was the curse on me. Not only had I been complicit with these events but I couldn't have the man I loved because of them.' Charlie felt that Iris was conveniently forgetting Robert was gay but then remembered that love takes many forms and he must not be dismissive of her emotions.

'I had no idea Iris, none, I am so sorry that I didn't have the sensitivity to see this too.'

'But there is something else,' Iris continued. 'My sight, as you know is very limited, but let me tell you what I have sensed. I believe that there is a bigger plan at work here, a tale which has not yet been told. Don't ask me what it is, I don't know, I'm not even sure myself but I must trust my instincts and I think in time all will be revealed to us. Will you trust me Charlie?'

He reflected on this for a while, his mind was overflowing with different emotions but eventually he smiled, 'Yes Iris I will trust you.' But then a thought came to him and his expression darkened again.

'But tell me this. You knew before I met Robert what the outcome would be, that we would only have a brief fleeting time with each other. Did you not think that we should have been warned so that we could have avoided being in the wrong place in January 1990, when the second bomb exploded in 1945?'

'My dear, don't you think I tried? Robert and I had discussed what we could do to stop your separation so that events in his past, your future, could be changed. He was so hopeful, it was what kept him going. We didn't know if this was possible but we did everything in our power.

We thought that if you were not in the house in Dulwich on the night in question then everything would be fine, you and Robert would stay together and Robert would never return to 1945. Robert's memories of your last few days together were very hazy and he did not know why you had been in Dulwich that night. It seemed easy to ensure we could change your future. I called you the day before and checked you were in Kennington. Do you remember dear?

To be sure I called your old friend Elizabeth and asked her to invite you out for dinner so that at the time of the bomb explosion in 1945 you would be safely dining with friends. I believed that this action was enough to ensure that whatever reason might have taken you to the house no longer happened. Of course though, I was wrong. For some reason you drove over to Hurst Court Road that night when you were never meant to be there and the awful winds came across time and blew you apart.'

'Elizabeth asked to see the house; we were just popping in for a few minutes on the way back from dinner. She thought she might like to buy it. So it would seem Iris, that if you hadn't arranged the date with Elizabeth we would never have been there. I have you to blame for our separation. Oh Iris don't you see what your meddling resulted in?' Charlie said bitterly.

Iris was deeply stung by Charlie's accusation, then reflected for a moment and replied, 'Well that is something else that I carry guilt for. Yet I also have the sense there was nothing more I could do. Perhaps faced with the prospect of Robert's history being wiped out time could not cope with the impending paradox and caused you to be there on that night. Or perhaps time could not cope with the paradox of two men from different times being together and finally dealt with it. I really do not know dear, these are huge questions for which I have no answer. I thought I had done my best. Forgive me Charlie. Also, reflect on this, if my plan had worked and Robert had not been propelled back to 1945, then I would never have met him in Dulwich Park in 1953, you would not have known your godfather Stephen and we could not have engineered your meeting together. Have you considered that possibility dear?'

'I'm not sure if I can cope with any more of this now Iris, this is all too much. I need to think.'

Iris said nothing.

Shortly afterwards she left, kissing Charlie on the forehead saying, 'I will be back before long, and I think we will need to talk more, and by the way don't forget how very loved you are, will you?'

$$\star\ \star\ \star$$

Chapter Two: A Letter

Over the next few days Charlie had various visitors. Elizabeth and Olga came together, he enjoyed that visit and a dwindling number of other friends did their duty calls. Some of them seemed to be able to be supportive and to offer him what he needed at the end of his life. Others seemed to be there for their own purposes, perhaps to purge guilt at not having supported him at an earlier point in his illness. One, a guy called Christian who he had briefly dated, sat there moaning all the time about his life and how awful it was he didn't have a boyfriend. Charlie gave instructions that he wouldn't be allowed in again.

He desperately wanted to see Iris and didn't know why she hadn't yet come back. He'd texted her twice but she'd not returned his messages. He was concerned that she was upset at discussing the story and didn't know how she would be feeling. He had also thought long and hard about her role in the events and come to accept that Iris was not to blame and had been doing her best to help.

The food trolley came round with its unsavoury looking offerings. Charlie looked at it but had no appetite, the morphine had seen to that. He was now very emaciated and weak, but at least the pain from his various tumours was under control and he had found some peace. He knew that he probably only had a week or so left to live and now the pain management team had got his morphine at the correct level he wanted to go home to die in his bedroom overlooking the beautiful garden where he would feel close to Robert, but he no longer had the energy to try and make any arrangements. So probably this is where he would slip away. He hoped he wouldn't be alone. He was no longer frightened, but he did feel very lonely and wanted to feel love around him now. At that point he needed Iris more than anyone else in the world.

Later on that afternoon his iPhone buzzed and he saw Iris's name come up on the display; the message read:

'Will see you tomorrow, much to tell Love I, xxx'

Charlie was pleased and that night he went to sleep quickly. He dreamed a little, sometimes of Robert, sometimes of the old dream where he was a bird and felt so loved and then once, in the early hours, he strayed into the dark dreams and saw the number 80 that he used to as a child. He woke with a start, sweating and frightened and eventually rang the bell for the nurse and got him to bring a sleeping pill. It brought a few more hours of blessed unconsciousness and also stopped any further dreams.

Iris arrived at 10.30am the next morning. She came into the room as radiant as a sunflower, kissed him and beamed, 'I have something to give you today. I know you will be pleased, it is something very special.'

As usual Iris was immaculately dressed, this time in a pink linen skirt and crisp white blouse, her hair well coiffed and wearing several pieces of what looked like very expensive jewellery. The only concession that she made to her age was that she walked with a stick, as one of her hips was rather sore.

She had brought some Cox's apples with her. She cut one up with a knife that was on the bedside cabinet and fed it to Charlie in small slices. The tart flavour was refreshing and it was the first solid food he'd enjoyed for several days.

'Now, firstly dear,' Iris started, 'let me tell you why I've not been to see you for a few days. I have been busy making very important plans and I wanted them complete before my return. I shall tell you more of those later but first I have something that Robert asked me to give you.'

Charlie's eyes opened wide and had more life in them than they had had for months. 'What is it?' enquired Charlie excitedly but with his voice quavering as he choked back his tears.

'It's a letter. I have never opened it. He sent it to me some years after he went to New Zealand with instructions that I was to give it to you when the time was right and that I would know when that was.' At that she opened her black Gucci bag and got out a large envelope with 'Charlie' written on the side in Robert's distinctive handwriting.

Charlie burst into sobs and for a few minutes they sat looking at the envelope on the bed. Then Iris said with tenderness 'I know you are probably too weak to read dear, should I read it to you? Are you happy for me to hear Robert's words?'

'Yes of course Iris. I would be honoured. It would feel exactly right.' So she carefully opened the envelope and took out four sheets of large white paper covered in Robert's beautiful and rather old-fashioned handwriting.

Napier, New Zealand, 25ᵗʰ April, 1979

My darling and beloved Charlie,

I wish I was with you now to hold your hand on your final journey but as I cannot be I hope that you will find comfort in my words, sent across the years with all my love. I want to tell you my story. I have given Iris instructions that you should only know the contents of this letter if I am dead and you are reaching the end of your life.

I firstly want to talk about my love for you. When we met it seemed like my world had suddenly come to life. I had always lived a shadowy, unfulfilled existence and on meeting you it was like the lights suddenly came on, the sun came out and the rain stopped. That was how it felt. I had never been able to express love either emotionally or physically and I was only really half a man. Uncompleted. Empty. You will recall when we met how repressed I was but you gently showed me how to love and how to feel totally at one with another human being. You were my sunshine, you were my completion, and you were my hero. You saved me from a loveless existence and the times I spent with you were the most magical period in my life.

I know we only had six short months together but that 6 months was wondrous and for the first time I felt totally satisfied as a man. Who can totally understand how one person falls in love with another? The first thing that I fell for about you was of course your wonderful blue-green eyes. They used to change colour you know. When you were angry they seemed to flash much more green, when you were happy a deeper, bluer hue. They are eyes that carry so much emotion and also hurt. It was that vulnerability that I ultimately found so special about you. I always had the sense that I wanted to put my strong arms around you and protect you from the harsh world.

Of course what I also loved, and what other people never saw, was that underneath the vulnerable exterior there was actually a very strong man who gave me a great deal of love and support.

Maybe Charlie you have wondered that perhaps it would have been better if we had not met because, I'm sure, your pain on our separation must have been as terrible as mine. For some years I did ponder this and then gradually I came to understand that having been loved is a wonderful thing, and even though that love was only for a brief, magical moment, my God I wouldn't have forsaken that moment for anything. I hope you think that too.

Now, as promised, my story. You'll know by now that I met Iris in Dulwich Park in 1953. I suspect she fancied me. I hope she never sees this letter (both Iris and Charlie giggled at this point), *as she will think me big headed.*

I was in great need of a friend. I had lost you eight long dark years before. For a long while I had desperately hoped that we could be reunited but that seed of optimism gradually withered and I was left with a cold desolate future. How could I live without you and without any chance of our meeting again? That day I had planned to take my own life, as I couldn't bear my existence without you any longer. I'm sure Iris will have told you the rest of the story of our meeting. What she may not know is how wonderful it was for me to meet her, and I grew to love her very deeply. She is the best friend I ever had and I know that she is a wonderful aunt and friend to you. She saved me that day. As our friendship developed and we realised what the fates had mapped out for all of us, I felt drawn closer and closer to Iris. Without her you and I would have never met.

I'm sure that you know by now I started calling myself by my middle name, Stephen, so there was no confusion for you. When you were a little boy I put money into a trust fund to make sure that you would have the best possible schooling. I didn't think your parents would be able to afford it and I hope this set you up well. I have also written a Will and when I die I will leave you a large part of my wealth. Do you remember the day we had lunch in Rye, the day we first kissed? I promised you I would pay you back for your generosity and I have. I always keep my promises.

I love you so much Charlie and so much wanted to look after you, but I have to bare my soul now and tell you how I failed to deliver on that love. I had intended that I would be present throughout your life making sure that there was always a guardian angel to help you over your trials and tribulations. But as you grew from a baby to a toddler and then to a little boy, I knew that seeing you growing up, knowing there was no possibility for us to be in love as we had been in 1989, my already broken heart would be ripped apart again if I stayed.

I wasn't strong enough to deal with this. I'm sorry, I know I failed you and I hope you can find it in your heart to forgive me now. Your big handsome hero as you used to call me wasn't tough enough to deal with this ultimate test.

Do you remember the last time I met you, as your Godfather, when you were 5 years old and I took you up for a spin from Biggin Hill in the Cessna? Perhaps you were too young to remember much of the day but I can see it clearly in my head now. It was a beautiful sunny summer afternoon and the little plane was barely buffeted by any winds. The view was amazing and we were able to see planes taking off from Heathrow below us to the west and at the same time see all the way to the coast at Southend to the east. Do you remember what I said to you? I do hope that at least some of my words stayed with you to give you strength through the years that were to come.

I said, 'Charlie this is a very special sunny day. We are flying up with the birds a little nearer to the heavens. Any time you are troubled, or anything bad happens to you I want you to remember this day and how beautiful it was and how excited we both were and recall this: that I told you that you are very loved, will always be very loved and are a very special and wonderful boy.

To know and accept that we are loved as people is the most wonderful gift that we can have in life. Will you promise me that you will do that?' You replied, 'Yes, Uncle Stephen, of course, I think I understand,' and smiled one of your big cheesy grins. I wonder if you do remember that day and how I tried to instil into you a message of lasting love. I do hope so. It was my spoken gift to you.

As you may know shortly afterwards I left England and went and lived in New Zealand. I never loved another man, but I married Ellen who I had met on the boat on the way over. She was a good and kind woman. I had really only wanted a friendship with her, but she proposed, she was very forward, and I was lonely and accepted. It was easier in those days for men like us to hide behind a cloak of normality.

I think in time I grew to love her. Not like the deep and special love I feel *for you but there was a love there. Please don't feel betrayed. We had 14 years together in a little Art Deco bungalow in Napier overlooking the sea. I found a degree of peace. I was content to have a very quiet life. We didn't have children and she died quite young. Why she tolerated the marriage in the way it was I don't know, I suppose she must have cared for me greatly. So these last few years I have spent by myself, with my thoughts and my amazing memories of you.*

I wonder sometimes if I will be alone for the rest of my life but I have no regrets about any of this. I have been loved and have found great fulfilment and happiness and although you have now been gone for over 30 years your memory is as fresh in my mind as the day we were forcibly parted.

Now I'm sure that you may have wondered why you could only ever know all these things when Iris knew the time to be right. It had to be when you were reaching the end of your story. Can you imagine if you got to see this letter before I died? Knowing how impetuous and romantic you are you would have come to find me. Can you imagine how awful for me it would be if we had met at some point even though your intentions were purely loving and good? There would have been a 40 year age difference and I could conceive of no way that you could love an older man in the way you had loved me before. I would have been totally devastated to be rejected and I hope you understand and forgive this too. Please find it in your heart to do so, my pride was too great and stubborn for me to even contemplate that possibility.

As I told you on that blue sunny day when we were close to the birds, you are loved and will always be loved. I adore you with every fibre of my body and I have some small sense, a hope, that one day, perhaps in heaven, we will be together again.

I love you so very, very much.

Robert

The only noise in the little room was Charlie's laboured breathing and the clicking sound of the morphine pump delivering its frequent doses of relief to his tortured body.

After some minutes had passed, and they had both composed themselves, Iris spoke: 'I hope now that everything is clear to you, why you could never meet again and why it has been so long for you to know everything?'

'I think so, but my mind is still spinning. What I have learned in the last days is just so huge, so complex and so impossible, sometimes I feel as if I will burst. But I've understood a lot through what you have told me and now what I have heard in Robert's letter. I know now how selfish I have been for all these years, thinking it was just my tragedy, my loss and I completely failed to see that there were other victims too.

Robert of course suffered terribly but do you know I spent years being jealous of all the men that he might be meeting in the 1940's. I never of course had any knowledge about your role in this but I can now also see that you loved him too and were unable to have him and that was your tragedy. Although poor Ellen married him she could never have him fully as a proper husband and she must have been desperately lonely within her marriage.

The most amazing revelation is that I now also understand one of my dreams. Often I have dreamed of being a bird and having a wonderful sense of being loved and cared for. I didn't fully remember what Robert told me in the plane that day when I was 5 years old, but the wonderful message stayed with me always. Quite often when I was troubled I would think of my dream, of being a bird and feeling comforted and loved. I never really knew why. Can you imagine what a wonderful gift Robert gave to me? I feel so small and humbled by this. I hope you and Robert can forgive me for my insensitivity and selfishness.'

'There is nothing to forgive sweetheart, you are just a human being, and we are all frail and all sometimes wrong. But actually all of us are good people just trying to make everything right when it was impossible to make everything right.

Robert tried to support you the best he could but ultimately was defeated by his own pride; that was his conflict. I loved Robert all those years, even after he went to live in Napier. I visited every year knowing he could never be mine, and please forgive me, I was insanely jealous of you for having his love. Finally, poor, dull, loyal and unglamorous Ellen. She sacrificed the possibility of having a proper marriage and the chance of having children for Robert. Can you see now Charlie there are no villains, no victims, just good but ultimately weak and fragile human beings?'

Charlie made no verbal response but reached out his weak hand to Iris's and squeezed it as hard as he could. She knew what it meant and felt very loved herself at that moment.

'Charlie I have something else to tell you. You remember when I arrived I said I had been busy making plans?' Iris looked rather pleased with herself as she said this. 'You are going home, I have all the preparations made. I have the Macmillan nurses set up to look after you and I have your room full of flowers.'

'That's wonderful Iris, you know how important it is for me to die at home, in the room where I first met Robert, overlooking my lovely garden. Thank you so very, very much, it is the most wonderful gift you could have given to me. You are a very special and amazing person and having had you in my life has been something of wonder, you have always been able to give me the support my mother couldn't, thank you so much, and by the way I reckon you're the most glamorous aunty that anyone ever had, look at you, 85 years old and still gorgeous!'

Iris blushed a little and thanked Charlie for the compliment.

'Perhaps I've always had to hide a little of my pain under my glamour and make up,' she added, but smiling as she said it. 'I think I should go now dear, I may be glamorous but I am an old lady and I am tired, forgive me. Tomorrow I have arranged for the ambulance to take you home and I will be waiting for you there.'

'Iris, there is one more thing that I need to ask you, is that okay?'

'Yes of course dear, anything.'

'You have explained so much to me, and I understand that one of the reasons that your destiny was tied up with mine and Robert's is your psychic powers. Can you help me with something else that troubles me? You now know about my wonderful dream of birds and love, inspired by Robert's amazing spoken gift to me. What you do not know is that when I was a little boy I had a recurring terrible dark dream as if in counterpoint to the light one. In the dream I nearly always saw the number 80. I dreamed of an awful place, it was a cellar, which stank of death. Sometimes in the dream

I would see the faces of other boys and I would know them to be dead, and sometimes in the dream I had the horrible and gut churning fear that I was about to die myself. There was a figure in the cellar. I never saw his face but he smelled like a man and I could sense his bulk. I think he was going to kill me. Whenever I had the dream I would wake up screaming just as he moved towards me with a piece of electric flex stretched between his outreached hands. It was the most terrible nightmare Iris. Occasionally I get a little glimpse of it now. I can see that there have been many complex and strange threads to my life, do you know what this means? It troubles me and I feel that I need to get this resolved before I can go peacefully.'

'It means nothing to me at all dear, I'm sorry but I can't help you with this one,' and she pointedly busied herself collecting her bag and mobile phone and stood up to go.

He saw two things in her eyes as she said this, one was fear and the other was that she was lying.

★ ★ ★

Chapter Three: Flowers in the Bedroom

The next day Iris returned to Charlie's house in Dulwich where he had been brought earlier that morning. She pressed the little old fashioned wind-up front door bell which he insisted on keeping although it didn't always work. On this occasion it tinkled brightly and a uniformed nurse promptly opened the front door.

'Good morning Mrs Wilson.'

'Please call me Iris. How is he, is he comfortable?' she enquired as she took her coat off. 'Sorry what's your name dear?'

'It's Grainne,' the nurse replied with a soft Irish burr. 'I've got his morphine pump set, so he's not in any pain. But you do understand how grave his situation is I think? He may only have a few days.'

'I do fully understand, I am prepared for that.'

Iris walked slowly up the stairs and across the landing to the back bedroom where Charlie had given instructions that he was to spend his last days. It was the room in which he had first met Robert so it was very special in his heart, and was also very pretty and filled with light. Iris had arranged for it to be covered in flowers. In one of Charlie's camper moments he had waved his hand saying, 'When I go I want there to be flowers like they had for Princess Diana!'

There were flowers on the bedside table, flowers on the chest of drawers, flowers in the little wooden fireplace. All white. That is what he loved. Their fragrance on entering the room was almost overpowering. She had committed to herself that they would be constantly fresh. There were also musky, scented candles burning on the mantelpiece. Charlie lay propped up on a mound of pillows, on immaculate Egyptian cotton cream bed linen, with his eyes closed and looking serene but very frail. On the pillow next to him were a couple of his favourite teddy bears.

Iris kissed him on the top of his head, very gently not wishing to wake him, but he must have only been dozing as one eye opened a little and he managed a half smile for her.

'Iris, I can't begin to thank you enough for what you have done, to be here in my own home, in this special place, with the windows open and the fresh air coming in from the garden.'

She settled herself onto the little cream Lloyd Loom chair that was placed by the side of the bed for visitors. 'Now dear I want to know how you're feeling and if there is anything I should be doing for you, although it looks like Grainne is looking after you well.'

The smile left Charlie's face and she sensed he had something of gravity to say. He started, 'Well there is something very important that you can do,' and he fixed her with his amazing eyes flashing green with what looked like anger to Iris. 'You can tell me the truth.'

'What in heaven's name do you mean? I've never lied to you. I may have not mentioned the odd romantic fling, but I have never lied, you know you can trust me completely.'

'I'm not speaking of your sex life Iris, please take me seriously and stop being flippant. What I'm alluding to is that when I spoke of my dark dreams to you yesterday you lied. You told me they meant nothing to you, but I saw a shadow cross your face, saw something that I think was fear in your eyes. I know you were lying and are frightened of something. Iris I need the truth.'

'Forgive me, I'm an old fool, I thought I was able to cover up my reactions and you would never know of the dreadful knowledge that I have, but I ask you this darling, would you grant me one last favour and allow that knowledge to die with me? You need not know, it is of no importance to you now.'

'I am not a child and although sometimes I have been fragile, I think you know that I have an inner core of strength and I'm sure I can handle anything you tell me.'

Iris thought for a few moments, sighed heavily, then replied, 'You ask a great deal of me but I suppose I must share this vile story with you. I ask God's forgiveness for what I have done and your forgiveness for burdening you with it now, but if you insist I will comply.' Charlie was rather thrown by the mention of God, as he knew Iris to be completely irreligious.

She went to the bedroom door and spoke to Grainne asking that they were not to be interrupted, reassuring her she would call if Charlie needed anything. 'Charlie, I need to tell you something that has weighed like decaying lead in my mind for years. I have done a terrible wrong but perhaps telling you this now may give me some peace. Firstly, you need to know how I was involved with something dreadful that happened many many years ago. So far back but still the pain of what I did cuts into me every day like a new and deep flesh wound.

I was busy that morning in 1972. Do you know that was the last day in my life I didn't carry a huge burden of guilt and knowledge? Funny the detail you remember isn't it? The before and the after. The before always seems like a sunlit carefree time and then the after, with its constant burden of foul knowledge that you would give an arm not to have.'

Iris then, slowly and with tremors of emotion in her voice, told him of what had started that day all those years ago when Rose had called her and had mentioned The Peckham Murders.

She reached the end of the story an hour later. 'Harry was repeatedly raped and beaten up in Wandsworth, he could not handle it and hung himself. After I found out it was actually Frederick that had killed the boys I carried terrible guilt with me for almost 40 years.'

Charlie was barely able to lift his head off the pillow. He was so weak but he managed a slight smile. 'I've heard everything, I understand it all and Iris how can I ever thank you for what you have done for me, for what you have given of yourself to protect me. One thing I don't understand though, if you knew I was going to meet Robert in my future, an event in Robert's past, surely you had to do none of this because our love had already happened, I could not really have been killed?'

'Charlie, I'm not some science fiction hero. I have no answers, only questions. How was I to know what to do? Do you think I wouldn't have preferred to know exactly what the effect of different choices would be? I had no idea. I felt helpless. It was an awful predicament, I had to act. It was the only way to be sure.'

After a pause Charlie said, 'Thank you again Iris, I think I just about understand now, just a little. This is a terrible dark story, but it is a great relief for me that I now know the meaning of 80, 80 Victoria Street, that terrible place which has haunted me all my life. How did I dream of it Iris, am I psychic too like you, does it run in the family?'

Iris replied, 'Maybe, perhaps you have a little sight too, and darling no thanks is required. My love for you has always been deep and I was prepared to do anything to ensure your safety. I will add that I was of course very scared that I would be caught and prosecuted for Frederick's murder. I wasn't willing to go to prison for an act that I considered just. I dragged his body down to the cellar and when I went back up to the street later I bribed the men with the bulldozer to start working on number 80 that same day. They weren't very bright and I flirted with them to get what I wanted, they never suspected anything.

Later that day they pushed number 80 down with the bulldozer. Everything collapsed into the cellar and Frederick was buried with it. They built an estate there shortly afterwards. The Salisbury Estate. Terrible, grey, life-draining place. God knows what phantasms haunt its occupants.'

'One question Iris which intrigues me? Where does a middle class woman from the suburbs get a gun from?'

Iris smiled. 'You must remember dear I always had a lot of lovers. The year before I killed Frederick I had a brief fling with Albert Davidson. You must have heard of the gang who ran south London for a long time in the 60's. He owed me a few favours and got me the gun with no questions asked. I hadn't planned to kill Frederick, it was really for protection, but when I did, I also kind of knew that I would always do it.'

Throughout the long story telling by Iris, Charlie had come to see with growing sadness that this beloved wonderful and strong woman who had killed to protect him was carrying a great load of guilt, but she clearly didn't know the whole truth.

'There is something that you don't know. Something I have never told anyone before. Do you remember that Christmas when

I was a little boy? When my father gave me that bloody cricket bat and I ran away?' Iris nodded.

'I was only 6 years old but I can remember every detail of that day. I can remember howling when I saw that I had the wrong present and how cross I was with my parents. I remember thinking that I could go and find Stephen in New Zealand. I cycled off on my little bike down the road determined never to come back.

I can still remember seeing into various sitting rooms on the way down the road, seeing the Christmas trees and the children happily playing with their families and feeling very envious. They seemed to be much happier families than mine. For some reason that I can't recall I decided to cycle into the woods where I often played with Susan.

I was half way along the path by the stream, when I almost collided with a man. I stopped about two inches from his feet; I hadn't been looking where I was going. When I jammed on the brakes I can remember the little wheels skidding but I stayed upright. I looked up fearing that I was going to be told off and then was relieved when I saw a familiar, rather toothless face that I knew beaming down at me. It was Uncle Harry. I didn't really know him very well but as he was family it felt safe. Harry said to me, 'Whoa, little man, what's the rush, aren't you meant to be enjoying your Christmas lunch?' At that I started crying again, so Harry leaned down and scooped me up in his arms. 'Come on my lad I've got something to show you.'

He carried me behind some bushes and laid me on the ground. 'I've got something special to show you Charlie, but you mustn't tell anyone because if you do you will get in trouble.' Charlie stopped for a moment clearly struggling with his recollections.

'He never actually touched me or did anything but he was exposing himself and I knew it was deeply wrong and I jumped up and ran back towards my bike. I climbed on and started to cycle off as quickly as possible, but Harry ran across my path and I fell off cutting my knee. I think he realised by then that he wasn't going to get anywhere with me and he carried me back to my parents. All the time as we walked up the road he was whispering, 'Don't say a word of this Charlie Rogers, if you do I'll kill you. My friends and

I will come and kill you and then we'll kill your mother, do you understand you little brat?'

'When we got back to the house Harry made it look as if he had picked me up from a cycling accident, he feigned his usual stupidity, I suspect much of it was an act.' Iris sat grey and stony faced but eventually managed to speak.

'All these years Charlie, almost 40 years I have held onto a flawed knowledge. In my stupidity I believed Harry to be an innocent and he was almost your abuser. He lived next door to Frederick you know, they knew each other. God knows what vile role he may have played in the boys' murders; we shall never find out. I now know the full depth of your story but Charlie do you fully understand my story? My love was so strong for you that I mothered you and dried your tears when your own mother failed, I enabled your love with Robert to happen, I sent a man to his death and for years carried a burning guilt because I thought he was innocent and finally I killed for you. I would willingly do this all again for you a hundred times because I love you so much, it was always my destiny to do these things I believe. But I am a tired old woman now and I am pleased to have at least been relieved of the guilt about Harry and to find some peace before it is my time to go. Your life and mine are so deeply entangled, I have made your story and you have made mine. We can regret nothing in life. I regret little, only that it has taken me all these years to find out the truth about Frederick and Harry but that of course was part of their game, part of their pleasure to manipulate me and cause me pain as well. All these things have helped to write my story. I am the person that I am because of them and I believe that every challenge, every difficulty that we have in this life prepares us for things that we face in our next lives. We become better people because of them.'

Iris, now silent, laid her head on Charlie's chest, she finally sobbed great racking sobs and her tears flowed and for the first time ever, it was he who comforted her.

★ ★ ★

Chapter Four: The Heart of the Matter

The following morning Iris woke early; the sun was streaming in through the bedroom windows and skylights. She had been so tired that she hadn't even drawn the blinds when she went to bed the previous night. She briefly showered, dressed and went downstairs for breakfast. As she was halfway through coffee her mobile phone rang and she saw 'Grainne' coming up on the display. She answered it immediately, 'Hello Grainne, how's Charlie?' but she knew that a call at 8.00am was not likely to be good news.

'Iris, you need to come now. He has deteriorated very quickly overnight and if you want to see him I think you should come straight away.'

'I'll be there as soon as I can.'

Iris quickly picked up her bag, walking stick and keys then got the lift down to the ground floor of her apartment block and asked the concierge to call her a cab. Within five minutes the mini cab was pulling up outside 'Hurst Court Road, Dulwich, as quick as you can.'

The traffic at that time of morning was painfully slow and Iris feared that she might not get there to see Charlie and make her goodbyes. But eventually she arrived outside his house, paid the taxi driver and walked up the drive as quickly as her 85-year-old frame would allow her. As she did Grainne opened the front door.

'Iris, thank you for coming so quickly. His breathing is very laboured and I think it's only a matter of hours if that.' Iris ascended the stairs and went straight into Charlie's room. She could see his pallor and hear his breathing, a terrible grating, wheezing noise. She saw no flicker of recognition on his face. She sensed he was deeply asleep.

She took off her coat and sat in the little Lloyd Loom chair where she had spent so much time telling Charlie her story and held his hand. 'Charlie it's Iris, I love you very much, you are not alone, I'm here with you.'

There was a very slight pressure on her hand and clearly he had recognised her voice. She was pleased that he would not feel alone. For the next hour she sat constantly holding Charlie's hand and frequently telling him how loved he was and not to be afraid. She felt very tranquil and also so pleased that she was able to be with Charlie now, when he most needed her. Tears and mourning could come later. She sat there for maybe an hour, occasionally dozing and drifting into light sleep.

In the future when she recalled what happened next she never really knew if she had dreamed it or if it had been a vision like her vision long ago in the Blitz. Something strange was going on. It was still a bright sunny day when Iris arrived at Charlie's house but now the colour of the light changed in the room.

It became a glorious golden pinky glow as if there was a huge sunset sky outside. At the same time she noticed that the smell of the room had changed. Previously it had been a combination of the scent of the numerous flowers and the stale odour of a sick room. Now these were both gone and all Iris could smell was the sea, the English Channel on a clear sunny day.

Now she smelt something else, an indefinable smell, but one she knew to be the smell of a man, and she knew straight away who the man was.

She felt a large reassuring squeeze on her hand. A man with a deep, familiar masculine voice, from so long ago, spoke. 'Iris, I've come to take Charlie on his final journey home.'

Iris gasped, and by that stage it was of no surprise to her that Robert was sitting on the side of the bed. This wasn't the Robert that she last remembered when she'd visited him in New Zealand. This was the young Robert when he was in his thirties and at the height of his handsome good looks; dark, swarthy and masculine and his wonderful sparkling eyes full of life.

Iris felt the old familiar sexual attraction that she had for him flicker through her and at the same time the remembrance of the sadness that she was unable to be with him. 'Robert, how, but how, I can't believe I am seeing you? Are you a ghost? Look at you, so young and handsome and me, a tired wrinkled old woman.'

'Iris you are still beautiful, you always have been and your beauty has grown with age, not wilted.'

'You always were the smooth talker weren't you?' but she blushed and appreciated his words.

'Iris, I have much to tell you before I take Charlie home, but I need him to hear this as well. Let me see if I can wake him.' Robert got up from the side of the bed and bent over and tenderly kissed Charlie on the lips. As he did Charlie's breathing evened out a little and to Iris's great surprise he opened his eyes slightly. They immediately fell on Robert. He could say nothing but tears started to trickle down Charlie's face and at the same time he looked very, very slightly less ill.

Robert spoke again: 'You both must listen to me now, there is not much time. Iris you too have a right to know everything that has been a part of your destiny.

Charlie, you and I have always been together, it was written in the stars and such great loves cannot be torn apart. I believe that if we wanted to be apart it would not be possible. We would be drawn back together. That is what is deemed and what cannot be broken.

I have only learned much of this since I left this strange place and went home, after my death in this dark England and I of course learned much of it through a wonderful psychic woman in *my* England,' and he winked at Iris.

'We come from a different England, a kinder, more gentle place where there have been no World Wars, an England where terrible missiles have not fallen out of the sky. It is also somewhere where our love for each other is valued as much as any other love. We had spent years as a couple, had a fierce bond of love and loyalty to each other and had promised to be together for all time.

We complemented each other and made each other whole. Our lives together seemed blessed, charmed and untouchable. Everyone who knew us thought we were the perfect couple and that only death would ever part us.

That was until the terrible wind came. You had dreamed of it my darling boy and I chided you for being silly and insecure. The terrible wind separated us, the bomb that exploded on the 22nd July, 1944 in this other, war torn London somehow blasted through the fabric of reality into our England and ripped us apart. We should have been deposited in this cruel dark dirty place together but somehow we were separated by the winds of time and you were reborn to Rose and David in 1955 and I was reborn to my parents in 1915. So my God what cruel fate! Not only separated but reborn and having to live a life in this England which is a dark shadow of our true beloved home. We then lived out our lives here, meeting again only to be separated once more.

When it was time for me to encounter 22nd July, 1944 in this England, the bomb fractured the weak point in time once more, and because of our destiny to be lovers, because it is written in the stars that we should be together, time tried to make a correction and we were flung back into each other's arms. Then the second bomb 6 months later finally sealed our fate and we were separated.

Time had become confused, on one hand trying to keep us together but on the other hand unable to handle the paradox. But you must understand Charlie that to us none of this is real, it is only a faded image of our proper home.

It is no more real than a photo is in an album, yes it is similar to the reality but it is in black and white, not colour, it is distorted. You and I have been dreaming a long dream, sometimes it became a nightmare and now you are to awake. When you wake Charlie you will be with me in the sunlit peaceful place where we belong.

This isn't the real England, at least not to us; perhaps it is to the people that were meant to be born here. This mirror image of where we come from is but a dark mirror where everything has gone wrong and terrible things happen. Charlie, I've come to take you home. We will be together now, nothing can prevent it. Loves such as ours are so strong because they have happened before, in another world, in another time. You do understand that don't you?'

Charlie was unable to respond, he was crying too much and also too weak but he squeezed Robert's hand slightly.

'And what about me?' ventured Iris. 'Have I too been ripped out of one England and projected into another? Please tell me.'

'Your story is different, yes there is an Iris there too and she is my beloved friend, as you have been here. You belong in both places. That is why you have psychic powers. Iris, without you and your astral sister, Charlie and I would never have been together. You have been the key that has unlocked the door for us.'

'Tell me this Robert, as you seem to know all. One thing I have never understood. Someone writing the word BELOW on a wall behind a mirror pointed me towards Frederick as Charlie's future killer. Below the desk where I sat I found the key to the house that held Frederick's secrets.'

'I know about this, this part of the story has been made clear to me by Iris in the real England … but do you really not know who did that?'

'No Robert, that's why I'm asking.'

'Iris, it was you, it was you in the place that Charlie and I come from. The same beautiful woman, the same wonderful loving friend. She gave much of herself, endured great physical and mental exhaustion to breach a passageway across the stars so that she could write the message to you to see in the mirror to save Charlie. When you dreamed, you saw fragments of a picture. You were never able to see everything. The other Iris saw everything and knew that Frederick was the killer much sooner; she was shown it in her visions.'

She found a wise woman who was able to teach her how to project herself through the astral planes. She knew that moment, when you could have either found or missed the key to 80 Victoria Street, was pivotal and that was the moment that she picked to help you. So Iris, you helped yourself, and you saved Charlie in all possible ways. That is your ultimate gift to him.

The other Iris has again given greatly, to help me to break through the veils between the worlds to be at Charlie's deathbed. Such acts require great power and this is drained from the spirit, from the soul. I can never thank you enough Iris. You are the key to our salvation and the solution to this trial. That is your importance to us.'

'So what of Frederick and Harry? Where do they fit in with all of this Robert?'

'The other Iris told me much, she saw that there was a twisted, dark and evil man in another distant, dark and shadowy version of England, even darker than yours. We know little of this place but we do know is that there was a man with ice in his heart who on seeing Charlie and me together reached out through the astral planes as he was determined to destroy our love, such great love, and love between men was abhorrent to him.'

'But you say 'person' Robert, but surely there were two of them?'

'Be patient Iris and I shall explain. He used the power that was generated by the bomb explosion that fractured the weak point in time in 1944 as a source of energy or a beacon, I'm not clear which. But something went badly wrong with his plans and when he entered this dimension he was shattered into two fragments, it was like a mirror breaking and each of the men he became was a fragment of the mirror, just like a shard of glass. The two fragments were then reborn into the men you know. In some ways the shattering reduced his powers, but it gave him two different aspects of evil to do terrible deeds with.'

'And what happens now? Is he dead, are they dead everywhere? Do I need to be concerned for Charlie that they could still be waiting somewhere for him? You have frightened me.'

'Iris, be calm, there is nothing to worry about. What also happened when the dark man was shattered into fragments was that something went wrong with the cycle of his time-line. The two of them now live, for infinity, being born, having ice and dark in their hearts and committing their dreadful acts. Then for all time Harry will be repeatedly raped and hang himself and Fred will be shot by you and will lie undiscovered in that terrible cellar.'

'But that's dreadful Robert, that means that the boys are suffering again and again.'

'No, understand me fully Iris, the men's time-line keeps looping for infinity round the same events. The boys' time-line happened once.'

Iris now fully grasped what Robert had told her. 'They seem to have learned what Hell is don't they Robert? Do you think that there is some kind of God out there who has seen what they did and has done this as a punishment?'

'I know nothing of any Gods Iris, all I know is that they are experiencing a hell which they truly deserve, and that maybe the universe has intervened to ensure this, I really don't know.

And understand this, each time they go through the loop, for eternity, their souls will be corroded more and more by their evil acts, as if eroded and burned by terrible corrosive acid. I suspect at some point, in a few million millennia's time, their souls will have become tortured fragments in permanent screaming agony.'

Both of them were silent for a while taking in the enormity of everything and just listening to Charlie's breathing.

After maybe half an hour Iris noticed that the red colour in the sky was starting to fade and Charlie's breathing was now barely perceptible. Bizarrely she smelt ginger nut biscuits, like she had used to treat Charlie to when he was a little boy. She sensed that the end was very close.

'I must say farewell to you Iris, my beloved friend, I thank you for everything you have done,' and Robert kissed her tenderly. The smell and taste of him lingered on her lips.

Charlie managed to whisper a few words to Robert. 'Perhaps I will get to have tea with Evita now, I wish I could tell Michael.'

Robert smiled again but said nothing.

Charlie had heard everything that Robert had said, and as Robert spoke, he gradually felt the illness slipping away from his body. He felt his youth coming back and the weight of the years falling away from his shoulders. As Robert finished he felt him pick him up in his strong arms, kiss him again and whisper, 'Now for the most exciting journey darling boy, we are going home together.'

Iris snapped completely awake and noticed Charlie's eyes start to close and she could see him slipping away. His breathing got shallower and shallower and then stopped and she could see that he was dead. The sunshine gradually returned to its previous colour, the smell of ginger nuts subsided and the scent of flowers came back. She picked up Charlie's favourite bear, the one that his sister had given him that Christmas all those years ago, and tucked it under Charlie's arm. 'Good night sweetheart, sleep tight,' and she kissed him gently on the lips.

A little later Iris started to make her calls to let Charlie's family and friends know that he was gone. Her first was to Olga. 'He passed away half an hour ago dear.' Olga immediately burst into tears and started sobbing loudly down the phone.

'Hush don't cry dear, he has found peace, and there is something else, I'm not sure, I may have been dreaming, it may have been the wishful thinking of an old woman but I think Robert came back to him at the end. Let us think about them being together now. I'm sure that they *are* somewhere. I don't think that the universe would allow them to be separated for too long do you?'

★ ★ ★

The End and the Beginning

Battersea, November 2010

Iris was entertaining her sister Violet for tea. Violet was 90 years old but keeping physically and mentally alert. Iris was pleased to see her; she had become so much easier to be with over the years since Frederick's death. She had blossomed and relaxed and was no longer the prim proper person that Iris recalled. Iris however, had got out her best bone china, as she knew Violet still liked things 'just so'.

They chatted and exchanged pleasantries. Then Iris changed her tone and started, 'Violet, it occurs to me that the years that we have left in this life may not be many and there is something I want to tell you.'

'I know what you mean Iris, every day I awake I'm surprised that I'm still here, but what is it dear, what's troubling you?' Violet had seen the expression on her sister's face and realised that something was on her mind.

'Violet, I want to tell you about Frederick and what happened to him in 1974, I think you have a right to know.'

'Stop Iris, there's no need for you to say anything. I know you've thought me stupid and repressed for many years but I knew much. I suspected what happened and have always known you probably dealt with him. There is though something that I should perhaps tell you. How do you think you found out about his ghastly acts in the first place? I found the list with the boys' names on it in Frederick's desk and put it inside a paperback book. Do you remember the night you took us to Gatwick for our holiday in Sorrento? I took the book from our luggage and deliberately left it in the boot of the car. You see Iris, I had suspected Frederick for a while. I had a little sight too you know, it runs in the family and I had had a glimmer, a slight instinct, nothing more. But I was too weak, too frightened of what people would think but I knew of your strength and determination and knew how you would fight to protect Charlie. After he disappeared I kept checking his bank statement and then I became sure you had dealt with him for he never drew any further money, I knew he must be dead. In my pathetic weakness I left it to you, my sister to deal with Frederick. Can you ever find it in your heart to forgive me dear?'

The two old women embraced and wept.

England 1940

Iris, now knowing the whole story, realises that she has a very important job to do. She knows how the story ended; she now needs to be sure that it will start in the right way. She goes to a shop in the village where she lives.

She buys a beautifully hand drawn set of Tarot cards and a greetings card with a little black cat on it. Her next visit is a house a few yards down the cobbled street; she needs to go and consult with a wise woman. She talks for hours with the woman who is old and wizened and by the end of the consultation she has the knowledge to take the next step.

On returning to her own house, she purifies herself by bathing in rose scented water. She clears her mind for the act by meditating for 3 hours. She is then ready for the huge summoning of personal power that will be needed to enable her to be successful in her deed.

She sits cross-legged on the floor, surrounded by a circle of candles and incense. In front of her is the Tarot pack and greeting card on which she has written her message. Using every fragment, every ounce of her powers, she summons up a huge wave of energy and she sends them through the walls that separate the worlds and across time to a young woman, to herself, in other, blitz-torn England.

★ ★ ★